AN INNOCENT BEAUTY . . .

Jason looked down at her upturned face. Her green eyes were sparkling, her cheeks glowing, kissed by sunshine. Involuntarily, his hands tightened on her waist. He wanted to do more than kiss her . . .

Jade felt her head swim and for a moment she thought she might faint . . . her heart was beating triple time, her fingers trembling. She felt weak and at the same time pulsing with an energy that drew her to him like a magnet to iron . . .

Praise for *Wildflower*:

"A delight from start to finish!"
—*Rendezvous*

Also by Jill Marie Landis from Jove

ROSE
SUNFLOWER
WILDFLOWER

JADE

JILL MARIE LANDIS

JOVE BOOKS, NEW YORK

JADE

A Jove Book / published by arrangement with
the author

PRINTING HISTORY
Jove edition / June 1991

ISBN: 0-515-10591-0

Jove Books are published by The Berkley Publishing Group,
200 Madison Avenue, New York, New York 10016.
The name "JOVE" and the "J" logo
are trademarks belonging to Jove Publications, Inc.

PRINTED IN THE UNITED STATES OF AMERICA

10 9 8 7 6 5 4 3 2 1

To Chelley Kitzmiller, whose vision of Li Po
was clearer than mine;

to Antoniette and Harold Nickless and Betty and Bill
Olson, my favorite aunts and uncles;

to the members of the Orange County Romance Writers
for their loving support;

to Mellisa Davis, Beth Anne Davis, and Jeffrey Landis
and their parents;

to Hillary Cige and Joni Friedman of Berkley Publishing
for putting my hero on the cover.

Gold is worth nothing much . . .
Peace and happiness are priceless.

❧ PROLOGUE ❧

Man cannot stir one inch
Without the push of Heaven's finger.

CHINA, 1874

Neither light of day nor the heat of the summer sun penetrated the interior of Li Po's cave. Tin oil lamps hung suspended from slender lengths of chain imbedded in the rock; their smoke stained the ceiling of the cave with ever-widening, black circles of soot. The cloying scent of incense weighed heavy on the air, yet even it was unable to disguise the odor of must and time.

An age-old, slate-topped table banked the back wall of the cave; a work space covered with blue and white porcelain jars, clay pots, and glass vessels filled with the grains and powders essential to an alchemist's work. Granular cinnabar, fine-dusted gold, slivers of jade and silver lay beside pieces of bark and snippets of pine tree boughs, baskets of peach pits, and dried cuttings from the divine herb, *chih*. A weathered basket with an unraveled rim housed a dozen or more eggs of tortoise and crane, ingredients vital in the mixing of medicinal elixirs.

A bulbous glass still with a triad of extended arms took precedence beside the instruments of weights and measures on the worktable. Hot coals burned brightly in a brazier, blinking like the glowing red eyes of a demon against the shadowed walls of the cave.

Everything stood in readiness. The hushed sound of foot-steps sliding over the earthen floor and a soft mumbling and grumbling grew louder as an ancient alchemist, stooped and white haired, entered his shadowed realm. Li Po paused for a moment inside the large room in the earth's interior and surveyed his worktable. His eyes, shaped like midnight black almonds, shone with inner light; they were quick to note that all was exactly as he had anticipated. The pine in the brazier had burned low until it was reduced to the fiery ash he needed to heat the still.

1

Stray white whiskers grew from the corners of the old man's mouth and chin like long blades of dried grass. They formed a pointed beard that Li Po repeatedly stroked as he whispered to himself in the flickering light of the cave. The villagers thought him a wizard. Indeed, his fame was renowned throughout the countryside. For generation upon generation Li Po's ancestors had been alchemists. His father's father had once served the emperor.

Only Li Po knew the truth.

He was no more a wizard than the humblest village beggar. He was a charlatan, a fake who had held the people enthralled with little more than explosions of sulfur and simple predictions for which he carefully orchestrated the outcomes. Whatever valuable secrets his ancestors had possessed had long since been lost to time. Had his father or his father's father truly been wizards they would still walk among the living—for it was well known that true alchemists possessed the very secret of life itself.

Now that he was stooped with age, he could see the doubt in the young men's eyes when they watched him. He could feel their disbelief when he tried to hold onto his power over them. Even the high-soled shoes he had ordered made in Canton so that he might appear taller than any man in the village failed to bring him proper respect anymore. He often heard the young ones laughing whenever he passed by.

For years he had tried to discover the elixir of immortality supposedly known to the ancients. Today he would try again, and hope that he would succeed before death claimed him.

The old man had taken great care with his appearance this day so that he might please the goddess of the stove. He had followed every prescribed precaution in order to insure success. On his head he wore a tall, nearly square black hat. The headdress was covered with gold and red beads. He had donned the sacred crimson alchemist's robe handed down from generation to generation. Unlike Li Po, whose wrinkled body showed all of his eighty-nine years, the robe had not aged, though it was hundreds of years old. The silk fabric, as red as blood, was emblazoned with dragons and tigers, lions and cranes. Stars, crescent moons, and images of the sun were worked in threads of spun gold.

Mingled with the images were symbols, characters of an archaic form of Chinese long since forgotten by most. He was happy the robe was red, for it insured success. Red was the color of the female deity of the stove, the goddess who blessed all those who transmuted metals, brewed medicines, or merely prepared meals.

Li Po's father had failed to rediscover the exact proportions of the magic life-extending elixir, but he had passed on one important clue to Li Po. On his deathbed, the father of Li Po whispered the same words his father before him had whispered with his dying breath. "The robe itself is magic, it is part of the transmutation."

After years of futility, Li Po had nearly given up, but then, a month ago, after his last miserable attempt to transform himself into a youth, he realized where he had gone wrong. As he had cursed himself, his forefathers, and then the sacred robe, he suddenly stopped in mid-sentence. He slipped off the robe and ran his long fingernails over the symbols. He stared at the ancient script, at the lions, tigers, cranes and dragons, and a revelation came to him.

Merely *wearing* the robe and mixing his own elixir would not insure success. The secret formula itself had been carefully embroidered on the robe in gilded threads. As he looked closer, even his faded vision could not miss the fact that the robe, which had been in his family for generations, was as new as the day it had been made.

The magic had kept the robe from aging.

It had taken Li Po almost a month to transcribe the ancient symbols into a formula that made any sense to him at all. Now he was ready to proceed. Not only had Li Po fasted as ancient custom dictated, but he had purified himself with jasmine perfume and burned incense at a shrine outside of the village. He knew as well as any that one must enter the mountains to produce efficacious medicines. And so he had come to his cave deep in the heart of the mountain outside of Sin Ngan Hien.

This night, even the stars were aligned in his favor. All he needed to do was believe. Disbelief assured failure.

With an iron ladle he measured the white-hot ash into the bed below the still. His blue-veined hands were steady and sure. Li Po thought of the many years he had conducted the *tan*, the search for the secret formula that would produce the life-extending elixir. He chuckled to himself when he realized what a cruel trick fate had placed on his ancestors. The correct proportions of gold and mercury that would assure his immortality had always been within their grasp. They were emblazoned on the robe. He reminded himself to hurry. Time was of the essence.

He was fast becoming a very old man.

Li Po sifted the cinnabar and then gold dust into the still while he repeatedly whispered the words of an incantation that had also been handed down to him.

"Gold, you will not rot or decay. You are the most precious of all things on earth. Make me a lusty youth. Help me escape the perils of life and pain of death. Let me live to be as old as the universe itself. I pray that once I have ingested the elixir of life that I will regain my lost years and live forever. Change me as easily as the wind changes direction before a storm. As I say these words aloud, make them so."

Li Po chuckled to himself—a rasping, choking sound—each time he repeated the line about the lusty youth. He alternately smiled and frowned as he bent stoop-shouldered over his worktable, sifting and measuring, mumbling and mixing. *Soon now*, thought Li Po, *I will achieve the status of True Man and live forever. Far past eternity will I walk the earth as I have these many, many moons. I will watch the stars rotate through the heavens again and again.*

And just as the philosopher Lao Tzu practiced magic, so too did Li Po.

Carefully he continued to sift ingredients into the glass crucible that topped the still as he chanted and chuckled over the words of his prayer. The old man's mind was so attuned to the moment at hand, his concentration so focused, that he failed to hear the muffled sound of hushed whispers or the scuffling feet of the half-dozen men who crept stealthily toward him through the shadows.

They were upon him before he was aware of their presence.

Li Po turned, his withered, parchmentlike skin bleached with shock until it was as white as his whiskers. The fire behind his eyes blazed bright with anger. He recognized these men; they were the bearded foreigners who rode the tall-masted sailing ships.

Quickly, he turned and lifted the vial of elixir that had simmered above the still. He swirled it, made a great show of holding it to the light and watched it shimmer. It pulsated with life and glowed irridescent in the darkness.

He had to stall these intruders while the liquid cooled, for to drink it now would surely scald his throat beyond healing.

One of the men started to creep toward Li Po.

With the elixir clutched in one hand, he raised his arms high in a dramatic gesture of power. The wide sleeves of the royal red robe fanned out to give him the appearance of a huge bat ready to swoop down upon them. The golden animals on the robe shimmered in the lamp light, moving and swaying within the garment's folds.

In unison, the men fell back a step.

Good, Li Po thought. *Let the spineless creatures quiver!* He reached down with one hand, scooped up a few grains of sulfur, and tossed them on the brazier.

They exploded with a shower of light and an ominous hiss.

The men scurried farther away.

For good measure, Li Po waved his arms and shouted curses at them.

Fiercely he stared at the burly *fon kwei*, the foreign devils who dared surround him in the inner sanctuary of his cave. They were certainly thieves of the lowest sort, for their clothes were strange and rough, tattered and filthy. Their faces were covered with thick, shaggy beards. One man wore an eye patch, another was missing his front teeth. Typical of other Caucasian devils he had seen, they reeked of grease, liquor, and unwashed flesh.

When Li Po spoke again, the strength in his tone belied his age. The words sounded clear and true against the walls of stone. "Be gone, devils! Take what you will and be gone!"

He glanced at the vial. It was still glowing, but the steam had died down. Out of the corner of his eye, he saw a shadow move; one of the men had ventured away from the others and was steadily creeping toward him. Slowly Li Po carried the glass vial to his lips, and just as he did, another man shouted and rushed forward.

In the struggle that followed, the vial fell from Li Po's hand. It fell to the ground, where it shattered into hundreds of tiny shards. The precious elixir mingled with the broken glass on the floor of the cave. The liquid seemed to pulsate. As if it were a live thing, the liquid danced. Its irridescence flared, wavered, and then died.

Before Li Po knew what was happening, the foreigners moved forward in a pack. Someone grabbed his arms, twisted them behind his back, and bound his wrists together.

Li Po began shouting, commanding, summoning the gods for help. But when the first devil remained unharmed, the others failed to heed him.

Helpless now, he watched while they threw all of his precious items into baskets and cursed him in their harsh foreign tongue.

Li Po hung his head in resignation. If he had only swallowed this latest elixir, he would now be immortal. Fit and youthful, he would have been able to fight the devils off.

As the men prodded him out of the cave and along the crooked path that wound down the mountain, Li Po realized with aching clarity that unless he could retain possession of the robe and escape his captors, he would remain a captive, powerless old man doomed to meet the fate of all mortals.

❊ CHAPTER 1 ❊

Good deeds stay indoors . . .
Evil deeds travel many miles from home.

SAN FRANCISCO, 1875

Although she was anxious to see her hostess, Jade Douglas was glad she had arrived before her old friend had awakened. She needed the time alone to collect her thoughts. Jade stared around her borrowed retreat, studying its overblown opulence. Fall sunlight, diffused by fog, barely lit the second-story room, but even the weak, early morning light could not diminish the shining surfaces of the various gilded frames, polished mirrors, and crystal droplets that adorned the wall sconces. Pausing just inside the door, Jade ran her fingertip over the textured wall covering flocked with gold highlights, and then crossed over to the high, four-poster bed swathed in crushed velvet curtains and spread—a veritable sea of emerald green.

Despite the richness of the room's appointments, there was a look of untouched perfection about the place that made it lifeless and uninviting. When she set her satchel on the bed, the faded, lopsided bag reminded her of an old tramp that had somehow crept into a place where it definitely did not belong. She quickly moved it to the floor.

The same muted light that filled the room highlighted the golden strands woven within the red of her hair. Within seconds of closing the door behind her, she had released the wild mass from the severely wound knot tied at the slender nape of her neck. Now, as she ran her fingers through the thick, shining tresses, they sprang to life with curl. Jade shook her hair once more, enjoying the way it swayed past her shoulders. She retrieved her button hook from the satchel, then sat on the edge of the bed and slowly unhooked the buttons of her well-worn shoes. Once they were undone, she sighed with relief, and slipped them off of her feet. They fell to the floor, the sound muffled by the thick Persian carpet. After tossing the hook back into the bag, she paused to admire the ornate detail

7

of the rug's green and gold pattern. She wriggled her stock-
inged toes, then stretched, arms skyward, and crossed the
room to linger before the window. She opened it and leaned out
to welcome the chill October air that chased away the
stuffiness of the room. Jade stood in silent contemplation,
relishing the tangy scent of salt on the air, and stared out at
wisps of fog that crept along and eddied about the other homes
that lined Powell Street.

How different San Francisco was from Paris, where she had
spent the last five years. Beyond the window lay a city grown
wild and unencumbered as a storm at sea. Miners, stock
brokers, bankers, and thieves moved shoulder-to-shoulder
with immigrants of every land along the crowded streets in this
sprawling city on the edge of the world. Fortunes were made
and lost in a day. Everyone in San Francisco was caught up in
the fever of speculation, even hotel maids and milkmen
purchased stocks on the San Francisco exchange. People were
afraid not to spend their hard-earned wages on a chance at
riches, not when so many of the city's most wealthy residents
had made their fortunes in speculation, even though just as
many had lost. The city was much larger than she remembered,
sprawling wherever it was not held in check by the water that
surrounded it. Compared to the ancient, winding streets of
Paris lined with aged stone buildings, San Francisco seemed
new, raw, and barely tamed.

Jade crossed the room again and reached down into the
satchel. When she found her hairbrush, she worked it through
her hair until it shone, then tossed it aside and slipped off her
faded, travel-weary gown. After she draped the dress over a
nearby chair, she donned a robe of rich, topaz silk to cover her
short-sleeved chemise and cotton knickerbockers. As she tied
the sash, she lowered herself to the floor and sat cross-
legged—back straight, body relaxed. Closing her eyes, she
tried to still the inner chatter that plagued her thoughts as they
tumbled one after another.

Jade took a deep breath and sat very still. Her daily
meditation period was a habit she had learned long before she
went to Paris to learn Chinese. These contemplative moments
had long been a custom of her grandfather, Philo Page. As a

small child, she had taken to sitting quietly beside her grandfather whenever he and his companion, Chi Nu, meditated. Before she was twelve, she was able to sit in silence for nearly an hour.

She had barely begun to breathe evenly—taking the slow, rhythmic breaths prescribed by ancient Chinese philosophers—when the bedroom door opened without so much as a warning knock and an effervescent Barbara Barrett swept in.

Casually wrapped in a satin dressing gown with matching ivory slippers, Babs was a picture of elegant dishabille—her luxurious brunette hair swept up off the back of her neck and tied with a wide ribbon in a loose, sensuous style. She looked as beautiful as Jade remembered her.

When they were both thirteen, Babs' figure had already blossomed, while Jade's had remained reed thin. Now, at twenty-three and nearly the same height, Babs was a stunning brunette with dark, flashing eyes and a complexion that glowed the color of ripened apricots. Jade considered herself lucky not to have inherited her father's freckles. Her skin was the palest ivory; beside Babs, Jade had always felt like an ugly duckling.

Babs halted just inside the room and stared down at Jade as if she could not believe her eyes. She took a tentative step forward then halted again. "What are you doing sitting on the floor?"

Jade smiled and stood up, careful to keep her robe modestly closed. She hurried to embrace her old friend with a warm hug. "Oh, Babs! I'm so glad to see you! You look wonderful. You're too good, taking me in like this."

Babs laughed and hugged Jade tight, then pulled back to study her carefully. Her expression sobered. "You look tired, Jade."

Leading Jade across the room, Babs sidestepped the satchel without comment and sat on the edge of the bed. She pulled Jade down beside her. The scent of Babs' expensive perfume heavily scented the air about them.

"You poor thing. If I had known you were arriving so early, I would have been up to meet you. I felt just awful having to cable you in France about your father's murder, but I knew you would want to return as soon as possible." Babs hesitated while she watched Jade's reaction to her words. "You did want to come home, didn't you?"

Jade nodded, reassuring her friend as the two held hands in silent solidarity. She stared down at Babs' well-manicured nails and was suddenly all too aware of her own uneven and neglected ones. "I suppose it was time I came back. My studies were at an end. I'm able to speak Cantonese fluently now, which is what grandfather dearly wanted. So yes, returning to San Francisco was the logical thing to do."

"But what a horrible thing to have to face," Babs said, giving Jade's hand a final squeeze before letting go. "You can't imagine Reggie's reaction to your father's murder—"

"Oh, I think I can." It was no secret that Babs' husband, Reginald Barrett, hated scandal of any kind. He had never hidden his disapproval of Jade. Even when the three of them were younger and he and Babs had first become engaged, Reggie's feelings were clear. To his way of thinking, Jade was too eccentric, too headstrong, and far too intellectual for a woman. A bluestocking, he always called her. "I know Reggie's penchant for keeping up appearances," Jade added.

Babs shrugged. "Well, one can never be too careful. There's nothing San Franciscans enjoy more than someone else's scandal. Have you received any details aside from the *Chronicle* articles I sent you?"

Bothered by disturbing thoughts, Jade was unable to sit any longer. She stood and began to pace, pausing here and there to gingerly touch whatever piece of bric-a-brac caught her eye as she spoke. "A few. I stopped at the police station this morning while I was waiting for a decent hour to come knocking on your door." She lifted the lid of a crystal bonbon dish. It was empty.

Babs brushed at a stray wisp of hair that had escaped the pile atop her crown. "We were out late last night, but you could have come right over. The servants are here to answer the door anyway."

"I met your maid when she let me in."

Babs leaned back on her elbows and jiggled her foot, admiring her fashionable slipper. "Doreen is utterly useless."

Jade paused for a moment and contemplated a Staffordshire

vase on a side table. She wondered if Babs truly meant the insensitive remark. The maid had struck her as very young, inexperienced, perhaps, but very pleasant and hardly useless.

"Well?" Babs prodded.

Jade started. "Well what?"

"What have you learned about the murder? What did the police say?"

"Not much. The detective on the case wasn't there, but the man at the desk was able to tell me that they think my father was connected to a kidnapping of some kind. I'm to meet with the detective in charge of the case later this morning to learn the details."

"This morning? But you just got here. Surely they'll give you time to rest?"

Jade shrugged. "It's not every day a caucasian is found in Little China with a tong war axe buried in his skull."

"God, it's awful, for a man to die that way, isn't it? I mean, I know there was no love lost between you and your father, but . . ."

Jade walked over to the window again, took a deep breath, and stared out at the city. Babs knew her well enough to know what a strain Fredrick Douglas' drinking and gambling had put on her childhood. The girls' mothers had been close; both women encouraged the children's friendship. Jade used to relish her visits to Babs' home; compared to her own, it was a haven, a place filled with love where both parents lavished affection on their child.

Fredrick Douglas had never hidden the fact that he had not wanted the burden of his only child. Jade and her mother had been the victims of his constant verbal abuse. After her mother's death, Jade's grandfather had urged her to study in France. He'd insisted that he needed her to help him catalogue and translate markings on the piece of his Chinese art collection. In reality, they both knew it was a way to escape from her overbearing and increasingly irrational father.

Looking back now, she wished she had possessed the foresight to return before her father had placed the very collection that was essential to her grandfather's dream in jeopardy.

"It's just horrible," Babs went on, unaware that Jade had not been paying attention. "God knows we're probably not even safe in our own beds. That's the trouble with having so many Chinese around. They're taking over the city, you know. I won't even have a Chinese servant in the house."

Jade spun around to face her friend. The Chinese she had known were hardworking and intelligent—fighting to make a place for themselves in a culture that was alien to their own. Amazed by her friend's prejudice, she held her temper, nonetheless. She was, after all, a guest in Babs' home. "Even the police aren't sure it was the Chinese that killed my father, Babs. It could be that the murderer just wanted it to look that way."

"But why? Why would anyone have wanted him dead?" Babs wondered aloud.

"You know my father wasn't the most scrupulous of businessmen, Babs," Jade said softly. He had made more enemies in business than she could count. Some he had duped through sales of bogus silver mine certificates, others he had outgambled, and then there were those whose properties he had gained through illegal real estate transactions. It could have been any one of them. "He was always involved in one scheme or another, always losing as much money as he made." She had been too young and frightened then to do anything about his thieving. Now it was too late.

Jade turned and crossed the room again. She stood beside the bed and toyed with one of the tassels on the satin braid that held the bed drapes swagged open. Babs had shifted on the bed and lay curled up on her side, her feet tucked beneath her dressing gown.

"Right now I'm more concerned with recovering Grandfather Page's Chinese collection than finding out who killed my father. The Hibernia Bank contacted me before I left Paris, and it seems that before he was murdered, my father managed to go through all of the money mother had inherited." She took a deep breath, nearly unable to relate her next bit of bad news. "He even took Grandfather's collection . . . my collection," she amended, "and used it as collateral against his debts. The bank is holding it until I can find a way to pay off the sixty thousand dollars my father owed them."

"Sixty thousand?" Babs sat up.

Jade shook her head. "Exactly. Where am I supposed to get that kind of money in thirty days?"

"Are you sure there's nothing left of your grandfather's estate?"

"Father sold everything off but the old adobe and the land around it, which he could not touch, but that was only because I was named on the deed when I was a child. Grandfather didn't leave a will, so everything that would have been mother's reverted to my father when she died. All that's left is the house and the land it sits on." She flicked the tassel once more before she dropped it. "I'm sure that wherever Grandfather is now, he hates knowing that. If there was any money left at all, I wouldn't have arrived here this morning, bag and baggage, on your doorstep."

Babs leaned back on her elbows. "Don't even think about it. I want you to stay for as long as need be."

Jade had no idea when her affairs would be settled, and at this very moment, she felt too tired to care.

"Maybe you should talk to them. Tell them you need more time," Babs suggested.

Jade shook her head. In his absent-mindedness, her grandfather had not thought to safeguard the collection for her. He had been a self-taught scholar of things Chinese, living not in the present but in the distant past, trying to understand a culture very different from his own. His dream was to find a way to house and display the collection of Chinese antiques he had collected over the years, so that the people of San Francisco could begin to understand the history of the many Chinese that lived and worked among them. He had passed his dream on to Jade.

She couldn't even imagine what state the adobe might be in. The house and grounds were in disrepair even before she left San Francisco, for sadly enough, crumbling adobe bricks had never taken precedence over Philo Page's studies.

Compared to the new homes she had heard were rising on California Street, the place was little more than a hovel of adobe clay. The surrounding garden had once been filled with native plants as well as exotic herbs and flowers able to withstand the climate. It was the place where she had planned to live, and yet, as much as she loved it, she knew she would gladly give it up if it meant saving the collection of Chinese lacquer, pottery, bronzes, and paintings her grandfather had amassed.

"Maybe if I ask Reggie, he might advance you the money you need," Babs volunteered.

Jade turned to her friend. "Sixty thousand dollars?" She shook her head, her eyes wide but dry. "I can't accept your offer. Besides," she said, shrugging, "Reggie has never been more than decidedly cool toward me. I'm sure my father's scandalous murder hasn't endeared me to him, not to mention what happened the night before I left San Francisco."

She had been eighteen then, emotionally drained, her nerves on edge. Caring for her mother had been an ordeal she had yet to put behind her when her father insisted she accompany him to dinner at Cliff House, the restaurant perched on a point across from Seal Rocks.

Determined to stand up to her belligerent, overbearing father as she had always wished her mother would have done, Jade agreed to accompany him to dinner because she felt it would be safer to tell him she was leaving for Paris if they were in a public place where he would not be able to vent his fury. She had asked that she be permitted to leave once the meal had ended and he had agreed, but once they reached Cliff House, the evening began to reel out of control.

As usual, he had gathered together a group of his cronies and began to drink heavily. Jade stayed until the meal had ended, then asked the manager to hail her a hack. Her father told her to sit down, that she was going nowhere until he said she could, and began to lash out at her verbally, seeking to humble and bend her to his will—as he had always done to her mother.

But unlike Melinda Douglas, Jade lashed back. She refused to let his irrational ranting upset her as she stood in a darkened alcove that did little to shield her from the startled, curious expressions of the other diners.

"I'm going now, Father, and tomorrow I'm leaving for France."

He took a menacing step toward her. "You will do no such thing. Get back to the table."

"Grandfather has arranged everything. He's found a traveling companion and a family I can live with in Paris. Now that Mother is gone, there is no longer any reason for me to stay."

Fredrick Douglas had grabbed her arm as she turned to go. "Where in the hell do you think you're going? After all the years and money I had to spend on you, don't think you're going to just walk away."

Jade fought to keep her voice low, tried to ignore the growing number of stares. "If you think I'm going to cower and crawl like my mother used to, think again."

He raised his fist, glanced over his shoulder, then pushed her away. "Go ahead and go!"

Jade stumbled back and fell against the window seat in the alcove. "I hate you."

He raged out of control until there was not a single person in the restaurant who could not hear him. "You're not even mine! I never wanted you." His face was flushed. Threatening to burst, the veins at his temples stood out blue and throbbing against his pale skin.

Laughter had bubbled up in her throat, uncharacteristically sarcastic and cold, as she spurned his cruel remark. There was no denying her flaming hair or emerald eyes, the even brows and finely tapered nose. She looked so much like Fredrick Douglas that she might have been an artist's miniature. He had used that taunt once too often to ever hurt her with the lie again. But this time he had said it before a crowd of onlookers.

"No," she said softly as she slowly stood up to face him again. "Sadly enough, I'm yours. But I wish with all my heart that I wasn't." She stood toe-to-toe with him and refused to cower now that she no longer had to submit to his tantrums to protect her mother. "I'm leaving. If you lay a hand on me, or try to stop me in any way, I'll have the manager fetch the police."

She wanted no part of him, his money, his schemes, or his twisted hatred. Then, just to spite him, to pay him back in kind for every harmful word he had ever inflicted on her mother, Jade lowered her voice to a menacing whisper and said, "I'm not coming back unless it's to dance on your grave."

Now, while Jade had been lost in memories of the past, Babs remained unusually silent for so long that Jade was afraid her friend had fallen asleep. "Babs?"

"You know, Jade," Babs said, propping herself up against the mound of pillows against the carved headboard, "I've been thinking."

Jade tried to remember what they had last discussed. "About Reggie?"

Babs waved the idea away. "Don't worry about Reggie, I can handle him. No, I've been thinking about your predicament."

"And?" Jade couldn't keep the suspicion out of her voice. In the past, whenever Babs got to thinking, it had only led to trouble for them both.

Abruptly, Babs sat up and scooted off the bed. She crossed over to Jade, took her hand and patted it sympathetically. "And I think you should rest." She pulled her dressing gown up and tightened the sash at her waist. "Don't worry about a thing." She turned and headed for the door. Before she left the room, she paused and looked back at Jade. "I'm going to send Doreen in with some of my things. You can't run around town looking like a pauper."

"Which is exactly what I am at the moment."

Babs mumbled something that sounded like, "Not for long," then said, "Leave everything to me," before she hurried out and closed the door behind her.

Jade exhaled, only just realizing she had been holding her breath. There was not much time left before she had to dress and meet the detective assigned to her father's case. She lowered herself to the carpet once again, folded her legs beneath her, and closed her eyes. But it was hard to clear her mind while it still echoed Babs' parting words, *Leave everything to me.*

The brick-lined path between the carriage house and the service porch of Harrington House was carefully manicured and edged with brightly colored blossoms. Pansies turned their faces skyward to drink in the fall sunshine as Jason Terrell Harrington III stood at the far end of the walk and surveyed its precisely laid herringbone pattern before he stepped onto the rich red bricks. When he did, the sound of the worn heels of his leather boots blended with the lilting jingle of the rowels of his spurs as he walked toward the servant's entrance to the grand mansion he could now call his own. Three stories high, the place loomed over the surrounding gardens and cast its shadow over the carriage house and long row of stables behind it.

As he reached the back door, J.T. paused, set down his satchel, saddlebags, and guitar, removed work-hardened leather gloves, and used them to beat the trail dust off his Levi's and the long duster that flapped around his calves. Then he knocked.

The summons rang hollow and went unanswered. Matt Van Buren, his father's lawyer, had alerted him to the fact that the house was unstaffed, the servants dismissed pending the immediate sale of Harrington House. Still, J.T. was not one to walk into an empty house, even if it was his own. He was relieved when no one appeared in answer to his knock. What he needed now was food, a good long bath, and a nap.

Jason pushed aside the edge of his long duster, reached down into the pocket of his denims, and hooked his finger around the key that would gain him entrance. It had been his father's home, yet the place held no boyhood memories for him. J.T. had never lived here. Nor, for that matter, had his father, who had built the mansion merely as a showplace little more than a year ago. J.T. had learned as much from Van Buren when the man wrote to inform him of his father's death and his own subsequent inheritance. J.T. hadn't mourned the loss of a man he had never really known.

The door swung wide to reveal a large service porch that opened onto the cavernous kitchen, silent now, but far from cold due to the warm fall sunshine that had burned away the morning fog. The attorney had promised to send around a grocer's delivery of foodstuffs and assured Jason the wine cellar was still well stocked. Jason was to make himself at home.

Home? He could never imagine this cold mausoleum as a

home, nor this city, for that matter. He had not been out of
New Mexico for three weeks, and yet he was already anxious
to return. He had come to San Francisco only to settle the
estate, sell off his father's coffee import company, the mansion, and stocks, and then go back home to New Mexico.

As he looked around the kitchen, he wondered why his
father had even built the place, for it was obvious no one had
ever used the shining new pots and pans lining the open
cupboards. Compared to the crowded, very noisy kitchen at his
uncle's ranch in New Mexico, this one had all the appeal of an
empty tomb. As he surveyed the place in the late afternoon
light, he tried to imagine his Uncle Cash Younger teasing Aunt
Lupita as she bustled about. It was as impossible as trying to
picture the ranch hands gathering here for cups of strong black
chicory and boisterous talk on cold winter mornings or after the
day's work was through. When his stomach rumbled with
neglect, Jason wished he could smell some of Lupita's tortillas
frying on the griddle, instead of the mustiness of a long
closed-up house.

He had lived with Cash and Lupita for fifteen years now,
although it seemed as if it were just yesterday that his mother
had taken him to New Mexico to live with her brother and his
wife. The sterile emptiness of the mansion made him thankful
he would never have to live in this showplace his father had
built for no apparent reason other than to impress others with
his wealth.

J.T. walked across the deserted kitchen and soon his boot
heels and spurs rang out hollowly in the long, wood-paneled
hallway. No paintings brightened the walls. The doors spaced
at intervals down the hall were all closed, casting the passageway in deep shadow. As he moved along, his saddlebags in one
hand, his guitar under his arm and satchel under the other, J.T.
took care not to bump his possessions against the close walls.
He didn't think it would do to scar up the place since he was
trying to sell it.

Walking down the darkened hallway was like strolling
through a tunnel toward the past, as he pictured the night his
uncle had told him the story of his parents' divorce. He'd been
working with Cash, herding wild mustangs into a box canyon

when they set up camp for the night. Cash had casually mentioned the rotten hand his sister had been dealt when she married Harrington, and J.T. immediately asked if Cash knew what had happened between them.

All his mother had ever told him was that she and his father had differences they could not resolve, but that his father was a good man, an upstanding citizen, and that it was because of her that they finally divorced.

Jason remembered the night as if it were yesterday. The crackling, open fire, the call of the night owl in the trees on the hillside behind them, even the crisp fall air was still as real to him as his uncle's words.

"Hell, yes," Cash had said before he flipped his cigarette into the fire, "you could say it was because of Louisa. It was because your ma wouldn't put up with his livin' part-time with his mistress. Harrington wouldn't give the woman up, either. Not for you, not for Louisa, not for nothin'. Let his wife walk out and take his only son and never put up a fight at all."

Since J.T. had taken his mother at her word—that his father had cared about him, that the money he sent to Louisa Younger Harrington's bank account was for Jason's upbringing and education, that he felt his son was better off living with his mother—he never wondered why his father had never contacted him personally. When he was a child, he had been able to rationalize that his father was an important man who was just too busy to see him. But once Cash had told him the truth straight out, when he learned that his father had placed his love for his mistress above any feelings he had for his wife and son, Jason's illusions vanished, and with them went any shred of respect or admiration he might have ever held for his father.

For years he had nurtured an image of his father that had been built on a lie, and there was nothing J.T. hated worse than a liar. Ever since Cash's revealing conversation, he became angry when he thought of his father and his desertion. His uncle often ribbed him about his unbending idealism and the resultant intolerance he displayed whenever anyone failed to live up to his expectations of them, but his emotional reaction to a deception of any kind was not something he was willing or able to change.

The long, paneled hallway opened onto a foyer as large a
the sitting room back home. Shaking his head, J.T. stared u
at the huge crystal chandelier that hung a good twenty fee
above him in the high open ceiling of the foyer. A wide
curving staircase that led to the second floor beckoned, so h
decided to choose a room of his own before he explored th
rest of the place and made himself something to eat.

❧ CHAPTER 2 ❧

When the blind lead the blind . . .
Beware the river's edge!

Jade glanced around the small but elegantly appointed Barrett library. Bookshelves reached from floor to ceiling, all of them covered with expensive, newly bound books, their leather and gilt spines attesting to the fact that they were more show pieces than treasured well-worn friends. She thought momentarily of her own box of books she had inherited from her grandfather, and knew she would not trade one of them for Reggie's entire collection.

"Miss Douglas?"

Startled out of her thoughts, Jade turned to her companion, Lieutenant Jon Chang, who sat directly across from her in a tall wing chair upholstered in burgundy leather near the fireplace. In a woolen jacket and plaid pants, his low-cut boots polished to a high, gleaming shine, Jon Chang appeared every inch a California businessman—except for the waist-length queue that appeared from beneath his bowler hat.

"Pardon me, Mr. Chang. I'm afraid my mind has wandered. You were saying?" Exhaustion made it hard to concentrate.

"I'm interpreter for the department's newly formed Raiding Squad. We work the back alleys of Little China to stem the opium trade. Since your father's body was found in Little China—"

"—with a tong war axe in his head," she completed.

"I was assigned to the case. Are you familiar with the tongs, Miss Douglas?"

Jade nodded. "They're Chinese associations established to address the grievances of their members. But I don't ever recall reading about Caucasians being involved in their disputes. Do you really have reason to believe my father's death had anything to do with the tong?"

"We are not certain. It may be that the murderer just wanted

21

it to appear that way. Do you know anyone who might have wanted to kill your father?"

Jade recalled what she had told Babs earlier. "My father was not the most ethical of businessmen, Detective."

Chang's expression was unreadable. "Certain things have come to light."

"Do you mind telling me what kind of *things*?"

"On the surface, it seems your father's last venture involved some sort of gold speculation."

"I'm not surprised. He was always involved in one sort of scheme or another," she said.

"So I have learned."

Jade stood, hoping that if she kept moving she would not feel so sleepy. "I think it may have been my grandfather's good name and wealth that kept the law from coming down so hard on my father. That, and the fact that no one could ever prove he had actually done anything wrong. Many of the men he duped were too embarrassed to try and recoup their losses. Perhaps someone finally took matters into his own hands."

"I have uncovered some most unusual news concerning your father's death, Miss Douglas." He reached into his pocket and pulled out a folded slip of paper covered with Chinese characters. "Do you read Chinese?"

With a nod, she reached for the small, neatly scripted page. "I read and speak Cantonese, Lieutenant," she said softly as she looked down at the page of Chinese characters. When his face registered surprise she explained, "My grandfather sent me to Paris to live with a missionary and his family recently returned from Canton so that I could learn from them." With a wistful smile she added, "I didn't know that he would not be here to welcome me home again."

"I am sorry for your loss."

She accepted his sympathy and then concentrated on the slip of paper in her hand.

Chang explained as she read. "This is a *chin hung*, a public notice. Originally it was posted on the bulletin wall on Clay Street in Little China. An informant turned it over to me just yesterday." He paused when she began to read aloud.

"It is believed that Fredrick Douglas has abducted one Li

Po, venerated wizard of Sin Ngan Hien. Be it known that if any man of any association can remove the barbarian Douglas, we will thankfully pay six hundred dollars. If he only wounds him, we shall pay three hundred. The combined associations shall pay one thousand dollars to the man who discovers the whereabouts of Li Po."

Jade tried to digest the meaning of the strangely worded notice. "The tongs *advertised* to have my father assassinated? Is that what *removed* refers to?"

"So it seems."

Stunned by the contents of the advertisement, Jade could not imagine the reason why her father would abduct a Chinese from the mainland, but she knew that if he had indeed been guilty of such a crime, money was somehow involved. "I still don't understand," she admitted quietly.

"We are trying to piece together your father's reasons for kidnapping this old man, Li Po, if indeed this notice is true. At least now the motive for your father's murder is somewhat clearer."

Chang continued, "Li Po was very old, somewhat worshipped by the villagers of Sin Ngan Hien. He was known as a formidable wizard. We are not even sure the old man ever reached San Francisco. My informants say he was smuggled into the country and then disappeared without a trace."

She handed the notice back to Chang. "What would my father want with an old man?"

He refolded and pocketed it. "Li Po was a wizard. An alchemist."

Jade crossed the room and sank down upon the settee. "An alchemist?" Things suddenly became all too clear as she recalled what her grandfather had told her of the Chinese emperors who always kept a resident alchemist at court. She thought aloud, "A man versed in the ways of ancient alchemy is capable of changing one substance into another. Many claimed they had the power to extend life, some said they could turn lead into gold."

And she knew very well what the word gold meant to her father.

"The last speculative venture your father attempted involved the sale of certificates, shares in a gold mine. He claimed the gold from this mine would prove to be of the highest grade ever found."

"So you think the alchemist might have been the key to a gold mine hoax?" It all sounded too incredible to be believed. "You don't think it's possible that the old man could really make gold, do you?"

Chang paused for a moment. Jade watched his expression as centuries of traditional beliefs warred with modern thought. "I believe it is highly unlikely. If anyone could change base metals into gold, then gold would become worthless, wouldn't it?"

"Or . . . the man who knew the secret would become the richest man in the world," Jade said softly.

Chang nodded. "I see you grasp what might have been your father's plan. I think Fredrick Douglas definitely believed in Li Po's ability—if the public notice is true."

"But to kidnap an old man . . . to bring him all the way from China . . ."

"You knew your father far better than I, who can only guess at answers. What do you think, Miss Douglas?"

Jade thought about the past, the business discussions she had overheard as her father and his associates sat around a crowded table. She thought about the diamond hoaxes, the silver mines in Nevada that never panned out, the import-export schemes. She thought, too, about the money her father had spent over the years—so much money that he had not only squandered his own funds, but the fortune her mother would have inherited as well. Most of all she thought of the abusive words and the harsh way he had always treated her and her mother.

She faced the truth without a hint of doubt. "I believe he was quite capable of it, Mr. Chang. I believe my father was capable of anything. But how would the tongs here in San Francisco have learned of Li Po's abduction?"

"Word could have reached the port at the same time Li Po did, especially if there were any immigrants or slave girls brought over on the same ship."

Jade sighed and wriggled uncomfortably in her borrowed finery. She felt like an over-dressed, long-necked goose. After suffering a round of insistence on Babs' part, Jade had agreed to wear her friend's polonaise walking suit for her meeting with the detective. Doreen had styled her hair in an upswept creation that was as unfamiliar to her as her elegant attire. She was afraid that one unthinking move might send hairpins flying or set the uncomfortable bustle askew. "It must have been easy for the tongs to find an assassin for six hundred dollars." She shivered involuntarily. Accounts of the hatchetmen who hacked men to death in the back alleys with meat axes, daggers, and snickersnees were legendary. It was even bandied about that such assassins were said to order wildcat in the Chinese restaurants because they believed it would give them superhuman power.

Trying to weigh the gravity of this new information and what it meant to her present situation, Jade asked, "What happens now? Doesn't this explain my father's murder?"

"There is no proof that Li Po was abducted. Until we find him, or his remains—"

"You think my father might have killed him?"

"All the more reason your father was assassinated in return. I should tell you there is little hope of finding the man or men who actually killed your father. The tongs protect their own."

Jade thought of the network of opium dens and warrens of Little China, the joy houses filled with slave girls and *fan-tan* parlors that served as fronts for the brothels. Her grandfather had not spared her sensibilities when he taught her about San Francisco's Chinese, both the good and the bad. Little China was a city within a city, a world within a world. Her father's murderer could easily take refuge there forever.

Jade rubbed her eyes. Lack of sleep had made them dry and itchy. She wondered what the unreadable lieutenant thought of her lack of energy or enthusiasm at this point.

As if he sensed her fatigue, Chang shifted in his chair and then stood. "I know you must be weary from your journey, so I will leave you now to think over all I have told you. If you come across any of your father's things that might be of importance, I hope you will let me know. We searched his hotel suite after his death, but found nothing."

Together they walked to the library door. As Jade opened it

and then followed Chang into the entry hall, they both came to an abrupt halt when they encountered Reggie Barrett on the staircase in conversation with his wife. Both Barretts were so intent that they failed to notice them. Nor did they realize their exchange could be overheard.

"What is she doing in there closeted with that man?" Reggie demanded, anger all too visible in the veins that strained against the starched fabric of his collar. As always, he was impeccably dressed, his hair slicked down with scented oil. His light eyes and patrician nose added to his undistinguished features. He appeared much the same as Jade had last seen him, except for deepened creases across his brow and the harsh, unexpressive line of his lips.

Babs tried to placate him. "He's a policeman, Reggie. A detective. Just calm down."

Jade had to congratulate Babs as she stood up to him, but Reggie would not be daunted. "Good grief! It's enough we have to have *her* here. Now there's a damned Chinaman running in and out and they're discussing her father's *murder*, no less! What next?"

Jade glanced over at Chang and moved swiftly to halt any further humiliation by interrupting the Barretts and introducing the lieutenant.

Reggie spared the man little more than a nod. Babs colored and tried to force a smile. Head high, Jade then led the lieutenant to the front door. Upon her return, she found that Reggie had disappeared upstairs without another word.

"I'm sorry you had to hear that," Babs said.

Fatigue and worry did little to numb the embarrassment and anger Jade felt. "I'm just sorry the detective had to hear it. I know Reggie is entitled to his opinion, but I'm just as entitled to my own, and I can't condone such open hostility toward a person merely because of the color of his skin. Reggie won't have to put up with such an unwanted invasion of his privacy, because I'll be leaving as soon as I can."

"Calm down, Jade. I absolutely refuse to let you leave before you have a decent place to stay. Reggie's tantrums never last long."

Fatigue washed over Jade again in waves. Where could she

go? The only other person she might appeal to was an old friend of her grandfather's, who had often brought him art pieces from the Orient, but she had learned that morning when her own ship docked that Captain Emery Lennox's vessel was not in port. She reached up and began to unpin her hair.

"Now, what did the detective say?" Babs wanted to know.

"I'll tell you over a cup of tea in my room," Jade promised. "Right now, I would just like to get out of all these clothes." As she mounted the stairs she could not help but ask herself the same phrase that Reggie had voiced aloud. *What next?*

Closeted in Jade's room once more, the two women shared a cup of bohea tea at a small table near the window.

Babs spoke abruptly. "What you need to do is marry an extremely rich man." As if the outcome was already settled, she sat back, folded her arms across her breasts, and waited for Jade's reaction, which was immediate.

"You can't be serious!"

Babs merely smiled.

"You are."

"Of course." Theatrically, Babs waved a hand in the air.

"I won't even think of it."

"There's no other way, as far as I can see."

"Look again," Jade said.

"Why not marry some old man with money? Make him happy and he'll pay off your debts. The collection will be saved and *voila,* your worries over."

Surprised by Babs' callous attitude, Jade wondered if she had truly changed so much, or if she was just seeing her friend clearly for the first time.

"You've become so calculating," Jade said, thinking aloud.

"Calculating, or realistic?"

"I'll find work," Jade said hopefully.

"At what? You have no skills worth selling except yourself."

"Babs!" Appalled, Jade flushed to the roots.

"I mean it. So, you've studied Chinese art. What choice do you have? You might become a governess, but what woman in her right mind would want a temptation like you around?"

"I'm hardly that," Jade assured her.

Babs grabbed her by the wrist and pulled Jade up and across the room until the two of them stood before the vanity mirror. "Look at yourself. You aren't the gangly redhead that left here five years ago. Jade, you're beautiful! You've filled out." Babs pulled the back of the silk robe Jade had donned once again, until it became taut and molded itself against her ample breasts. "Your hair has gone to red-gold and your eyes . . . well, they've always been your best asset." Babs let go of her and then walked away mumbling, "If you'd just wear some decent clothes."

Jade stroked the fine silk of her robe. It had grown thin in spots, as fragile as rice paper, but she loved it. "My clothes are fine."

Babs reached behind her and lifted the rumpled dress Jade had been wearing when she arrived that morning. "Fine for an old maid or a Chinese coolie. Silk pants and Mandarin jackets just aren't the fashion these days."

"What do I care for fashion?"

"Obviously nothing."

"Stop mumbling," Jade warned. "Besides, I do own a few nice things."

"All hopelessly out of date, I'll bet. Did you buy any new gowns in Paris?"

Jade thought of the simple life she had shared with the Reverend Bishop and his family in a modest section of the city. She pictured her dour gray wool skirts and much-worn blouses. "I didn't need new clothes there." She was thoughtful for a moment, before she said, "I could teach."

"Oh yes. And make barely enough money to feed yourself. And where do you intend to live? You'll need an entire staff of workmen just to make the old adobe liveable."

"How do you know?"

"Reggie was out that way hunting last year and told me the place had nearly fallen down."

Jade couldn't hide her disappointment. Things were worse than she thought. "I was thinking of offering it to the bank. At least that way it would seem as if I'm trying to pay off the debt.

Maybe then they would turn some of the oldest pieces over to me."

"Don't you think that if they had wanted that crumbling old house that they would have suggested taking it over by now?"

"But I haven't even had time to correspond with them yet. I've only received the one letter."

Babs rolled her eyes toward the ceiling.

Jade sighed as she rubbed her temples. Even the hot tea had not relieved her fatigue. "I won't give in without a fight." She wished she had the nerve to tell Babs that she would like some time alone, but she did not feel right about ejecting her hostess from her room.

They remained still for a time, the only sound in the room the rhythmic tick of the standing clock in the hallway outside. The smell of Babs perfume mingled with the tang of the salt air that drifted in the open window.

Babs pushed aside her cup and saucer, rested her elbows on the table, and stared at Jade. "I want you to think about my plan, Jade. Think hard and carefully."

Jade felt her heart harden as she looked over at Babs. "Don't you think I've seen enough of marriage to know I don't want any part of it for myself?"

"You can't compare every marriage to your parents'," Babs said softly. "Look at Reggie and me."

"You've been in love with Reggie since you were twelve."

Fingering the hem of her robe, all the while ignoring Babs, Jade wished the answers to life and love were as easy for her as they had always been for Babs, but the only real affection she had ever known had come from her grandfather, her mother, and Babs. Her parents' dismal marriage had been all too real—a nightmare instead of a dream.

How many times had she watched her mother pace the floor, wringing her hands, praying that Fredrick Douglas would come home, and wondering aloud what mood he would be in when he finally arrived? And how many times had she and her mother cowered in fear in the pantry, or in Jade's room, while he spent his drunken rage shattering dishes and glasses, cursing, and berating them at the same time?

As if Babs sensed Jade was lost in the past, she asked softly,

"Did your father ever beat you? I know how cruel he was, but did he ever physically hurt you?"

Jade denied it with a quick shake of her head. "No. He never touched me, in love or in hate. At times he could be almost caring—almost. Then he would begin drinking and his mood would radically change. He was so volatile that whenever things did not go his way—and that was often—he would take his anger out on my mother and me." She sighed and drew a length of hair over her shoulder. "My mother loved him more than life itself. She did anything he asked, and was always crying and pleading with him to stay with us whenever he threatened to leave. When I grew up it was so evident to me that he had only married her for her money that I realized my mother must have known it all along, too. But she didn't even care."

Babs reached out and squeezed Jade's hand. "I know how proud and stubborn you've had to become, but I know if you'll only think about it, you'll see that my plan is the only way, because to be blatantly honest—"

"Which I know you will be," Jade quipped.

"—you're already twenty-three. Soon you'll be an old maid. You'll just have to learn to use your charm to catch a man. A very rich man," she amended.

Abruptly, Jade stood up and walked away from Babs. "This is ridiculous."

"No, it's not. You haven't a choice if you intend to save that collection. I know everything about who's doing what to whom in San Francisco, so it won't take me long to come up with a list of eligible widowers."

"How can you sound so mercenary?"

"I thought you'd do anything to that junk."

"Within reason."

"Can you think of any other way?" Babs asked.

The answer came in a tight whisper. "There's still time."

"You're right of course, but honestly, Jade, it's the only way if you insist on recouping your grandfather's collection of Chinese hodgepodge. Lord knows why you even care."

"You're mumbling again. Besides, it's a valuable collection of artifacts, not hodgepodge, which by rights belongs to me.

My grandfather's dream was to see that collection housed in a museum where everyone would benefit from it and learn about the Chinese."

"Who cares about the Chinese anyway?"

"I still refuse to let the Hibernia Bank sell even one piece of grandfather's things in order to pay my father's debts."

Babs ignored her sharp tone and prattled on. "What's wrong with marrying someone for money?"

"Please, Babs. Stop it."

"It would be simple." With a snap of her fingers, Babs stood up and began to pace around Jade, who sat resting her head in her hands. "A most excellent catch passed away a month ago. Jason Terrell Harrington, Junior. He owned a monstrous new mansion across from the Stanford's on Nob Hill. Died without an heir, or so everyone thought, but it seems he had a son no one even remembered. The news came as quite a shock, stirred up rumors for weeks."

"Babs, I'm really tired, do you think—"

Babs lowered her voice and leaned close as she passed Jade again. "Her mother actually *divorced* Harrington and took the boy away over twenty-five years ago. Seems he grew up on some cattle ranch in Arizona or Mexico or some such dusty place. I can't recall which. He's nearly thirty now. Exactly thirty, I think, and fresh off the farm. He didn't even want to come to settle the estate—just asked his father's attorney to send him his money. Can you imagine? Here he has inherited a fortune, a mansion, and guaranteed standing among some of the richest people in the world, and he doesn't want any part of it. He should be in San Francisco by now."

Jade knew that there was no stopping Babs now. "I had forgotten how thorough the rumor mongers were in this place."

"Harrington's lawyer is Matt Van Buren. Matt's a member of Reggie's club."

Babs' eyes took on a faraway look and she stood lost in thought, tapping her index fingernail on her front tooth. Jade's worry deepened. "I know that look. What are you thinking?"

"I think it's time to go shopping," Babs said.

Jade yawned. "I'd much rather take a nap."

"You can't wear my clothes forever. Come on now, put on the pink stripe that Doreen brought in. The color will cheer you. We'll go shopping a while, not long I promise, then you can rest. The fresh air will revive you."

"I don't think so."

Babs walked back over to Jade and stood, hands on hips, staring down at her. "I'll send Doreen in to help you." When Jade was about to protest again she added, "And I won't take no for an answer."

Shadows blurred reality as they so often did whenever he was dreaming of the past. In the strange way of all dreamers, Jason was both observer and participant. He saw himself as a youth of fifteen, smooth-skinned and lanky, strolling along the stream that crossed the homestead near Athens, Georgia, where he had lived with his mother and her maiden aunt.

His childhood sweetheart, Nettie Parsons, walked beside him, her fingers resting lightly, properly, against the crook of his arm. She appeared as radiant as always, her blond hair parted and coiled into perfect ringlets that bobbed with every dainty step she took as they ambled along. The spring day of his dream was a warm, sunny one. Bird song surrounded them and the world seemed reborn. Nettie's gown was of a bygone era, a hoop-skirted confection covered with hand-painted roses. The blushing pink satin highlighted the roseate glow of her complexion. His dream was complete in every detail, down to the hint of jasmine that always scented the air about her.

J.T.'s heart contracted just as it had when the dream had been a reality. He knew what he was about to say to her, and willed himself to stop. But the Jason in the dream failed to obey his command, and the scene was played out just as it had been fifteen years before.

"I'll be leaving soon, Nettie," he said.

He watched her lips pout as she began to protest, her languid southern drawl as melodic as he remembered it. "You just can't leave me, Jason. Tell your mama you'll do no such thing, now, you hear? I can't live without you."

She paused along the bank of the stream, concentrating on the water lapping against the sandy creek bottom. He reached out to touch her shoulder. He would tell her that he would not go to New Mexico Territory with his mother, that he would stay in Georgia until she turned sixteen and her father gave them permission to marry.

If he left her behind, he knew what would happen. There were better prospects, wealthy plantation owners' sons who could give her everything her heart desired. But none could love her more.

Fifteen years ago, he had left her. Now, his dream was giving him a chance to stay.

But the past continued to unfold without alteration. When Nettie felt his touch, she turned to him just as she had so long ago, her eyes luminous with unshed tears. His own heart was near to breaking.

"In a year or two I'll send for you, Nettie. We'll get married just like we've planned, I promise."

She sniffed and accepted the handkerchief he handed her. "You been promising to marry me since we were seven years old, J.T. I just don't know how you can go off now and leave me this way."

"Mama needs me more than you do right now, Nettie. She's sold the place and is dead set against anything but moving to my uncle's ranch. There's nothing to be done for it. As soon as I see mama safe and settled there, I'll come back for you. How's that?" He reached out and wiped away one of her stray tears.

She sniffed again, and then, with her customary resiliency, Nettie brightened and smiled, her sadness behind her for the time being. "I guess so, Jason, but I want you to remember that you'll be takin' my little bitty ol' heart along with you. So be careful with it, will you now, honey?"

As the vision faded, Jason tried to recapture his dream, but when he reached out to Nettie, he jerked himself awake. When he woke up to find his hat pulled low over his eyes, he reached up and pushed it to the crown of his head, then sat up and looked around. The last thing he remembered was walking into the master suite, dropping his things in the corner of the expansive room, and then stretching out on the sleigh bed that dominated the center of the room.

J.T. stretched, then swung his feet over the edge of the bed. While he rubbed his hand across the stubble that shaded the lower half of his face, his stomach rumbled. He ambled out of the room and down the hall, unable to shake the remnants of the dream. *What would Nettie think of this place?* he wondered. Despite the years that had passed, despite the impossibility of the notion, he could imagine the perfect hostess Nettie Parsons would make as mistress of Harrington House. The place would be a fitting background to her beauty. As he descended the wide, curved stairs and assessed the fine workmanship in the graceful curve of the handrail, he silently admitted to himself that Nettie still inhabited a special place in his heart, and always would. To him she represented all that was the ideal of southern womanhood—purity, regal grace, loyalty. It was Nettie's own unbending convictions that had forced the permanent rift between them. That, and his own beliefs. Shortly after he and his mother moved to New Mexico, the War Between the States had erupted. Although he had been raised in Georgia, J.T., like his Uncle Cash, had refused to take sides. But his decision not to fight had cost him Nettie, for she had expected him to return to Georgia and join the Confederate Army. When J.T. refused, after trying to explain to her that he did not believe in fighting against his own countrymen—no matter what their beliefs—and that Cash needed him on the ranch, she wrote back to tell him that under no condition could she continue to love a man who would not fight to defend the Confederacy.

He had written to her after that, but his letters had returned unopened. As demanding as the ranch was, he had little time to waste writing letters that would only be returned, and so soon he stopped writing at all. There had been a girlfriend or two, young women he'd met in Taos, ranchers' daughters he'd danced with at gatherings, whores he'd paid for in Santa Fe, but there had never been anyone in his life he had loved as much as he had Nettie. After fifteen years, he doubted there ever would be.

J.T. paused in the foyer. The entryway reminded him of the vestibule of a church with its high, vaulted ceiling and double doors. He stood for a moment with his hands jammed into his pockets, studied the two long panels of stained glass that bordered the front doors, shook his head, and then headed for the kitchen again.

"I can't believe I let you talk me into this." Jade shifted uneasily on the carriage seat, careful not to crush the bustle of the second gown she'd had to don that day. "Where exactly are we going?" If indeed they were going shopping, as Babs had insisted, the driver was headed in the wrong direction.

"I told Harry to swing by Harrington House."

Jade straightened, suddenly wary. "Why?"

"To welcome Jason Harrington III to town, why else? Doreen told me that the neighbors' maid told her that their yard man had seen him ride up to Harrington House on horseback not an hour ago."

Jade frowned and glanced out of the carriage window. "It's very crass of us to go calling on him before he has had time to get settled."

"In this city, anyone who hopes to take advantage of an opportunity has to act and act fast. Besides," Babs added, drawing herself up smugly, "the Elite Directory states, 'It is a rule of people of quality to call on persons newly arrived in the city.'"

"But, a lady doesn't call upon a gentleman," Jade countered.

Babs waved away the comment. "He won't know that."

"You hope."

Jade watched with mounting suspicion as the Barretts' shining, black-lacquered carriage entered the gate to Harrington House. When it halted before the towering double doors, Babs opened the door and urged Jade forward with a shove. Harry, the driver, hopped down from his seat to assist her.

"Get out, Jade."

"Honestly, Babs, I don't think we should do this." Jade twisted her gloved hands in her lap as she tried to ignore the heat from the rush of blood that stained her cheeks.

"Out! If you start to get cold feet, just keep thinking of that Chinese collection you're so set on rescuing from the bank, and pull yourself together. I've been over and over this."

"I haven't agreed to anything. In fact, I refuse to meet this man. I have no intention of duping someone into marriage."

For a moment Babs appeared perplexed. She wrinkled her brow in thought, sighed, and just as Jade was certain she was about to capitulate, Babs said, "I'll be right behind you. Let's get out, shall we?"

Jade stayed put.

"All you have to do is meet him. *I* want to meet him. The least you can do is come with me."

Harry shifted from one foot to the other, carefully watching them both between worried glances at the front of the imposing structure behind him. Carriages passed by on the street outside the fenced lawn while a steady breeze from the bay blew up California Street.

"Whenever you start a sentence with 'all you have to do,' then I know we're headed for trouble. Remember the time you decided we should take that dinghy out in the bay and row around the ships in the harbor? We were caught in a riptide that nearly carried us out to sea before we were rescued. My father locked me away for a month."

"Pooh. You make it sound worse than it really was," Babs said.

"It couldn't have been any worse unless we had drowned. We were gone for hours without food or water, and I ended up with my skin sun-scorched!"

"This is different."

"How?"

Babs smiled. "You're on dry land. Now let's get out."

Jade knew Babs well enough to know she would not be dissuaded once she set herself to a task. It would be best to meet Harrington and get it over with, rather than stand outside his door and argue for an hour with Babs. With her skirt gathered in her hands, Jade stepped out of the carriage, taking care not to miss the step. The Barretts' driver took her hand and helped her down.

Babs hung back. As soon as Jade stepped aside to let her out, the brunette slammed the carriage door shut. Furious, Jade spun around and made a grab at the handle.

Babs stared at Harry with a cool expression that brooked no argument. "A hideous headache just hit me. Get back up on the box, Harry. Now."

Jade grappled with the door handle, which was now locked

She gritted her teeth. "You open this door, Barbara Barrett, or I'll never speak to you again as long as you live, so help me God!"

"Drive on, Harry," Babs called over Jade's tirade. "I'm doing this for your own good, Jade. All you have to do is meet him, let him get a look at you all dressed up, and ask him for a ride home."

Harry glanced back, hesitant to drive away while his mistress' friend continued to cling to the door handle. Babs reached out of the window, grabbed Jade by the wrists, and forced her away from the carriage. "Now, Harry, now!" she called out.

Her temper blazing, Jade tried to quell a flurry of nervous flutters in her stomach as she watched the carriage speed down the drive.

It was a long walk back.

Jade turned and looked at the oversized doors. Her blush failed to recede. Standing alone outside of Harrington's front door, she felt humiliated. She should have known Babs would not rest until she had forced a meeting.

Jade turned again when she heard another carriage roll by. For a moment she thought about walking back down the long drive and waving down a ride, but hesitated, afraid she might find herself in a worse predicament.

She raised her hand to knock, dropped it to her side, then stood staring at the door once again. It took a few moments more before she decided that Harrington could easily have one of his servants drive her back to the Barretts', where she intended to immediately pack her meager belongings and move out—onto the streets if necessary. At least there she would not have to put up with Reggie's disapproval and prejudice, or Babs' scheming.

Jade squared her shoulders and tilted her face to take full advantage of the late afternoon sunlight. She straightened the jaunty princess hat, then smoothed her perfectly fitted white kid gloves. Babs had seen to every last detail.

She took a deep breath, then licked her lips and raised her hand again to grab the ring that dangled from the mouth of a brass lion's head. Its feline eyes glowered at her forebodingly as she rapped the knocker in a series of loud bangs and waited for someone to answer the door.

❧ CHAPTER 3 ❧

Easy to bend the body . . .
Not the will.

She did not have to wait long.

The door swung wide, astonishing her at first, for any well-trained houseboy knew better than to open a front door more than halfway. Trying to show as little curiosity as possible, Jade's gaze flickered over what hardly passed as a decently dressed servant.

Spatula in hand, the man stared back at her with a questioning half-smile. She was amazed to find him rude enough to wear a hat indoors. It was not even a fashionable bowler, but a wide-brimmed, high-crowned Stetson that had seen better days. Dust was caked here and there about the tired hills and valleys of the hat. The brim shadowed his eyes, but did not hide the fact that they were a clear, rich blue. The lower half of his face was covered with the stubble of a dark blond beard—a good two days' worth at the very least. A dark shirt, open at the neck to reveal his deeply tanned skin, was half-hidden beneath a creased leather vest. Faded denim trousers molded themselves to long, well-muscled legs, almost to the point of indecency. The glowing glint of teasing humor in his eyes sparked her indignation. He was like no hired servant she had ever seen—he looked more like a drifter pressed into service.

She straightened, faced him squarely, and in a steady voice that belied her inner turmoil said, "I've come to see Mr. Harrington. Please tell him I'm here."

His voice was deep, somewhat gravelly. The words were strung out in a low, lazy drawl. "And who might be calling?"

She watched his lips twitch slightly at the corners and wondered what kind of a man would welcome this impertinent servant into his employ. What in God's name must J.T. Harrington be like?

39

"My name is Jade Douglas." She wished she had her hands clenched tightly about Babs' slender neck right now. Instead, she opted for twisting the drawstrings on her reticule.

He stepped aside and indicated that she follow him. Hesitantly, she walked into the wide entry hall and quickly assessed the high-vaulted ceiling, the chandelier that dangled from it with its deluge of crystal droplets, the marble floor beneath her feet. Her attention was drawn to the sound of the spurs attached to the man's boots. She cringed at the thought of those spurs scraping against the highly polished marble or the shining oak floors that stretched beyond a series of doorways that ringed the foyer.

"Mighty neighborly of you to call, Miss Douglas."

Overawed by her surroundings, she jumped at the sound of his voice, realizing she had nearly forgotten him. His drawl seemed to have lengthened. The intent way he was staring at her did little to quell her uneasiness. Were they all alone? She tried again. "I would like to see Mr. Harrington. Now."

The smile no longer merely teased his lips. It eased across his face and became full blown to reveal a wide grin. This was no grizzled older man. He was much younger than she had first assumed. His grin lightened the dark look of him, subtracted years from the creases of his sun-darkened face.

Jason Harrington stared just as curiously at Jade, and could not believe his good fortune. He had almost ignored the incessant knock when he had first heard it, but now, as he stood staring down at the green-eyed beauty next to him, he forgave the intrusion and forgot all about his grumbling stomach.

J.T. had never believed in love at first sight. He realized as he marveled at his immediate, overwhelming attraction to Jade Douglas that he had never been knocked off his feet by the sight of a woman before. While he stared back at her, he absently ran his fingers over his stubbled jaw. He'd never experienced vanity before either, but just now he wished he'd taken a bath and shaved the minute he had arrived.

He wondered what had brought her to his door, then immediately decided he would not mind taking the rest of the afternoon to find out. "What do you want with him?"

Jade stiffened. "Pardon me?"

"Why do you want to see J.T. Harrington?"

Jade tensed and took a step toward the door. "If you aren't going to call him, then I'll be going."

Jason couldn't resist looping his thumbs in his back pockets and rolling on his heels. He eyed her speculatively again and decided she was clearly the best looking woman he had ever laid eyes on—with or without the fancy clothes. Then he slowly shrugged and said, "Whatever you want with J.T. does concern me, Miss Douglas. I *am* Jason Harrington. J.T. to my friends." He started to extend the hand that held the spatula, switched it over, offered the other, and continued to smile down on her while she decided whether or not to take his proffered hand.

For a moment Jade stared, speechless. The strong, lean fingers, the sprinkling of golden hair across the back of his hand and up the arm that showed below his upturned sleeve— her gaze captured it all, even to the crescent-shaped scar above the base of his thumb. Jade caught herself staring, and wondered at her own reaction. Recovering quickly, she made it clear she had no intention of touching him, and watched him push the brim of his hat upward with his thumb until the disreputable thing rode upon the back of his head. No longer shadowed, his **azure** eyes stared down at her with undisguised amusement and a hint of admiration.

Jade experienced a deep sense of foreboding. The obviously empty house loomed about her, the silence nearly deafening. Each breath she drew was magnified by the cold wood and marble emptiness. He was staring at her the way a cat might stare at a cornered mouse. Her feeling of unease intensified as he closed the front door behind her.

Jade finally found her voice and asked, "Where are the servants?"

"Out of a job, it seems. The place is for sale. Now, what can I do for you, Miss Douglas?"

He was direct, asking her again like that. Too direct, when it came right down to it. She watched him assess every inch of her. While she stood motionless, wondering what he would think if she turned on her heel and walked out without another word, he looked her up and down and up again. Didn't he know that his slow perusal was not only embarrassing, but improper?

Without pausing to think of the consequences, she decided to pay him back in kind. Her gaze traveled away from his eyes, past the open collar of his shirt, down the neat row of buttons on his vest, jumped the crotch of his denims to his sadly scuffed boots, then shot hastily back up to his eyes. There. Let him taste a little of his own medicine.

It would have been easier if her cheeks had not tinted with color when she avoided staring dead center at the front of his pants. What started as a swift once-over had taken forever because of his height. At five-foot-ten she was in the habit of meeting men eye-to-eye, if not actually looking down at some of them. But Jason Terrell Harrington had to be at least six-foot-three. At least. She was forced to look up at him.

Under his rough exterior and well-worn clothes there was an all too easy sensuality about him—one that tempted her to guess what he would look like washed, dressed, and groomed like a gentleman. Jade paused to wonder where the idea came from, for she had certainly never entertained thoughts of a man in such terms before. While she lived in Paris, she had been intent on her studies. Neither the urge nor the opportunity had ever arisen. Before that time, there had only been her mother to care for, and her grandfather's dream.

The only thing that kept her from running out the door and down the drive was the fact that J.T. Harrington stood three feet away waiting for an explanation.

Her mind whirled and the words nearly stuck in her throat, but she finally managed to blurt out, "I . . . I've come to welcome you to San Francisco."

Even as the words escaped her they sounded absurd. She watched the man wage a silent battle against outright laughter as the lines about his eyes deepened and his lips twitched. He rubbed a hand over his square jaw.

Jade straightened, affronted by his show of humor at her expense. "And now that I have, I'll be going."

Jason stepped between Jade and the door. "No need to be hasty, Miss Douglas."

When he leaned against the dark wood and casually crossed

his booted feet, Jade glanced around, searching for another exit. She had no idea which door would lead her to the rear of the house.

"At least stay until you tell me why you're really here."

"I have."

"I don't believe you."

"Why not?"

"Your eyes tell me you're lying. They're very open, very honest."

"I'm staying with a friend, Barbara Barrett, and she suggested it would be the polite thing to do to come by and welcome you to San Francisco."

His eyes took in the empty room and flashed back to Jade. "A friend? Where is your friend, Miss Douglas?"

Her expression darkened. "She became ill, quite suddenly in fact, and had to leave just as we arrived. I knocked only because I thought that perhaps one of your servants could take me home. I'm sorry now that I did, because I see I've inconvenienced you."

He didn't budge, except to cross his arms over his chest. "Tell me more about this *friend* of yours. The one who so mysteriously left you on my doorstep."

Jade knew he had every right to be suspicious. After all, hadn't Babs indeed meant for her to meet him because of his money? The fact that she wanted nothing to do with such a plan could not help her now. She would have to do some fast talking to convince him that her visit was as innocent as she claimed, at least on her part.

"I've just returned to San Francisco myself, and my hostess, Barbara Barrett—her husband is Reginald Barrett—maybe you know him?" When he shook his head, she continued anyway. "Well, Babs decided we should welcome you to town and see if we might be of any assistance to you."

One brow slowly arched as his gaze turned skeptical. "Help me how?"

What now? she wondered. She took stock of him again. His stance and mocking smile were beginning to irritate her. She had given him a reason for her appearance on his doorstep, and as implausible as it sounded, she wondered what right he had demanding further explanation of her. Too tired to deal with J.T. Harrington any longer, Jade drew herself up and managed what she hoped was a frosty tone. "Why, it's obvious, Mr. Harrington, that you need all the help you can get in the way of social introductions and refinement. Polish, if you will."

Jason could not help but laugh. He hoped his mother was not looking down on him now, for she had spent hours and taken great pains to see that he became versed in the refined manners and strict code of ethics that all southern gentlemen were supposed to live by. "So, you decided before meeting me to make a silk purse out of a sow's ear? Is that it, Miss Douglas?"

For the first time that afternoon, Jade found herself smiling. He was disarming, she would grant him that. Babs was not here to defend herself, Jade decided, so she said, "It was my friend's idea."

"And now that you've seen me, I guess you would agree."

"Really, Mr. Harrington, I—"

"Stay for a bite to eat," he said as he lifted the spatula again, "then I'll see you get home safely, if that's really what you want." Despite her protests, he couldn't believe her sudden visit was as innocent as she claimed.

"That's definitely what I want." Knowing full well that they were alone in the house, Jade knew she should insist on leaving, but when she looked up at Jason Harrington and found him waiting so expectantly for her answer, she found herself wanting to stay. "You have no cook," she said.

"I can cook."

"You?" Somehow she couldn't imagine this man at home around pots and pans.

Her challenging tone provided Jason with just the excuse he needed to keep her with him a while longer. He stepped around her and headed for the kitchen, hoping she would follow him. "Come on. I'll prove it to you."

Jade watched him as he left her standing alone in the foyer. She turned around and glanced back at the front door, then toward Jason Harrington's retreating figure. There were things she should see to, but it was too late in the day to contact the bank, and she knew that finding a place to stay would have to wait until the morrow. What harm would there be in staying a few moments longer? "Mr. Harrington, I can only stay a—"

She heard him call out from farther down the hallway, "It's J.T. Call me J.T. or Jason."

When he disappeared around a corner, Jade rolled her eyes and hurried after him.

J.T. tried to keep up a running conversation with Jade Douglas as he prepared a simple meal of ham steaks and fried potatoes. As he sliced the potatoes, he paused to look over at the woman seated on a tall stool beside the butcher block table in the center of the room. He could tell by the uneasy expression on her face that he would have to keep up a steady stream of talk or she would likely bolt, which made him wonder why she had really come in the first place. She stared around the overly large kitchen, and he could see by her wide-eyed gaze and the way she fidgeted on the stool that she was as uncomfortable in the grand atmosphere as he.

As the late afternoon sunlight streamed into the windows it highlighted the sunset color of her hair. Arrested by the sight, Jason paused, a handful of potatoes suspended above the frying pan. He smiled at her.

She shifted again and looked away.

He dropped the potatoes in the pan, careful not to spatter himself with the hot oil, and then picked up his spatula again. "You said you were staying with this disappearing friend?"

Her chin went up a notch. "I am. Her name is Barbara Barrett. She knew you were in town because her husband is a member of your attorney's club."

"So it *was* a legitimate social call."

Offended, she stiffened. "Of course, I told you it was."

"What about the nonsense about helping me fit in?"

She crossed her arms and shook her head, but could not hide a grin. "I still think you are decidedly lacking in tact and manners."

J.T. smiled. "I have to admit, I have been teasing you a bit, Miss Douglas. And as far as my appearance," he added, glancing down at his none-too-clean denims, "the next order of business was to have been cleaning myself up."

She colored with embarrassment and stared down at her folded hands.

"Are you from San Francisco originally?" he asked.

"I was born here, but I've been away, studying."

Her silly excuse for a hat was still squatting atop the unswept pile of thick red-blond hair that she had tricked into some sort of fancy 'do.' He wondered how she would react if he reached out, as he wanted to, and removed that bit of fluff and feathers and pulled the pins from her hair.

There was something childlike and vulnerable about her that even her fancy get-up could not disguise. For all her outward polish and poise, there was an insecurity about her, something in her eyes that revealed an underlying unease with him that gave J.T. cause to wonder why. Whenever he would catch her eye, she would look away and stare down at the plate he set before her, or toy with her silverware.

"Do you plan on staying in San Francisco now that you've come home, Miss Douglas?"

"Please, call me Jade."

He was silent until she looked him directly in the eye. Hers were deep green and innocent. "Were you named for the color of your eyes?"

She shook her head. "No, actually, my given name was Melcena, but my grandfather loved Chinese art pieces. He took to calling me Precious Jade when I was a baby, and the name stuck. It seems I've always been Jade."

"And so, Jade, are you going to live here permanently?"

"It's my home. What about you?"

He turned the potatoes, scraping the crispy, brown edges from the side of the pan. "No. I'll be leaving as soon as I clear up my father's estate." He glanced at her momentarily, hoping he might see disappointment in her eyes. If she'd come to cozy up to him because of his inheritance, it was best to let her know she was wasting her time. She was studying him carefully.

"Leaving for . . ."

"Back to New Mexico. I live with my Uncle Cash and his wife, Guadalupe, near Taos. We breed horses. I'm planning to use the money I've inherited to build up Cash's stock and fix up the ranch."

He sensed discomfort in her silence and so continued. "The ranch is in a canyon fed by natural springs. You should see it this time of year."

"It must be lovely."

"It is. Since the day I saw the ranch I knew why my uncle wanted to live there. A natural spring from the Sangre de Cristo Mountains keeps the place green, and the altitude keeps the water cool, even in summer. There's a timelessness about the place that's hard to describe. I often wonder if it isn't because of the ancient pueblo nearby." He thought of home and how he enjoyed nothing more than to ride the open range, where the only sounds he heard were the creak of his leather saddle and the jingle of his spurs.

J.T. reached out and filled her plate with potatoes and added a slice of warmed ham. She picked up her fork and took a bite of potato. He couldn't take his eyes off her face. Her complexion brought images to his mind of the flowers in his aunt's garden—her skin was clear and white as a primrose, her cheeks sun-kissed with the soft pink of desert verbenas. Jade's hair made him think he was staring into the last rays of a New Mexican sunset.

Despite the sophisticated dress and the cool demeanor she had momentarily affected in the hallway, she was the most beautiful woman he had ever laid eyes on. He found himself wondering how he could get her to open up to him—and why he even wanted her to, knowing he would be leaving so soon. "I found a place in Monterey on the way here where I plan to buy more palominos."

She sighed and rested her chin in her hand, then set her fork aside.

"Don't you like it?" he asked, pointing his own fork at her plate.

"It's delicious," she said, "but I think I'm too tired to eat. It hasn't been a very good day."

"Want to talk about it?"

"No."

The silence lengthened. She fidgeted again. What he knew about her didn't amount to a pile of pinfeathers.

"Mind telling me what you were studying?" J.T. asked.

"Chinese. For five years I lived with a missionary family in Paris who had been stationed in China."

"What about your folks? Didn't they want you home before now?" He couldn't fathom being away from his aunt and uncle or the ranch for more than a few weeks. Even the short time he had already been on the trail was beginning to wear on him. Home was a place he valued above all others; everything he needed was nestled in the spring-fed canyon in the mountains of New Mexico Territory. At least it had been, until he found himself face-to-face with Jade Douglas.

Jade shrugged and toyed with one of the fabric-covered buttons that fronted her gown. "Grandfather has been dead for three years. My mother passed away just before I left, and my father . . . well, my father was far too occupied with his business to care. I returned only after I learned of his death." Her expression was shuttered.

He wondered how she could speak so casually of her father's death, and then realized he had not anguished a moment over his own recent loss. "What did your father do for a living?"

"Whatever was profitable." She shifted. "You have to know San Francisco to understand. Speculation is a way of life here for some, and has been since the gold rush. My father was adept at using people's dreams to further his own."

"Was he on the good side of the law?" *Was her father responsible for the wary look behind her eyes?* he wondered.

"Somehow he was always one step ahead. If he was selling shares in a silver mine, there really was one available, but not as abundantly lined with ore as he would claim."

"So he was pretty well set for life?" With a quick glance around the room, he wondered how many coffee beans his father had imported to accumulate such wealth. When he saw Jade's wistful smile, his attention centered on her again.

"My father wasn't immune to reinvesting in many of the kinds of schemes he found so lucrative. There is always a bigger shark in the sea, and he fell prey to some of them."

She made no further comment, so J.T. decided not to press her. He watched her lift her head, stare around the now dimly lit room, and frown. Abruptly, she stood.

"I have to go." Her stunning green eyes met his full on at last. "Thank you for the meal."

"It wasn't much, and you hardly ate any of it." He looked at his own empty plate.

"It was delicious."

When she smiled to reassure him, he felt his heart trip inside like a newborn, stumbling colt. He watched the tint of her cheeks deepen from a soft sunrise pink to a deep rose red. When she cast her gaze downward again, he was treated to the sight of her thick golden lashes. In that instant, he knew he couldn't let her just walk out of his life, no matter why she had come knocking at his door.

She picked up the gloves she had set aside and he waited until she drew them on. He watched her work the soft leather over her fingers, could almost feel the fingers that stroked and smoothed the kid over the back of her hand, and somehow knew what it would feel like if she were ever to touch him so tenderly. He cleared his throat. "I have an appointment later—dinner with my father's attorney. As you said, I need all the help I can get—"

"Jason, I . . . I'm sorry. I was mad at Babs for leaving so abruptly, and I'm afraid I tried to take it out on you." She glanced at the matted curls that sprung from beneath the wide-brimmed hat that still rode the crown of his head.

He shrugged off her apology. "I was thinking that since you offered, maybe you wouldn't mind staying while I wash up. Maybe you could pick out something for me to wear? The closet upstairs is full of clothes that look like they've never even been worn."

His expression shadowed. Knowing that his father had never lived here, he wondered why the man had even bothered to stock the closet with clothing. "I'd be obliged if you would join Matt and me for dinner."

Jade glanced around the kitchen again. While they had talked, the October afternoon had dimmed to twilight. She really *had* to go. If anyone but Babs knew that she spent the afternoon alone with this man, her reputation would be ruined. Not only would she have to deal with the notoriety of her father's murder, but with a scandal of her own as well.

"I'm afraid I've really overstayed my visit. You don't understand San Francisco, Jason. I shouldn't even be here with you like this."

"It's broad daylight," he said, knowing full well he should have taken her home an hour ago, but instead of giving in to convention, he found he wanted her to stay.

"It's a big house," she countered.

"You said you came to help me, now I'm asking you for it. Please stay and choose something for me to wear, then go to dinner with us."

"I'm not dressed for dinner out. This is a day dress."

His easy smile was back. "See how much I need to learn? Here I thought you were in your very best. We'll have Matt take us by your friend's house so you can change."

Jade wondered why her *friend* had not come back for her yet. She could just imagine Babs' delight when she arrived at the Barretts' escorted by not one but two men. Babs would be certain her plan was working, and Jade would have to spend the evening assuring her that it was not, that she still wanted no part of it. She had already let J.T. talk her into spending more time with him than she had intended. Besides, if she arrived home accompanied by both Jason and his lawyer, Reggie would probably have her trunks out on the front stoop before morning, which after the way he acted earlier, would not bother her in the least.

"I'm sorry, Jason, but I have to go now." She stepped around the butcher block and started down the hallway, hoping he would follow. The walls soon echoed the sound of his spurs. She paused long enough to admonish him. "You shouldn't wear those things in the house."

"No?"

"No. Definitely not. Does your aunt let you wear them indoors?"

"Yes."

Although she could barely see him in the darkened hall, she could tell by the sound of his voice that he was laughing. She tried to imagine his home in New Mexico, and all she could conjure up was a place where tall, dust-coated men tracked spurred heels across the floors. He was, after all, leaving for good, so what did it matter what he did to the place?

J.T. followed her, straining to see the beguiling twitch of her bustle in the darkened interior. He caught the delicate fragrance of her perfume as it wafted in her wake. Its citrus scent reminded him of lemons. If he were back home, he would know just what to do—he had never been at a loss with the women in New Mexico, but things had been different with them. They were country born and bred, none as sophisticated as Jade Douglas. It had been years since he'd been with so poised and delicate a lady. He was aching to kiss her, curious to see how she would respond to his arms. She seemed so fragile, he was half-afraid to touch her. Worried that the underlying current of uneasiness she'd shown around him would turn to fear, he held back as they continued down the hall.

But by the time they reached the foyer again, he knew he had to kiss her—had to experience the touch of her lips against his, even if she became so insulted she would walk out of his life as suddenly as she walked into it.

But then again, perhaps she would stay a while longer.

There was only one way to find out.

Dusk had settled heavily. Away from the warm kitchen the house had chilled, tainted with the smell of the damp sea air. Jade stood silently by the door while he lit the lamps.

When he returned to her side, he reached out in the wavering light as if to open the front door. His eyes were riveted on her face. She was definitely one of the most beautiful women he had ever seen. Alluring, vibrant, there was a quality about her that made her seem as if she belonged to another place and time.

He stepped closer, half-expecting her to back away. Afraid to hesitate any longer, he reached out and drew her up hard against him. Her eyes widened until they were emerald pools of fear. She gasped just before his mouth captured hers.

Startled, Jade fought to hold him off as his lips began to play against hers, lightly at first, then with increased demand. Before she knew what was happening, his tongue probed her lips. Startled, she opened her mouth to protest and felt his tongue seek out her own. A ripple of pleasure traveled along her spine, down to the tips of her toes and up again. Shocked, she leaned against him, surrendered to the overpowering mastery of his kiss, and although the very nature of its intimacy shook her, she found herself wondering why she had waited so long to experience something so very wondrous.

Jason had expected her to slap him. He was astonished when she clung to him instead. As soon as her arms slipped around his neck, he moved with her until she was trapped hard against the solid surface of the door. He heard her moan, felt her stiffen, and leaned into her until he was pressed full length against her. When his hips nudged hers suggestively, he found her resistant but pliable. As she obviously did not know how to proceed, J.T. took control. The kiss went on—long, warm and wet. Jade Douglas, he found, proved to be an excellent student.

Finally, when his heart pounded with an uncontrolled rhythm that matched the hectic beat of the pulse at the base of her throat, he ended the kiss. Jason nipped at her lower lip before he raised his head. Jade stared up at him, dazed, as if she did not recognize him. He thought fleetingly of what he might have missed had he not followed his own instincts. A man had to reach out and take what he wanted, no matter where he was.

Releasing his relentless grip on her upper arms, he let Jade go long enough to move his hands up to cup her face between his palms. She was still silent.

He could not resist tasting her once more, and so lowered his lips to hers. This time he kissed her softly, briefly, and then whispered against her mouth.

"I take it you'll go out to dinner with me after all?"

❈ CHAPTER 4 ❈

*The door to virtue
Is heavy and hard to push.*

"Absolutely not!"

Jade blinked furiously, spread her palms against his chest, and attempted to push him away again. This time J.T. complied, released her, and stepped back so abruptly that she had to lock her knees to keep from sliding back down the door. The image of herself as nothing more than a puddle of beribboned strawberry satin at his feet strengthened her resolve. Shaken, she pulled her shattered nerves together and took a deep breath.

"The least you can do is be gentlemanly enough to let me out of here!" She tried to keep her voice from shaking, but failed.

"The least you can do," he countered, "is tell me why you're really here." After kissing her, he was more confused than ever. If she had come to ingratiate herself with him, to try to use her feminine wiles to get to his fortune, she displayed none of the expertise needed for the task. She was innocent—the way she kissed told him as much. And then there had been her statement about the missionaries she had lived with in Paris. Missionaries? He'd never seen one, but somehow he knew the alluring Jade Douglas was not of missionary stock.

"Please." She tried to twist away from him. "I have to go."

"I don't think so," he said softly as he thought, *at least not until I've taught you a lesson.* "I was brought up to know better than to let a lady go out at night all by herself. You can wait here until Van Buren comes by with the carriage to pick me up for dinner. Then we'll take you home."

She opened her mouth to protest, but before she could utter a word, Jason let go of her arm and grabbed her wrist. When she found herself following him up the sweeping staircase toward the second floor, she abruptly halted in the middle of the stairs and tried to pull out of his grasp.

He stopped two steps above her and looked down. "What?"

"Where are you taking me?"

"Why?"

Her pulse jumped erratically as her mind flashed on an image of her mother. She straightened and refused to cower or show the fear that was causing her heart to pound and her throat to dry up. "You're dragging me upstairs like some . . . cave dweller, and you want to know why?"

Because I'm afraid you'll leave while I change, J.T. thought. *Because if it's a quick tumble and cash you want, I don't want you out on the streets searching elsewhere.*

"All I want you to do is look over my late father's clothes and choose something for me to wear for dinner tonight." He held up his hands in imitation of a man with a gun aimed at his ribs. "Honest. No bad intentions. Just pick something out and I'll see that you get home."

After the way he had surprised her with his kiss, Jade was not certain she could trust him, no matter how honest he appeared. "Are you certain that's all?"

"No. I'm asking because I would like you to stay a little while longer, Jade."

Seconds passed as they stood on the stairs, gazes focused on each other. She could never remember a time when anyone specifically wanted her for herself. Her grandfather wanted to protect her and to broaden her education—he needed someone to carry on after he was gone. Her mother had always used her as a support, as a shoulder to cry on whenever she was in despair. Babs had been her friend, but she had involved Jade in all of her schemes. Her father had never wanted her at all.

Now this man, a man the likes of which she had never seen, a man who could alternately be rough and gentle, was asking her to stay a while longer—asking merely because he wanted to be with her a while longer.

"All right," she said softly. "I'll stay until Mister Van Buren arrives, as long as you promise you'll take me home then."

He nodded, and took the stairs two at a time, trusting her to

follow him. His spurs blinked silver in the lamplight as Jade
slowly followed him up the stairs.

Jade ran her hand over the smooth, curved footboard of the
oversized sleigh bed in the master suite. The mahogany bed
was highly polished and swathed in a plush, royal blue velvet
spread that matched the swagged draperies at the long windows
that lined the walls. She studied the bed, the focus of the huge
room, and although she had heard of the beds that resembled
horse-drawn cutters, she had never actually seen one before.

Not only the huge bed but the entire master suite was
pretentious. She walked around the room, her feet moving over
the thick Turkish carpet without a sound. A scrolled hat rack
stood beside the double-door wardrobe that was filled with an
ample selection of clothing, all of which appeared to be new.
Nervous in such questionable surroundings, Jade took a seat in
one of the tufted armchairs gathered about a pedestal table in
a corner of the room.

She then proceeded to tap the toe of her shoe in rhythm to
her fingertips as she absentmindedly drummed them against
the tabletop. There was nothing in the room that hinted of the
personality of its former resident, but Jason's few possessions
were scattered about. None of them blended with the luxurious
surroundings. A battered guitar was propped against the wall
near the doorframe, while a sagging, raveled satchel slumped
like a tired traveler near an ornately carved umbrella stand. His
boots were where he had tossed them, the toes curled slightly
upward. The heels were sadly worn. He had draped his
saddlebags over a chair in the corner.

She tried to still the nervous flutter that had taken up
residence in the vicinity of her midriff. The intimate sounds of
a man shaving—of Jason shaving—the razor stropping against
the strap, water slopping in the basin, the occasional humming
of an unrecognizable tune, were sounds that she had never
listened to before. They seemed twice as loud in the cavernous
master bedroom adjacent to the bath, and twice as intimate as
they would have been had they belonged to any other man.

Jade crossed her arms protectively before she recognized the
defensive gesture for what it was and hastily uncrossed them.

It had taken her years to learn to stand up to her father, and now, in a few hours, her newfound courage had been shaken. But this time her fear was not the result of verbal abuse, but of uncertainty. Everything Jason Harrington did was perplexing when she compared him to the only two men she had ever known well—her father and grandfather. Callous and volatile were words she would use to aptly describe her father. Academic and absentminded best suited her grandfather. She searched for words that might apply to Jason Harrington and decided she needed far more than two. Curious, spontaneous, and overwhelming all came to mind.

Perhaps his unabashed honesty and his polite request for her to "please wait right here" were the reasons she had not bolted from the room after she carefully studied the wardrobe of the late Mr. Harrington and selected the clothing Jason should wear to dinner. Now, as she sat uneasily on the edge of the chair and pondered her immediate attraction to this arresting stranger, she tried to dismiss the intimate sounds issuing from the dressing room and bath.

Unable to quell the nervous flutter in her midsection, Jade jumped to her feet and walked to the window. Drawing aside the heavy draperies, she gazed down on the darkened grounds, the long drive, the ornate iron gates guarding the boundary to Harrington House. In the distance, a golden glow haloed the tall gas lamps that lined the street. Now and again, a carriage rolled past the gates, the rythmic clip-clop of horses' hooves barely audible from inside the mansion.

A splash of water alerted her to the fact that Jason was still washing, but surely he would be finished soon. Once again she glanced at the oversized bed where she had laid out what she considered proper attire for an evening on the town: black trousers, vest, matching coat, a white linen shirt with wing-tipped collar, and a black silk tie. Diamond shirt studs had been carefully tucked into a lacquer box in the top dresser drawer. Jade had found them easily and set the box alongside the clothes.

As she rubbed the rich black wool of the formal jacket between her fingers, she wondered how much the exquisitely tailored clothes would alter Jason's rough good looks.

Determined not to have him find her in the room when he reappeared, Jade turned, intending to quietly slip downstairs and await him in the sitting room off the foyer. Instead, she found herself face-to-face with Jason. Clean shaven, his strong, square jaw was now smooth, his wavy dark blond hair still damp but tamed into place. He was remarkably handsome. More so than any man she had ever seen in her life. Bare to the waist, he towered over her, his thumbs hooked casually in the pockets of his low-riding denims. His chest was wide, the muscles well defined beneath a mat of dark blond hair that veed down to a line that divided his taut abdomen before it disappeared into his waistband.

Embarrassed at her own unabashed perusal, stunned at the half-naked state he so casually assumed, her gaze dropped to the floor. He was barefooted. Jade would never have guessed that the mere lack of shoes would make a big man seem somehow vulnerable.

"I was just going downstairs to wait for you." She let her gaze plumb the light blue depths of his eyes. Her throat suddenly dry, she tried to swallow. "I've laid out a suit that should do well for dinner. That does, of course, depend on where you are going to dine."

He took a step toward her, lessening the slight distance between them. A smile quirked the corners of his lips. "I don't have any idea."

Jade felt the blood rush to her cheeks. "I think I'll wait downstairs."

Without another word, she turned and fled the room. Jason's spontaneous laughter echoed behind her.

Getting dressed took him longer than he expected, what with fiddling with the small studs that were meant to hold the tuck-fronted shirt closed and then trying to squeeze his feet into a pair of his father's dress shoes. Frustrated, sweating, and grumbling to himself, Jason finally shoved his own weathered boots back on and gave up on buttoning his collar. He carried the blasted thing downstairs where he expected to find Jade waiting impatiently.

Instead, he found her sound asleep in the dimly lit sitting

room off the foyer. He paused in the doorway, content to study
her in silence. She had tried, it seemed, to assume a proper,
ladylike position in the center of the settee. Her skirt was
carefully spread out around her. It took up all the space about
her on the small piece of ornately carved and elegantly
upholstered furniture. He assumed she meant for him to sit
elsewhere before exhaustion had claimed her. Now she was
slumped over, the feathers of her once jaunty hat askew. He
was looking about the room for something to use to cover her
with when he heard the sound of a carriage on the drive.

Jason hurried to the front door, careful not to step too
heavily across the foyer and awaken his sleeping guest. He
opened the door just wide enough to step outside, and waited
in the darkness to greet his father's attorney. The air held the
tang of salt and moisture. Not a star was visible.

Matthew Van Buren was not what J.T. had expected. At the
very least, he thought the attorney would have been a few years
older. Instead, he found himself greeting a well-dressed man a
few years younger than himself.

"Van Buren?"

"That's right." The sandy-haired lawyer sized Jason up from
behind wire-rimmed spectacles, and then smiled as his new
employer shifted his shirt collar and a handful of studs from his
right hand to his left. "Your father always called me Matt."

"Thanks." Jason nodded. "Friends back home call me J.T."

They shook hands in greeting and Van Buren waited
expectantly to be invited in. Jason cleared his throat and
glanced at the door.

"You find everything you need?" Van Buren asked.

Jason raked his hands through his hair. "Yeah, fine."

The silence lengthened awkwardly between them.

"Well . . ." the attorney tried again, obviously uncomfortable with the odd situation as his client kept him standing on
the front steps without explanation. "If you're ready, we can
go." He looked doubtfully at Jason and then at the buggy that
loomed at the bottom of the stairs.

"Actually, I've decided not to go. I hope you don't mind."
Jason inhaled, intrigued by the sea-scented air. "I'm a lot more

tired than I thought. Just got in a few hours ago, and after unpacking, well . . ." He shrugged and left the rest unsaid.

Matt Van Buren looked disappointed, then he brightened. "Of course, if that's what you want. You're certain you'd rather stay in?"

Jason rocked forward on his toes, then back on his heels. "Sorry, but I feel like turnin' in early," he assured Matt as he stretched. He knew as sure as he was standing there that the woman asleep on his settee would be furious when she discovered he had sent away her promised means of transportation, but at the moment that threat did not bother him at all.

"Well then." Matt left to retrieve a tall bottle from the buggy seat and then returned and handed it to Jason. "Here's a welcome gift. Tomorrow will be soon enough to go over everything."

Relieved, Jason reached behind him for the door handle, pushed open the door, and stepped back inside. "Not too early."

Matt looked curious but managed to smile in return. "Not before nine, then." He turned to leave, and Jason began to close the door before Matt had cleared the porch. When the lawyer paused on the bottom stair and turned, Jason found himself holding his breath.

"So you found the groceries I had sent over?" Matt asked.

"Yep. Just right. Plenty left, thanks." Jason smiled, one hand on the door, the other on the frame.

"Good night then, J.T.," Matt called out as he climbed up onto the buggy and took up the reins.

"*Adios.*"

Jason closed the door and leaned against it. He let out a sigh of relief and then walked toward the sitting room.

The whalebone corset bit into the underside of her breasts and forced Jade awake. She shifted, then wondered why she had gone to bed fully dressed. When she opened her eyes, she realized she was not in her room at the Barretts' but sprawled face down on the settee in Jason Harrington's parlor. Without uttering the groan that welled up inside her, Jade cautiously peered around, hesitant to move. A timid fire was burning low in the fireplace directly across from her. It emitted a low light, barely enough to silhouette the man sitting on the floor with his back resting against a chair.

Jason. She watched him as he sat staring into the fire, uncertain whether to move and call attention to herself just yet or not. Inwardly she chided herself for getting into such a predicament as she continued to study him in silence. The tableau was such a peaceful one, the aura surrounding him one of such quiet contemplation and contentment that Jade was loath to disturb him. Nor was she eager to call attention to herself or her situation.

She became aware of the satin-smooth finish of the cushion beneath her cheek just as she realized the scene—one of a striking man in quiet contemplation before a fire—was something she had never witnessed before. Of course, she had always imagined such a blissful setting, had even dreamed childish dreams that one day she would awaken and find herself part of a normal, loving family. But upon awakening, her dreams would always be shattered as reality became a home filled with anger and dissension.

The firelight played upon a man at ease with himself and his surroundings. He appeared larger than life in this room filled with fragile, elegant furnishings. His presence gave her the feeling that somehow the outdoors had been brought inside. He stared into the fire so intently she wondered what he was seeing, what he was feeling, and suddenly she needed to know. Jade began to straighten, then she saw him move. He picked up a half-finished champagne bottle on the floor beside him. Her breath caught and held as he lifted it to his lips and swallowed a goodly portion.

The quiet moment of reverie fled as Jade recognized fear brought on by her experiences of the past. At least when Fredrick Douglas had been drunk she had known what to expect. *Was* Jason drunk? And if so, what could she expect?

Jade realized how very alone she was. Her gaze flickered to the darkened corners of the room and back to Jason again. Shadows filled the place, along with an ominous silence broken only by the sound of a tall case clock that stood just inside the doorway. She gauged the distance to the door and knew it would be impossible to slip away unnoticed. The rustle of the voluminous ruffles and yards of fabric gathered into her skirt would give away her every move.

Her heart pounded in her ears. Her mouth was dry, but Jade knew she could not feign sleep forever. Nor could she stay in this house with him any longer.

Before she could bring herself to sit up and straighten her clothing, before she drew another breath, Jason turned toward her. In the dim light of the fire, she saw him smile.

His voice was soft, his tone as warm as the flames behind the grate. "Have a good sleep?"

Jade pushed herself upright and used her hands to examine the damage she had done to her hair. "I . . . yes . . . I have to go."

"It's raining." His words were uttered in so low a tone she could barely hear him.

"Did you say raining?"

He turned and uncrossed his booted feet. With a nod he confirmed it. "Yep. Has been for about an hour."

Jade groaned. As she took in his casual position, the open neckline of his shirt and missing collar, she wondered aloud, "What happened to Mister Van Buren? Shouldn't he have been here by now?" She stood, shook out her skirt and overskirt, tried to straighten her bustle without calling attention to it, and then rearranged the drooping feathers that bobbed before her eyes.

"I guess he took a notion not to come."

"Well, I guess then you better take a notion to take me home, or else I'm walking out the door by myself. What time is it?"

"It's nearly eight o'clock."

Jade's eyes widened. "I slept for two hours?"

"You must have needed it."

She thought of the day she had had to endure and knew it was no surprise that she had fallen asleep. In no mood to put up with more, she wondered why Babs had not come back to get her, or at the very least sent her driver around to pick her up. She glanced at Jason again and frowned.

"You have no intention of taking me home, do you?"

"No."

He had not moved. She might have panicked if it hadn't been for the innocent smile curving his lips and the lazy way he rested his arm on the chair behind him. He did not quite fit the image of a man who was about to ravage her.

Jade tried to recall what happened in the one dime novel she had read abroad, but none of the heroine's adventures came to mind. She decided to ask him outright.

"If you aren't taking me home, then what exactly do you intend?"

"I intend to find out what you want from me. What are you really doing here, Jade Douglas?"

She hated the fact that her eyes filled with tears. She'd be damned if she let this man make her cry. Nor could she tell him the truth—that the whole idea had been part of Babs' crazy scheme, how she had refused to go along with it but then she'd literally been dumped on his doorstep because she had trusted her friend. An explanation would lead to a discussion of her dire straits, and her problems were her own—not his, not anyone else's. She would find a way out of her predicament, and if she had to, she would give up the collection rather than prostitute herself.

"I told you what happened. If you don't care to believe me, that's your problem, not mine." She snatched up her reticule and headed for the door.

He stood and followed her.

She could feel him close behind her as she turned the lock and opened the door. It was raining, just as he had said, and much harder than she imagined. It seemed a full-fledged storm had hit San Francisco.

Her head ached. The tightly laced corset was killing her, and she wanted nothing more than to let her hair down, slip into a comfortable robe, and go to sleep. The clock chimed half past the hour.

She rubbed her temples and felt the cool mist of rain.

Jason reached around her and closed the door.

"Listen," he said, his tone contemplative, "you may as well go upstairs and try to get some sleep. I counted more than sixteen rooms up there with beds in them." He was certain now that whatever her motive had been for stopping by, it was not to seduce him. He had given her enough chances and she had not taken them. Now, the storm would force them together for even longer.

"I think I'll try my chances out on the street, if you don't mind."

"That's what I'm afraid of."

"What do you mean?"

"You can't go out in that rain," he said, avoiding a direct answer to her question.

"I can and I will, because what you are suggesting is impossible. I will not stay here a moment longer and I will positively not sleep here. I thought you were a gentleman."

"I'm still trying to figure out what you are," he said.

Heedless of the rain, Jade shoved past him and ran outside. The front steps were slippery and slowed her down some, but she was still able to dash across the porch and start down the drive. Beneath, the ground was quickly becoming a quagmire. With each step, her feet sank deeper into the muddy ground. Bunching her skirt in her hands, Jade kept running, heedless of the mud sucking at her shoes. Rain streamed down her face, into her eyes, and beneath the high collar of her gown. She chanced a glance over her shoulder. Jason was but a few steps behind. Suddenly, she found herself pitching forward, and let go of her skirt.

Before she hit the ground, Jason caught up with her, grasped her arm, and pulled her upright.

Jason held tight to her arm and spun her around. Jade glared up at him, blinking furiously to drive the rain out of her eyes. It was pelting down in sheets, driven by a steady wind that blew in off the sea. His wet shirt clung to him like wallpaper to a wall, emphasizing the well-defined muscles of his chest and shoulders.

"Listen!" He reached out and grabbed her by both shoulders and held her at arm's length as he shouted above the rain. "I promise to keep my hands to myself. You go on upstairs. Pick any room you want. I'll stay downstairs and stretch out on the floor if it will make you feel any better."

"That's just impossible!" She wanted to believe him,

wanted to get in out of the pouring rain. Babs' gown was fast becoming soaked, the once perky feathers of her hat were drooping sadly. Her hair was slowly sliding down her neck. "I can't spend the night here. We are unchaperoned."

"We've been alone since afternoon and nothing's happened. I think you ought to be able to trust me by now."

Nothing's happened? She had been intimately, thoroughly kissed for the first time in her life and he dismissed it as *nothing*? Did that mean he had felt nothing?

Jade tried again. "If anyone were to find out . . . and what about Babs? She must be worried sick. I'm sure she would have come for me if it hadn't been for the storm." She tried to hide the doubt from her tone. There really was no telling what Babs was thinking.

"If I get you out of here early in the morning, no one will ever know. Besides, if this friend of yours was so all-fired worried about you, why didn't she come after you earlier?"

They were shouting over the pounding rain. It ran in rivers down his face and onto his clothes. They were fast becoming soaked to the skin, and still she wouldn't budge. Tired of arguing in the rain, Jason swept her up in his arms and marched back to the house.

"Put me down this instant!" Jade tried to wriggle free. He tightened his hold. When he was well inside the foyer, J.T. set her down and then locked the door.

"I'll take you home first thing in the morning. It's bound to have stopped raining by then." He leaned close to emphasize his next words. "Just remember, Miss Douglas, you're the one who came calling."

Jade watched as he swung around and crossed the foyer with a slow, casual stride. He paused on the second stair and turned. There was something arresting about the look of him towering there, dripping wet at the bottom of the imposing stairway. The white linen shirt clung to his well-muscled chest and taut abdomen.

"I'm going up to bed. You can sit up all night, or find a place to sleep, I don't care, but I've had a long day in the saddle and I'm ready to bed down."

He reached up as if to tip his hat to her, then realized he

wasn't wearing one. He nodded in her direction instead. " 'Night, Miss Douglas."

Jade watched him mount the stairs. When she was certain he meant to keep his word, she turned abruptly and peered through the stained glass panel that framed the front door. Outside, muted by the translucent emerald glass, sheets of rain continued to fall. She sighed and wandered back into the sitting room.

One glance at the uncomfortable settee and she nearly faltered in her reserve. Then she spied the lush, willow-patterned Oriental carpet where Jason had sprawled earlier. It would serve him right if she ruined it. Jade slipped her soggy reticule from her wrist, knelt down, and then took off her hat and placed it carefully on the floor beside the settee. Thankful for a reprieve, she pulled out her hairpins, finger-combed her tangled hair, and tried to shake it free. Tamping down the sodden ruffles of her skirt, she stretched out before the fire and tried to make herself as comfortable as possible. Jade was determined not to think about the fifteen empty beds upstairs, or about the one that was occupied.

❈ CHAPTER 5 ❈

Words spoken may fly away . . .
The writing brush leaves its mark.

The sound of horses' hooves and carriage wheels on the drive were real, not part of his musing. Jason threw back the covers and stood up, gave a quick glance out the window, then reached for his trousers. A carriage had stopped at the front door. J.T. thrust one long leg in his trousers and hopped toward the door as he fought with the other pantleg. He nearly tripped and fell before he reached the door, but managed to yank it open and head downstairs without stopping to grab his shirt.

An incessant pounding began at the front door as Jason bounded down the stairs, both hands groping to close his fly. Barefooted, bleary-eyed with sleep, he managed to fasten all but the top button before he flung the door wide and glared out into the morning light. A weak-willed sun tried to burn off the morning's fog. The lawn and shrubbery near the house winked with raindrops left behind by the storm.

A pert brunette with snapping brown eyes and the determination of a wild bronco glared back at him.

"Where's Jade? What have you done with her?"

Before he could answer, she shoved him aside, searching for some sign of his reluctant houseguest. Just as he was about to tell the persistent woman it was none of her business where Jade was, they both spied the object of her search rising from the floor in the front parlor.

The brunette turned and headed toward Jade. Jason followed close behind, unwilling to miss the exchange. He found a safe haven and casually leaned against the doorjamb, his thumbs hooked in his pockets.

Although he was only half-dressed, he noted that Jade looked much the worse for wear. Her fine gown was water-stained and crumpled, her bustle misshapen. Her hair stood out like a wild sunset-red nimbus about her head, while deep shadows underlined her eyes. A throw blanket she had appropriated from the wing chair was tangled in a heap near the hearth. The half-empty champagne bottle stood nearby. Her pheasant-feathered hat and reticule were forgotten beside it.

He watched with undisguised humor as the flabbergasted brunette took in the scene. With her hands on her hips, she stepped close to Jade and hissed sotto voce, "Good God, Jade! I didn't think you would go this far!"

Jade blinked, put a hand against her forehead, and managed to mutter, "What are you doing here, Babs?"

"Me? I came to get you out of here. Now!"

"It's nice of you to return after the way you left me here yesterday."

Jason smiled from where he lazed against the doorjamb. "Can't you ladies at least stay for breakfast?"

The woman Jade had called Babs hastily grabbed up Jade's hat and bag and then took the other girl by the arm. She dragged her silent companion across the room and paused momentarily before him. He snuck a glance at Jade, and was not surprised to see her fuming silently as she stared at the floor. Her face flamed as bright as her hair.

Babs drew his attention once again as she addressed him icily. "I would suggest you put something on. A reporter from the *Chronicle* is on the way over to interview you—he's doing a piece on new arrivals in town."

"It's nice to make your acquaintance, too, ma'am."

Too angry to speak to either of them, Jade frantically tried in vain to twist her hair into some semblance of order.

"There's no time for that," Babs snapped. She pulled on Jade's arm and led her past Jason into the foyer.

Just as Jason wondered whether Jade needed to be rescued from the termagant who had her in tow, Jade took a stand and refused to budge. "What do you mean, reporter?" she demanded.

"What I mean is that a reporter from the *Chronicle* stopped by my house to interview you, bright and early I might add, and I had to pretend you were still upstairs asleep. As a matter of fact"—she shot a quelling glance at Jason—"that's exactly where Reggie thinks you've been since yesterday afternoon—

sick in bed. When I told the reporter you weren't up yet, he let it slip that he was on his way here to interview the *other* new arrival in town." She got a better grip on Jade's arm and yanked. "Let's *go*!"

Jade gave Jason one last parting glare and followed Babs out the door. Barbara Barrett's driver sat staring straight ahead as if his employer had threatened him with a fate worse than death should he chance to glance in their direction. Jade climbed aboard, too embarrassed to meet Jason's teasing smile, and stared ahead as stiffly as the driver on the box. The door slammed shut behind Babs and the carriage was away a second later, which proved not quite soon enough.

J.T. watched as the first carriage swerved to avoid hitting a second vehicle making its way up the drive. As the carriages neared each other, he could have sworn he saw Jade and her captor dive for the floor of theirs.

Fighting hard to bite back a laugh, he waited patiently on the stairs, the damp brick cold against his bare feet. The second carriage pulled up in the spot just vacated and the door swung wide to reveal a short, portly man dressed in a three-piece suit and bowler hat. Head down, he scribbled furiously over a notebook, then descended with a bound and hurried up the steps. He stopped abruptly in front of Jason.

"I'm here to see Jason T. Harrington III. You can tell him Arnold Peterson of the *San Francisco Chronicle* has arrived to interview him." He pulled himself up ramrod straight, expecting Jason to leave to do his bidding.

Jason had no intention of telling the worried-looking man who he was just yet. On close inspection, he could see the hair oil stain that had seeped through the reporter's hat to form a second hat band. Peterson stood staring up at him. Jason was tempted to tell him J.T. Harrington was not at home, but his mother had taught him his manners, so he honestly admitted, "I'm J.T. Harrington. What can I do for you, Mr. Peterson?"

Pop-eyed, Peterson stared up at Jason, then down at his bare feet, then back up to his bare chest, and then at the half-open front door, as if he expected the real J.T. Harrington to appear and set things aright.

"You?"

"Yep."

Peterson cleared his throat and ran a finger around the inside of his collar. "It might be easier if we went inside." His curious gaze flicked to the half-open door.

Jason obliged him. "Fine with me. Come on in."

The little man stepped inside first and waited for Jason to close the door. Too late, Jason realized his tactical error as Peterson headed directly for the sitting room. Quick to note the champagne bottle and the rumpled blanket near the fireplace, the reporter scribbled furtively in his notebook. J.T. stifled the urge to rip the thing from the man's hands.

"I like to sleep on the floor," Jason volunteered without having been asked. "Reminds me of sleeping out on the open range."

Peterson made another note and took a chair near the fire. Jason suddenly found himself regretting the game he had played with Jade Douglas last night. It had not been fair to use the rain against her—not when there were at least three vehicles in the carriage house he might have used to drive her safely home. He was surprised she had not thought of it herself—but then, why should she? She had been naive enough to trust him to tell her the truth, and he had only meant to teach her a lesson by avoiding it. She would think twice about finding herself alone and defenseless with a man again. But now this pompous little man was intrigued by the signs of what had been an innocent occurence and was furiously noting every detail.

"Do you know anyone here in San Francisco?" Peterson asked, peering up at Jason from beneath the brim of his hat.

Jason knew the other man had seen the carriage leaving as he arrived, and furthermore, he believed a man's business was his own. "My attorney."

"Pardon me?"

"I know my attorney."

"Who is . . ."

"Who is none of your business."

Peterson looked nonplussed. "Do you plan to stay on here, Mr. Harrington? Take up the reins of the Harrington Import business?"

"Nope. I intend to sell out."

"So, you plan to return to . . ."

"My home."

"Which is . . ."

"In the New Mexico Territory."

"And you don't know anyone here outside of your attorney, nor do you have plans to stay on. Is that correct?"

Jason wondered at the little man's gall. He stifled the urge to pick him up by the lapels and carry him to the door. "I don't know any more folks than I told you I did half a minute ago. You're beginning to sound like a detective to me, Peterson. What is it you really want?"

"Just the story, sir, just the story. Is it true your mother and father were divorced some twenty years ago?"

"Is that any of your business?"

"And what happened to your mother after that?"

"She died." *There*, he thought, *that should shut the man up*. But bluntness had no effect on Peterson at all.

"You're a cattleman?"

"Nope. Horses. I plan on expanding my uncle's ranch."

"I see."

J.T. sensed the man's frustration, but he could not answer questions that he felt concerned no one but himself. Nor could he lie. Teasing was one thing, but he could not abide outright lying, so he avoided saying anything at all.

"Might I ask the identity of the occupants of that carriage?"

"What carriage?" Jason frowned.

"The one that just left here."

"No, you might not."

"Are you married, Mr. Harrington?"

"No. Are you, Mr. Peterson?"

Just as Arnold Peterson seemed to have reached the high point of frustration, there was another knock at the door. Jason excused himself and went to answer it. He was relieved to see Matthew Van Buren standing expectantly on the porch.

"I need help," Jason whispered to him as ushered Matt inside. "Let's see if you can start earnin' your keep."

Matt swiftly put an end to the interview by introducing

himself and informing Peterson that Jason had a very important appointment within the hour.

"Might I continue the interview soon, Mr. Harrington?" Peterson asked.

"You might," J.T. mumbled.

"We'll contact you if Mr. Harrington has any newsworthy announcements," Matt added as he deftly ushered Peterson out the door.

The ride home from Harrington House had been short, but fraught with tension. Babs was certain that the reporter from the *Chronicle* had not recognized them. Jade had tried to ignore her friend's ranting while she concentrated on finger-combing her hair into some sort of order. Babs made certain that Reggie had departed for work before the two of them snuck up the back stairs to Jade's room, where Babs left her alone and went to order a tray of food sent up.

Jade hastily changed into a flowing Chinese robe and long, silk pajama pants, then pulled one of her satchels out of the closet and began throwing what clothing she possessed into it. When a quick knock on the door heralded Babs' return, Jade took a deep breath and bade her enter. One look at her friend's smug smile warned her that Babs was in rare form. She could almost see the brunette's mind at work.

"What are you doing?" Babs asked when she spied Jade's bag.

"I'm leaving. I can't stay here another minute." She turned on Babs. "How could you do it? How could you leave me there? I made an absolute fool of myself, and I'll never forgive you for your part in it. This time you've gone too far."

Babs took a deep breath and then smiled. "Just calm down and tell me everything. When's the wedding?"

Jade turned back to her packing. "There'll be no wedding," she said softly.

"But you spent the *night* with him!"

"No, I spent the night at his *home*. I did not sleep with him, Babs. At least in that respect he's a gentleman."

"I know you didn't sleep with him, but who else is ever going to believe that?"

At that Jade spun and faced her friend with a pointed stare. "Who is going to find out? Or do you plan to tell anyone about this?"

"Don't be a fool, Jade. *Harrington* knows. And that little ferret of a reporter probably knows by now. What about the servants?"

Jade drew the belt of her robe tight and ran her hands through her hair. "He doesn't have any servants." She watched Babs for a moment as the other girl considered the situation. At Babs' look of skepticism, Jade crossed the room and took hold of her friend's hands. "Nothing happened. You have to believe me. I stayed for a meal. We talked. I helped him choose clothes to wear out for dinner, and then it started raining. He refused to take me home in the downpour."

"But he looked perfect to me. Just what you need—rich, handsome, virile, and available." A frown creased Babs' brow. "Isn't he?"

For a moment Jade was taken aback. Jason Harrington had not admitted to being married. But then again, she had not asked.

"He didn't mention a wife."

"I don't imagine a man alone with a beautiful redhead would bring it up. Didn't you ask?"

Jade let go of Babs and began to pace the room. "I don't believe this is happening. I should have never gotten in your carriage yesterday in the first place." She swerved abruptly and faced Babs again. "This was *your* idea, remember, not mine. I was so nervous I don't know what I said at first. Whatever you're planning, whatever twisted scheme you've devised, you can forget it." When Babs looked about to argue, Jade snapped her satchel closed and began sorting through the box of books on the desk near the window.

A month ago her life had been simple. She had time to study, all the serenity she needed, and companions knowledgeable in all the things she valued. Regretfully, she realized now she had taken those days in Paris for granted. When would she ever be left alone with her books again?

Babs waved toward the satchel and shook her head. "Don't be crazy. You have nowhere to go, Jade. Besides, that man was looking at you like you were a sugar plum and today was Christmas."

"Forget it." Jade began folding a dress and stuffing it into the satchel.

"How can you forget it now? I never told you to spend the night there. I only wanted you to meet him and get a ride home, not disappear for the entire evening and leave me to whisk you away in the nick of time—"

"Then why didn't you come after me?"

"Jade, please calm down."

"You seem to forget you're the one that left me there in the first place. And then that reporter showed up out of the blue! What a terrible coincidence."

Babs was suddenly contrite. "Let's not argue, Jade." She walked over to stand beside her friend and put a hand on Jade's shoulder. "Your only worry is how discriminating Harrington will be and whether or not Peterson saw us."

"Peterson?"

"The reporter."

Jade contemplated Babs for a moment. "How well do you know this Peterson?"

Babs colored. "Not well at all. Whatever gave you that idea?"

"Just a thought," Jade said softly. "I'm beginning to think you would go to any lengths to see this through, Babs."

"Please trust me, Jade. I got you into this, and now I want to get you out of it. Put your things away and settle in, please? You have nowhere to go, and I'd feel just awful if anything happened to you."

The truth of the matter, Jade thought, *is that indeed, I have nowhere to go*. She shook her head and sighed. Babs was waiting for her answer, standing apologetic and subdued at her shoulder.

Jade shrugged. "I'll stay until I can find somewhere else to live, but I'm telling you right now, Babs, I'm still very upset. And just remember, I won't be part of any more of your plans."

Jason turned and smiled thankfully at Matt Van Buren as he finally closed the door on Arnold Peterson. "I don't know what

I'd have done if you hadn't come along. I was plumb out of patience."

"Glad to help. If anyone at the *Chronicle* can uncover any gossip about anyone it's him. Peterson is one of the best."

Jason frowned, recalling the near collision of carriages in the drive, and wondered if he should enlighten his attorney as to the strange events of the night before. Hesitant to start a fire where there might not be a flame, he remained silent on the issue of his mysterious redheaded caller and instead nodded toward the stairs.

"Come on up while I change, then I'll rustle up some breakfast. I'm not used to doing business before I eat."

Matt smiled amiably and jogged up the steps behind Jason. "I thought we'd go out."

"For breakfast? There's plenty left from what you sent over."

"People take their meals in hotels and restaurants here in town—sort of a habit that came on with the forty-niners.. There's every sort of food imaginable, from home cooking to Chinese or Italian—anything you'd like. I thought you might enjoy What Cheer House. It's clean, and they have good simple food."

"At this point, it doesn't matter. I could eat a whole side of beef." Jason paused, frowning down at his dress trousers and bare feet. "Do I have to dress up?"

Matt laughed. "Not at all. Wear whatever you're comfortable in."

Twenty minutes later Jason had donned his own comfortable Levi's, a clean flannel shirt, and a jacket lined with sheepskin. The men were seated in Matt's open carriage. Interrupting himself to point out interesting sights as they passed, Matt outlined his plans for the sale of the property Jason now possessed, and appraised him of the money and other assets that would come to him as soon as all the transactions took place.

Attentive to Matt all the while, Jason stared at the passing kaleidoscope of sights and sounds that was San Francisco. Matt skillfully guided the carriage along the Embarcadero, the street that fronted the wharf. Flags of every color and description flew from the forest of mizzen masts of the ships harbored along the waterfront. Jason could not begin to identify them all. Matt pointed out the brothels, gin mills, and honkytonks clustered in the six blocks between Pacific, Kearny, and Broadway. He warned Jason to stay away from the district at night, unless he wanted to run the risk of being shanghaied and wake up to find himself halfway to Manila.

The exhilarating sights and sounds of the city could not keep Jason's mind from slipping back to the memory of Jade Douglas. She was a looker—that was for certain—and he had nearly convinced himself that her impromptu visit had had no other purpose than what she had claimed; she and her friend had only wanted to welcome him to town, but things had gone awry when the brunette had suddenly left Jade on his doorstep. Even with as little fashion knowledge as he had, he could tell that her clothes were made of fine fabrics. She obviously had money of her own. A woman who had intended to please him, to butter him up in order to get at his money would not have been as determined to leave as she had. At least he didn't think so. There was no way J.T. could dismiss her innocence. The more he thought about it, the more he believed her excuse for showing up stranded on his doorstep. Besides, he had seen her friend Babs for himself. She had seemed spontaneous, to say the least.

Jason found himself wanting to ask Matt about Jade Douglas, but he knew that would only lead to questions about where and how they had met. Ruining Jade's reputation over his own curiosity wasn't what he wanted at all. Instead, he tried a different tack.

"Do you know anybody named Barrett?"

"I know a Reggie Barrett. Why? Has he offered to buy the place? I know he wants to move up in society, but I know he hasn't the assets he would need to buy Harrington House."

"Just curious. I think Peterson mentioned the name."

Matt stared at him for a brief moment and then changed the subject. "What do you think of San Francisco so far?"

"Too damned many people in one place if you ask me. Can't be healthy," Jason mumbled to himself. Away from the waterfront, his interest was immediately taken by an overwhelming building he had seen from the hilltop but had forgotten until now.

Six stories high, the structure covered an entire city block at the end of Montgomery Street. Forced to slow his carriage due to congestion about the building, Matt pointed out the entrance where foot traffic, riders, and even carriages passed beneath vaulting arches held aloft by ornate columns. Jason had never seen the likes of the place anywhere.

"That's the Palace," Matt volunteered, "just finished. Quite a story behind it, too. William Ralston, the man who built it, owned the Bank of California. Spent years and a fortune on this place, then two months ago, after the bank failed, he went swimming in the bay and drowned. Never got to see it open."

Jason craned his neck and held his hat on the back of his head as he tried to view the upper stories. "That's a damn shame."

"There's a big function to be held there tonight in honor of General Philip Sheridan. How about coming along?"

"With you?" Somehow Jason could not picture himself moving among men who were used to invitations to such an ostentatious place.

"Yes. It would be a great way for you to meet people, get the word out about how anxious you are to sell the house and the coffee import business. The top two hundred men in San Francisco—Leland Stanford, Ben Holladay, James Phelan—they'll all be there. Reggie Barrett will be most likely be there, too."

Unimpressed by names, Jason was determined not to go until he heard Matt say, "The women are going to arrive late in the evening for dancing and socializing." Matt leaned forward, expertly guiding the rig through the crowded streets. "Be a chance to meet some of the fair ladies of San Francisco."

Would the exclusive guest list include Miss Jade Douglas? Jason decided it might just be worth putting on his father's blasted suit again to find out.

"J.T., I hope I'm not intruding," Matt began hesitantly, "but there's one delicate matter your father left unsettled that I think you need to consider."

Jason stiffened, well aware of the delicate matter that Matt alluded to. "Spit it out."

"As you're well aware, your father died intestate—without a will. As his legal heir, you have inherited everything, but your father's sudden death left the woman he had lived with for nearly twenty years virtually penniless."

Jason's heart hardened of its own volition. His father's whore. The woman responsible for ruining his parents' marriage. The reason his mother had suffered divorce and he had been raised without a knowing his father.

He owed her nothing.

"I suppose she's after money."

Matt looked grave. "Not at all. In fact, she's never even contacted me. I went by and visited with her two weeks ago, and she asked if you had responded to my telegram. I told her you were on the way to California. That's all she asked about."

"So?"

"So I think that your father would have wanted you to see her provided for. I think you at least owe her a visit. Meet her. Talk to her."

J.T. slid to the edge of the seat and leaned forward, resting his forearms on his knees. With his head down he said, "I don't think so." He stared at the floor of the buggy and tried to dispel the feeling that his mother would somehow be ashamed of him at the moment. Reneging on his previous thoughts, he said curtly, "Send her some money." Then he added, "Whatever she needs."

"I still think you ought to meet her," Matt said softly.

Jason slapped his thighs, leaned back again, and crossed his arms over his chest. "I'll think about it."

CHAPTER 6

Blessings come in pairs . . .
Ills never come alone.

The newly completed Palace Hotel at the corner of Montgomery and Market streets was so imposing that Jade forgot her nervousness and became immersed in seeing all there was to see. As the Barretts' carriage rolled into the hotel's cobblestoned Grand Court, Babs regaled Jade with information about the place. There were seven hundred rooms in the eight-story building that enclosed an area of two and a half acres.

"Can you imagine? Four hundred and thirty-seven bathtubs and a water closet in every room? This place has its own artesian wells, five *hydraulic* elevators, and a dining room one hundred and fifty feet long." She squirmed in her seat, edging toward the window, nearly crushing Jade in her enthusiasm to see the gaslight streaming from the windows.

"It is awesome," Jade admitted as she tugged her skirt—another of Bab's gowns—from under Babs' weight on the seat. After much apologizing on her friend's part, Jade decided to stay at the Barretts' until the end of the week. As always, her anger at Babs disintegrated when she thought of the many years of friendship that stood behind them.

After a light luncheon and a long nap, Jade was refreshed enough to consider attending the after-dinner ball for Lieutenant General Philip Sheridan—the Palace Hotel's first social affair of any importance. At first she had vigorously declined, but when Babs reminded her she might very well run into some of her father's business associates who might help her discover something about his death, Jade decided it was worth wedging herself into another stoutly boned, long-waisted corset and donning one of Babs' dresses. She had balked at having her hair rolled and curled, merely tying it back in a simple but elegant figure-eight coil at the nape of her neck.

"Reggie said he'll look for us by the door to the ballroom, but if we should get separated in the crush, let's plan to meet at the refreshment table at midnight," Babs suggested.

Jade agreed and reached down to lift the heavy overskirt of pink poult-de-soie draped over verticle rows of white tulle ruffles. As soon as she stepped out of the carriage, assisted by a colorfully garbed hotel footman, Jade adjusted one of the many silk roses that were sewn onto the low-cut neckline.

She walked alongside Babs until the crush became too great and they were separated. Choosing a quiet alcove off the ballroom floor, Jade surveyed the room. She recognized Leland Stanford, the railroad king, stagecoach monarch Ben Holladay, and James Phelan, millionare real estate and liquor tycoon, milling about among the other guests. Three hundred gas jets flooded the palatial dining room with light. The ceiling was held aloft by rows of cream-colored columns; both ends of the room were draped with red, white, and blue bunting. Baskets abundant with flowers lined the tables, interspersed with silver trays with pyramids of desserts.

A virtual regiment of waiters in swallowtail coats and white lisle gloves moved among the crowd, while a uniformed military band filled the great hall with music. Jade smiled to herself and found her toe beginning to tap in time to the music.

"Jade!"

She whirled at the sound of her name. Babs was hurrying toward her, with a white-haired gentleman in tow.

"Oh, Jade, I'm so glad I found you! I was just telling Mr. Ashbury here all about you and he is so anxious to get to know you. Mr. Harold Ashbury, this is Miss Jade Douglas."

Babs looked about to burst with excitement. Jade ignored her as she studied the hopeful Mr. Ashbury. His swallowtailed coat was of expensive cloth, as was his tuck-fronted shirt. The man was bald and freckle-headed, with a hooked nose, rheumy eyes, and blue-veined hands. He leaned forward from the waist, peering at her curiously, inspecting her as closely as one would a piece of merchandise. He had to be nearly seventy.

"Babs, I—"

"Isn't it *delightful* that I ran into Mr. Ashbury just inside the doorway? He's recently widowed and you're here without an escort. The dear man said he'd be thrilled to have your company for the evening." Babs leaned close to Jade. Still smiling, she hissed through her teeth, "He's nearly deaf as a post but rich as Croesus."

"I can't . . . ," Jade began, trying not to look at the over-eager Mr. Ashbury while he focused on her décolletage. "I won't . . ."

She felt someone move close behind. "Miss Douglas would love to attend to Mr. Ashbury, but she has promised to introduce me to San Francisco society. Isn't that right, Miss Douglas?"

There was no disguising that low, gravelly voice, or the words laced with the soft hint of a drawl. Jade turned and found herself face-to-face with Jason Harrington. And she could not think of a thing to say.

Babs smiled widely. Jade wanted to deny his words and tell him she would have nothing further to do with him, but one look at Harold Ashbury convinced her not to. Besides, there was still a score to settle with J.T.

"I . . . I'm afraid Mr. Harrington is correct," she began hesitantly. "I'm pleased to have met you, Mr. Ashbury, but I did promise . . ."

The old gentleman looked so crestfallen that Jade almost relented. But with a parting smile for Ashbury and then a warning scowl meant for Babs, Jade took Jason's arm and stepped onto the dance floor.

He was an excellent dancer. His movements were fluid and graceful. He led with confidence as he whirled her about the dance floor. Tonight he was dressed in a suit of elegant black wool and satin-edged lapels and pockets. His black satin tie was perfectly tied, his diamond studs winked against the crisp white shirt. A gold-buttoned black vest completed his attire. The sight of him was utterly heart-stopping. She could not help but notice the sly looks the women around them gave him. Their interest did little to douse her anger. If anything, it infuriated her more. He was probably used to women swooning at his feet. Well, not Jade Douglas. She intended to let him know that she would do no such thing.

She glanced down and nearly laughed aloud when she

noticed that he was wearing his old boots. Even though the
had been polished, they still looked worn.

"You're smiling about my boots?"

"I couldn't help but notice."

"I told you I needed your help. None of the shoes at th
house were big enough." He shrugged without missing a bea
"I had to make do."

"How did you get in here?"

He smiled down at her and squeezed her hand. "Glad to se
me?"

"No," she lied.

"Matt Van Buren brought me. He's around somewhere."

"You had your nerve, Mr. Harrington, duping me int
staying at your home last night." She assumed her iciest tone
"I can't understand why you did it. What did you stand t
gain?"

"I think that would be obvious." The twinkle in his ey
alluded to his meaning.

"How dare you!" She stopped moving without warning an
his foot collided with hers.

"I suggest you keep dancing. You're making a scene."

Jade glanced past him and noticed that more than one coup
were regarding them intently. They began dancing once agai
"Babs berated me all the way home. I gave her all the san
sorry excuses you gave me, and she reminded me that yc
probably had a stable full of carriages. Is that true?"

J.T. was taken by the furious gleam in her eyes and the col
that anger added to her cheeks. He was only half-attentive
her words.

"Is what true?" he murmured.

Jade groaned. "That you have a stable full of carriages."

Patiently, he smiled down at her as one might at a curio
child. "Not completely full."

She tried to pull away. He jerked her closer to his ches
off-balancing her so that she had to cling to him in order not
fall into the other dancers.

"Let me go."

"Not until I've apologized."

"It's a little late for that," she sniffed.

The music ended. They remained on the dance floor, intent upon each other as dancers around them exchanged partners and waited for the orchestra to begin again.

"I'm sorry, Jade. It was damn selfish of me to have kept you there last night." His tone was a hushed whisper meant for her ears alone. "I realized that today when the reporter showed up at my door. I assumed"—he didn't know how to say it without offending her—"I thought that you—"

"You thought I was a slut." Jade used the word she had heard before but had never dared to utter. Her face was crimson. Unable to meet his gaze, she concentrated on his shirt front.

"You've got a way with words."

Once again, she tried to break his hold. The music started. He pulled her closer.

"Dance," he commanded.

"No."

His punishing grip on her hand brooked no argument. "Do it."

She followed his lead again.

"I'm not finished," he said. "I knew you were innocent the moment I kissed you. From then on, I wanted to teach you a lesson. Never put yourself in such a vulnerable position again."

"Your game might have ruined my reputation forever."

"I realized that too late. And I'm sorry."

Although her anger had slowly subsided, there was nothing more she wanted to say to him. She danced in silence.

J.T. tried to cajole her into a better humor. "Come on. You have to admit it wasn't all that bad."

"Sleeping on the floor soaked to the skin? Waking up looking like a wild woman, with a reporter on my heels?"

He laughed aloud. At the warm sound she found herself smiling.

"It was all so very wonderful," she said sarcastically. But her eyes danced with merriment.

His good humor mellowed her. She realized that this was their second dance, and she could not even remember the first one ending. Jade let herself relax in his arms and flow to the lilting music of the waltz. It seemed impossible to stay angry with him. It was nice to put her problems behind her for a while and rely on someone else to take the lead. And it was heavenly to feel his arms around her.

All too soon, the waltz ended and Jade found herself staring up at Jason. When he smiled, she stepped out of his embrace, embarrassed to have been caught staring. The sun had tinted his skin a deep gold, just as it had lightened his brown hair with dancing highlights. His eyes were bright blue, mirroring his easy smile.

"Let's take a walk," he said, grasping her elbow and guiding her across the floor as easily as he had led her through the steps of the dance.

They moved past male guests sporting unrelieved black or navy military uniforms and women gowned in tarlatan, crepe, and silks. Crystal chandeliers set the room aglow, potted palms filled every corner and alcove, Haviland china graced the refreshment table, and rich carpeting covered all but the dance floor.

Before they reached the other side of the room, Jade felt Jason stiffen and followed his gaze. "Who is that woman?" he asked, his voice low but charged with feeling.

"I don't know," she admitted, curious to see who had claimed his attention. She tried to see over the moving crowd and then caught a glimpse of the woman Jason was staring at so avidly. She was diminutive in height, blond, and dressed in a daringly low-cut ballgown of midnight silk. The shocking contrast of ivory skin and white blond hair against the unrelieved black created a stunning portrait. A diamond choker about her neck matched the teardrops that dangled in her ears. The woman was clinging to the arm of a portly, balding man with thick mutton-chop whiskers.

"Come on." Jason pulled her along as he elbowed his way through the crowded room.

Jade immediately let go of his arm, and he stopped abruptly to look back. "You go ahead," she said.

He took her by the hand and held on tight. "I want you to go with me."

"Why?" She got no answer from him. He was already

moving forward. When they reached the other couple, he drew
her up alongside him and held her there, one hand around her
waist.

"Jason," she hissed, unwilling to make a scene.

He squeezed her waist.

She complied with a stony silence as she waited to see
exactly what would come of his interest in the blonde. At
closer range, Jade noted that although the woman was still
beautiful, her complexion was hidden by thick powder, her
cheeks rouged, her lips suspiciously red.

Jade was certain Babs would have immediately labeled the
woman a tart. She held her opinion in reserve.

"Nettie?" Jason said, drawing the attention of the petite
blonde and the man beside her.

For a moment Jade was certain the woman was not going to
admit that she knew Jason, but there was no denying her
flabbergasted look of recognition.

"Jason Harrington?" the woman squealed. "Jason Harrington, as I live and breathe I can't *believe* that's you standin'
right here in front of me after all these years!"

Her southern drawl was as thick as molasses on a cold day.
Silent, Jade watched as the woman Jason called Nettie took
command of the situation. The blonde quickly turned to the
older man at her side.

"Winslow, this is Jason Harrington. He's from back home in
Georgia. I haven't seen him for years now. We grew up
neighbors in Athens. Jason, this is my *very* dear friend,
Winslow Winters."

Jason coldly shook hands with Winters, then remembered
Jade. "Nettie, Winters, this is *my* very dear friend, Jade
Douglas." He smiled down at her.

Aware of his forced smile, Jade was tempted to drive her
heel into his foot. She tried to wriggle out of Jason's grasp. She
didn't know what he was up to, but she wanted no part of it.
All the while, Nettie Parsons preened and batted her lashes at
Jason. Jade stiffened. J.T. stood mute.

"Why, Jason, whatever are you doin' in San Francisco? I
thought you were still livin' out in the desert someplace?
Mexico, was it? Or Texas?"

"New Mexico."

"That's right. You moved there just before the war, didn't you?" Then, with a smile that reminded Jade of a cat who had just been in the cream, Nettie pouted prettily and turned to Winters. "I never dreamed all the time we were growin' up together that Jason would turn out to be afraid of fightin'. He didn't serve in the war. On either side."

Jade colored, embarrassed for Jason, quelling the urge to reach out and slap the woman herself. She wished there was something she could do to defend Jason, but was afraid he might be too proud to stand for that. Even though the War Between the States had ended nearly ten years before, feelings often ran high on both sides. It did not matter to Jade in the least that Jason had not taken sides and put on a uniform to kill his own countrymen. She could not imagine this man being a coward. Surely he had his own reasons for avoiding service. And those reasons were his alone.

Winters dismissed Nettie with a frown. "You'll have to excuse Nettie. She does tend to speak her own mind. Nettie, Mr. Harrington here just inherited his father's fortune. Coffee bean holdings, wasn't it, Harrington? Quite extensive, I might add."

"That's right," J.T. answered stiffly.

Nettie immediately tried to look contrite. She deftly snapped open the lace fan that dangled from her wrist. "Jason, I'm sorry if I spoke out of turn. I forget my good manners once in a while."

Probably most of the time, Jade thought. Nettie's obvious about-face when she learned that Jason had inherited a fortune disgusted Jade. She couldn't help but notice that the woman was eyeing her closely, studying her gown while the men were occupied in conversation. She guessed Nettie was at least thirty, but it was hard to be certain with all the face powder the woman wore. She turned to see how Jason was faring and was surprised to note a change in him. Jade was thankful that the icy stare he concentrated on Nettie was not directed at her. Nothing about his current demeanor reminded her of the easygoing man he'd been a few moments ago. The look he gave the southern woman was one of utter distaste.

"How is it you find yourself in San Francisco?" Jade asked Nettie as she tried to fill the tense silence.

"Winslow insisted we see the Pacific. He works for the railroad, you see, and so we travel quite extensively."

"You're from the North then, Mr. Winters?" Jade wondered if Jason was going to say anything else or if she should make excuses for them both so that they might leave.

"Philadelphia."

Jade immediately turned to Nettie. "With your feelings running so strong for the South, how is it you find yourself in a room full of Yankees? I would have thought it might be distasteful for you, after all you must have suffered during the war."

Nettie Winters glared at Jade for a moment before she regained her composure. "Why, because I believe in letting bygones by bygones."

"And I, like the Chinese," Jade said slowly, "believe that we should let every man sweep the snow from his own doorstep and not trouble himself with the frost on his neighbor's." She turned to Jason and for Nettie Parsons' sake, beamed up at him. "I would really like a glass of champagne, Jason."

The hardness never left his eyes. Nor did the tight lines about his lips. "Of course." He turned to the other couple and, with a courtly bow, bade them both good evening.

As he escorted Jade across the room, Jason tried to calm down. Seeing Nettie after all these years, and so close on the heels of his dream of her, had been a shock. She had not aged well at all; there was a hard look about her, a callousness that no amount of beautiful clothes or face powder could hide. He felt like a fool. All this time he had imagined Nettie as the picture of southern womanhood—virtuous, long-suffering, probably widowed at an early age. Yet here she was on the arm of some Yankee entrepreneur after she had given Jason up because he refused to join the Confederate Army.

"Jason?"

He glanced down at the young woman beside him and smiled. Jade was like a breath of fresh air compared to Nettie.

He let the sight of her brush the cobwebs of the past from his mind.

Reaching for two champagne flutes from a forty-foot-long refreshment table, he handed one to Jade, and after a silent toast, drained his glass. He ordered a whiskey as Jade took a sip and enjoyed the effervescence of the bubbling wine.

"Tell me about her," she said.

He had visibly relaxed as they carried the drinks to the open balcony doors. They stepped outside and, instead of finding themselves alone, became part of the stream of guests strolling along the balustraded walkway that rimmed the courtyard below. Gaslights flickered every few feet along the outer walls as Jason directed Jade toward the balcony railing and leaned back against it. He took another swig of whiskey and then looked at Jade. She was waiting expectantly for an explanation.

"Nettie lived on the neighboring plantation near Athens. I left Georgia when I was fifteen and never saw her again." He finished his drink just as a waiter passed by bearing a tray ladened with refills. Jason exchanged glasses with the man and stared down into his whiskey for a moment.

Seeing Nettie tonight on the arm of her traveling companion, a man who was not even her husband, had been a stunning revelation. He cursed the irony of it all. Who would have ever thought, after holding her memory sacred for all these years, that on his first trip out of New Mexico he would run into her and have his idyllic image shattered?

His noble visions were of Nettie standing behind the Confederacy, enduring hardships and suffering for the cause she had believed in so deeply that she had sacrificed the love they had for each other. How often had he wondered if she had married, only to lose her husband to the war? He was so convinced that she and her family were impoverished, that at one point after the war he considered going back to Georgia to find her. Only the thought that she would still consider him a traitor and reject him again kept him from going.

But it seemed his Nettie had faired quite well after all, if the diamonds she was wearing were any indication. Slowly his anger at Nettie turned inward as he found himself blaming her for not living up to the ideals he had attributed to her.

"You were in love with her, weren't you?" Jade asked quietly.

Jason looked down at the woman beside him. Her upturned face mirrored her concern. Determined to lighten the mood, he shrugged. "I was. But that was a long time ago."

She wondered how many others he had loved, how many women had loved him. Jade felt a disturbing sadness in her heart. "Then why were you hanging all over me like that in front of her, if not to make her jealous?"

He laughed aloud. "Was I that obvious?"

"Yes. And I don't appreciate being used."

He leaned down and whispered near her ear, "I will never do it again."

Chills ran down her spine.

He wanted to put Nettie out of his mind. "Did I tell you how beautiful you look tonight?"

Jade almost protested his compliment. In her mind's eye she would always be the awkward, gangly young girl who was too tall, whose hair was too curly to tame—the way she looked before she left San Francisco. Instead, she blushed—because she could not help it—and simply thanked him.

"It must be Babs' dress," she admitted.

"On the contrary. I think it's what's in the dress."

"Watch your manners," she warned.

"It suits you. So does smiling."

His voice was low and warm and struck a chord in her somewhere near her heart. She felt herself being drawn toward him like a thirsty hummingbird drawn to nectar.

"I like your hair better when you leave it hanging loose."

Had he stepped closer, or had she? "I prefer wearing it that way, too, but it's not socially acceptable for a woman my age."

"And we know you always do what is socially acceptable."

He was teasing her now. She could hear it in his tone.

"Not always. My father often accused me of being too much of a bluestocking, an intellectual female who cares more for studies than anything else."

"Are you?"

Jade nodded. "I'm afraid so."

"You make it sound like a curse."

She was twenty-three years old and had only received her first kiss yesterday, and had to agree with him. "Sometimes it is."

Jason glanced down into the courtyard below. Carriages were still arriving and departing—the cobblestones rang loud with the sound of horses' hooves, and carriage wheels mingled with the voices of the guests promenading on the seven tiers of balconies.

"What do you study?"

Jade was staring up at him so intently that for a moment she could not even formulate an answer. "China," she finally blurted out. "Chinese culture and art."

"Do you mind if I ask why?"

"Why what?"

"Why you study China."

"Oh." No one had ever asked her before. Babs had always ignored her interest in things Chinese, for she found them embarrassing. The Chinese in California labored at the lowest tasks. Babs, like most Californians, could see nothing worthwhile at all about any facet of Chinese culture. Jade's most eccentric habits had developed from her studies. "I suppose because my grandfather was so dedicated to learning all he could about the Chinese. He was already here in forty-nine when the Chinese immigration began. At first, they immigrated to work the gold mines. Later they were hired to lay the transcontinental railroad lines. The first Chinese who arrived were either ex-convicts, adventurers, or rebels who had fought against the Manchurian emperor."

When she noticed he was trying to suppress a smile, she stopped. "I'm sorry I'm boring you."

"Not at all. I was just thinking that if I had had such a beautiful teacher when I was in school I would have paid better attention."

"Where did you go to school?"

"In Athens. My mother hired a male tutor for me. Then when we moved to the territories, we were out on the ranch, miles from any civilized place. My uncle taught me everything

I needed to know about horse breeding and ranching. He's a wonderful man, accident prone, but the kind of man I'd like to be someday."

"You must be anxious to get back."

"Actually, I find I'm enjoying myself more than I imagined I would. Because of you."

He turned toward her again and stepped close. Jade caught her breath, afraid he might kiss her again. Hoping that he would.

"Would you believe me if I told you I think I'm falling in love with you?" His lips were so very close to hers that she was afraid to move, to breathe.

"Do you fall in love with every woman you meet?" she whispered.

"No, only the ones who appear on my doorstep." He reached out to touch her and brushed his fingertips against her bare arms. J.T. felt her tremble; felt the blood surge through him. She was so very beautiful—so wise and at the same time so untutored. He longed to make her his, all the time knowing that she was not the kind of woman he could merely love and leave. If he toyed with Jade Douglas, he would be playing for keeps.

He brushed a quick, innocent kiss across her lips and started to pull away, but the effort took more strength of will than he possessed. As their lips met and held, he dropped his hands to his sides, unwilling to test his own resolve any more than he had to. Jade swayed toward him, placed her palms against his chest, and opened herself to his kiss.

It was slow and sweet, and Jason savored every moment of it. A tangy lemon scent drifted on the air about her; the soft rustle of her gown added to the unique spell she was weaving around him. He wanted nothing more than to take her in his arms, but he was all too aware of where they were and how her reputation might suffer because of him.

Reluctantly, he was the first to pull back.

His voice was rough with emotion as he said, "I think we should go inside."

Unable to speak, she nodded in agreement. As they were about to reenter the ballroom, Babs and Reggie appeared in

the doorway and Jade thanked the gods that they had not come
looking for her a moment sooner, or Babs would be announcing a wedding and Reggie would be demanding an explanation.

"Jade, I'm so glad we found you," Babs said. "I was
worried that you might be alone, but I can see Mr. Harrington
has kept you well occupied."

Very well occupied, Jade thought.

"I'm fine," she assured Babs. "We were just coming back
inside."

"I thought that the four of us could go downstairs and view
the art collection in the foyer. Reggie and Mr. Harrington can
become acquainted and we can chat."

Jade suspected what that little *chat* would be about, but
Jason agreed to the idea after he told them both to call him J.T.

The lifts were crowded with curious guests and a sizable
group stood waiting their turn, so Reggie suggested they take
the stairs. Babs and Jade preceded the men down the wide,
circular staircase.

"Jade, he's just perfect if you ask me!" Babs whispered in
her ear.

"Stop that," Jade warned. "He'll be leaving here soon to go
back to his home in New Mexico." She did not want to give
Jason the impression they were talking about him, so she
ignored Babs and moved to the edge of the stairs to look down
on the floor below.

Only half-listening to Reginald Barrett, J.T. was watching
Jade as she walked down the stairs with her friend. The opulent
surroundings suited her well—her striking coloring and regal
bearing set her off like a glowing jewel. For the first time he
noticed she was not wearing any jewelry, and thought it
perceptive of her to realize how much more alluring she was
unadorned. She was as radiant as any diamond.

He watched her intently as she rested her hand gently upon
the polished banister and moved gracefully down the stairs.
Then he began to take in the sights and sounds around
him. Waiters and bellmen moved unobtrusively among the
guests. The walls were decorated with elaborately designed
wall coverings. Each landing contained more of the exotic

potted palms. Jason had never seen anything like it, even in the South before the war. He let his gaze move upward, past the crystal wall sconces to the section of the circular staircase above them. A movement caught his eye.

In the time it took his heart to beat twice, he watched paralyzed as one of the heavy urns containing a palm began to topple over the edge and plummet toward them. Jade was directly beneath the hurtling object. He shoved Reggie out of harm's way and made a diving leap toward Jade.

His weight knocked Babs back against the wall, while it propelled him and Jade downward. Jason tried to turn with Jade in his arms to absorb the shock of the fall. He had no time to think as he held onto her tightly. They tumbled down a half a dozen stairs to the landing below.

When the huge urn hit the staircase, there was a sound of splintering wood and porcelain. Shards of the container flew out in all directions as loose soil showered them all.

Babs screamed.

The crowd in the foyer below reacted with surprised gasps and shouts. Jade shook her head, opened her eyes, and stared down at Jason Harrington. She was sprawled atop him, safely locked in his arms.

A puffed sleeve of her gown was torn away, the bodice ripped near the underarm. She tried to catch her breath, tried to fight the dizziness that assailed her, tried to ignore the sensations sweeping through her as she lay atop him. She could feel his warm breath against her cheek.

Jade planted her open palms against his shirt front and pushed herself up until she was straddling him. When the world came into focus, she wanted to die when she realized she was virtually sitting astride Jason's crotch. She slid off of him until she was seated beside him on the floor.

He groaned.

Her heart fluttered with fear.

"Jason? Are you all right?"

❈ CHAPTER 7 ❈

By a long journey we know a horse's strength;
So length of days shows a man's heart.

"Jade! You could have been killed!" Babs rushed over and stared down at the tangle that was Jason and Jade. "We could have all been killed!"

J.T., still stunned by the fall, shook his head and tried to clear his vision. Reggie Barrett hurried to join them on the landing.

"Get up, Jade!" Chagrined, Reggie glanced at the gathering crowd and admonished her in a whisper, "Good God, you're making a scene!"

Jade ignored him and smoothed Jason's hair back off his forehead. "Jason? Are you all right?" He had paled, even beneath his tan.

He tried to sit up. "Yeah. Right as rain. Help me up, Barrett."

With Babs' help, Jade got to her knees and Reggie quickly righted Jason, who stared at the broken urn that had made a shambles of the staircase. Had the oversized pot hit them, they would have indeed been killed. He glanced up the stairs to the landing, but all he saw was another mob of curious onlookers peering over the railing.

Babs brushed dirt off of Jade and tucked the torn fabric of her sleeve into the top of her bodice, while Jade watched Jason to be sure he was all right. Reggie merely stood there looking thoroughly embarrassed. The hotel manager was working his way through the crowd. Jade noticed him just before she saw a short man in a plaid suit at the front of the mob staring at them.

She heard Jason groan and gave him her full attention. "You are hurt!" she said.

"No," he whispered, "I'm not, but I want to get you out of here right now. That ferret of a reporter is staring at us. I don't intend to answer any of his questions."

Matt Van Buren forced his way through the crowd and ran

95

up the few remaining steps to the landing. "Jason? Are you all right?"

"I'm fine, but we need to get out of here. Will you get us a carriage?" Without waiting for comment from the Barretts, Jason turned to them and said, "I'll take Jade back to your house. She's badly shaken."

Jade did not protest, not when it seemed as if her knees would not hold her upright any longer. As she let Jason lead her through the parting mob, she became more and more aware of the curious stares of the onlookers. The room buzzed with whispers. The manager halted their exit as he apologized profusely and assured them that he would be happy to have them spend the night as guests of the hotel, free of charge.

Jason declined and led Jade to the door. They stood in the crowded courtyard while Matt had his own carriage brought around instead of a hotel hack. When Jade began to tremble uncontrollably, J.T. slipped his arm about her shoulders. Fear of what might have happened to her shook him to the core. He tried to dispel her trembling.

"Did you bring a wrap?"

She shook her head. "It was not very cold when we left the house. I forgot it." The weather had turned chilly, but she trembled more from fear than anything else.

"I'll have you home soon. Here." J.T. slipped out of his own coat and drew it over her shoulders. He pulled the lapels closed. He fought the urge to draw her near, and let go of the coat. When the carriage arrived, he helped her in, then joined her in the darkness.

He was as good as his word, and soon they pulled up before the Barretts' residence. Before he opened the door, Jason lingered inside the close confines of the carriage, watching Jade as she tried to regain her composure.

"Feeling better?"

She nodded. "I think so. And you?"

"I'm fine, but I'm probably going to regret playing the hero tomorrow."

"I'm starting to feel a little stiff in places myself," she said, laughing. Jade snuggled inside his coat, all too aware of the scent of soap and hint of bay rum that clung to it.

He was pleased to note her good humor had returned. "What a disaster." He shook his head.

"Do you think the reporter saw the whole incident, or just the part where I landed on top of you?"

He laughed. "That's the part he'll remember, if I don't miss my guess."

J.T. reached out for her hand and held it between his own. His were warm and dry and somehow comforting. When she realized how safe she felt with this man, she remembered her uncalled-for fear of him just yesterday.

As he sat beside her, Jason realized what it felt like to be responsible for a woman for no other reason except that he wanted to. "Will you be all right alone until they get back?"

"Of course," she said, knowing full well that she would relish the peace and quiet. Babs was certain to return in a state of near frenzy after all the excitement.

"I'll walk you to the door."

When they climbed the front stairs and reached the landing, Jason rang the bell and waited with her until one of the servants answered. Jade started to draw his coat off of her shoulders. He reached out for her and would not let her go when she stiffened and tried to draw away.

"I'm coming back here first thing in the morning to see how you are," he promised.

She shook her head. "That's not necessary. Aside from being spattered with dirt from head to toe, I'm fine. Besides, by tomorrow you might not be able to move. You took the full brunt of the fall."

"You noticed."

"That was all I noticed—everything happened so fast. Someone on the floor above us must have bumped into that urn." Lamplight spilled over them from the doorway. She let her eyes roam over his strong features—his finely drawn lips, the deep-set eyes, the sharp lines of his jaw. "I owe you my life, Jason." She did not add that the Chinese believed once a man saved a person's life that he was responsible for that person forever after.

"You owe me nothing. But I will ask for some of your time. I'm coming to get you in the morning, so that you can show me some of the countryside. Do the Barretts have a horse you can ride?"

"Horse?" If there was one thing Jade knew little about and did not care to know better, it was horses.

"That's usually what one rides."

She could not fathom why his remark had caused him to stifle a smile. "I hate horses and I'm a terrible rider," she admitted.

"I love horses and I'll teach you."

"I don't think—"

"You owe me your life, remember. All I'm asking for is your company. Or would riding together be frowned on by San Francisco society?"

"Not in broad daylight . . ."

"Then I'll see you in the morning." He hoped he was not pushing her too fast, but as he watched her stand there in the yellow-gold lamplight, with her hair a wild nimbus framing perfect features set in flawless ivory skin, J.T. wanted nothing more than to taste the sweetness of her kiss again.

Jade stared back, too haunted by his gaze to move away. Just hours ago, he had kissed her in a way she had never even imagined. And now he was staring down at her in the same way he had before. She knew she should move, wanted to draw off his coat and hand it to him, but some force greater than her will compelled her to stand mute before him.

At the same time, J.T. lost the battle raging within him. Before she was aware of what he was doing, he pulled her up hard against him and kissed her. It was another deeply disturbing, soul-shattering exchange that set her knees knocking and his own heart pounding. He kissed her long and expertly, holding her so close he could feel her heart beating. The wild tempo matched that of his own. With aching slowness, J.T. slipped his tongue between her lips.

Her initial resistance ebbed as he expertly held her in his arms, his lips moving tenderly over hers. She gave herself up to the wonder of their blending. Radiating warmth began to spread upward from somewhere deep inside to set her nerve ends tingling. Just as she was about to slip her arms about his neck and hold on for dear life, the exchange ended and Jason stepped back.

"Tomorrow," he whispered, hating to leave her. Knowing he must.

"Tomorrow," she promised, even as she wondered what she was doing prolonging their time together. Nothing could come of this relationship. Nothing at all. He was leaving as soon as he could. She was setting herself up for heartache. And she knew it.

Jade handed him his coat and watched him jog down the stairs knowing the few short hours until morning would seem like forever.

Alone inside the carriage, Jason slipped off his silk tie and stuffed it into his jacket pocket. He unclasped the studs at his cuffs and collar and deposited them with the tie, then settled back against the tucked leather seat.

His mind was whirling. Jade Douglas had set his whole life upside down since the moment he opened the door and found her on his doorstep. It seemed disaster followed in the beautiful redhead's wake. First the storm, then tonight's accident. He shook his head and wondered if her life was always so eventful.

He thought about what she had told him, about her years with the missionary family, her scholarly habits and the interest in the Chinese culture that she had inherited from her grandfather. It was easy to imagine her as a little girl walking hand in hand with her grandfather as he taught her what he knew. The many hours she must have spent with the elderly man would account for her quiet self-control. She had no doubt been the apple of her grandfather's eye. J.T. had never known anyone like her. Chinese culture, this city—everything she cared about was foreign to him.

As the carriage sped toward Harrington House, Jason told himself he was a fool for pursuing Jade. They were from two different worlds. No matter how natural and unassuming she was, she was used to the city, to a sophisticated way of life. Why would she consent to give up living in San Francisco for a life on an isolated ranch in New Mexico?

Just listen to yourself, he thought, *you've known the girl a little over one full day and you're trying to picture her in New Mexico.* And marriage? He hadn't given the institution a serious thought for fifteen years. Perhaps the sight of Nettie, seeing her for what she really was, instead of the idealized symbol of conviction and virtue he had worshipped all these years, had freed his heart.

He shrugged and crossed his feet on the seat opposite him. J.T. rarely smoked, but tonight he needed something to help him relax. He pulled a thin cigarillo from his coat pocket and lit it. The match flared in the dark interior of the coach, and soon the rich heavy scent of tobacco filled the confined space. He sighed and shook his head.

Nettie Parsons. It seemed she had profited well from the war. He could almost hear his Uncle Cash's horselaugh now. When he first moved to the ranch he had told Cash and Lupita all about Nettie in glowing terms and about how she had promised to marry him. Then, when the war started and Jason chose not to join the Confederate Army as Nettie had expected, he shared his pain with them when she rejected him.

Cash claimed that any woman who really loved him would have stood by his decision. Jason disagreed. As much as he had loved Nettie, he valued her idealism and the fact that she could not give up the cause she believed in, even for the man she loved. He understood when she wrote and told him she could not betray all she believed in. He felt the same way about his own beliefs.

Still, the war years had not been easy for J.T. Even in the far canyons and mountains of New Mexico, the repercussions of the War Between the States had been strongly felt. Many men left the territories to serve on both sides. Those who stayed behind were most often older or infirm, or men like his Uncle Cash who could not afford to leave his ranch in the hands of a green youngster like Jason. But J.T. had been tall and strong—a strapping youth accused of cowardice on more than one occasion. It mattered little to his critics that he and Cash were raising horses for both armies. He had not donned a uniform and taken sides.

During the war years, his trips to Santa Fe for supplies dwindled until he became a near recluse in Canyon de las Bolsas. It was easier to live alone with his convictions than to face those men who did not understand his objection to a blood fest between Americans. He could not condone men of the same country killing each other for any reason.

He shook his head and his bitter laughter filled the carriage. Little Nettie had done quite well for herself, if the portly railroad Yankee she had hung on tonight was any indication.

He wondered if he would ever dream of Nettie again.

The carriage entered the drive at Harrington House and before long stopped at the entrance. J.T. stepped out and thanked Matt's driver, ground out the butt of his cigar in the drive, then let himself into the empty house. Thankful that he had tomorrow's ride with Jade to look forward to, he felt his way through the darkness. His boot heels rang out hollowly in the emptiness.

A predawn chill lingered in Jade's room, but she forced herself up and out of bed. When she stretched her arms high overhead, every muscle cried out from the bruising she had taken in last night's fall. Barefoot, with the hems of her loose silk pants brushing the floor, she padded softly to the window seat and lowered herself into a comfortable sitting position. The window in her borrowed room faced east and she was glad of that, for she enjoyed watching the sunrise. She closed her eyes and took a deep breath, hoping to relax and slip into a contemplative state. Now that she had a room to herself, she enjoyed the freedom of being able to meditate whenever she wished. In Paris, she had shared a loft above the ground floor with the missionary's three daughters. Early in her stay with the good minister and his family, she became aware that their great knowledge of the Chinese language was equal to their lack of appreciation for Chinese philosophy and their total objection to the religious practices of the East.

Those periods of silent contemplation she had once shared with her grandfather, she was forced to spend alone. When she retired for the night and the lights were doused, she would lie quietly in bed beside the sleeping girls and review the day. Whenever she awoke before the others, she would stay abed and use the quiet moments in thought before the day began.

Now it was a joy to be able to sit and await the dawn and think about all that had happened since she arrived home. As she sat in silence, waiting for the first rays of sunlight to beckon her to open her eyes, Jade became more and more determined to take control of her situation. Ever since she had returned, she had allowed Babs' vivacity to lead her where she did not really want to go, just as had happened for years. But things were about to change.

On the journey from Paris, she had decided that she would attempt to follow the philosophy of Chuang Tzu, a Taoist philosopher. She had memorized the passage she most subscribed to: "The pure men of old acted without calculation, not seeking to secure results. They laid no plans. Therefore, failing, they had no cause for regret; succeeding, no cause for congratulation. And thus they could scale heights without fear, enter water without becoming wet, and fire without feeling hot. The pure men of old slept without dreams, and waked without anxiety."

So she had laid no plans. She knew only that she wanted to retrieve her grandfather's Chinese collection, somehow pay off her father's debts, and find a means of support. But unlike the "pure men of old," she had not scaled any heights, nor had she awakened once since her arrival without anxiety. She wondered how long it would take before acting without calculation brought results, and then promptly decided she could not wait any longer to find out.

After all, she shrugged and smiled to herself, this *was* San Francisco in 1875, not China in 400 B.C.

As the daylight began to intensify, she planned her day. She had promised to go riding with J.T. She also promised herself it was the last time she would see him. Then she convinced herself she was only going so that she could ride out and visit her grandfather's adobe. That was easier than thinking about never seeing Jason Harrington again.

She thought back to the night before when Babs had come in after the grand reception to see how she fared. Jade had asked permission to use one of the Barretts' horses. Babs had immediately demanded all the details.

Babs had been too excited to sit still. She began combing out her hair with Jade's brush. "What in heaven's name do you want with a horse, Jade? As I recall, you hate them."

"I don't hate them," Jade had tried to explain, "I just never wanted to be around them after the time you decided we should go out for a carriage ride without your father or a groom."

Babs had the good sense to look sheepish. She shrugged. "I was only nine. How was I to know how hard it was to control a carriage horse?"

"We were nearly killed. Anyway, after that I never wanted to know any horse very well."

"We're talking about horses, not distant relatives."

Jade thought of the Chinese belief in reincarnation and laughed. "Who knows? Anyway, Jason wants to see the sights and I thought it would be a good time for me to go out to the adobe and see what sort of state it's in."

"*Jason?*"

"Mr. Harrington."

Jade's borrowed hairbrush was forgotten as Babs threw it down on the dressing table. "This is *wonderful*, Jade. He must really have taken an interest in you. I told you not to worry! Why, before you know it, he'll be asking for your hand and you'll be living in high style."

"Babs—"

"You can be married right here and—"

"Babs!"

"What?"

"Stop."

Babs pouted prettily. "Oh, pooh. You're no fun."

"I'm only going riding."

"Do you have anything decent to wear?"

"Yes."

"Let me see it. I don't trust you."

"No. It's late. Now get out of here and let me go to sleep. He's coming over very early."

"Don't wake me up."

"I wouldn't think of it." Jade was determined not to have Babs there to greet Jason.

Jade opened her eyes and put her thoughts of yesterday aside. The sky had lightened, but the sun had not been able to break through the fog. Rubbing her arms to ward off the chill, she crossed the room to the armoire. She quickly stepped out of her silk trousers and robe and slipped into knee-length knickerbocker drawers and a waist-length chemise of cotton. Without fussing overlong, she brushed out her heavy, unruly hair and tied the entire mass at the nape of her neck with a long length of black ribbon.

She refused to wear the heavy corset or to strap on the bustle Babs loaned her until she could get one of her own. Instead, she pulled on a simple walking skirt with braid trim about the hem and topped it off with a neat, white French waist blouse. She pulled on her tassled boots and then donned a gray waterproof cloak. She fluffed the attached cape and straightened the hood she left dangling behind her.

Rifling through the top drawer of her vanity, she found her kid gloves and pulled them on, smoothed back loose tendrils of hair that had escaped her ribbon, and quietly slipped out the door.

She paused in the kitchen long enough to search through the baskets and bread box until she had the makings of a simple picnic: bread, cheese, and apples. Then she even helped herself to a bottle of Reggie's red wine. She wrapped the food in a dish towel and tied the makeshift bag shut.

The stablehand was already up and currying the horses. She told him she wished to have a gentle mount saddled, and watched—well out of the way—as he readied a bay mare. The stablehand, who looked no older than fifteen, easily hefted the cumbersome saddle and began to rig up the various straps and buckles when he suddenly stopped and slapped his hand against his forehead.

"Damn!" he grumbled to himself, before he snuck a glance at Jade. "I reckon you'll be wanting a sidesaddle, right, ma'am?"

Jade frowned. She didn't want to ride at all. Her only experience had been in the runaway carriage or when she shared a ride with her grandfather. Then she had used a conventional saddle. She looked down at her uneven skirt, longer in the back than the front due to the lack of a bustle, and shook her head.

"I'll use the one you've already put on," she said.

The boy smiled and rechecked the cinches. "I'll lead 'er

down the drive and around the front for you ma'am." He nodded politely.

She thanked him, and followed him out into the fog. They stood near the front entrance to the Barrett's, alternately looking up and down the street, but able to see little through the mist.

They heard Jason's horse approaching before they saw him.

Jade smiled up at him as he drew his horse to a halt before them. She thought him handsome last night, but as he appeared out of the fog he was even more imposing astride a huge palomino stallion. He was casually but sensibly dressed in navy blue Levi's, a creamy yellow shirt, leather vest, and waterproof duster. J.T. dismounted and handed his reins to the groom. He then took the reins of the mare from the groom, and held the horse still while Jade mounted. Or tried to.

Whispering softly, she held her hands out in front of her as if to ward off a sudden attack. "Nice horse. Good old horse," she whispered. She stared up the stirrup dangling a good four feet above the ground and groaned. Jason linked his fingers together to form a step.

"Here," he said. "I'll boost you up."

She hiked up her skirt and stepped onto his hands. J.T. could not help but admire her neatly turned ankles and calves when she raised her skirt and stepped trustingly onto his hands. He made certain she was well settled in the saddle before he took the liberty to tuck the hem of her wrap beneath her calves.

"Be sure to keep your cloak from flapping. It might spook the horse." He immediately sensed that his casual warning alarmed her.

"Spook?" She could barely say the word.

Jason smiled up at her as he smoothed the horse's mane. "You'll be just fine. What's the mare's name?"

"Name?" She looked dismayed.

"Daffodil," the stableboy volunteered.

"Perfect," Jason laughed. He turned to Jade. "How can you seriously worry when you're on a horse named Daffodil?"

"Names can be deceiving," Jade said, tightening her grip.

"Just relax."

He could not help but smile again. Blushing furiously, she

straightened her skirt again as best she could, but the tops of
her boots and ankles were plainly showing. She looked away
from Jason, who sensed her embarrassment and mounted his
own horse.

Aware of her fear, he walked his horse beside hers. The
golden stallion clearly wanted to run but contented itself with
head tossing, blowing, and an occasional nip at Jade's mount.
Jason kept the big animal under a firm hand as they ambled
down the street.

A smile teased his lips. "Am I suitably attired?"

She was staring at the ground, watching every step the horse
took, silently praying it would not bolt down the street.
"What?" Her tone reflected her irritation.

He noted her distraction and kept up the banter, trying to put
her at ease. "A Chinaman came to the back door before dawn
with two huge baskets hanging off a pole across his shoulders.
He said he'd take my laundry and have it back by tonight, so
I gave him everything but these."

"You look fine." She did not look up. "You shouldn't pay
more than ten cents a piece," she added as an afterthought.

"Where are we off to?" Jason asked, squinting as if it would
help him see through the fog.

"Out of town. I would like to visit my grandfather's house.
It's been deserted for nearly four years now."

Considering her fear, he was surprised she had gotten so
many words out. "Is it far?"

"Not really. The city has spread out so that it seems much
closer now."

She wished she could relax, but she was busy trying to keep
her seat. The saddle creaked and groaned with each step
Daffodil took. Jade wondered if and when the saddle might
come loose. She clenched the reins in a death grip while she
held on to the pommel as well. She thought that riding a camel
might be just as comfortable and prayed silently that Jason
would not want to go any faster. For the moment, he seemed
content to walk his own horse silently beside hers.

Jason snuck glances at the woman beside him and decided
he had never seen a person less at home on horseback. She
looked as stiff as a board as she leaned forward over the

pommel, fighting every step. He bet himself that beneath her kid gloves her knuckles were white. He found it hard to imagine anyone who was afraid of horses, but then, the animals were his life. Obviously, Jade had nothing but fear and distaste for them.

"Loosen up on the reins a bit."

"What?" She glanced over at him in disbelief and then quickly concentrated on the ground again.

"Relax. Enjoy the ride. Try not to fight the movement of the horse. Anticipate it and go with it."

She took a deep breath and tried to relax. It did not work.

He edged the stallion closer and the mare shied away.

"Don't!" Jade squealed.

"Steady." He reached out and grabbed her horse's bridle above the bit and stopped the mare just as he did his own. He slipped his hands over hers and took command of her reins. As she released the death grip on the pommel, he smiled his reassurance. "Hold these lightly. Let the horse know when you want it to stop or turn. Use the insides of your legs and your knees, too."

She blushed again.

Jason chuckled deep in his throat.

"Miss Douglas, I believe your sensibilities are too great to allow you to become an expert horsewoman."

"Don't worry about my sensibilities. Worry about me falling off."

He laughed again. "We'll take it slow. By the end of the day you'll be more comfortable."

"By the end of the day, I'll just be glad to be alive."

The sun slowly burned the fog away just as they reached the hills surrounding the Page adobe. The fall-yellowed grasses, the dense, low-growing sage on the hills, and the gnarled oaks that fanned out across the landscape had not changed since she had seen them last. Nestled in the hollow between hills dotted with oaks, the house was a two-story structure surrounded by low wall that defined the gardens. A balcony lined the second floor and provided the roof for the veranda below it. Every door opened onto the balcony or the veranda. Two outdoor stairways banked either end of the house.

The sight of the chipping whitewashed walls and dilapidated

roof did little to dim the feeling of relief that washed over Jade at her homecoming. Jason's guidance had helped to make her more at ease on horseback, and as she followed him down the hill, she gave her horse leave to go at the quickest trot of the morning. Breathless, she slowed the mare before the garden gate that was hanging open on its hinges, and led the way as they rode through.

He watched her carefully as she began squirming beneath her cloak. Wriggling slowly, she seemed to be balling material in her hands from the hem up, inching it toward her head.

"What are you doing?" He asked.

In a barely audible voice she replied, "I'm trying to get this cloak off without spooking the horse."

"We're standing perfectly still," he reminded her. "That horse isn't going anywhere. What I meant was not to let the ends flap wildly while we were riding."

Jade had the entire cloak wadded up about her neck like a thick shawl. She shrugged sheepishly. "You mean I can just take it off?"

He held out his hand.

She untied her cloak and handed it over to him. Jason shook his head and brushed out the folds before he hung it over the front of his saddle.

He remained silent as Jade took in the shambles that had once been a well-tended garden. The wild grapevine had escaped its trellis and extended about the place. Weaker plants had been choked out by the honeysuckle and barberry. The toyon—called California holly because of its round berries that turned red in December—had grown wild and much in need of pruning. The stately walnut and sycamore leaves had yellowed. Many had already fallen to litter the ground below. The paths, benches, and rocks situated about the garden had all but disappeared beneath the overgrowth.

Jade sighed and looked at the door. She could almost see Philo Page now, with his stray wisps of hair on his bald head, his shoulders stooped from constant reading, his spectacles riding on the tip of his narrow nose, as he stood in the open doorway and called out a greeting. Whenever she arrived on one of her frequent visits, he always met her with some bit of information, a new book, or news of the arrival of a prized object from the Orient. Sometimes Emery Lennox, or one of the other sea captains who supplied the antiques, would be with him. And always, Chi Nu—Philo's friend, chief caretaker, cook and groundskeeper—would be right behind him to welcome Jade home.

Now they were both gone.

Her eyes misted and she blinked away the tears.

"Are you all right?"

She gave a start, surprised to remember she was not alone, and tried to smile at Jason. "Thank you," she said softly.

"For what?"

"For letting me take this all in without saying anything."

J.T. wondered at her quiet thanks. It seemed only natural to hold his silence while she studied the changes that had occurred while she had been gone. He would have done the same. He could not wait to ride into Canyon de las Bolsas and feast his eyes on his home again.

Jason dismounted before the hitching rail at the edge of the veranda. He walked to Jade's horse and reached up for her. Thankful for his assistance, she put her hands on his shoulders. He grasped her waist. She gave herself over to him and he lifted her down, but did not immediately release her.

Jade tried to step away, but her legs would not hold her. With her muscles trembling with fatigue, she could do little but cling helplessly to Jason.

"I feel so foolish," she said. She could not seem to force her legs together.

He looked down at her upturned face. Her green eyes were sparkling, her cheeks glowing, kissed by sunshine. Involuntarily, his hands tightened on her waist. He wanted to do more than kiss her. He wanted to feel himself moving inside her, awaken her to the pleasures that she, in her wide-eyed innocence, had never dreamed of.

Jade felt her head swim and for a moment she thought she might faint, but she was too interested in the feeling Jason's very touch inspired. The way he was looking at her evoked responses identical to his kisses—her heart was beating triple-time, her fingers were trembling. She felt weak and at the same time pulsing with an energy that drew her to him like a magnet to iron.

He was as addictive as the opium smoked in Little China.

She could get used to this gentle man, to having him beside her always, but her inner voice told her that he would soon move on, just as it reminded her that she had much to accomplish. Her grandfather's dream had yet to be realized. Jason Harrington was not part of that dream. Nor had he any intention of becoming part of her future.

A sudden gust of wind blew through the garden and the branches of the walnut groaned in protest. The sound broke the fragile spell that held them in its grasp. Jade pulled away from Jason, bewildered by her intense reaction to him.

She did not know what to say.

Did he feel the way she did? Had the brief, innocent exchange moved him also? Dying to know, but far too shy to ask, Jade avoided meeting his eyes and waited for him to move away from her.

"Jade?"

"What?" she whispered.

He put his forefinger beneath her chin and lifted her head until she looked at him.

"Are you all right?"

She tried to find her voice. "Yes."

"Sure?"

She wanted this moment to last forever. She wanted nothing more than to stand alone with him in the garden and stare up into his eyes. She felt fully alive for the first time in her life, felt the very blood singing through her, welcomed the sunshine and breeze against her skin. For the first time she knew why she had been born a woman. But she was experiencing it all with a man who would never become part of her life. It seemed so very sad.

"Jade, I—"

She put her fingertips to his lips. His expression had grown so serious, the look he gave her so apologetic, that she did not want to hear whatever he was about to say. She would allow nothing to spoil the glorious moment.

With a determined effort, she smiled up at him. "Let's go inside."

CHAPTER 8

*Life is a dream walking
Death is a going home.*

The inside of the house was several degrees cooler than the air outside, as was the way with adobes. The clay walls were three feet thick and able to keep the interior warm in winter and cool in summer. In places where the whitewash had flaked off, the adobe construction was visible: straw, bits of shell, and twigs had been worked into the clay. With many of the windows broken and the wooden shutters missing, the inside of the house was damper and colder than usual. Jason left the door standing open as they walked inside and crossed the main room that was the core of the lower story.

With the exception of a few sticks of simple wooden furniture, there was nothing left of Philo Page's possessions. Jade did not know what she had expected to find, but it was certainly not this bleak, yawning emptiness.

She walked through the house with Jason close on her heels, pausing to open connecting doors and peer into bare rooms. The floorboards, although warped in a few places, were in better shape than the roof. The upper floor had been subjected to water damage from the leakage.

Jade paused before the door of one of the upper rooms and recalled the first time she had entered it. She had been seven years old, but still remembered it well. Philo Page had been to San Francisco to call on his daughter because he had not seen her for some time. Jade would never forget his visit, because it coincided with the beginning of both the best and the bleakest years of her life.

It seemed as if her mother had been crying for days. Jade had tried to comfort her—singing her favorite songs, carrying her cups of tea, holding her hand. Nothing had helped. When Grandfather arrived, Jade had run to greet him, begged him to make her mama happy again. Philo Page had left Jade in the hallway to wait while he talked to his daughter. Driven by worry about her mother, Jade listened at the door. It was years before she was able to comprehend all they had said, but the conversation was still vivid in her mind.

"Oh, Papa," Melinda Douglas had cried. "He has another woman. I'm certain of it."

Philo's words had been bluntly honest. "Come home with me. Leave the bastard. He's a gambler who married you for your money, girl. You realize that now, don't you?"

Jade's grandfather had been a wealthy man. Fredrick Douglas had indeed married her mother for the money she stood to inherit.

"I love him, Papa. I love him more than anything," her mother had said.

"More than Jade? Do you know what you are putting that child through, acting like this? If you aren't going to stand up to him and demand he give that woman up, then at least come out of this room and show some mettle. Look at you, lying about, wallowing in self-pity."

Clinging to the doorknob, trying to see though the keyhole, little Jade listened to her mother's heartrending sobs.

Philo Page paced the room, alternately trying to console and reason with his daughter. Finally, he said, "At least let me take Jade home with me for a few weeks. The poor child looks so drawn. She doesn't know why you're upset and I don't think she should be exposed to this turmoil."

"But Papa—"

"You know he won't mind. He barely knows she's alive."

There was more quiet sniffling before he added, "It will give you time to pull yourself together."

He took Jade with him that day. She remembered being held securely before him on his horse, his saddlebags filled with her clothes. She had spent the long summer in his care and thrived at the adobe, roaming the garden and listening to Chi Nu's endless stories of the faraway place called China.

Before she was tucked into bed the first night she was to spend there that glorious summer, Grandfather Page had led her by the hand to the same door she stood before today.

"What's inside?" she had whispered.

"Treasures," he answered solemnly.

He held a silver candelabra aloft as he pushed the door open. Jade would never forget what she saw that night in the shimmering candlelight. A long table stood directly in the center of the room. She moved toward it in silent awe, for it was indeed covered with treasures. There was a gilded bronze statue of a camel laden with bundles and goods that her grandfather patiently pointed out as a roll of silk, a sheep, a hare, and a pheasant. There were lacquered bowls that gleamed with such a high-polished shine that she thought they were still wet. One lacquer box lay open to expose a dragon necklace carved of green jade. He told her that jade was called *yu* and that the beautiful stone was believed to preserve the dead and bring life.

There were rolled scrolls that proved to be paintings of strange-looking people on odd-shaped horses. He unrolled one of the paintings and spread it on the floor, then the two of them dropped to their knees to inspect it closer. He asked her what the painting made her feel. "The horses are running through the woods. The men are hunting."

"But how does it make you *feel*?" he asked a second time.

She studied the painting carefully. The men on horseback seemed to be fleeing. The forest was sparse, the trees bending in the same direction the riders traveled, giving the scene an aura of urgency. There was nothing in the background at all. "It makes me feel scared. They're running away. I think someone is chasing them."

"Very good, Jade. Always remember that Chinese artists are not trying to paint objects—the horses, trees, or hunters. They are trying to convey an idea, a thought, or a feeling. Do you understand?"

"Yes, Grandfather," she had said, pleased with his praise. And she had understood.

So began her lessons in things Chinese.

She spent summers with Philo Page and Chi Nu, and many weeks during the year as well. Often, when she was not at the adobe, she would spend time with Babs and her family. Her mother became more and more reclusive, but when Fredrick

Douglas was at home and had days when he was not drunk or irrationally angry, Melinda Douglas was almost gay.

When he was drinking, or worse yet, living away from home, Melinda would weep and withdraw. Then Jade would escape to her room, study the books her grandfather had given her, and pray that summer would come early.

When J.T. reached around her and pushed the door open, she was drawn back to the present. Jade stood on the threshold and looked in at the empty room that once held her grandfather's treasures.

"How long has this place been empty?" Jason tested the floorboards before he entered the room.

"Four years now."

"There's been no caretaker around, obviously."

"Obviously," she agreed. "My grandfather had an old Chinaman that was his caretaker. He and Chi Nu became best friends. It was Chi Nu who taught my grandfather about Chinese philosophy and religious beliefs. He came here in forty-nine to work the gold mines."

"What happened to all the furniture?" Jason watched her expression darken with anger.

"My father must have sold it. Grandfather deeded the house to me years ago. I'm sure he did not think he needed to worry that anything would happen to the furnishings or his art collection, but he was a bit absentminded where details were concerned. He did not mention them in his will."

Jason could not imagine her father purposely taking the personal belongings from Jade. "Perhaps your father had them stored for you?"

"My father looked out for himself. He couldn't sell the house, but it seems that he took everything else of value and either sold it or used it for collateral."

Jason shoved his hat back off his forehead and sauntered to the window that overlooked the garden.

"If you need any money to buy your things back, I'd be happy to—"

"No!" Jade quickly colored, her anger apparent in her tone. His suggestion was all too close to Bab's idea that she marry him for his money. She could never use Jason or any other man for that matter. "No." She shook her head emphatically and hoped he believed her. "I don't need your money. As a matter of fact, I'm going to visit the bank as soon as we get back to town and make arrangements to take over the care of my grandfather's collection." She wasn't sure how she would do it, but was determined to follow her new resolve to take control of her own affairs. Somehow she would convince the bank that she fully intended to reclaim the Chinese pieces. Perhaps they would take the adobe in exchange.

Outside, Jason's horse whinnied. He crossed the room and paused for a moment beside her. He smiled down at Jade and stared at her intently.

"What are you looking at?" she wanted to know.

"If you keep frowning, your face will freeze that way."

She laughed. "I'm sorry. I was just thinking."

"Well, I don't believe in thinking on an empty stomach, so I'll go down and get the picnic. I'll meet you in the garden."

"I'll be right down," she said, thankful for some time alone in the house.

She wandered back downstairs and into the kitchen. The place was as bare as the rest of the house except for a wooden worktable and the brick oven built into the side wall. The windowpane was missing. Jade started when she heard a rustling sound in the dead leaves scattered on the floor near the open window. She stood perfectly still, listening, and watched a meadow mouse scutter across the floor and disappear through a hole in the floorboards.

As she stared after it, she remembered the tiny cellar below the kitchen. The trap door to the storeroom was directly under the worktable. It took but a push and a pull to move the table out of the way. Jade brushed aside the leaves and dust that covered the door and carefully slipped her fingers into the recessed handhold and lifted the trap door. She pulled it upward and stepped back. The door fell open with a heavy thud.

The smell of must and mice crept up from the hole in the earth. It was dark down below, but if she remembered correctly, the room wasn't so large that the light from open kitchen windows would not fill it. She brushed her hands together and then turned around so that she could descend the ladder that led to the underground room.

The stale, damp smell of earth rose up to meet her; the air below the ground was considerably chillier. She paused for a moment, suspended on the ladder halfway between the opening and the dirt floor below, and listened carefully. She thought she heard rustling again and prayed it was only the little meadow mouse and not a rat.

Jade reached the ground and waited for her eyes to grow accustomed to the dim light that filtered down from above. The wooden shelves that lined the walls were still intact, but all that was left on them were a few jars of preserved peaches and tomatoes. Afraid to move too far from the ladder, Jade stayed where she was and let her gaze take in the rest of the room.

It was perfectly square, carved out of the earth beneath the adobe. There was nothing in the tiny room but the shelves and their meager supplies. It was a perfect hiding place, one she often used as a child when she wished to tease her grandfather into searching for her. Chi Nu would feign ignorance of her whereabouts when she went below with a book and a candle to hide, but Grandfather always knew where she was. He let the game go on until he was certain she was ready to be found.

A perfect hiding place.

Jade thought of all she had learned yesterday from Detective Chang. Her father had been murdered for abducting a Chinese alchemist.

If he had kidnapped the alchemist, Fredrick Douglas must have hidden the old man. What better place than beneath the floor of a deserted house outside of town?

To catch a fish one does not climb a tree, she thought. Her father would never have kept the old man in San Francisco, not when there was a chance of anyone finding him. Slowly, she moved away from the ladder and began to check the floor for any sign that might lead to a discovery. The hard-packed surface was smooth. As far as she could tell there was nothing on it. If only she had a candle. She heard footsteps above, and was about to call out to Jason when her eye caught the sheen of a scrap of fabric near the ladder.

Just as her fingers closed over the glittering object, the trap door closed with an angry, thunderous sound and she was cast in darkness.

"Jason!" she screamed at the top of her lungs. With the cloth in her hand, she felt her way to the ladder. "Jason, I'm down here. Open the door!"

She heard stealthy footsteps overhead and listened in terror as they moved farther and farther away.

"Jason! Help me! Why are you doing this?" She tried to calm herself as she carefully climbed upward. This was no time to panic. Surely he had not meant to harm her.

She nearly fell off the ladder when the toe of her boot caught in the hem of her skirt. Her heart was tripping doubly fast now, her breath coming in quick gasps. Shoving the strip of fabric in her waistband, Jade continued climbing. She reached the top of the ladder and pushed up on the door. When she got ahold of Jason Harrington, she would box his ears.

She shoved at the thick planks, but the door did not budge. It was heavy, but not so heavy that she could not open it. Not unless the latch had clicked shut.

Jade beat on the underside of the door and shouted again. Damn him! If this was Jason's idea of a joke, she could not see the humor in it. She tried screaming his name again, and then stopped. He would open the door when he was good and ready and not before. *Two could play at this game,* she thought, trying to keep her mind off the scampering sounds below her. She thumped the underside of the door with her fist one last time and then hugged the ladder rails and waited for Jason to open the door. It wouldn't do to exhaust herself.

She closed her eyes to shut out the darkness that surrounded her, and tried not to compare the smell of the place to that of the inside of a grave.

At one time, the garden around the adobe had been lovely. Jason could appreciate it even now that it was overgrown. The huge oak in the center of the garden shaded most of it from the late morning sun. The wild tangle of vines and bushes had not yet obliterated all of the winding paths.

He tried to find a clearing where they could spread out the picnic Jade had made, and then decided on a spot near the old tree. It was on the sunny side where the deep covering of leaves were no longer moist from the fog. When he spied a particularly striking oak leaf, one that was dappled with color, he bent to pick it up for Jade.

Afraid to lay out the food and leave it while he went back to find her, J.T. carried it back with him. He thought she was coming right out, but she had not followed him. She must have needed more time alone. He could sense that as he roamed through the old place with her and watched her eyes brim with unshed tears, but now his stomach was rumbling and she had been alone inside for nearly half an hour.

He paused outside on the veranda, listening for the sound of her footsteps, thinking she might still be upstairs. But the place was quiet. There was no sound of her walking overhead, so he went toward the back of the lower story and walked into the kitchen.

"Jade?" He did not see her anywhere.

"Jason! Open this door immediately !" He heard her muffled cry, walked to the back door, and yanked it open. There was no one outside. Frantic pounding came from below the center of the room. J.T. set the picnic bundle on the scarred wooden table and hunkered down. He could just make out the outline of a trap door fitted into the planked floor when he heard her cry out again.

"Jason! Please!"

"Hold on, Jade." He felt around the floor until he located the nearly undetectable finger holds and the latch. He yanked the door up and stepped back.

Jade was on the ladder just beneath the opening, shielding her eyes from the light. Within seconds, she squinted up at him, her face mottled red, her green eyes blinking furiously.

He reached down to pull her out, but she pushed his hand aside. She climbed out on her own and angrily brushed off the front of her cloak, then at the dust clinging to her hair.

"How in the hell did you get stuck down there? And how did the door get locked?" he demanded.

She slapped him as hard as she could. "Damn you, Jason Harrington! How could you do that to me?"

"Me?" He shouted back. "What do you mean me? I was out in the garden waiting for you to come out."

"I don't believe you. Nor do I think this is very funny!" She turned away and headed toward the front door.

"Jade!"

His voice was so demanding she immediately halted. She paused in the doorway, her back to him, then turned around and glared. "What?"

He crossed the room quickly and grabbed her shoulders. Slowly and distinctly he said, "I did not lock you in that cellar."

She searched his face for the truth and found it. Her eyes widened in panic. She licked her lips. "Then who did?" she whispered.

He released her and both of them looked around the empty room. Their minds working together, they glanced at the upper story and Jason put his finger to his lips warning her to be silent. Jade nodded and followed him on tiptoe as they crept across the room.

J.T. grabbed her hand, anxious to find the culprit who trapped her, unwilling to let her out of his sight. He pulled her out the back door. They ran to the front of the house, but no one was in sight.

She stood patiently beside him while he flipped open his saddlebag and pulled out a gun and holster. Deft fingers strapped on the gunbelt and whipped the rawhide tie around his thigh.

"What are you doing?" she demanded.

"What does it look like I'm doing?"

"I thought you were against bloodshed."

"I'm against war, Jade. I'm not stupid." He shook his head then looked left and right. "I'm not going to look for whoever trapped you in the cellar without a gun."

"Trapped me?" Myriad thoughts flew through her mind. She was unwilling to believe anyone would want to hurt her intentionally. "Maybe the door just slammed shut."

"Then how did the latch turn?"

She wondered why anyone would want to frighten her. And if it were true, where had they gone?

"Come on. Let's have a look around."

Jade fought the urge to cling to his hand. Instead, she lifted her skirt and tried to keep up with his long-legged stride.

Quickly they surveyed the downstairs and then exited to the veranda. Outside, they each looked toward a different staircase.

"I'll go left," Jade whispered and pointed to the left staircase.

Jason shook his head. "You're staying with me."

"But with the double staircases, whoever is here can go down one while we go up the other."

He pondered a moment, trying to come up with a safe plan and failing. "I don't want you left alone. Whoever did this must have had a reason. There's no sense in putting you in their path. We go up together or not at all."

She was about to argue until she remembered the cellar. She wasn't about to be caught unaware again. "All right," she agreed, "but I have a feeling we won't find anything."

Just as she predicted, the rooms upstairs were empty. After a thorough inspection they went back downstairs, where Jason collected the picnic bundle after he unhitched the horses and had Jade wait with them outside the back door.

"We'll ride over and look inside the barn and the shed before we go, but I'm as sure as you are we won't find anyone," he admitted. "Would you still like to picnic in the garden? I found a nice spot under the oak tree."

She shook her head. "No. I want to leave."

Jade's preoccupation with what had happened overrode her fear of the horses. She mounted up with Jason's help and took the reins like an accomplished horsewoman. Jason smiled, proud of the mettle she had shown.

One thing was certain. The girl needed a keeper. Again, he thought about the predicaments she had been in during the short time he had known her and added this latest escapade to the list. Coupled with the falling urn of the night before, he almost convinced himself that someone was out to kill her. He glanced across at Jade, who was riding along in silent preoccupation, and wondered what she was thinking. Her golden-red brows knit in concentration as she rode along, totally unaware of the attractive picture she presented against the open blue sky. Her long hair had seductively slipped out of the ribbon to curl in a wild tangle about her face. Her cheeks had turned a delightful shade of pink and a dusting of freckles bridged her nose. The touch of California's autumn sun had been good for her.

They rode to the top of the hill where they had stopped to overlook the adobe earlier. Jason reined in his horse and dismounted.

"What are you doing?" she asked.

"I'm starving. Let's have this picnic." With a level stare he added, "And while we're eating, you can tell me who might have locked you in the cellar. And why."

Jason leaned back on his elbows, his long legs stretched out before him and crossed at the ankles. He lay on the ground across the cloth they had spread between them and ate the bread and cheese while Jade sat on his coat and told him what she had learned of her father's death since she had returned.

"Why didn't you tell me before that your father had been murdered?"

Jade looked away and brushed the hair back from her face. "It's not something I go around announcing. My father double-dealt people all his life. I should have expected something like this."

He could not imagine anyone as sweet and open as Jade having the type of father she had described to him. "Why would his killers want to murder you?"

"If the tong killed him to avenge the alchemist, I would have thought it ended there. I can't imagine why they would want to harm me. I don't know anything about any of this."

"Perhaps they think you could lead them to the missing alchemist?"

"But I just returned to town. I didn't know anything about it. And how would killing me help them find anything?"

"Maybe they think your father sent the information to you?"

"He never wrote to me." Her tone was matter-of-fact, not wistful, for she had no love for her father. She had hated having to tell Jason about her father's treacherous scheme, and his morbid death. She would not drag in her childhood, nor would she have him feeling sorry for her.

"I can't help but think that whoever locked you in the cellar today probably tried to kill you last night."

Her eyes widened and she shuddered visibly. "The urn . . ." Startled by his revelation, she thought of last night and how close she had come to harm. If Jason had not been there, she would have been seriously hurt, if not killed. Until today she had never given a thought to her own safety. What had her father gotten her involved in? It was as if he were reaching out from his grave to harm her.

"Someone may be watching you," he added. "How else would anyone know you would be here today?"

"We weren't followed, were we?"

"Not that I know of." He had not meant to frighten her so severely, but as he saw her pale, J.T. wished he had ahold of the man responsible.

Jade Douglas' life was far more complicated than he ever could have guessed. And he definitely needed no such complications in his own life. Still, she tugged at his heartstrings. He watched the sunlight shimmer in her hair. Her prim white blouse and skirt were a far cry from the finery her friend had loaned her. It was nice to see her own choice was more to his liking. She was a simple girl at heart, one who had led a sheltered life of learning and spent most of her time with an old man. Like himself, she had grown up without a father's love.

He let his imagination wander. What would she think of the ranch? He would love to show it to her, to teach her to ride with him. Cash and Lupita would welcome her with open arms. They had wanted him to settle down for years.

"Jason?"

"What?" Startled out of his reverie, he realized she was perched on her knees, shaking out the dishtowel and recorking the bottle of wine.

"I found this in the cellar." She pulled the length of satin out of her waistband. Jade's mysterious shining object turned out to be a length of red silk shot through with golden threads.

"What's that?" he reached out and rubbed the material between his fingers.

"It's silk. I found it on the floor. It looks like the belt from a Chinese robe."

"Your grandfather's?"

She shook her head. "Not that I know of." Jade quietly tucked the piece away in her pocket. She did not recall seeing a robe or Mandarin coat of red and gold among her grandfather's things, but that did not mean he could not have acquired one after she left home.

He reached into his duster pocket. "I found this for you."

He handed her a giant oak leaf, bent, but not broken. It was as soft as leather—some of the water that had kept it alive was still trapped inside. The leaf had turned the color of burgundy. It was flecked with gold and orange.

"It's beautiful, Jason. Thank you."

He was pleased that she seemed genuinely delighted with his simple gift. He shrugged. "Thank you for riding out with me."

It was early afternoon when their picnic ended. Relieved that he had not tried to kiss her again, willing to admit that she would have given in again if he had, Jade asked him to take her back to the city. They rode back in silence. She was lost in thought worrying about how to convince the bank that she would soon have the money to claim her collection, while J.T. worried about her safety.

She insisted on riding straight to the bank, and he insisted upon accompanying her. He tied the horses' reins to the hitching rail while she tried to tame her hair into place.

"How do I look?" she asked, trying to see herself in the wide glass window that fronted the Hibernia Bank.

"Like an upstanding citizen. Go give 'em hell. I'll wait for you in the lobby."

"Really, Jason, you don't have to wait. I can get back to Babs' on my own. You must have things to do."

"Not really," he lied. He had intended to use the afternoon to contact horse breeders he had written before he arrived, but there was no way he would leave Jade unaccompanied after what had happened earlier.

She promised to be as quick as possible, half-certain the loan officials would not be very encouraging, given her circumstances. Jason was already occupied studying the well-appointed interior of Richard Tobin's bank.

Jade was pleasantly surprised when she was immediately ushered into the office of Arvin Arnold, vice president of Hibernia Bank, and given a seat across from him at his scrupulously neat desk. Every paper was stacked neatly in one even-edged pile. Pen and inkwell were lined up diagonally off the corner of the stack. The *Chronicle* was precisely folded and lying off to the side. The trim young man in his severe black wool suit and crisp linen shirt leaned forward, elbows on the desk, and steepled his fingertips. He smiled.

Jade took a deep breath and explained her dilemma. "I'm sure you are aware that some of my grandfather's collection of Chinese art pieces was delivered to you as collateral against my father's debts. I was told I still have thirty days left to settle the debt or lose the collateral." Her stomach churned as she waited for him to reply.

"As I understand it, that was the agreement."

"You do realize those items were not my father's to use?"

"I'm sorry, Miss Douglas, but our lawyers went over your grandfather's will. He left his house and the land around it to you. Nothing else."

"But it was always understood those things were to have been mine."

"I understand your position, but your grandfather failed to name them as yours in his will. Actually, the will itself was so old it was signed even before your mother died. Everything but the adobe went to her, and since she was no longer living, to your father."

"But it was all a mistake."

"That may be, but legally, your father was in his rights to give us the collection as collateral." He arched a brow and added, "For what it's worth."

Just as Jade had hoped, the bank was not interested in the Chinese pieces. Not as much as she was. "Then I would like to trade the house and the land around it for the collection."

He stared at her in puzzlement. "Why would you want to do that? It has to be worth far more."

Mr. Arvin, it seemed, was unaware of the antiquity of any

of the pieces. Nor would he or the other bank officials have cared even if they had known. To most San Franciscans, the collection was mere Chinese junk—castoffs of the past that meant nothing to them. To the average man, the items looked exactly like others readily available in Little China.

Her grandfather had always told her that no one knew the true value of his collection, and that it might be years before anyone in California learned to treasure Chinese art.

"If that's the case, I'll sign it over to you now," she said. The adobe had been part of her life for as long as she could remember, but she would willingly sacrifice it to save the bronzes and paintings, the pottery, lacquerware, and silks her grandfather had amassed.

He stood, glanced out the glass window on his door, then leaned against the desk with his fingers splayed. "Miss Douglas, why be hasty? Why not stop and think about what you can do with the land? Get some advice from a third party."

All she could think of was Babs and her ridiculous scheme. When she started to protest, he cut her off.

"You've just returned to town and I'd hate to see you rush into anything. Take your time. You have nearly a month to retrieve the Chinese goods. As a matter of fact, we value your standing and your grandfather's past business with us so much that I know the board would agree to let you take possession of the pieces as soon as you find a permanent residence. We'll look upon you as a caretaker of sorts—until you can work something out, that is."

She wanted to jump up and grab the man and hug him for sheer joy. A valued customer? She hadn't a penny to her name, but it was true, her grandfather had done all his business through the bank. Still, she could hardly believe her good fortune. "There must be some mistake."

He smiled again. "None whatsoever." Arvin Arnold crossed the room and took her hand. He began to pat it consolingly. "Just let us know when you're finally settled and we'll have the crates delivered."

"Where are they?"

"In our warehouse, safe and sound. Now just remember, we

are more than willing to deal fairly with you, Miss Douglas. Hibernia Bank means to please."

Stunned, she got to her feet and thanked him as he walked her to the office door. "It was nice to see you, Miss Douglas. Please feel free to come to me whenever you need to." Arvin glanced out at Jason, who was still waiting with hat in hand, casually leaning against the ledge beneath the teller window as he spoke to the man behind the bars. "And please, give my regards to Mr. Harrington."

J.T. could not help but smile when Jade raced up to him, aglow with jubilation. She looked like a little girl with gumdrop money.

"I can't believe it!" she cried, her face wreathed in smiles. "They said I could have the collection back as soon as I have a place to live and that my standing was good with them and that I shouldn't sign over the adobe until I was absolutely certain what I wanted to do!"

"Whoa! Slow down!" Carried away on her cloud of enthusiasm, he put his hands on her waist and swung her around full circle before he set her down. "Well, little lady, it looks like you struck gold today."

She sobered and shook her head in disbelief. "It's a miracle all right. Mr. Arnold couldn't have been any nicer. I still can't believe it."

For a moment Jason had seen a completely different side to her and was intrigued. She had never been as carefree. Jade smiled up at him so trustingly that she made him wish he could see that she was always this happy, made him want to be responsible for her happiness. He was amazed at himself when he realized he wanted to spend the rest of his life making her smile.

He glanced around the lobby of the bank and lowered his voice before he said, "You have a beautiful smile."

Suddenly embarrassed, she held her hands to her sunburned cheeks and her radiant smile dimmed. It had been all too easy to share her joy with him. It was time to tell Jason she could not see him again. The longer she was with him, the more she wanted to do exactly the opposite, but now that she would recover the collection, she had to see to the means to keep it.

And besides, any day now Jason's own business would be settled and he would be leaving for New Mexico. She could not let her dependence on him go any further. "I think I had better get home now."

Jade was silent on the way home, the realization that the time had come to say goodbye to Jason forever weighing heavy on her mind. As they rode along together, she studied him. This is what love would have been like if her life had not become so very complicated. He was gentle and understanding, a truly kind and compassionate man—nothing at all like her father. Here was a man she could live with, but their paths were far too different.

All too quickly they reached the Barretts', where the stablehand ran to meet her at the foot of the drive and walk her horse back to the stables for her. She was thankful for the time alone with Jason.

"Would you like to go riding again tomorrow morning? I haven't been to the seashore yet."

She would have liked nothing better than to go down to the beach with him, to introduce him to the tide pools, to walk along the shore and watch the waves. The ocean always gave her such a feeling of serenity. She would find it healing now. They could spend an afternoon at Woodward Gardens, where they would leave the windy city and dusty streets behind while they laughed over the collection of natural curiosities and zoological specimens. It would be heaven to walk through the conservatory and view the flowering plants. There were so many things she would have liked to have done with him. But it was better to say goodbye to him now and have done with it.

She paused at the foot of the stairs that led to the front door. The slight afternoon breeze had intensified. The air smelled of the sea. She wondered if Babs was inside trying to peer out at them.

Jade fiddled with a button on her cloak. "Jason, I think that it's best we don't see each other again."

There was a slight pause before he said softly, "Best for who?"

His disappointed tone surprised and dismayed her. She had wanted this to be simple. She wanted to remember the happy hours they had shared together, not a quarrel.

"Best for both of us. I have so much to think about, so much to do to put my life in order—just as you have. You'll be leaving for New Mexico soon, and I have my future here to think about."

He would have argued with her, but everything she had said was true. Still, he did not want to admit it. "You won't even spare a few hours tomorrow for a short outing?"

Sadly she smiled and shook her head. "No. Besides, I don't think I'll be able to sit down for a week after today's ride."

He pulled off his weathered hat and impatiently tapped it against his thigh as he frowned down at her. She watched the muscle jump in the side of his jaw and knew he was wrestling with a decision. "I don't usually give up so easily."

"I didn't think so. But I'm very sure about this, Jason." She hoped she sounded more sure than she felt at the moment.

J.T. wasn't certain that what she wanted was right, and that uncertainty made him angry. How could she dismiss him so casually when he found he was beginning to care deeply for her? Obviously she shared none of the same feelings for him. He jammed his hat back on. He'd be damned if he would stand there any longer making a bigger fool of himself than he already had.

"If your mind's made up, then I'll be moving along."

"Jason, I hope you understand. I've enjoyed the ride today. I—"

"Forget it. You don't need to explain. I get the idea." Without another word or parting gesture, he turned away from her and started back down the drive.

Jade felt her heart sink to her toes and willed herself not to cry as she watched him walk away. He was a proud man and she had hurt him without meaning to, but there was no alternative. She watched as Jason mounted up. He was about to leave without so much as a goodbye.

"Jason!" She had called out to him before she could stop herself.

He turned in the saddle to look back, his jaw rigid, his lips drawn together in a taut line.

"Be careful," she said softly.

He gave no indication that he had even heard her as he rode away without a word.

❁ CHAPTER 9 ❁

The pen can kill a man
No knife is needed.

Parting with Jason took the excitement out of the good news Jade had to share with Babs about her trip to the bank, but determined to let her friend know that she had gained access to the Page collection again, Jade went directly to Babs' room. The only sound she heard in answer to her knock was a muffled, "Mummmph mmmum."

Unwilling to let anything dampen her spirits, Jade opened the door and breezed in, much the way Babs herself might have done. "I have the greatest news! You'll never believe how understanding Mr. Arnold was to me at the bank. What in the world!—"

She stopped dead still in the center of the room and stared down at Babs, who was stretched out on the bed. The bedroom suite was overblown with decoration; the button-tufted chaise, love seat, and side chairs were all highly ornate rococo pieces. The bed was draped with tassled velvet draperies drawn back to reveal Babs, who languished inside, one arm draped carelessly above her head, while the other dangled limply over the edge.

A wrapper frosted with lace covered her from neckline to ankle. Matching satin slippers adorned her feet. Her face was coated in a stiff white paste that left only her eyes, lips, and nostrils visible. Jade was hard pressed not to laugh as she gazed down at the ghoulish sight. Babs' hair was hidden beneath a thick turban, but the smell of olive oil hinted at the reason; an olive oil wrap was well known to revitalize dry hair. The additional scent of bitter almonds gave Jade a clue as to the nature of the paste Babs had spread over her face. Bitter almonds, rose oil, alcohol, and egg white went into a concoction that was supposed to leave the skin glowing with radiance and health.

Jade had never partaken of such treatments, but while she

129

had been in France, she had received more than one letter from Babs that attested to their success. After her initial shock, Jade ignored Babs' unsightly state.

"I spoke directly to the bank's vice president, who told me that as soon as I have a permanent residence I can send for the collection, and they would leave it in my care. He assured me they considered me a valuable customer and"—she shrugged—"for some reason he seemed convinced that I would find a way to pay off the debt in time. I'm certain, now that I think about it, that dealing with my grandfather must have outweighed any problems they ever faced dealing with my father."

Babs' eyes widened and she shook her head furiously. "Mummmph mummba bewabba papon!"

"No, really. They were wonderful. But don't worry, I won't have the crates delivered here. And the adobe is out of the question right now." She paced the room as she talked and unbuttoned her cloak. Shrugging out of it, Jade carefully draped her wrap across an empty chair and then glanced at Babs. Her eyes were still wide or perhaps, Jade thought, she had to hold them open that way. "Jason and I rode out there, and it was a worse mess than I expected." She carefully avoided mention of being trapped in the cellar. Babs would no doubt want to go back to see if they could find any clue as to why or how Jade became trapped. "I won't be able to move out there right away, so you'll have to put up with me a few days more until I can work something out."

"Mummmup put!"

Jade folded her arms and stared thoughtfully at the ceiling. "I was thinking of putting an ad in the *Chronicle* for a governess position. I could teach French lessons, you know."

Babs began flailing a hand about wildly until Jade took notice of her and crossed back to the bedside. "What do you want?" she asked.

Babs pointed to a side table across the room. Jade went to it and began lifting objects.

"Hairbrush?"

Babs shook her head.

"Jewelry box?"

The shaking intensified.

"Combs?"

"Puppa." Babs said through immobile lips.

"The paper?" Senna picked up the *Chronicle* and carried it over to Babs who grabbed it away without moving a muscle more than necessary. She paged through it until she found what she was looking for, folded it back with a vicious snap, and thrust the paper at Jade.

"Where?" Jade squinted.

"Agggh!" Babs growled.

Jade scanned the page until a headline caught her eye:

MILLIONAIRE HEIR WELCOMED TO TOWN IN STYLE

by Arnold Peterson,
Society Reporter at Large

San Francisco's newest Heir to Fortune has left his Desert Hideaway, moved into his Mansion on Nob Hill, and has already been greeted in the Style Befitting a Sultan. This Reporter will Stand Behind his Word and Observation that Another Newly Arrived Member of San Francisco society has Taken her Welcome Duties to Heart. Not only was this Flame-Haired Temptress seen leaving the Millionaire's Mansion well before most of Polite Society is even Abroad, but this reporter has seen with his Own Eyes the Evidence of a Night of Unbridled Lust. When questioned yesterday, the Coffee Bean Heir skirted the Issues while Your Diligent Reporter observed a parlor floor littered with bedding and Empty Champagne Bottles.

This evidence could only lead me, and no doubt You as well, Dear Reader, to agree that Something More than a Traditional Greeting was Exchanged. It is of further note that the Persons In Question also ended An Evening of Dancing at the Palace Hotel Entangled in a Compromising Position at the Foot of the stairs. Quite a lot of Work for one short day.

It seems our Hero was already so Enamoured of his Lady Love that he Leapt at the Chance to save her From Certain Harm when one of the Decorative Plants at the Palace nearly missed Landing Atop Her before the Heir did. The events of yesterday only led this reporter to Wonder what might be happening between the Millionaire and his Light o' Love at this Very Moment.

Jade slowly sank to the edge of Babs' bed as she read the article, her pulse beating rapidly. She was humiliated by the sordid gossip columnist's portrayal of her innocent association with Jason, and then she thought of him with a start. Had Jason seen the article yet?

She turned to Babs, who was scrunching up her face to crack off face plaster with every ridiculous move.

Jade was filled with rage. She stepped away from the bed. Babs swung her legs over the side and sat up. "You are the reason I'm in this mess!" Jade shouted.

"As I said yesterday, I never *told* you to spend the night with him!" Her wrapper had slipped down her shoulders. Babs yanked it up as she marched behind her dressing screen. After a session of water-splashing in the wash bowl, Jade saw Babs reach for a towel thrown over the top of the screen. She soon reappeared, her face clean but her hair still turbaned. "This is no time for us to argue. We have to do something. It's too late to steal every last paper before they are delivered. Could we burn the publishing house?"

"Be serious. Couldn't I sue this man for such slander?"

Babs smirked. "Only if it weren't true. He wrote what he saw. Can you deny that you *didn't* leave Jason's house early yesterday morning? No. Did you end up on top of him in the lobby of the Palace Hotel last night? Yes. Heavens, Jade, what did you two *do* today?" Babs arched a brow as she crossed her arms.

"Nothing," Jade whispered, everything suddenly becoming quite clear. "We just went riding, but . . . but then Jason insisted on going with me to the bank."

"Where they were suddenly *so* magnanimous that they gave you what you wanted, carte blanche. Now you know why they were so accommodating."

"Jason." The realization hit her hard. "Was it because of Jason?"

"Of course. After reading this, and then seeing that he was

with you, they decided you were a good credit risk with over a million dollars behind you."

Jade took off her spectacles and rubbed her eyes. "The vice president had a copy of the *Chronicle* on his desk." She felt like she could easily throw up, but that would only upset Babs further. She tried to calm her heaving stomach. "God, Babs, how could I be so naive?"

Babs crossed the room and stood beside her friend. She looked down with pity and put a hand on Jade's shoulder.

"There's only one thing left to do."

Jade sighed, certain she would not like hearing what Babs considered her only option.

"He'll have to do the honorable thing and ask you to marry him now." Babs smiled triumphantly. "And you'll say yes."

Jade covered her face with her hands. "No. Absolutely not. Besides, once he sees this he'll never speak to me again."

Jason finished feeding and watering his horse, but his pent-up ill humor needed release, so he decided to muck out the stall as well. Halfway through the task, he stripped off his vest and shirt and hung them over the gate. It felt good to use his stiff muscles. He was still aching from the fall he'd taken last night. The hard work also gave him a chance to think.

Jade had been right to end their friendship, and that in itself irked him. She belonged here in the city and he belonged on the ranch. He wouldn't be happy here, he knew that much. He needed to live where the sky was close enough to touch and the land wide enough for him to see for miles. It wouldn't be fair to ask Jade to give up her home unless he was willing to do the same. Still, he couldn't help but wonder if there wasn't something they could do to work out their differences. He knew that with a woman like Jade he'd be willing to try.

He'd worked up a sweat filling a wheelbarrow with manure and was ready to spread fresh straw in the stall, when he heard a carriage coming up the drive. He waited, listened expectantly, and wondered if he should go around to the front of the house himself when he saw the vehicle turn past the corner of the drive and pull into sight. It halted in front of the stables. His first thought was that Jade had come to her senses and had decided that whatever time they had left together was enough.

He was more than surprised when the liveried negro driver jumped off the box and opened the door for Nettie Parsons. She stepped out of the carriage like a queen, pausing at the bottom to let him take in the sight of her and then, without a word or nod to her driver, she walked toward J.T.

There was a gleam in her eye and an invitation that no man could mistake. Jason watched her swaying hips as she walked toward him. Her blue eyes wantonly took in his half-dressed state as her tongue flicked out to moisten her rubied lips.

"Jason," she said, her voice low and seductive, "you are certainly a sight for my sore eyes."

He leaned on the shovel and crooked a brow suspiciously. "What a surprise, Nettie. Where's your Mr. Winters this afternoon?"

"At a business meetin'. He's always at one sort of meetin' or another. I have to keep myself amused most of the time."

"And you think you'll find me amusin'?" he said, slipping into the familiar cadence of a southern drawl.

"I 'spect I just might at that." She fluttered her lashes and looked him up and down. "I always did like to see a man sweat. I like to see the muscles play under the skin, the way they all bunch up tight and then let go. That kind of thing can make a girl shiver all over, you know, Jason?"

He shook his head. "I really wouldn't know." As he watched her look him over like he was a slice of white cake at a Sunday social, Jason felt nothing for her but disgust. She hadn't even the decency not to wear red. He did not care much for the fashion of the day, and he cared even less for the overblown gown Nettie wore. It was of cranberry red velvet, a heavy, tassled thing with a fitted bodice that emphasized her already lush curves. The gathered train in back covered a bustle that twitched provocatively with her every step. Instead of the brace of diamonds she had worn the night before, she was wearing a set of ruby earrings and a matching pendant.

She sidled up to him and reached out with her gloved hand to trace his bicep with a long-nailed fingertip.

"My, my, Jason. It's been quite a long time."

"As I recall, Nettie darlin', it's been forever."

He could hardly believe this accomplished temptress before him could ever have been the virginal coquette he had loved so long ago. She made him wish he'd had her back then and been done with it, instead of holding to his principles.

"Were you always such a whore, Nettie? How is it I never saw that in you?"

J.T. had the satisfaction of hearing her gasp just before she slapped him.

He laughed when he realized she could no longer hurt him.

She looked mad enough to spit fire as her blond ringlets bobbed from the crown of her head. "No, I wasn't always a whore, mister high and mighty. But I learned how to survive, and I came out on top. That's what counts in this world."

"Not to everyone. I'd wager there are a few people left with ideals."

"So, you're a moralist, are you Jason? You don't mind takin' your daddy's money even though you never saw him after you were five years old? And I suppose you think that brassy redhead you were with last night is as pure as the driven snow. You can't fool me and neither can she. Besides, I read all about the two of you in today's paper, so don't go puttin' on airs."

"What are you talking about?"

"You don't know? Everyone's talkin' about it at the hotel. How that woman latched onto you as soon as you got here, how she jumped into your bed the first night you came to town. I may like livin' high and doin' what it takes to get there, but I've never had to advertise it in the paper. Or don't you read the newspaper, Jason? It's been so long I don't recall whether you ever learned to read or not."

"Get out of here, Nettie, and don't come back."

"Don't worry, Jason. I'll be glad to. It's just too bad that Amazon got her claws into you so fast you can't even realize what she is." She sashayed back to the carriage, lifted her skirt, and paused with one foot on the step, giving him ample time to catch sight of the turn of her shapely ankle. "I'm happy with Winslow. He's the type of man every woman is looking for—rich and malleable."

Jason watched her carriage swing out of the stableyard. He

pulled a kerchief out of his back pocket, wiped the dirt and sweat from his brow, and then threw down his shovel. After he collected his shirt and vest he hurried into the house, intent on taking a bath and locating a copy of the *Chronicle*.

It did not take him long to accomplish both tasks, and within two hours, J.T. was standing outside Matthew Van Buren's room at the Occidental Hotel on Montgomery Street with a crumpled copy of the *Chronicle* in his hand.

Matt looked genuinely pleased and surprised to see him, but when he saw the paper in Jason's hand, his smile faded.

"So, you've read it. I tried to find you this morning, but you weren't home."

"We went riding."

"I take it the 'we' means you and the lady in question?"

"She's not in question. She's not anything except innocent of this whole affair."

"Come in," Matt said as he took Jason's hat and ushered him into a well-appointed room, one of the 412 the hotel offered along with a main hall, reading room, and telegraph office near the Montgomery Street entrance. "Maybe you had better tell me the whole story from the beginning."

By the time they had each finished two cups of strong coffee liberally laced with brandy, Jason had told Matt the whole tale.

"It sounds to me like you're both crazy. You refused to take her home and she did not put up a fight?"

"No, she did put up a fight. She even went out in the storm, but got drenched by the time she was halfway down the drive."

"What were you thinking about?"

"I don't know. In the beginning I guess I was thinkin' about what any red-blooded man would given the circumstances, but after I kissed her—"

"So you did kiss her?"

"Once."

"Only once?"

"That night. Then again at the dance. And after."

"In public?" Matt probed.

"We were out on the balcony at the Palace."

Matt shook his head.

"What should I do?" J.T. asked. "Could I write something in rebuttal?"

"It would only keep the gossip alive. You could let it die down and forget it."

"Will it die down?" J.T. said.

"In time. Of course, Jade's reputation will never be the same."

"That's what I was afraid of." Jason stretched and stood up. He ran a hand through his hair, then paced over to the sideboard where he helped himself to more brandy. This time without coffee. "I think I should marry her."

Matt looked startled. "Don't do anything rash. How do you feel about her?"

J.T. returned to the settee and stretched out again. He faced Matt honestly. "I'm falling in love with her."

"Does this happen often?"

Jason laughed. "That's what she asked me last night. The answer is no."

"How does she feel about you?"

How did Jade feel about him? "I guess amiable would be the right word. She has a lot on her mind right now." He paused, looked down at his hands, then back up at Matt. "Someone killed her father. Did you know about that?"

"The whole town knows. I'm surprised Peterson didn't mention it in his article. Come to think of it, you really don't know this girl, J.T. How did she end up on your doorstep anyway? I hear her father, Fredrick Douglas, was a grand schemer, a man who married into money and set out to get richer as fast as possible. It might be best to just ignore all this. After all, you are going back to New Mexico as soon as everything is settled here. Let her fend for herself."

Jason shook his head, denying Matt's suggestion. "Jade's the innocent party in all of this. I don't care who her father was—she was practically raised by her grandfather, and from what she's told me, she hasn't had any contact with her father for years. As to how she ended up on my doorstep, that's still a bit fuzzy, but it seems her friend Barbara Barrett was with her, took sick, and suddenly left Jade there alone."

"That explains it. Barbara Barrett is well known for her

adventurous escapades. Once she decided she wanted to see what we did inside the Union Club, so she dressed as a man and walked right in." Matt laughed as he filled Jason in on the details. "Reggie is a member there, and I guess Babs' curiosity got the best of her. Aside from rooms for members who reside there, we have parlors, a reading room, dining room, billiards, a game room, and a small saloon. Babs bellied up to the bar and ordered a whiskey, belted it down and then took such a fit coughing that the short wig she was wearing fell off and out tumbled her hair."

Jason shook his head. It sounded exactly like something Babs Barrett would have done. "That's why I think Jade's a victim of circumstance."

"Still and all, marriage is a serious proposition."

"I wouldn't have suggested it if I had not already been thinking along those lines," J.T. admitted. He sat up straight and leaned forward, elbows on his knees. In a low voice he tried to explain. "My mother left here twenty-five years ago in disgrace because she wouldn't put up with my father's unfaithfulness. She divorced him and went back to Georgia. But she was the one who lived out her life in shame just because she stood up for what she believed and got a divorce. She might as well have had an affair. I've seen first-hand what it's like for a woman to be talked about, to be whispered about behind her back. To be cut off socially. Jade doesn't deserve a lifetime of that. Besides, I couldn't leave knowing I was the one to blame."

"Like I said, it'll die down."

"And like you said, they won't ever really forget."

"It sounds like your mind is made up; you're going to propose to her."

Jason nodded, convinced. "I am. Don't look so sorry for me, Matt. You've seen Jade. She's a beauty. And she has a heart and mind to match."

Matt reached out and gave him a hearty pat on the back and a handshake. "Then I wish you all the best of luck, J.T. . . . All the best."

"There's one more thing I'd like to take care of today," J.T. told him.

Matt sobered. "Just name it."

❧ CHAPTER 10 ❧

To know the road ahead . . .
Ask those coming back.

Jason reigned in his stallion, and stared down at the slip of paper he held crumpled in his right hand. Matt's bold writing stood out clearly in the late afternoon light. He glanced around at the homes lining the street that ascended Rincon Hill, and then behind him toward the waterfront and the ships in the bay. The dwellings around him appeared older and more comfortable than the palatial structures like his father's on California Street. As he had ridden up the sharp slope, the gathering evening fog had dissipated until, rising above it, he was able to see clearly again. J.T. carefully matched the house numbers with the slip of paper, and continued on up the street. A sporty carriage rumbled past as he studied the large homes and well-manicured lawns that sat askew on the hillside. Finally, he found the one he was looking for.

It was a two-story white-framed house with what appeared to be a newly added bay window. Millwork adorned the facade. Jason left his horse tied to a hitching post at the curb, opened the low, white picket gate, and slowly walked up the front walk. Before he stepped onto the porch, he tipped his head back to look up at the second story. Snowy lace tie-backs hung at every window. After one last look at the paper in his hand, he folded it into a square no bigger than an inch and slipped it into the pocket of his dark suit.

Peoney Flannagan. A rather unassuming name for a mistress, Jason decided. He stepped up onto the porch and wondered how many times over the years his father had tread the same path.

When he had asked Matt for the woman's name and address earlier that day, his attorney had appeared genuinely surprised and somewhat relieved. J.T. wondered if Miss Flannagan had

139

somehow worked her wiles on Matt to get the man to encourage him to see to her welfare.

Before he raised his hand to knock on the door, Jason nearly turned around to leave. He didn't want to be here, didn't want to see the woman who had usurped his mother's place in his father's heart. He could not even hazard a guess at her age—his father had lived with her for nearly twenty years—but had the creature been very young when she met his father, she might now be only a few years older than J.T. He may not know how old she was, but he had a firm picture in his mind of what she would look like—hennaed hair, or perhaps a frowsy blonde, heavy makeup, rubied lips, kohl around the eyes.

Perhaps Miss Peoney Flannagan had already found herself another paramour, another rich sponsor who was happy to see to her future now that the elder J.T. Harrington was out of the way.

Jason knocked loudly and firmly on the door, and tried to see through the thick lace curtain hanging over the oval window set in the polished oak. He waited a good thirty seconds before he knocked again.

Not only had she found a protector, he decided, but it seemed Miss Peoney Flannagan had gone out.

Just as he turned to leave, he heard soft footsteps echoing through the room just inside. There was a pause as a bolt inside was slipped back, and then the door began to open.

Jason took a deep breath, cursed himself for coming, and wondered what in the hell he was going to say to this woman.

A short, plump, brown-eyed woman with thick silver hair piled in a chignon high on her head stared back at him. He was about to ask her to call Peoney Flannagan to the door when he became arrested by the look of shock and wonder that came over her face. As her hand fluttered to the cameo broach pinned at the throat of her high-collared, black bombazine gown, her eyes began to glisten with tears. She clutched the edge of the door for support and opened her mouth to speak, closed it again, and then shook her head. One lone tear began to trickle down her cheek.

"Jason," she whispered.

Jason Terrell Harrington III simply stared back at the woman on the other side of the threshold.

Then slowly, he nodded. And took off his hat. Nervously, he began to spin the thing in his hands. At the same time that he wished he had never knocked on the door, he found himself silently cursing Matt Van Buren.

"Come in," the woman finally managed. She stepped back and swung the door wide. "Come in and have a cup of tea."

"I really can't stay," he found himself saying, even though he stepped inside.

She extended her hand. Jason stared down at it as if it was a snake.

"Your hat," she said softly.

He handed it to her.

"Please sit down." Indicating a small parlor off to the right of the entry hall, she seemed unable to take her eyes off him. "I'll be right back."

Before he could protest, she was gone, moving off toward the back of the house. Perhaps, he thought wildly, he had jumped to conclusions. Perhaps the little woman who was the picture of innocence and gentility had gone to summon the real Peoney Flannagan. Perhaps, he took a wild guess, the woman he'd just seen was his father's mistress's grandmother.

He ran his hand over his hair and then unbuttoned the front of his coat and shoved his hands into his pockets. Uncomfortable in the small, crowded parlor, Jason did not take a chair, but began to look around. The smell of fresh baked bread permeated the place along with a hint of cinnamon. It reminded him of his mother's home in Athens and brought back memories he had not had in years, memories of warm cookies and tarts and flaky apple pie.

Careful not to bump into any of the small tables scattered about the room, he wove his way between a settee and a tall wing chair and stood before the fireplace. An enormous gilt-framed mirror that stretched to the ceiling hung behind the objects crowded together on the mantel.

Amid candlesticks, figurines, and vases filled with fern fronds was a scattered line of daguerreotype pictures printed on thin copper plates and set in a variety of velvet cases and

tarnished silver frames. He peered closely at the one set to the
far left of the mantel and then picked it up. He tipped the
daguerreotype and tilted it until the mirrorlike image revealed
the likeness of a small child in a long white gown staring
solemnly back at him. His heart sank to a point somewhere
near the pit of his stomach.

It was a likeness of him. He recognized it because his
mother had possessed an exact copy of it herself. If he
remembered correctly, it was in a trunk filled with her
keepsakes at the ranch in New Mexico. Gingerly, he set the
picture down and looked at the next. It was another picture of
him, but in this one he was wearing short pants, dark woolen
stockings, and a shirt with a sailor collar. For some inexplicable reason, as he realized what the pictures meant, his eyes
filled with tears and J.T. began to blink furiously. With his
hands still buried deep in his pockets, his fingers balled into
fists, he proceeded to walk slowly along the length of the
mantel, and as he did, he saw himself grow older in each
daguerreotype. The progression ended abruptly with a photograph taken when he was fifteen.

He distinctly remembered the day his mother had insisted he
have that last portrait done. They had been about to embark
upon their journey to New Mexico. She was certain the
situation between the Union and the Confederacy was about to
become all-out war and had made provisions for them to live
with the Youngers. But before they left Athens, she had
insisted he go for his yearly session at the portrait studio. As
always, his mother wanted one portrait of him alone, and one
of the two of them together. J.T. realized now that he had
never really questioned her as to where his pictures had
disappeared to, except for the one time when she had replied,
"I'm keeping them safe for you in a memory book."

He reached out and ran his finger over the frame of that final
picture. All the time she had been sending them to his father.
And for all those years his father had been bringing them here,
to this house, where his mistress proudly displayed them on her
mantel. Beside the final picture was a photograph of a face so
very like his own that the two might have been mistaken for
each other, if the viewer had not looked closely and noticed the

silver hair where Jason's own was lightened by the sun. The same light blue eyes stared back at him, the same strong jaw, the same broad shoulders. He stared at the picture of his father and then looked away, only to see his own reflection in the mirror above it.

He was the very image of his father, and he could not even remember the sound of the man's voice.

He turned away from both reflections—that of the past and his own in the mirror. Carefully, Jason began to study the rest of the parlor. A faded ruby rug patterned in gold and black floral borders carpeted the room. Two wing chairs and a rocker were drawn up near the fireplace, each companioned by small footstools upholstered in finely executed needlework. Enormous vases filled with cattails and dried seagrass flanked the fireplace.

Everywhere around the room he saw touches of comfort mingled with refinement. Cabbage rose pillows were propped invitingly against the back of the settee. Still-life paintings and seascapes stood out against the worn but once gilded wall covering. An étagère covered with china plates and tea cups stood in one corner behind another low, comfortable chair.

Coupled with the mouthwatering scent of bread and cinnamon, the appointments in the crowded, well-lived-in room gave the place an overwhelming feeling of hominess. It was a far different dwelling than the edifice the elder J.T. Harrington had built for himself on California Street. Jason was all too certain, as he stood staring around the charming little room, that this was where his father had truly lived.

"There you are."

The silver-haired woman's melodious voice startled him into turning around. He watched her walk through the doorway carrying a tea tray lined with embroidered white linen cloths and covered with cups and saucers, a plate stacked high with cookies, and a white tea pot with a slow trail of steam ascending from its spout.

"I really—" he began to protest, suddenly awkward in her presence. He had invaded her privacy, his late father's privacy. The sight of his own pictures so carefully displayed on the mantel had shaken him as nothing else could have. During all the years Jason had spent hating his father for what he had done to his mother, the man had been charting Jason's growth through the pictures his mother had sent him.

The woman looked up at him, her eyes once again glistening with unshed tears. As he stared down at her, J.T. could not help but notice the red-rimmed eyes, the pale complexion, the slightly trembling lips. It was obvious she had been crying in the kitchen and had taken the time while the water boiled to come to terms with her tears. She gave no indication that there was anyone other than herself at home.

This small, brown-eyed wren of a woman with a massive pile of shockingly silver hair was indeed Peoney Flannagan, the woman his father had chosen over his wife and son. She was the opposite of everything J.T. expected. She had to be over sixty years old. The severe black dress she was wearing was an obvious sign of mourning for his father. He watched her bat away a tell-tale tear as she sniffed and adjusted the tray in her hands.

Jason sat down on the rocking chair near the fire.

She set the tea tray on a low table beside him and took her own place on a wing chair on the opposite side of the table.

"You look exactly like your father," she said as she deftly poured him a cup of amber tea. "It gave me quite a start when I saw you standing at the door."

"I'm sorry. I didn't know." He took the cup and saucer from her and carefully set it on his knees. The dainty handle of the china cup seemed far too small and fragile between his thumb and forefinger, but he carefully lifted it to his lips and tried to take a sip. He burned his tongue.

"This must be hard for you," she tried again, "coming here like this."

He nodded.

"Your father loved you very much. He waited for your picture to arrive every year. It was the only time your mother ever communicated with him. To your father, it was better than Christmas. He would bring the daguerreotype home and set it in place on the mantel, then he would look at them all again. My, how he could go on and on about how you'd changed."

"Yet he never came to see me," Jason couldn't help but remind her.

Peoney Flannagan glanced down and stared into the dark brew in her own tea cup as if she could see the past in the steaming liquid. She drew a deep breath and said, "Your mother forbid it. He wrote and asked permission to see you every year, but she would deny his request. She was kind enough to send the portraits, though, right up until she died."

"Why didn't he write to me?"

"And say what? It had been ten years. He didn't know you, Jason. Didn't know if you hated him or not, didn't even know what to say." She shook her head and passed him the plate of cookies. Jason took three and set them on the saucer he had balanced awkwardly on his knees. "It was the only time I ever knew Jason—your father, that is—to be afraid. He was terrified of really finding out how you felt about him."

Peoney took another sip of tea and stared levelly at him. "Would you have come?"

"I probably wouldn't have even responded."

She sighed. "It would have wounded him deeply. I'm sure that's why he never even tried. It was far better not to know what the outcome of any communication to you might have wrought."

They were silent for a few uncomfortable moments. He could see that she was hard-pressed not to stare at him. Finally Jason said honestly, "You aren't at all what I expected."

Peoney smiled. "You thought perhaps I was an opera star in red satin that showed my ankles?"

He shrugged. "Something like that."

"Did your mother ever tell you about me?"

"No. My mother's maiden aunt used to refer to you as 'that woman.' She was even more embittered than my mother. You would have thought she had been the one my father had thrown over."

"Will you listen if I try to explain?"

Too many years had passed for Jason to think anything Peoney Flannagan might say would sway his opinion of his father's infidelity. J.T. knew that had he ever taken the vow of marriage, hell would have to freeze over before he deserted the woman he had chosen as his wife. Cash always told him that things weren't always black and white, that the color gray had been invented for a reason, but Jason had never been able to reconcile the thought. Now this woman, "the other woman" in his father's life, was asking him for a chance to tell her side of the story.

He set the teacup on the table and leaned back in the rocker. Pushing the footstool aside with his toe, he crossed his legs at the ankles and folded his hands on his lap. "Go ahead," he said softly. The least he could do was hear her out.

"Your father's people were from New York. Wealthy, powerful, established. We met when we were twenty, and your father was taking over the reins of business from your grandfather. We fell in love, and Jason asked me to marry him. My family was poor, and to make matters worse, we were Irish." She set her own cup aside.

Jason began to slowly rock to and fro, lulled by the warm tea and the soft words as she told the story. "His family forbade it. They quickly arranged a marriage between Jason and your mother. She was from a wealthy but impoverished southern family that was all too willing to see the marriage take place as soon as possible. Your father, whether you want to believe it or not, was a man who always kept his word. Or fully intended to. He gave me up and set out to make a go of his marriage.

"You were born shortly afterward, in forty-five. In forty-nine, during the gold rush, he came out to California. What Jason didn't know was that I was already here. I had come out with my brother, and instead of striking it rich in the gold fields, he built a boarding house which I cooked for, cleaned and managed. There was no housing then, and the place was crawling with men who would pay a fortune for a clean bed and a good meal. You can probably guess what happened."

He nodded. "My father stayed at your boarding house."

"He knocked on the door, and I was as surprised to find him standing there as I was to see you here today. The old feelings we had tried to deny were stronger than ever, but I can tell you we both fought it. He lived in a hotel. I refused to see him. But somewhere along the way, we caved in.

"When your mother arrived out here with you a few months

ater, we had already begun living together." The look she
ave him begged him to understand and forgive her without her
aving to say a word. "Jason tried to explain to your mother.
Ie told her he would always provide for both of you, that he
would never shame her publicly, that he would even live with
er, but that he could never give me up completely."

"So she divorced him," J.T. said.

"Yes." Peoney nodded and stared down at her clasped
ands. "She took you back to Georgia, and he never saw you
gain." She indicated the mantel with a nod. "Except in those
ictures. I like to think that he fully intended to write to you
omeday, to see you again . . . but he died so suddenly." A
eep shudder shook her. "His heart gave out one day while he
vas at his office."

"Can you tell me something?" he asked.

"I'll try," she promised.

"Did my father live here all the time?"

Her voice was a mere whisper. "Yes."

"Why did he build the house on California Street?"

Miss Flannagan blinked rapidly and cocked her head to the
ide like the wren she reminded him of. "Why, for you."

Jason sat up abruptly. "Me?"

"Well, that, and he felt that it would be a good investment.
he wealthiest men in San Francisco were beginning to build
here. He got a lot of enjoyment out of planning the place,
taffing it. For a while he tried to persuade me to live there, but
knew I could never show my face outside it, not with us
ving together like this—"

"Why didn't you ever marry him?"

"He stopped asking."

"What?" Jason was flabbergasted. After the divorce, his
ather would have been free to marry Peoney Flannagan if he
ad wanted.

"The harm had already been done. Marriage wouldn't have
hanged anything between us, nor would it have saved my
eputation at that point. I wanted your father to be free to
hoose in the event that he ever changed his mind and tried to
in your mother back for the sake of having you with him
gain." She shrugged and gave him a wistful half-smile.

"After a few years it didn't seem to matter one way or th
other, and eventually, he stopped asking. By the way, did yo
find the diamond studs and the clothes? I had Matthew tak
them to Harrington House for you. Your father never coul
resist going down to Baloun and Lambla's, the tailors, for
new suit. He had quite a collection that he had never eve
worn." She dabbed at her eyes with a snowy napkin.

J.T. remembered the diamond shirt studs Jade had found i
the dresser drawer. They were worth a tidy sum, one tha
would have kept Miss Peoney well-supplied with cash for quit
a while, yet she had Matt deliver them to Harrington House

He indicated the suit he had on and said, "I found the suits
and I've even used the studs. Thanks."

"Do you like Harrington House?"

It was a moment before Jason responded. He was sti
thinking about her previous statement. "Well . . ." She wa
staring at him expectantly, as proud as if Harrington House ha
been her own gift to him. "It's . . ."

"Go on."

"It's lifeless—too big for me. As a matter of fact, I have
up for sale. I'm going back to New Mexico."

"You aren't staying here?"

"No. I'm selling out."

She looked quite sad. "I thought that after what I read i
today's paper . . ."

Jason stood up and walked back to the mantel and stare
down at his father's picture. "The story about Jade Dougla
and me."

"I thought perhaps you would get married and stay here."

He didn't know what to say to her. He certainly didn't thin
he needed to explain himself to his father's mistress, but the
for some inexplicable reason, he sat down in the rocker agai
this time hunched forward with his arms on his knees. "I a
thinking of marrying her. Matt doesn't think it's all that gre
of an idea."

"Why not?"

"I hardly know her."

"Do you love her?" she asked.

He stared hard at Peoney, at the cameo pinned beneath the high, starched collar of her dress. "I think I do."

"Does she love you?"

"I have no idea."

"You won't know until you ask."

"I guess not," he agreed, shrugging.

"May an old woman give you some advice?"

"I may not take it," he said.

"You may not like it," she said.

"Go ahead."

"If there's no one you left behind, and if you care a fig for the girl, you should offer for her hand. She'll be virtually ruined here now unless you marry her. That won't matter to some, but when you mentioned the name Jade Douglas, I recalled her family. Her grandfather, Philo Page, was a wealthy man—one of the first Americans to settle here. He was a bit eccentric as I remember, but well thought of. She comes from respectable people. She'll never be able to hold her head up amongst them again if you don't do right by her. I know."

As he sat listening to her gentle admonition, Jason could not help but think of the two women in his father's life and the scandal each of them had had to face because of their relationship with the same man. In that instant, he let go of the hate and resentment he had always fostered toward his father's mistress. She was only a woman, and an old one at that—a woman of flesh and blood who had made the mistake of falling in love with his father and of not being able to give up that love.

He found himself saying, "Matt told me that since my father died without a will, there is no provision for your future."

"I'll manage somehow. I don't expect anything from you, Jason."

He glanced at the long line of pictures of himself on the mantel and then at the last one of his father. "My father would have wanted me to see you secure."

Her voice was choked with tears as she said, "Whatever you think, dear."

"I'll send Matt over with a bank draft in the morning." When he stood up, the rocking chair was set in motion.

"That was your father's favorite chair," she said, fighting to keep her voice from breaking. "I wasn't a bit surprised when you chose to sit in it."

He realized how comfortable, how relaxed he'd been as he had sat in the low rocker, rocking back and forth. He couldn't recall ever having sat in one before.

"Thank you for the tea and cookies, Miss Flannagan."

"I'm so very glad you called, Jason. Because of the pictures, I feel as if I know you, but it's wonderful to meet you at last."

He didn't know what to say, so he followed her to the entry hall in silence. She went to get his hat as he waited by the front door.

"It was nice meeting you, ma'am," he said as he took back his hat. He could finally admit to himself that the experience he had so dreaded had turned out to be enlightening, and not so terrible after all.

"Take care of yourself and your young lady," she said as he stepped out the door.

With a nod, J.T. signaled his goodbye. "I intend to."

Reggie Barrett was predictably mortified over Arnold Peterson's column in the *Chronicle*. Jade decided that her time would be best spent out of his way, so she kept to her room. Her self-imposed isolation gave her time to go through a box of papers of her father's that Detective Chang had delivered while she and Jason had been out riding the day before.

Aside from unissued copies of certificates for silver and gold mines that were worthless, there was no other evidence of any of her father's latest business schemes and certainly no clue as to whether or not he had been behind the abduction of the Chinese alchemist, Li Po.

Rather than infuriate her host any further, Jade had dressed conservatively. Her white, high-collared French waist blouse and gray skirt gave her a look of staid gentility, so she wore them instead of her comfortable Chinese garb. After carefully twisting her hair into her favorite figure-eight loop at the back of her head, she resisted holding it in place with chopsticks—as she sometimes did—and instead used some tortoiseshell combs that had once belonged to her mother.

She paused from leafing through her father's papers to stare at herself in the oval mirror above the desk. She shook her head. If she had indeed grown as beautiful as Babs insisted, she certainly could not see it. She had far too much hair for her oval face, her bottom lip was too plump, and because she had not worn a hat yesterday while she was riding, there were freckles across her nose and cheeks.

As she had a hundred times that day, she thought of Jason and wondered what he was doing. Would he be leaving soon? Did he care a whit about the scandalous article or not? He did not care what anyone said about him. If that had been the case, he would have never stayed out of the war conflict.

He knew the truth of what had really happened that night at his house, and perhaps the truth was enough for him. She hoped so. She had only herself to blame for becoming the center of such a scandal; she should have never listened to Babs, never have gotten into her friend's carriage that day they went to Jason's. But it was too late to cry over her lack of judgment now. *Slander cannot destroy an honest man, for when the flood recedes the rock is there.* Or so claimed the Chinese proverb. She knew she was strong enough to survive until the flood receded, but she wasn't sure about Reggie Barrett.

Babs was taking this latest crisis in stride, no doubt because she was responsible. But Jade realized the time had come to leave the Barretts' hospitality behind. On the morrow she would find a room elsewhere, although she could not even hazard a guess as to where.

She turned back to the certificates spread across the bed, and began to refold and stack them. The image of Jason's warm gaze and teasing smile danced into her conscience and Jade paused once more. She leaned forward and rested her chin in her hand as she let her mind wander. Was she experiencing the stirrings of love? She had never dreamt this would happen to her—but what else could explain this persistent urge to think of Jason Harrington, the realization that she thoroughly enjoyed herself in his company, that she was able to share her worries and joys with him? He made her laugh. He was protective and caring, warm and considerate. She thought of the night he had lied to her to keep her at his home, and shook her head with a wry smile on her lips. He could be very trying, not to mention stubborn, but she could not hold him to blame. He had no idea where his teasing would lead.

There was no doubt that she was physically attracted to the man. His kiss had proven that. What other wonders of the flesh might he have introduced to her had she been at all receptive? Jade felt her cheeks grow warm just thinking about it. She tried to banish him from her thoughts and concentrated on her father's papers again, but to no avail.

Was she turning away happiness by dismissing Jason's growing friendship? He had said he was falling in love with her. Did he say that to every woman he was attracted to? Nettie Parsons might have been his first love, but how many others had he had since?

If his words were true, he did not give his heart casually. Shouldn't she heed them? She looked down at the stack of certificates and wondered if this was all she would ever have in her life. A box of worthless papers and a few crates of inanimate objects. The collection had meant everything to her grandfather, but it would offer her small comfort on a cold, lonely night. Was she destined to grow old alone and become a reclusive scholar like Philo Page?

It was far too late to worry herself with such indecision. She had been frank and final with Jason yesterday. She had told him emphatically that she did not want to see him again, and had angered him with her decision. By now he had no doubt read or heard of the scandalous article concerning them both.

He was probably glad to be rid of her.

Weary of confinement, she stood and stretched, set down her spectacles, and walked to the window to see who might be in the carriage she had heard on the drive. The overhang that formed the portico below blocked the visitor from view. She hoped it was not the reporter from the *Chronicle*, although she wondered if the man would dare to show his face here. There was the sound of a knock at the door. "A clear conscience never fears midnight knocking," she whispered aloud.

After a slight pause, Reggie's voice echoed quite clearly

from below, "You have your nerve coming here in broad daylight. Haven't you done enough?"

Although she could not hear the visitor's low response clearly, she recognized Jason's voice. Jade did not hesitate to rush to his defense. She was out the door and down the stairs in seconds. Breathless, she stood in the entry hall, ready to fend off Reggie's verbal assault on Jason.

Drawing herself up to her full height, meeting Reggie eye-to-eye, she assumed her iciest, most reserved tone. "Thank you, Reggie, for greeting Mr. Harrington. I would like to speak to him alone."

Reggie turned scarlet. The veins in his neck bulged. His narrow nose became more beaked as his eyes widened. "Absolutely not! I will not have you creating a scandal here in my very own home."

Jason took a step forward and in a low, menacing tone that brooked no argument he said, "Apologize to the lady, Barrett."

Reggie failed to apologize, but he did fall silent.

Jason ignored him and turned to Jade. "I want to take you to dinner. We need to talk."

She could not believe he had come. She had spent the last twenty-four hours convincing herself she would never lay eyes on him again, and now here he stood, more handsome than she remembered, defending her before Reggie. Suddenly self-conscious, her hands flew to her hair.

"You look fine," he said with a warm smile. "If you get your coat we'll be on our way." He nodded at Reggie as if to dismiss him, but Reggie was not leaving.

"You realize, Harrington, I have nothing against you, but this is a very sticky situation. Very." Reggie tugged on his collar. "I'm extremely upset."

Jade almost felt sorry for Reggie. It seemed he would not hold the embarrassing situation against Jason. Jason was wealthy now, and socially conscious Reggie Barrett would never blame him for the humiliating gossip. Only her.

"Get your wrap, Jade," Jason said again.

She glanced once at Reggie, then back to Jason.

"I'll be fine," Jason assured her.

"I know that," she said as she finally smiled. "I was worried about Reggie."

When J.T. smiled, too, she relaxed.

"He'll be all right," Jason said.

Jade lifted her skirt and fairly flew up the stairs. In less than two minutes, she was back with her cloak in her hands.

❋ CHAPTER 11 ❋

Every day cannot be a feast of lanterns.

Once they reached the carriage and were safely inside, Jade became increasingly nervous. She now knew for certain J.T. had seen the disgusting *Chronicle* article. Seated opposite him, she fidgeted on the plush upholstery in the closed carriage and wondered what to say.

"Jade?"

The sound of his deep voice over the rhythmic pounding of horses' hooves and carriage wheels startled her out of her deep reverie. "What?"

"I asked where you would like to go for dinner."

"Oh." She was not hungry, but it would be far easier, not to mention safer, to be in a public place while they had their "discussion." She nearly suggested the Cliff House, then decided they should probably avoid any location where they were likely to become the topic of conversation. "Have you ever had Chinese food?" she asked.

"Is it edible?"

Jade nodded with a wry smile. "Not only edible, but delicious. At least I think so."

"Fine."

She gave him directions and he passed them on to the driver. Then she asked him, "Is this your carriage? One of the carriages that was not available the night you forced me to stay at your house?"

"It's Matt Van Buren's, on loan. And I did not force you to stay at my house. As I recall, the rain forced you to stay."

"I don't want to argue about that," she said, pausing long enough to look out the window to check their progress. "What's done is done."

"Look, Jade, if it's any consolation, I'm sorry as hell this all happened. I'm sorry about the article in the paper. That's why

155

I wanted to talk to you alone. I think I've come up with a way to put the gossip to rest."

"How?"

She was only visible in the dark confines of the carriage when they passed beneath a gas streetlamp. Her expression was unreadable. J.T. wiped his slightly sweaty palms against his thighs—he had donned woolen dress pants of unrelieved black, along with a matching vest and jacket, and now found the outfit far too warm. He nervously adjusted his hat and wondered if the occasion warranted removing it. He set the hat upon his knee.

J.T. cleared his throat. He looked out the window. He looked at Jade. He still didn't know how to begin.

It had been forever since he had thought about marrying anyone. Now he was about to ask a woman he had known for four days to be his wife. He figured it was enough to make any man jumpy.

He took a deep breath. "I think we should get married."

Unable to hide her surprise, Jade gasped. "What?"

"We could get married." Jason cleared his throat again. He was definitely going about this the wrong way. "I mean, will you marry me?"

"Marry you?" she whispered.

He didn't say anything else. J.T. moved to her side of the carriage and sat down next to her. Before she could move or say anything, he reached for her.

Jade had not recovered from his shocking proposal when she suddenly found herself in his arms. She stiffened and held him at bay. "Is this the only way you know how to settle things?"

"Can you think of a better one?" he asked.

"Talking, for one."

"Somehow I'm not very eloquent tonight." He tried to pull her close.

She resisted. "Try."

"I want to kiss you."

"I want you to stop this carriage and let me out."

"Jade, please."

"Jason, no. Absolutely not. We can't solve one crisis by creating another. I would have never agreed to come with you if I had thought this is how we would end up. You asked me to dinner. You said we had to talk. Start talking."

"I think we should get married. What do you say?"

"I—" She did not want to sound mindless, but for the life of her, she did not know how to answer him. "Because of the article?"

"Hell, no. Because of the way I feel when I'm with you. When I kiss you." He moved his hands up and down, stroking her upper arms, gentling her. "Because of what I feel when I touch you and think about what it would be like to have you beside me for the rest of my life."

For a man who claimed he was not eloquent, she thought he was doing a commendable job. A chill shot down her spine as he leaned close and kissed her on her cheek, slightly in front of her ear. She felt his warm breath against her face, shivered when his tongue graced the outline of her ear. Jade weakened for a moment and let down her guard. He raised his head and stared down at her mouth. As he began to lower his lips to hers, she locked her arms again and held him off.

"It's so sudden. I . . . we don't really know each other," she protested weakly.

"We'll have a lifetime to get to know each other."

"We have only known each other four days!"

"I know what I like," he said.

"Well, I don't."

"You don't know what I like? I'll teach you." He laughed as he tried to kiss her again.

She pushed him away. "This is serious, Jason. Or are you making a joke?"

He looked down at her and his tone sobered. "I would never joke about something like this, Jade."

Uncertain, she stared back at him and wished it was not so very dark in the carriage. Just then, the vehicle drew to a halt. Before the driver could open the door, Jason drew a polite distance away.

"We've arrived, sir," Matt's driver announced, holding the door open for them.

"Thank you, George," Jason said. He and Jade climbed out and he dismissed the driver. "Please give Mr. Van Buren my thanks. We'll see ourselves back. Now," he said as he turned to Jade and held his arm out like a proper escort, "let's see this Little China of yours while you think about my proposal."

Although it was evening, the shops and stores that lined the streets were still open for business. They passed vendors selling their wares in the open beneath the light cast through shop windows. A cobbler lined his customers' shoes on the sidewalk. Another man sold noodles from a pot bubbling on a brazier placed precariously atop some crates.

"Which way?" Jason asked as they worked their way through the crowded streets.

Jade paused until she could get her bearings and then pointed to the corner. "A half a block that way," she directed, and they moved on.

When they reached the restaurant, Jade took charge. Deftly, she spoke to their host in Cantonese and Jason noted her ability with awe. They were seated in a far corner of a room that was filled with Chinese diners, as well as half a dozen other caucasians.

"You speak Chinese," he said, still amazed, half-afraid to ponder all she knew that he did not, to contemplate their myriad differences.

"Not very well, but I'm doing better. Grandfather's friend, Chi Nu, taught me a little, but I refined my speech when I lived in Paris. The missionaries were as unwilling to forget what they had learned as I was determined to gain a better knowledge of Chinese, so we were well suited and spoke in Cantonese most of the time."

They were served tea in a small brass pot, and Jade poured some of the steaming brew into two small bowl-shaped cups. J.T. watched in silent appreciation of her natural grace. She ordered food for them both, and then quietly sipped her tea as she stared across at him.

Jade could not help but smile as she watched Jason silently taking in every detail of the place. He ran his hand over the lacquered table, stared up at the multicolored hanging lanterns with their swaying red tassles, and peered curiously at the platters of food the waiters carried past their table. He seemed totally alien in the surroundings, more so than any of the other

Caucasians in the room. For one thing, his great height and build made him more noticeable. He had taken the time to dress for the occasion and looked more handsome than any man in the room. Suddenly, she felt rumpled and plain beside him. If ever a man could be called beautiful, she realized Jason was that sort of man. Still, his good looks did nothing to diminish his masculinity. If anything, the strong line of his jaw, his even lips, the deep-set blue eyes shadowed by sun-gilded brows, all attested to his strength.

Jason looked up and caught her staring. When he toasted her with his tea and smiled back, Jade's heart melted. She wished desperately that she had let him kiss her again in the carriage, then forced herself to think rationally. He had just asked her to marry him. Why?

J.T. watched Jade watch him. He could not help but grin. She was so fresh and natural, so unassuming, that it was impossible for her to hide her thoughts. Her open, guileless expression gave them away. She had on the same skirt and blouse she had worn riding, but he found he liked the outfit far more than the heavily bedecked gowns he had seen her in before. The crisp white blouse with its high-collared, modest neckline was closely fitted and emphasized her full breasts. Without the bustle, her skirt hugged her trim figure, leaving no need to guess what lay beneath.

Although she was studying him speculatively—and the warm look in her eyes told him she did not find him physically wanting—her deep emerald gaze could not hide her doubts. He wanted to put her at ease, but before he could speak, the waiter delivered two bowls of steaming soup and procelain soup spoons to their table.

"Look," he said, leaning forward as he alternately blew on his soup and sipped up the shovel-shaped spoonfuls, "I know this is sudden. I can see where you might want to wait and think about my proposal, but given the circumstances, I think we should be married as soon as possible."

"But wouldn't a sudden marriage look as if we were guilty? That we *had* to marry? I'm not guilty of anything."

"No, but you've been tried and condemned by the press and everyone else all the same." He set down the odd spoon and leaned closer. He thought of the conversation he had had earlier with Peoney Flannagan. Then he thought of his mother. "Jade, I know all about gossip. My mother divorced my father twenty-five years ago and took me to Georgia to her family home. Do you know what happened?"

She shook her head, intent on his every word.

"No one ever forgot that she had been divorced. The gossip never ended. Whenever anyone referred to my mother, they whispered behind her back and called her 'that divorced woman.' She was excluded from so many outings that she soon declined those she was asked to attend. She was punished merely because she stood up for what she believed and divorced my father rather than live a lie and stay married to a man who didn't love her."

Jade thought of how Babs had whispered the word *divorce* the day she had first talked about Jason. She remembered how she had wished her own mother had had the courage to divorce Fredrick Douglas. Instead, Melinda Douglas had stayed married, and Jade had grown up with a father who made it all too clear that he did not love her and with a mother who was so busy grasping for her own happiness that she did not have time to pay Jade much attention at all.

"It sounds as if you had an unhappy childhood," Jade said. Perhaps that was something they had in common.

"Not really." He shrugged off her words. "My mother was treated unfairly, but she always saw to it that I had everything I needed. The stigma of divorce did not pass itself on to me. Of course, I never got to know my father." He was silent as he thought of the row of pictures on Miss Flannagan's mantel.

Jade watched his eyes take on a faraway look, as if he could see beyond the walls of the restaurant to some other time and place. Then he began again. "It was during the war that I learned how much malice and hurt gossip could cause."

"Because you didn't serve."

"Yes. On the rare occasions that I went into Sante Fe, I was called everything from a yellow-bellied snake to an out-and-out coward. I knew why I stayed out of the war, and it certainly wasn't because I was afraid. Uncle Cash needed me. He was expanding his herd and couldn't afford to pay for any more help. They had given me a home when my mother died, and I felt there was no way I could leave them high and dry. Cash had a broken arm at the time." Jason smiled as he thought of his uncle and added, "He's always busting up one part of himself or another. More importantly, I stayed out of the war because I didn't believe in killing other Americans just because of their political persuasions." He leaned across the empty table, his voice barely above a whisper. "Look, I'm trying to tell you that I know firsthand what harm gossip can cause."

She fell silent when the waiter reappeared with another course.

"What's this?" Jason asked, poking the unusual, crisp-fried food with his fork.

"Egg roll."

"What's inside?"

"Just taste it," Jade said, using the chopsticks she had requested to lift the golden egg roll to her lips.

"Do you think it's too late to get a steak anywhere?" Jason asked, turning the roll up and down, looking at each end before he took a bite.

"Eat," she commanded.

J.T. took one bite and stared down at the mixture of cabbage and pork that spilled out of the opening. He set the egg roll on the plate and looked across at Jade again.

"Can I get back to my argument?"

"Are we arguing now?"

He rolled his eyes and shook his head. "I've never met a woman like you. You're intelligent—"

"I didn't ever see that as a particularly attractive asset before," she interjected.

"You're beautiful."

"I'm too tall."

"Your hair reminds me of a wild sunset."

"Too curly. So far you haven't given me one substantial reason. You say I'm beautiful—I don't happen to agree with you, but you're entitled to your opinion. Besides," she added, setting down her chopsticks and staring across at him, "virtue becomes a wife, beauty becomes a concubine."

"An old Chinese saying?"

She nodded.

"You have both virtue and beauty."

"You still haven't convinced me."

Jason watched her shake her head, her dark eyes sparkling with the humor of their exchange. She had gotten into his blood faster than any woman he had ever met. He wanted her, wanted Jade Douglas so badly it hurt, but unlike the women he had paid to have in Santa Fe, this was one he wanted to keep. Jade wasn't a whore he could use and leave. She was a lady—refined, cultured, intelligent.

He decided to appeal to that intelligence. "Some marriages are arranged, aren't they? At least we know each other. I think we deal well together."

She thought of the blood-stirring, nerve-shattering kisses they had exchanged. "*Deal* well together?"

"I can talk to you like I never have with anyone else," he finished. Then, at the risk of losing her, he added, "I'm in love with you."

She could not believe he had said it. Wanting to clear her name was one thing. Telling her he was in love with her was something else altogether.

"What about you? How do you feel about me?" he asked her outright.

For the first time since she had met him, Jason Harrington appeared to be nervous. Did her answer really mean so much to him? Jade thought about his question. More than that, she thought about how she felt whenever they were together. If they had gone a block farther in the carriage tonight, she would not have been able to keep herself from letting him kiss her. She wasn't certain whether it was love or intense physical attraction to him that made her feel so alive whenever she was near him, but when she thought about her life—the way she had never been attracted to any man before, the magnetic way she had been drawn to Jason—the more certain she became that she did indeed love him.

"You drive a hard bargain, Mr. Harrington," Jade whispered. "I have never been in love before," she said truthfully "so I have nothing to compare my feelings with, but if loving you means that my heart feels about to burst each time I look at you . . . If it means that I find myself thinking about you all day long . . . ," she smiled and said softly, "then, yes, I must be falling in love with you, too."

"So, what do you think?" He was about to burst with the excitement of her pronouncement. "Will you marry me?"

She reached over and stole Jason's egg roll, since he seemed to be ignoring it.

He stared, mesmerized as she licked her fingers.

Unaware of his fascination with her lips, she said, "There are so many things we haven't even discussed. Where will we live? I know you are anxious to return to New Mexico."

"I've thought about that. I won't try to fool you, Jade, this is no place for me. But I wouldn't object to bringing you back here once a year for an extended visit."

Knowing how much he hated the city, certain that his life at the ranch must be demanding, she knew what a sacrifice he was making to even offer.

"I have some things I must take care of first," she said, thinking of the collection. Earlier this evening, everything seemed so confusing. Now, as she listened to Jason, she became all the more determined to contact the bank and let them know she would be willing to give up the adobe and land to pay off her father's debts. She would even sign over the art pieces if the land did not cover the debt.

Surely Grandfather would forgive me for abandoning his dream, she decided. There was little else she could do, unless she was willing to forgo the happiness she was certain she would know as Jason's wife. It was time to dream her own dream and let go of the past.

J.T. began again. "I can't leave here until the mansion is sold and I've bought the new horse stock I promised Uncle Cash I'd take back to New Mexico. That should give you plenty of time to get your business in order."

She couldn't believe she was sitting with him, casually discussing the possibility of a future that she could not even have imagined five days ago.

A waiter interrupted and the main courses were laid out before them. Jason turned his full attention to the meal. Jade explained each dish and its ingredients as he poked and prodded at the vegetables, sticky white rice, and small portions of meat with his fork.

Jade ate heartily, deftly picking up even the smallest grains of rice with her chopsticks, while Jason tasted and examined each piece before he ate it. At long last they were finished and Jade suggested they take a horsecar back to the Barretts'. With eight horsecar companies in the city, it was easy to find a line on any major street.

Jason stayed close beside Jade as they walked through Little China. As they passed a red and gold building covered with detailed ornamentation at the corner of Dupont and Green Jade told Jason that it was the Chinese theater. A performance had just ended, and as they strolled by, a crowd exited the building. Jade was intent on moving away from the pressing throng and momentarily forgot to be sure that J.T. was right behind her. Before she knew what had happened, she was being jostled along with the boisterous crowd.

She tried to stand on tiptoe to see what had become of Jason but he was nowhere in sight. Somehow she found herself in the center of a tight knot of men, bobbing along in the crowd like a cork in an angry sea. There was something odd about the way a small phalanx had formed about her. They were all men, most of them dressed in nondescript peasant garb, none of them looking directly at her. Fighting to stay calm, Jade tried to stop moving until Jason could catch up to her, but when she did she received an abrupt shove from behind.

"Stop that," she said in Cantonese, furious that someone would treat her so rudely. She pushed back.

J.T. did not know when they had become separated, but the moment he realized Jade had been swept away with the crowd his pulse quickened and he felt for the gun he had tucked into the back of his waistband. After what he considered to be two attempts on her life, he had been determined to be on guard whenever they were out together. Now it seemed he had done a poor job of protecting her.

He could easily see over the heads of most of the crowd, but in the sea of humanity, he could not tell Jade from the rest. In the daylight, her bright hair would have given her away, but in the darkness it seemed she had been swallowed up by the crowd. If anything happened to her, J.T. knew he would never forgive himself.

He kept moving, certain she must have traveled in a forward direction, unwilling to believe she had been abducted. He tried to convince himself she would be waiting for him at the next corner, smiling up at him with a horsecar ticket in her hand.

When he reached he corner and the crowd opened up, Jade was not there.

He spun around, carefully checking every direction. Then he spotted what appeared to be three men heading down an alleyway at a fast clip, and ran after them. His boot heels rang out loudly in the narrow passageway as he ran past closed doors and darkened windows. Somewhere in one of the apartments along the alley, a child's cries turned to screams. A door slammed. The men ahead of him began to run. J.T. took up the chase.

Caught between her captors, Jade struggled to break free. When they had first turned into the narrow alleyway, she realized with terrifying clarity that they meant her harm. But by then it had been too late. Shoved ahead of them, she was halfway down the alley when she heard the echo of boot heels behind them. The Chinese had on soft-soled, flat slippers.

"Jason!" She screamed his name at the top of her lungs, praying the man chasing them was J.T.

The man behind her leapt forward, slammed into her, then wrapped his hand around her mouth. Jade tried to bite him, to fight and scratch and beat him off, but the man who held her was the largest of the three.

The sound of Jade calling out his name spurred Jason on. He slipped the gun out of his waistband and fired into the air. Two of her captors sprinted toward the end of the alley and then separated, escaping into side alleys. The man holding Jade gave her a vicious shove backward as he let her go. Her last glimpse of him revealed a gap-toothed smile and a wispy manchu beard. She stumbled backward and hit her head against the brick wall. As she fought for breath, the well-trampled earth in the alleyway rushed up to meet her, and she lost consciousness.

Jason's first reaction was to follow the men who had taken flight, but when he saw Jade crumple to the ground he fired again in an attempt to bring the man down without killing him. Darkness hampered his aim and the man escaped.

Concern for Jade sent Jason rushing to her side. Gun in hand, he lifted her into his arms, intent on getting her into the light so that he could make out the extent of her injuries. Before he had taken a few steps, she moaned and feebly tried to push away from him.

"Shh, Jade. It's all right. It's me, Jason."

He felt her go limp again and held her close. A small crowd had gathered at the end of the alley. He pushed his way past the curious onlookers until he stood in front of a well-lit store, and then he asked an aproned vendor in the doorway for water.

The man disappeared inside and came back with a cup of tepid tea.

Jason thanked him and sat down on an upended barrel, still holding Jade tight in his arms. Afraid to put his gun away, he gently laid it on Jade's stomach. Then he accepted the tea from the shopkeeper and pressed the cup to her lips.

"Drink this," he said, careful not to pour it down the front of her as he kept one eye on the crowd.

Jade moaned and opened her lips to the soothing liquid. She opened her eyes and met Jason's worried gaze. He pulled the cup away.

She blinked, shook her head, and in a voice that denied her words said, "I'm all right. Really."

"Are you sure? Can you sit up?"

She looked at the crowd of Chinese that surrounded them and groaned, "It looks like we've done it again."

He picked up his gun and helped her to a sitting position, but was reluctant to let her leave his lap until he was certain she was all right.

"Miss Douglas?"

Both Jade and Jason looked up.

"Detective Chang," she said.

Jason stared up at the Chinese policeman. "Am I glad to see you."

The detective stood within a circle of burly, blue-uniformed

San Francisco policemen. It was an incongruous sight—the lithe, well-dressed detective standing in the ring of huge caucasians holding axes and rifles at the ready.

"We were here to raid an opium den when we heard a gunshot and ran down the street to see what had happened. I never thought to find you here, Miss Douglas."

"Is there somewhere we can go to get her off the street?" Jason asked.

Chang nodded. "Follow me."

Jon Chang lived above a jewelry shop in Little China, which they reached by traveling through a narrow labyrinth formed by building walls, then through an inner courtyard which opened into the back of the jewelry store. Here, in the bowels of Little China, the over-crowded conditions and cramped housing shared by the Chinese was all too evident. Jason carried Jade up a rickety wooden stairway that led to Chang's third-story room. The cloying scent of air heavy with grease surrounded them as they passed open doorways. People stared out at them from every portal.

J.T. was more than thankful that he was accompanied by Chang. He would never want to venture into this place alone.

Chang ushered Jason and Jade inside and put a pot of water on the stove while J.T. set Jade down on a straight-backed chair before taking a seat himself.

"Tea will be ready soon," Chang told Jade. "Now, perhaps you should tell me what happened tonight and why your companion found it necessary to fire those shots."

Jade introduced Jason and told Chang what she could remember about her near-abduction. Jason then related his part in the escapade. Chang listened attentively to them both.

"It seems, Miss Douglas, that you are not safe here in Little China. Although I thought that with the death of your father the tong would be appeased, it seems this is not so. I have heard nothing from the underground network concerning you. Nothing further about the missing alchemist, either, but that doesn't mean they might not want to abduct you in order to gain more information."

Jason arched a brow at Jade and crossed his arms over his

chest. "This isn't the first attempt on Jade's life. A huge potted plant came hurtling over the stairway at her two nights ago at the Palace Hotel. Then yesterday, someone locked her into the cellar at her grandfather's adobe." He hated seeing her so shaken, her face blanched of its usual healthy glow.

Chang remained outwardly cool. "You did not contact me about these attempts on your life, Miss Douglas. Why?"

Jade sighed. It was all so complicated. "Because, I thought the falling urn was just an accident until yesterday, then when I got back from riding out to the adobe, well—" She had returned to learn about the horrid news article and the locked trap door seemed of little consequence then. "I just did not get around to letting you know."

"Miss Douglas, I must warn you to stay out of Little China. If you do not, I cannot guarantee your safety."

"Don't worry. She won't come anywhere near this place again, if I have anything to say about it." Jason stood, his brows drawn into a frown, his eyes dark with concern.

"Did you happen to find anything when you visited the Page adobe, Miss Douglas?"

"Nothing," she said with a shake of her head, then amended her reply. "Nothing but a red silk belt. It must have come from my grandfather's things. There was nothing else that might lead us to Li Po."

"Who in the hell is Li Po?" Jason asked.

Jade and Chang both answered at once.

"The alchemist."

An overwhelming sadness swept over Jade, replacing her earlier fright as it receded. Her father seemed to be ruining her life from the grave. Not only had he put her so deep in debt that she was forced to give up her only inheritance and her grandfather's most precious treasures as well, but now some one was trying to kill her. And what if they had harmed Jason? Perhaps it was a godsend that he had asked her to marry him and move to New Mexico. She could no longer journey into Little China, nor would she ever feel safe anywhere in San Francisco.

She looked up and found Jason watching her intently concern etched on his features. She smiled tiredly and stood up. Not only had her own life been ruined, but she had unwittingly drawn him into the web of danger. And what had he done in return? Offered her his love, his name, and his protection.

Suddenly, she wanted to get out of Little China. Wanted to see that Jason was out of harm's way. "I don't think I will stay for that cup of tea, Detective; I hope you will excuse me," she said.

"Of course, Miss Douglas. I understand."

Chang walked them down the stairs, through the winding entrance to the courtyard and all the way to the corner, where he waited until they boarded the horsecar. To further shield her from harm, Jason gave Jade an inside seat. He watched as the driver of the horsecar chatted amiably with the passengers. The man seemed to know all of the regular riders by name. At one point the car's weight was not equal to the plodding hay-burner's strength, so the male passengers jovially disembarked and helped push the car along a few yards. They were far enough out of Little China that Jason felt confident about leaving Jade's side for the few moments it took to get the horsecar moving up the steep hill, but he made certain he walked along beside her.

Once he was reseated in the car, he drew her close to his side and sat with an arm possessively draped around her. She smiled up at him before she allowed herself to lean back into the warmth of his embrace.

Although there was the continuous breeze blowing in from the sea, the night was relatively warm for October. They rode in contented silence listening to the clip-clop of the plodding horse. As more and more passengers disembarked, the remaining riders' voices became hushed. There were two other couples left on the open-sided car, but neither paid Jason and Jade any attention. Jade blushed when the pair a few seats in front of them exchanged a kiss. She looked down at her hands.

"Jason," she whispered, still unable to shake the melancholy feeling that had descended on her.

"Umm?" His lips gently grazed the top of her head.

"About your proposal—"

"I've been thinking about that myself," he whispered back.

Jade's throat tightened. He would take it all back now before she had a chance to sample happiness.

"Have you decided?" he asked.

Jade knew she would be a fool to let this gentle, caring man slip out of her life. She might never have another chance to discover love again.

Jade faced him squarely in the darkness. "I'll marry you, Jason," she said.

"And move to New Mexico?"

"Wherever you want."

"I love you, Jade." He said it simply, because it felt so good to admit it to her and to himself.

It was the first time anyone had ever said *I love you* to her. Her father most certainly had not, her mother had been too preoccupied with her own problems. Grandfather Page treated her with love and understanding, but had never told her he loved her in so many words.

"No one has ever told me that before," she said, her voice breaking on the words of admission.

"Get used to it," he warned. "I plan on making it a habit."

❈ CHAPTER 12 ❈

Water and words are easy to pour . . .
Impossible to recover.

Jason Harrington straightened his cuffs and then his black silk bow tie as he stood outside the Barretts' house waiting for someone to answer his knock. He felt his right coat pocket for the hundredth time and found—just as he had each time before—that the long velvet jewel case was still there. He shoved his hands in his trouser pockets and rocked back on his heels, tilted his head skyward, and realized he hardly ever saw stars in San francisco. It seemed the night sky was perpetually blanketed with clouds or fog.

He would give anything to be standing on the veranda of the ranch in Canyon de las Bolsas watching the stars instead of waiting for someone to usher him into his own wedding. Determined not to let his nerves get the best of him, Jason reached out and banged the brass doorknocker again. It was bad enough he had been dealing with a severe bout of prewedding jitters all day without having to agonize alone on the Barretts' front stoop.

He tried to picture Jade's expression last night when he told her that he loved her. She was as trusting as a child. His heart ached for her when she confessed that no one had ever said those words to her before.

Love was something he had always taken for granted. His mother had loved him enough to give up her own security to see that he lived a decent life away from his father's infidelity. The Youngers loved him enough to take him in when his mother died. Even if they had not ever told him outright that they loved him, he knew they cared for him as if he were their own son.

A wry smile twisted his lips. The women in Santa Fe had loved him. They said so every time he'd made love to any of them. Of course, they swore they never said as much to any of

171

their other customers, but still and all, Jason had heard the words spoken aloud.

No, he couldn't imagine having lived the kind of life Jade Douglas had—ignored by her parents, dependent on an old man and a scatterbrained girlfriend for companionship. He was definitely doing the right thing. Jade Douglas deserved to be loved and cherished, and he intended to see to it for the rest of his life.

Jason took a deep breath and wondered if he had the right house. From the way no one was responding to his knock, he was certain he was at the wrong address. Quickly, he stepped back and surveyed the front of the house. Like every other structure on the street, the place had a wide bay window and stretched up three stories high. He checked the numbers near the door. No, this was definitely the right place.

Just as he was about to pound on the door with his fist, a blushing maid opened it wide and stepped back to let him in. He nearly laughed aloud while he watched her stare up at him in awe, her mouth open, her eyes as wide as silver dollars. She didn't say a word.

"I'm J.T. Harrington."

She did not budge.

"The groom," he added.

She bobbed a quick curtsey and continued to stare.

"Maybe you should close the door?"

She did.

"Will you tell Miss Douglas I'm here?"

The girl finally found her tongue. "Yes sir, right away sir." She giggled aloud, bobbed again, and then without taking her eyes off him, backed toward the stairs.

The stairway was serpentined with evergreen tied with satin ribbons. The foyer itself was filled with vase after vase of fresh flowers in yellow and white hues. The heady fragrance of so many blossoms in such a small area was nearly overwhelming.

J.T. suddenly remembered the top hat he'd taken from his father's supply and doffed it before he walked into the drawing room unescorted. More flowers were spread about the room. Another maid was lighting one of what appeared to be hundreds of candles. Jason nodded to a woman seated behind a pianoforte in the corner, then paused before a long mirror above the fireplace and nervously smoothed back his hair. He hoped the black formal wear was correct and wondered if the maid who answered the door had thought him ridiculous in the hat. That might account for her odd reaction to him. From the looks of the decorations the Barretts had supplied, the wedding ceremony that was supposed to be a simple affair might prove far more elaborate than he expected.

"Jason! Welcome!"

He was surprised at the sound of Reggie Barrett's ingratiating tone. Yesterday evening the man had not exactly welcomed him—now he was hosting J.T.'s wedding. Jason could not find it in his heart to greet Reggie enthusiastically, but he did manage to extend his hand and exchange a polite greeting.

"Your attorney will be bringing Judge Cartwright," Barrett explained. "And of course, the women won't be down until we are all in place."

"In place? I thought this was going to be a very simple ceremony."

"Let's see," Reggie said, studying the parlor carefully, "if I remember correctly, and I had better"—he said confidentially to Jason—"we are to wait near the bay window while Babs descends the stairs and precedes Jade into the room. Then Jade will walk in and stand beside you. The judge will stand with his back to the bay window. Mr. Van Buren will stand beside you. Luckily we don't need to remember to do anything but just stand there."

"What does it matter where we stand when we'll be the only ones here?"

Reggie shrugged and ran his finger around the inside of his loose collar. "It matters to Babs, which means it matters a great deal."

"Isn't someone supposed to give the bride away?" Jason asked.

Reggie fidgeted again. "That's exactly what I thought, but Jade can be very obstinate at times. For some reason, she declined my offer. Said she doesn't want to be given away."

Jason thought he knew why Jade would be opposed to having Reginald Barrett escort her into the room, if the man

had always been as hypocritical with Jade as he had with him
for the past two days. J.T. silently saluted her decision.

"Would you like to sit down, Harrington?" Reggie offered.
"How about some sherry to calm your nerves?"

"How about some whiskey?"

Reggie cleared his throat. "Well, yes. I think I have some
here somewhere." He walked to a table covered with crystal
decanters and poured Jason a liberal dose of bourbon.

Jason pulled on his watch chain and checked the time. *Seven
o'clock.* He took the heavy crystal tumbler from Reggie and
tossed back the liquor. "What time is this supposed to start?"

"Seven thirty. I heard Babs tell Jade she told you to be here
by seven just so you wouldn't be late."

Great, Jason thought. That left him to suffer an uncomfortable half-hour of conversation with Reggie Barrett.

Jade stood before the full-length mirror and held her breath
as Babs cinched and laced her corset strings. She held her hand
lightly against her midriff and took shallow breaths until Babs
stopped grunting and tugging and tied a bow with a flourish.

"There! That ought to hold you. Until Jason unties it that
is." Babs snuck a glance at Jade out of the corner of her eye
and chuckled knowingly.

Jade felt her stomach lurch. She pressed the palm of her
hand flat against it and shook her head at Babs. "Take it off. I
can't stand this corset. I'm too nervous to deal with it."

"You need it to mold your figure into the style of the dress,"
Babs argued.

"Well, I won't wear it or the bustle," Jade replied.

"Jade!"

Jade shook her head. "No, Babs. I have to think
about . . . well, later."

"About Jason's undressing you?"

Jade nodded, her face flaming. "Without having to battle a
corset and bustle."

"I wouldn't worry about his ability if I were you," Babs
said.

"Why do you insist on tormenting me?"

Babs tweeked Jade's glowing cheek. "Because you are so

teasable, dear friend." Then her expression grew serious. "Jade, there's nothing to be frightened of. You love Jason, don't you?"

"I think so." Jade twisted her hands together. "I hardly know him, but what I know of him I've come to love." She began to pace as Babs went to the armoire and took out the white tulle dress Jade had worn to the ball at the Palace Hotel. "I didn't set out to love him. I didn't even want to meet him, if you remember correctly." She shot a meaningful glance at Babs before she smiled again. "But he is such a gentle man, so very opposite my father. And he seems to genuinely care for me. Can you imagine it, Babs? I never dreamed this could happen to me."

Babs signalled her forward and slipped the dress over her head. From deep inside the folds Jade continued talking. "I guess this must be love; I'm even looking forward to going to New Mexico with him."

Jade's head appeared through the neckline, then she wriggled her arms into the puffed sleeves.

Babs began working the buttons closed. "Of course it's love." She stepped back and studied the dress where it had been mended. "I wish you would have agreed to a new gown for tonight, Jade. It's your wedding after all. This only happens once or twice in a lifetime."

Jade shook her head. "This dress is beautiful, Babs. Besides, I didn't want to buy a dress that Jason would have to pay for later. I don't want him to think I'm marrying him for his money. In fact, I'd be happier if he was as poor as I am."

"Please, Jade, stop. If the two of you were penniless, everything would be quite dismal."

With a faraway smile, Jade shook her head and thought about her near-escape last night in Little China. Whenever she had needed Jason, he had been there. "I think that together we can overcome anything."

"Hold your hair up," Babs directed, "I can't see the buttons."

Jade did as she was bid.

"Are you certain you won't wear your hair up? You are a little old to wear it loose like this, you know."

"Jason likes it this way."

"Well, I guess that counts for—"

A timid knock at the door interrupted Babs, who called out, "Come in, Doreen."

"Oh, mum," said the wide-eyed Irish maid, "he's here. I never seen a man so beautiful, mum. Tall as a mountain in a high black hat. Eyes the color of an Irish sky, he has. Dressed all in black with a sparklin' white shirt and diamond studs a twinklin' against a broad chest that any woman would be proud to cozy up to—"

"Doreen! Really! Hold your tongue," Babs commanded.

The girl shook herself and curtsied. "Yes, mum. Anyway, he's here."

"Thank you, Doreen. See if there's anything the chef needs and then check on the gentlemen again. We'll be down exactly at seven-thirty."

Babs stepped away from Jade and eyed her carefully from the crown of her head to the tips of the white satin slippers. "Exquisite. Now, for the flowers." She went to the vanity and took up the wreath of baby's breath and miniature white roses and motioned Jade forward. Long white ribbons trailed down the back. She positioned the wreath on her friend's head, then gave Jade a warm hug.

"You are a beautiful bride, Jade. The most beautiful I've ever seen." Her eyes misted with tears.

Overwhelmed with emotion, Jade felt tears smart behind her own eyes and hugged Babs to her again. No matter what her faults, Babs had always been the dearest friend Jade could have ever wanted. Last night, when Jade and Jason announced that they wanted to be married as soon as possible, Babs had thrown herself into the preparations.

She had insisted they marry in her parlor, ordered and placed all the flower arrangements, planned the ceremony, hired the pianist, and secured a French chef to prepare the wedding supper to follow the ceremony. She was up before dawn orchestrating the preparations. Jade would have objected except for the fact that Babs thrived on organizing social events.

Jade had suggested they be married simply, in the judge's

chamber, but Babs would not hear of it. "We'll do this properly Jade, so that your wedding day will be unforgettable. It's bad enough you are already twenty-three, but there's no sense in denying yourself a grand evening."

After Jason had left them alone that evening, Jade took Babs aside. "I can't afford a grand evening, Babs."

It was the first time Jade had ever seen Babs genuinely angry. "I want to do this for you, Jade, as my gift to you both. Besides, it's the least I can do."

"You don't owe me anything," Jade told her. "You have always been there for me when I needed you."

It was the first time that Jade could ever remember seeing Babs at a loss for words. She was deeply touched by her friend's feelings. Graciously she accepted Bab's offer to stage the wedding and take charge of the entire affair. Only when it came to spending money for a new gown did Jade balk.

There was a second knock at the door and Babs called out, "Who is it?"

"Doreen again, mum."

Babs sighed and rolled her eyes. "Again? Come in then."

Doreen slipped in and gave Jade a long box covered in navy velvet. "Your gentleman said to give this to you, mum.

Jade held the box reverently and stared at it. "Oh, Babs! I didn't think of getting anything for Jason." Not only had she not thought of it, Jade realized, but she had no money to buy him anything even if she had remembered that a bride and groom exchanged gifts.

"For heaven's sake, open it!" Babs looked about to rip the box from Jade's hands.

"I'd like to be alone." Jade gave Babs a look that brooked no argument. This was a special moment, and she did not want to share it with anyone.

Babs shook her head. "You are such a sentimentalist, Jade. I'll have to content myself with being surprised. I'll be back to collect you in twenty minutes."

"Doreen, would you wait outside the door for a moment?" Jade asked.

The girl curtseyed and promised to wait. Finally alone, Jade walked to stand beside one of the lamps so that she might have a good look at the gift Jason had chosen for her. Slowly she opened the jewel box and stared down at a set of pearl and emerald earrings and a matching necklace. She lifted the rope of heavy pearls with an emerald medallion in the center and then gently lay it back in the box. A small card carefully lettered in neat, even script read: *These pearls reminded me of your flawless skin, the emeralds of your eyes.*

Overwhelmed by the thoughtfulness of his gift, Jade felt she had to send J.T. something in exchange. She snapped the lid closed and set the jewels on the vanity while she crossed the room to her bureau and opened a small lacquer box. She owned nothing of real value except her mother's wedding ring and the adobe. By tomorrow she would not even own that. Inside the box lay a few French coins she had saved as mementos of her days in Paris, as well as the object she sought. She drew out a piece of Chinese copper cash—a small round coin with a square hole in the middle and the Chinese symbols for good fortune on either side of the hole.

Hastily she went to her desk and bent over her pen and paper. Carefully she dipped the pen into the inkwell and wrote, *Jason, Accept this as a token of my affection and know that my heart is yours. Jade.*

She carefully wrapped the copper cash piece in the note and handed it out to Doreen with instructions to give it to Jason. She closed the door and went to put on his precious gifts.

Jason stood in the drawing room half-listening to Reggie Barrett converse with Matt Van Buren and Judge Cartwright about the state of financial institutions in San Francisco since the August market crash. The nearer the time came to seven-thirty, the quieter he grew, until he found himself unable to add anything more than monosyllables to the steady conversation. Matt tried to turn the conversation his way once or twice, but finding it impossible, left Jason alone with his thoughts.

It's normal to be nervous, he told himself.

But I'm thirty years old. Nearly thirty-one. What right do I have getting married at my age? And to a girl seven years younger?

Old men marry young girls all the time.
I'm not that old.

"It's time gentlemen," Reggie said.

J.T. took a deep breath and looked at Matt. He felt like a man going before a firing squad. Matt was struggling not to laugh. The lawyer stepped close to Jason and whispered, "You look like you're about to be shot."

Jason shook his head. "I never thought I'd be this nervous. I've never been so nervous in my life."

"I hear every groom goes through it. That's why you have a best man. By the way, do you have a ring?"

Jason reached into his vest pocket and pulled out the delicate gold band he had purchased when he bought the pearls and emeralds for Jade. He planned to give his mother's wedding ring to Jade as soon as they returned to New Mexico. For now, the thin gold band with tiny flowers engraved around it would have to suffice.

"It's not much," he said, as he handed it over to Matt, "but I have another one for her at the ranch."

The woman seated at the pianoforte began to play a lilting tune. Jason shoved his hands in his pockets and glanced toward the open double doors that lead to the foyer and the stairway beyond. When his fingers came in contact with Jade's note and the copper token she had sent down a few moments ago, he held it tight and felt a sense of calm settle over him.

He knew he was doing the right thing. He was doing something honorable by marrying Jade, and he knew in his heart that he was getting the best end of the bargain. She made him feel alive, able to take on the world. They were right for each other. As his apprehension fled, he squeezed the token for good measure and pulled his hands out of his pockets.

Barbara Barrett's maid appeared in the doorway and signaled Reggie with a nod. The men took their places: Judge Cartwright stood before the bay window, Jason stood to his right with Matt beside him, and Reggie stood far to the left, leaving room for Babs.

The pianist began to play the wedding march and Doreen burst into tears. All eyes turned to the doorway and they watched as Babs entered the room. Even Jason had to admit she was a stunning woman. Nearly as tall as Jade, she moved with the assurance of a woman who knew she was beautiful. Her dress was the color of a mountain lake. Pearls were clasped about her throat and shone luminously at her ears. Carrying an intricate lace fan, she walked regally through the room and took her place beside Reggie, then turned to face the door.

The sound of the music intensified. Jason could not take his eyes off of Jade when she paused on the threshold. She was a vision, an angel in white wearing a crown of flowers. A nimbus of red-gold curls swirled in a rippling mass to her waist. She seemed ethereal, unaware of her earthly surroundings as she held a small bouquet of yellow and white flowers in her hands. Jason watched her as she hesitated in the doorway. His heart swelled with pride when he realized she was wearing his gifts to her. The emeralds caught the light and sparkled, but he had been wrong—they would never match the radiance of her eyes.

Jade looked so vulnerable standing there all alone, that without thinking of anything except putting her at ease, Jason left his place and crossed the room. As a courtier of old might have done, he bowed and then held out his arm to her. Jade laid her hand upon his sleeve and let him lead her to the wedding party waiting near the window.

Tears she could not hide filled her eyes when Jason crossed the room and gallantly escorted her to the others. Any doubts she had about marrying him fled when she realized that he sensed what she was feeling as she stood alone in the drawing room doorway. Everything seemed to come into focus in that one instant in time, and she knew her life would never be the same. No longer would she think of herself as alone. From this day onward Jason would be a part of her life, and she a part of his. His recognition of her need, his caring act of coming to her when she felt so alone to escort her across the expansive room, proved to her that she was not making a mistake. It was as if someone had sent her a sign that all was well.

Jason looked down at the woman at his side as they stood before the judge and felt his blood run hot in his veins. He wanted her as he had never wanted a woman before. He wanted her, not for one night, but for a lifetime—and because of that he knew that he would be willing to wait until she wanted him. They had known each other less than a week, and although he hoped with all his heart that Jade would wish to consummate their union, he would understand if tonight was still too soon. As he tried to cool his racing blood, tried to ignore the touch of her hand on his and the subtle fragrance of orange blossoms that surrounded her, he told himself they would have the rest of their lives together. But deep inside he hoped he would not have to wait too long to claim his marital rights.

As Judge Cartwright read the words of the ceremony, Jade thought about her future with Jason. She was determined to make this marriage work. She intended to love and honor Jason just as he promised to love and honor her. She agreed to the word "obey" as well, but in her heart she knew she would never be like her mother. It was hard to imagine Jason forcing her to do anything that she did not want to, and as her thoughts drifted to the night ahead, she felt her face flame with color. She surreptitiously glanced at him from beneath lowered lashes. She could only guess at the mysteries of intimacy and what the night held in store for her, but she was more than willing to be Jason's wife in every way.

As the judge droned on, she thought of the Chinese custom of buying wives, then of arranged marriages. In many cultures a man and woman met and were married on the same day. She may not have had much time to get to know Jason, but at least she knew him well enough to determine the kind of man he was. She did not find him wanting. He was gentle, kind, and understanding. He had given her no reason to fear him or the night that lay ahead.

Jason and Jade stood before the judge and said yes to every vow. For better or worse, for richer, for poorer, in sickness and in health. When he slipped the ring on Jade's finger, then held both of her hands in his, their lives became inexorably entwined.

The time came for them to seal their vows with a kiss. Jade waited to see what Jason would do. Finally, when he did not move, she peered up at him, her eyes shining through her tears. He smiled down at her, placed a finger beneath her chin, and tilted her face toward his. He took Jade's flowers and handed them to Babs, who was fighting to hold back tears.

Then he took his wife into his arms, and before the entire gathering left no doubt as to the depth of his feeling for her.

Jade felt herself melting in his arms as she did each time he kissed her. Whenever he touched her, she became more than herself. As the parched soil of the desert welcomes a rain shower, so too did she welcome his kiss. Unmindful of the others, she gave herself over to him and slipped her arms about his neck. She clung to him, felt his hand at the small of her back and leaned into his embrace as close as her voluminous skirts would allow. Their kiss went on and on as Jason's lips moved expertly over Jade's. It was not until Matt cleared his throat that they became aware of the others in the room.

Gradually, J.T. let her go until she was able to stand alone again. He tried to hide his amusement, but failed when he gazed down at the heightened color of her pinkened cheeks. He took both her hands in his and looked down at the gold ring on her finger. She was his. Jason felt as if he owned the world.

The wedding feast was elegant and the conversation subdued in the candlelit dining room. Heavy crystal goblets glittered at each place setting as they reflected the dancing flames. Babs was so elated with the French chef that she had him present each course to the gathering as if each platter was an honored guest. Babs clapped and exclaimed over the dishes. Jade could not help but smile when the chef introduced the *saute de volaille reduit* with a flourish. The French words made the dish sound far more glamorous than sauteed chicken in cream sauce.

Jade glanced up at Jason. He viewed the proceedings with an arched brow and a dubious half-smile, obviously as unimpressed as she. But Babs wanted to prove how very cultured she had become. Reggie preened each time he was asked to taste a dish. Although she owed them much, Jade could not help but be relieved to leave the Barretts' home. Babs had changed during the time Jade had been in France, so much so that it was slowly dawning on Jade that, except for shared girlhood memories, they had very little in common.

Whenever he was unaware of her doing so, Jade watched Jason. He stared long and hard at each selection before he tasted it. Very often he would cut into a portion and carefully inspect it before he actually put it in his mouth. Jade made note of his finicky manner for the future.

She had little appetite, although the chicken, the potatoes Provençale, and the dessert of rum banana fritters were indeed delicious. Champagne flowed throughout the meal. Reggie and Judge Cartwright tried to outdo each other in toasts to the newlyweds. Babs, replete from the rich meal and lulled by the wine, was uncharacteristically quiet. Jade wondered when it would be polite to end the gathering, but decided it was up to Babs, as hostess, to give some sign that the celebration was over.

One part of her wanted the meal to end. On the other hand, she knew that this night would be unlike any other. She was married to Jason now. She intended to do right by him and be a wife to him in every way.

Although they sat side by side all evening, they had not done more than exchange polite pleasantries. Instead of being relieved by his undemanding silence, Jade became more nervous with each passing moment. It wasn't until Matt asked Jason if he had plans for a honeymoon trip that Jade felt J.T. reach beneath the table and take her hand in his. He squeezed her fingers gently, his gaze secretive. A wave of heat suffused her, one Jade knew was not entirely from embarrassment.

"As a matter of fact, I do. I'm taking my bride to Monterey early tomorrow morning. I've been meaning to go after some stock to add to the herd."

"And tonight?" Babs asked, staring over at Jade.

Jade blushed, and even Jason paused for a moment before he said, "We're staying at Harrington House."

"Oh." Babs looked disappointed, "I thought you might be staying at the Palace tonight. But then again, with a mansion like yours, who needs the Palace? By the way, Jade, when you are ready to hire help, be sure to let me know. I have contacts to all the best cooks in San Francisco. If you offer enough, you'll surely be able to steal one away from someone."

"I don't think—"

"I'm sure we'll manage until we go to New Mexico," Jason said with a nod to Babs, "but thanks anyway."

"Surely you don't mean she'll have to cook *herself*?"

Before Jason could answer, Matt stood up, champagne glass in hand. "How about one final toast to Jade and Jason?" He raised his glass in a salute. "To a long life together and every happiness." Everyone joined in.

Then Jason stood. Without hesitation or the self-consciousness that might have stopped another man, J.T. raised his glass. "I'd like to make a toast of my own." He turned to Jade as everyone else lifted their stemware in salute.

"To my wife."

Jade could not help but note the meaning behind the warm, suggestive glance he gave her over the rim of his glass. She lifted her glass and shyly returned his look.

Jason drained his glass and Jade followed suit.

It was time to go. Jade took one last look around the guest room to be certain she had not forgotten to pack anything. Her heavier boxes of books and personal belongings had been delivered to the mansion earlier in the day. All she had to carry with her was a small tapestry valise that contained her hairbrush and other toilette articles.

"Do you have everything?" Babs asked from the open doorway.

Jade looked at her friend and knew that their friendship had now altered. From now on, Jason would take precedence in her life. They were no longer children. The things they once had in common might have changed, but they still shared memories of those years.

"I think so." Jade crossed the room and took hold of Babs' hands. "Thank you so much, dear friend, for everything you've done for me."

A frown marred the brunette's features for a fleeting second before Babs forced a smile and said, "Just remember that I only wanted to see you have the best, Jade. You deserve it, no matter what you think."

Babs' uncustomary nervousness was all too obvious. "What do you mean?" Jade asked.

"I can't help but remember how lonely you were and how much you had to put up with when you were a child. I know it colored your picture of marriage. For a while I didn't think you would ever consent to marrying anyone. That's why I had to do what I did."

Jade was suddenly wary. "Are you referring to the day you left me on Jason's doorstep?"

Babs pulled away from Jade and twisted her hands together. "Well, that—and one other thing."

Despite every intention to stay calm, Jade felt her temper rise. "*What* other thing?"

Babs fiddled with a stray curl. "What would you say if you knew the reason that reporter was so anxious to interview Jason the morning you were there was because I sent an anonymous note?"

"*What?*"

"Now Jade, please don't be mad. I did it for you."

Jade's mind reeled with the ramifications of Babs' unthinking act. She remembered asking Babs if she had known the reporter, Peterson, and Babs had told her no. It was the worse kind of deception, one Jade doubted she could ever forgive. If not for Babs' meddling, Jason would never have felt obligated to ask her to marry him.

Jade felt dirty. A cheat.

Even though she was not a party to the shameful plot, she intended to tell Jason the truth immediately.

"I have to tell Jason." Jade tried to shove past Babs, who still blocked the doorway.

"Absolutely not. Stop and think, Jade. It will ruin everything."

"I don't care! I have to tell him before this goes any farther. Now get out of my way."

❈ CHAPTER 13 ❈

*The light of one star
Illumines the mountains of many regions . . .
So one unguarded expression
Injures a whole life of virtue.*

Matt Van Buren took Judge Cartwright home, and Reggie invited Jason into the drawing room for brandy. Anxious to collect his bride, J.T. excused himself and took the stairs two at a time until he reached the upper landing. He continued down the hall past paintings in ornate, gilded frames, side tables covered with lace cloths, and vases of flowers. Following the low sound of women's voices, he continued on until he stood just outside Jade's room. Her words reached him before he stepped into the women's line of vision. The frantic, angry sound of Jade's voice made him pause.

"Babs, I have to get downstairs. Now." Jade sounded angrier and far more determined than he had ever heard her. "I can't stand this anymore."

Jason was about to go to Jade's aid when he heard Babs say, "You'll be a fool if you tell Jason the truth now—not when you no longer have to worry about a thing. Everything worked out according to the plan. You've married your millionare and you'll have all the money you need to pay off your father's debts."

Jason stood rooted to the floor as overwhelming reaction to Babs' callous words ripped through him. Jade had married him for his money. The whole affair had been one great sham, and he had been fool enough to fall for it. He balled his hands into fists and stared up at the ceiling as anger, humiliation, pride, and revulsion roiled through him. Above all, Jason experienced a searing hurt—one that tore through his heart before it compelled him to move, forced him to step into the open doorway and face the conniving beauty he had just taken as his wife.

Unaware of him, Babs stood in the doorway. She whirled around as he pushed past her. J.T. then grabbed Jade by the

187

arm. Forgetting the strength behind the fingers that bit into her tender flesh, he ignored her look of pain and confusion and shoved her toward the door.

"Jason?" Her eyes were wide and pleading. "What is it? What's wrong?"

Babs grabbed his sleeve in a futile attempt to stop him. "Jason, I don't know what you heard, or what you think you heard, but—"

He found he had to force himself to speak. "I heard enough." He was not certain he could say any more, but discovered as he ground out the words that the release helped him vent some of his towering rage. "It seems I've bought myself a wife. I've come to collect."

He dragged Jade into the hallway.

"Jason, stop!" She tried to break away, tried to pull her arm out of his punishing grasp. "You're hurting me. Let me explain," she cried out. "I was just coming down to tell you—"

He spun around and glowered down at her. His eyes were dark and wild with anger. "Oh, really? And just *what* were you planning to tell me, Jade?" He gave her a shake and took pleasure in the fact that she winced. "How big a fool I've been? How easy I was to trap? Were you going to tell me now, or after you were well-ensconced in Harrington House? After you'd slept with me?"

She finally jerked out of his grasp and fell back against the wall. "I didn't know, Jason! Believe me, I didn't know Babs sent that reporter to your home!"

Babs had followed them into the hall. She began shouting in an effort to make him believe Jade. "It's true, Jason. She had nothing to do with Peterson finding out she spent the night at your house. It was all my idea."

"No?" His brow rose sardonically. "And I suppose she doesn't know how she arrived at my doorstep alone that first day! You two orchestrated the whole thing, and I was stupid enough to believe her when she told me you had just up and left her there, Babs."

He turned back to Jade, who was still pressed up against the wall. J.T. shook his head. She was a consummate actress. Her expression of wide-eyed innocence was still almost convincing, even now that he knew the truth. Jade had paled to the color of her dress and her lips were parted. One hand rested at the base of her throat while the other was braced against the wall. He turned his fury on Babs and she took a step back into the guest room. "Were you behind the trap door that closed poor, defenseless Jade in the cellar at the adobe? Oh, yes! How could I forget? Hiring the thugs that dragged her through Little China was very inspirational. I fell for that one like a rock off a cliff."

Jade laid her hand on his sleeve in an attempt to calm him. He stared down at the fingers that clutched the dark material as one might stare at a venomous snake.

"You choreographed the whole thing so that I'd feel sorry for her," he said as he shot a glance at Babs and then stared hard at Jade, "so that I would feel protective, chivalrous." He clamped a hand around her wrist and pulled her fingers off his sleeve. "God, what a farce."

Jade was trembling so hard she did not think her legs would hold for another second. As she stared up at Jason, she realized this was a nightmare she couldn't, wouldn't, let herself believe in. Her Jason Harrington was kind and gentle. He was like no man she had ever met. But the enraged man he had become in the last few seconds reminded her all too much of her father. She refused to accept what she saw. She tried to reach through his rage again.

She spoke in slow, even tones as she tried to soothe him to some degree of calm. "Jason, I don't know what you heard, but you have this all wrong. Please, let's go home so that I can explain it all to you. Please!"

"*Home?* My *home* is in New Mexico. Not here." J.T. stared down at her, his pulse racing, as he tried to think of a way to hurt her as much as she had hurt him. She had struck where he had always been the most vulnerable—when he had only wanted to do the honorable thing by her and make up for the hurt he had done her reputation. Instead he had made a fool of himself by marrying a woman who had no scruples, a creature who had duped him into falling into her trap. His smile twisted as he stared down at her in the dimly lit hallway. Jade was still as beautiful to him as she had been moments ago when they exchanged their vows, but now he saw her for the callous, conniving bitch she really was. He wanted nothing more than to walk away from her without another glance, to turn away from the stricken look she feigned and hide from the glistening emerald eyes and full lips that still made his traitorous body ache. But unable to leave her there, he pinned her to the wall with his stare.

"It wasn't like that, Jason. Believe me! I was going to the bank tomorrow to settle my father's debts. I'm giving up the adobe and the land. I don't even want Grandfather's things."

"Shut up," he snapped, holding up his hand in warning, refusing to listen, afraid to listen to her honeyed words. "It was all a lie," he whispered, not caring whether she heard or not. "The visit to the bank—nothing was settled that day, was it? You're still deep in debt and figured I was the only way out. But, that's the way you planned it all along."

"I don't want your money." She shook her head in denial as her tears began to fall. "I never did," she whispered.

"She didn't, Jason," Babs interjected. "She never wanted to trick you."

J.T. glanced at Babs with a look of hatred that most men would have feared. He had forgotten the woman was still there. He knew that if he did not leave now that his anger would drive him past all reason. He turned away and stalked down the long hallway. Jade ran after him. He could hear the rustle of her gown and the sound of her soft footsteps behind him. She grabbed his arm.

"Jason, please! At least listen to me. Give me a chance."

He swung around, fists clenched, legs spread.

She did not flinch.

"Please," she whispered. "You have to believe me."

"Why should I?" he ground out.

"Because I'm telling the truth."

He leaned down until he was nearly nose-to-nose with her. "You don't know the meaning of the word truth."

Jade closed her eyes, took a deep breath, and drew on her inner strength. He was hurt, she knew that; she had to choose her words carefully, lest she wound him more. *The swiftest horse cannot overtake the word once spoken*. If ever there was a time to guard her words, this was it. She could not risk defending herself with anger. That would only drive him farther away.

Just as surely as she refused to let him go, so too did she refuse to cower before him. He had to hear the truth.

"Jason, I agreed to marry you because you said you loved me. Was that a lie? Is that how you can walk out on me now?"

J.T. stared down at her, stunned. Her reminder only served to reinforce the lengths to which he had let her manipulate him. He had been fool enough to tell her he loved her, now he was fool enough to realize he still did. But he would be damned if he'd let Jade know it. He would not tell her he loved her again. Not until hell froze over. Never, ever again.

But she was waiting for him to say something.

So he lied.

"Don't delude yourself. We all play our little games. I only wanted your body, Jade. I would have said anything to get you into my bed."

She recoiled as if he had slapped her. Her gaze dropped to the floor. Had she been so starved for affection that she had believed his profession of love? Unwilling to believe what she had just heard, Jade covered her ears with her hands. But her logical mind could not be silenced. Of course he did not love her. She should have seen it sooner. Why would a man like Jason Harrington—a man who could have any woman he wanted with just a smile—want her? Suddenly ashamed, she wished he would go, wished he would walk out of her life and never come back. She would do nothing further to stop him.

The scent of her perfume assailed him in the narrow hallway. J.T. stood staring down at the crown of her head, looked upon hair as vibrant as a red-golden flame. She still wore the wreath of flowers—white, fragile, as delicate and innocent as he once thought she was. Her ivory skin still intrigued him. He still wanted to touch it. The pearls and emeralds at her ears and throat glistened in the lamplight, further testimony of the depths to which he had fallen for her.

He watched her breasts rise and fall with every breath. She was poised there before him, unable to look at him, unwilling, it seemed, to argue anymore.

She was waiting for him to leave her.

As he stared at her, Jason realized he could no more leave Jade tonight than he could admit aloud that he still loved her.

She was his wife.

He was the only man who could lay claim to her now. The only man who had the right to spread her pale thighs and lie between them. He was her husband, for better or worse. She might not care anything for him now, but he fully intended to make certain that by morning she would feel something for him. Even if it was hatred.

"Do you have all your things?" he asked abruptly.

She looked up then, her tear-filled eyes reflecting hope. Her voice trembled. "It's right here. Babs?"

Silk rustled behind him. He watched as Jade reached out and took her valise from the other woman. Babs silently stepped aside and waited. Jade shifted the heavy bag in her hands. Jason took it from her with one hand while he grabbed her arm with the other.

"Jade?" Babs called softly. "I'm so sorry."

Jade turned her back on Babs and set out to go with Jason. Always before she had forgiven her friend—called upon the past to forgive the present. But Babs had gone too far this time. No memory could erase what she had done to Jade, or more importantly, to Jason. Jade was determined to prove her sincerity to Jason, even if it meant never speaking to Babs again.

She tried to keep up as Jason dragged her down the hallway without a backward glance.

When her foot caught in the hem of her heavy gown, she almost tripped headlong down the stairway. Jason jerked her to her feet. She stifled a whimper of pain as her arm twisted and she tried to keep up. At the foot of the stairs he flung open the front door and half-dragged, half-carried her down the steps to his waiting carriage. He tossed her inside and barked orders to the driver of the hack he had hired for the occasion.

Jade dragged herself to a sitting position, scooted away from Jason, and tried to straighten her clothing. The mended sleeve and bodice had torn anew, exposing her white shoulder and the curve of her breast. Her garland of flowers sat crookedly. With trembling fingers she reached up and drew it off, the travesty of the last few moments made mockery of the touch of wedding finery.

She stared over at Jason. His jaw was set, his lips thinned, his eyes hooded and narrowed as he gazed out the window to avoid looking at her.

Her voice was calm and steady, her sure tone belying her inner turmoil. "If you'll just listen to me for a moment—"

He turned on her viciously. She refused to turn away. "I am warning you, Jade. Shut up."

The October air was heavy with dampness. Without a wrap of any kind, she was soon shivering. Jade crossed her arms and hugged them to herself. She tried to convince herself that she was not frightened of Jason, for after all, he had never given her reason to be, and that she was only shaking from cold.

Out of the corner of his eye, J.T. saw her shivering like a wounded animal on the far side of the seat. It mattered little to him why she quaked. He hoped she was more frightened than cold—good and scared would delight him.

The bitch deserved it. His emotions were leashed on a tight rein in the confines of the small carriage. To put her out of his thoughts, he stared out the window and watched as block after block of the city swept past. The carriage lurched as the driver began the steep ascent up Nob Hill. J.T. refused to look at her, but he was more aware of Jade at that moment than he had ever been before.

As the carriage hurried toward their destination, thoughts raced pell-mell through Jade's mind. She berated herself for ever agreeing to marry a man she did not really know. How could she have foreseen the towering rage he had exhibited tonight? Not even love could force her to stay with a man like her father, and if Jason proved to be as ruthless or as cruel, she would sooner leave him forever. She would annul the marriage and forget her dream of love before she led the life her mother had. She should never have agreed to this marriage, she concluded. She knew that now.

But it was still not too late to make up for her mistake.

When the carriage drew up beside the curb, Jason opened

the door. Rather than step out ahead of her and offer her his hand, he simply commanded, "Get out."

She voiced no argument, afraid that he was mad enough to shove her out if need be. Jade stepped down and waited for him on the curb. He grabbed her valise, paid the driver, and then marched up the stairs ahead of her.

Jade refused to follow him like a wounded puppy with its tail between its legs.

Jason turned at the top step and stared down at her. Silhouetted by the lamplight behind him, he was an imposing figure. Still, she screwed up her courage and stood her ground.

"I refuse to go in there with you."

"You're my wife. You'll do anything I say."

"Absolutely not—"

He was off the steps in seconds. He grabbed her about her hips and threw her over his shoulder, then bent and picked up her valise. He held her tight, even as she struggled, fumbled with the key, and then kicked open the door. Jade squirmed and screamed. She pounded his back with her fists. J.T. carried her as if she weighed nothing. Once he had dropped her valise and locked the door behind them, he set her down.

"Get upstairs."

"Jason, get out of the way. I'm walking out of here now, and tomorrow I'll have this marriage annulled. If you aren't willing to calm down and listen, I refuse to stay here with you."

"You want me to listen to more of your lies? You think I'll swallow them as easily as I did everything else?" He raked his fingers through his hair and leaned back against the door, emphasizing his unwillingness to let her go. His angry expression faded as he stared down at her, and for a moment he allowed his disappointment and hurt to slow. "I guess I was a pretty easy mark for you and your friend, huh, Jade?"

"I never lied to you." She denied his words with a shake of her head.

Jason did not heed her. "If you needed money, why didn't you just take a tumble with me and then ask for it? I'm used to dealing with women who get paid for it, Jade. Santa Fe is full of them. But that wouldn't have been enough, would it? You wanted it all." He shook his head and said half to himself,

"And I thought Nettie was bad." He stared back down at her and said, "No, Jade. I was the fool. I believed your innocent act, I felt protective, possessive . . . Do you do this all the time, Jade? Just how many men have you duped with your innocent act? How many?"

"I've never . . . None, Jason! None."

"I don't believe you."

"I—"

"How many men have you spread your legs for in order to get at their bank accounts?"

The shock of his words ripped through her, erasing her pain and fear. Anger quickly settled in their place. He thought the worst of her. All she wanted was out, now that she knew Jason was determined not to believe her. Why should she try to convince him any differently? He was still blocking the door. She wondered if she made him angry enough would he change his mind and throw her out.

Pushed to the limit, she let her own brewing anger erupt. Her head came up. Her eyes blazed with fury. "Hundreds!" she screamed at him. "I've been with hundreds of men. Thousands! You won't listen, so why should I even bother to explain?"

She could see that for a moment he was taken aback. He stared at her in stunned silence. Then, his face darkened. He became the predator she had so feared.

J.T. shoved away from the door. "I think I deserve having the pleasure of your company for at least one night."

She watched him as he took one menacing step after another until he stood directly in front of her. He reached out and wrapped her hair about his hands and pulled her up close. She tried to hold him off but failed. All too clearly Jade realized that the night he had proposed and she had held him at bay in the carriage it had not been because of her strength, but because he did not press her. Now she knew that she was no match for his great strength. Before she could utter a word of protest, his head came down and he ground his lips against hers.

Dipping with his weight and the force behind his kiss, she was soon draped over his arm. He pressed her hips to his with his free hand and continued the onslaught of the kiss until Jade was forced to open her lips and receive his marauding tongue. Her traitorous body betrayed her as it had every time he had kissed her; she felt a burning heat radiate outward from the secret place between her thighs until it became all-consuming. Seeking release, she involuntarily pressed her lips to his in answer to his demands.

"That's it, Jade," he said against her lips, "drop the innocent pretense. It's time we got down to business."

She tried to pull back, to argue, but he covered her mouth with his. Finally, once he had rendered her breathless, Jason scooped her up and carried her upstairs.

He shoved open the door to the master bedroom. The room was pitch dark, the moonless night adding nothing to the gloom. Jade struggled in earnest, trying to break his punishing hold on her. Finally he set her down.

"Hold still! I don't want to hurt you, Jade. I'm sure you're much better at this than you let on, so why play the offended virgin now?"

Over the pounding of her heart, Jade tried to reason with him one more time. "Jason, don't say or do anything you are going to regret—"

"The only regret I have is ever having found you on my doorstep."

It infuriated her when her eyes flooded with tears. She looked away and bit her bottom lip to still its uncontrollable trembling. Her brief, golden dream of love was gone, ended when Jason's love for her had been shattered by Babs' incriminating confession. Jason was innocent of the whole affair, and now he was demanding no more than what he thought he deserved. In his eyes she was a cheat—a woman who had schemed and manipulated to get his money. She understood, but hesitated to give him what he wanted.

Before he touched her again, before he kissed her into acquiescence, she had to get out.

Jason tried to see her finely sculpted features in the darkness. He sensed her hesitation and wondered why she was playing coy. He had married her, and even though the sun would have to burn itself out before he ever told her he loved her again, he knew it would be a long time until he got her out of his blood. And after all, he thought, this was his wedding night.

He intended to have her.

Jade made the slightest movement and he lunged for her as she tried to run past him. Hampered by darkness, he misjudged her close proximity and crashed into her, his forward momentum carrying them both to the ground. As they fell backward, Jason tried to spare her his weight and twisted until he was nearly beneath her, much the same as he had done when they fell down the stairs at the Palace.

Jade instinctively clutched his sleeves. She felt his muscles bunch beneath the fabric, knew he had not meant to harm her, and after they hit the floor, she tried to relax and catch her breath.

He could feel her breath, warm and enticing on his neck. Shaken by the fall, she was panting, reminding Jason of a woman in the throes of passion. He kissed her before he knew what he was doing. Jade was still too stunned to resist. Their tongues warred with each other—sparring, striking, receding. Jason grasped her face between his hands and held her immobile as he deepened the kiss. Jade arched, trying to shake him off, but only succeeded in arousing him more. He pressed her down until he was more on her than off, and she was nearly paralyzed beneath his greater weight. She could feel his erection, the height of his passion, and her fear mounted.

She gasped for air as he pulled away long enough to tear off his jacket and work at the waistband of his pants.

Realizing his intent, Jade struggled to sit up.

"No!" He barked out the harsh command. "Stay where you are."

She shoved at him.

He reached down and slid her torn dress and chemise off of one breast. Without pausing to be gentle, he lifted her breasts and began to knead them until she moaned. His lips were everywhere, kissing her ear, sliding along the column of her neck, playing across her breasts until they found a puckered nipple. His mouth and tongue were never still as his hands continued to tear away her gown. The mended side seam was soon rent all the way down. He pulled the garment aside, exposing her frilly chemise.

Jade refused to give in to myriad sensations that swept over her in wave after uncontrollable wave. Thoughts jumbled one on the other. As hard as she wanted to fight, still she could not deny the fact that this man was no stranger. It was Jason. Only an hour ago she had anticipated their lovemaking. If she had not looked forward to this very moment, she might have fought harder—might have wanted to stop him, but the sensations he was evoking, the pleasurable pain of his exquisite torture, was unlike anything she had ever imagined.

If only he loved me, she thought. If only the gentle, caring man she had known over the past few days was the one ministering to her now instead of using her body to vent his rage and hurt. But as hard as Jade tried to deny it, she still loved him. Still wanted him.

Realizing as much, she would do nothing to stop him.

Once he had torn away the bodice of her gown and captured her full, ripe breasts in his hands, Jason knew there was no way he could stop until he had buried himself inside her. Maybe then he could get her out of his heart. But he had never raped a woman and he would be damned if he did now.

He continued to kiss her, kept his hands roving over her full, lush breasts. She moaned low in her throat and soon he felt her relax beneath him, felt her go slack as he tore off her gown. J.T. felt no rush of joy when she stopped fighting him. He did not want her lying as cold and still as the jewels that still hung about her throat. In his twisted thoughts he was convinced that perhaps if she truly was innocent she would fight him to the end.

But now she was all too acquiescent. He'd be damned if he'd let her lie there beneath him like a broken doll. Before he took his own pleasure, he would be certain he brought her to heights she had never reached before. That way, at least he would have the satisfaction of knowing that she would never forget him.

"I'm glad you've decided to see this my way," he whispered into her ear before he bent his head, drew one nipple between his teeth and bit it gently. He heard her moan again and swelled with power. He ground his hips against her.

Jade felt him hard and heavy as he nudged his hips against her pelvis. She fought her panic by being as still and receptive as possible. Showing him any sign of the passion he had stoked in her was out of the question. She could not let herself feel, for if he knew the power he held over her she would be all that much more vulnerable.

It was their wedding night. A nightmare of a night, but the first and last they would share. She would let him have his way and be done with it. He felt he had been duped. She felt she owed him that much.

J.T. hated the way she did not respond to his touch. It angered him further when he reached out and felt her heart beating like a captured sparrow beneath his hand. He slipped his hand between her tightly closed legs, played his fingertips up her thighs past the silken garters that held her stockings, up her bare leg, until he reached the short pantaloons she wore. He shoved his hand into the waistband and soon found the warm recesses he sought. Deep inside the silken nest at the apex of her thighs she was hot, wet, and ready for him. When she flinched and tried to squirm out of his reach, he refused to let her move. When his fingers invaded the tight warmth inside her, J.T. had to keep himself from groaning in anticipation of sheathing himself in her.

Gentleness was not something he had intended to show her this night. He began to delve deep inside her dewy moistness until she could not help but follow the rhythm of his hand, writhing her hips up and down in imitation of his movements. Soon she was panting again, and he doubted if Jade even knew what she was doing when she reached out and clung to his shoulders.

He braced himself on one hand and let go of her long enough to tear open the buttons on his trousers and drawers. His heated shaft burst through the gap—throbbing and ready. Gathering her ponderous skirts in his hand, he shoved them up about her waist and then, without preamble, he plunged himself inside her.

Jade held tight to his arms and pressed her face against his starched, pristine shirt front. The diamond shirt studs were rough against her cheek, but they did not even bear notice when, before she expected it, he had driven his shaft into her. She felt as if she had been torn asunder, could feel the foreign length and weight of him invading her, plunging to the very mouth of her womb. As he broke through her virgin wall, she bit down hard on her lip to keep from crying out.

It was too late to cry. Tears would be a foolish waste of time. Just as he had refused to hear her out earlier, she reckoned he would not heed her tears now.

By the time Jason realized what he had done, it was too late. Her body's virginal resistance and then the way her tight sheath enfolded him was all the proof he needed. Despite what he had thought, he knew now he was the first man to have known her intimately.

Shame washed over him, followed close on its heels by anger. He was furious with himself for what he had done. Angry at her for having let him do it. Why had she given in to him?

Except for an occasional shudder, she was as still as a stone beneath him now, her face hidden in the hollow of his neck, her hands clutching his sleeves. Her hair was spread out on the carpet around them. Jason almost pulled away from her, intent on starting over. It would be so easy to draw her into his embrace, to gentle her, to beg her to forgive him as he carried her to the bed. But she had deceived him.

And he had gone too far to turn back now.

Besides, she and her friend had tricked him into this marriage, and he'd be damned if he'd let her know he still cared for her.

For now, she was tight and hot and his. Without thought for her comfort or pleasure, he began to move his hips, to seek his own release. He drove into her faster, harder, farther, with all the fury that had built inside him over the past hellish hour. Unmindful of the fact that she was on the hard floor with little but the carpet to keep his weight from crushing her, he quickened his pace and grasped her hips, tilting her to receive his seed. He heard her catch her breath and moan. Satisfied that he had broken through her facade of reserve, he climaxed.

Jade did not move when he finally rolled away from her. The air against her exposed skin was cold. She shivered. At least he was no longer hurting her. Thankful for the darkness, she kept her eyes closed anyway, unwilling to risk looking at him, afraid of what she might see in his eyes. She heard him get up, listened to the sound of his footsteps as he left her there with her dress up about her waist, the bodice rent and torn.

He was moving about in the dressing room, stripping clothing off of hangers, slamming doors. Finally, she heard the outer door close behind him and his footsteps recede down the hallway.

Jade levered herself up and sat dazed, trying to see through the darkness. She did not hear him anymore. He was indeed gone. Reaching out, she used the footboard of the bed to pull herself up. Her skirt fell into place around her ankles. Sticky moisture clung to her thighs; she wanted it off. Like a sleepwalker, she felt her way into the dressing room. There was a small lamp on the washstand inside, and she soon found matches in a small case beside it. She lit the lamp and turned the wick down low. Only then, in the weak lamplight, did she dare to look at herself in the mirror. As if they were chiding her, the emeralds winked back at her.

Her lower lip was bruised and bleeding where she had bit it. Like a madwoman's, her hair stood out about her head and shoulders, the unruly curls protesting Jason's careless treatment. She found a washcloth and poured tepid water out of the pitcher into a matching washbowl. Jade washed her lip and pressed the rag against it until the bleeding stopped.

Then she stripped away her dress and threw it into the corner. She untied the pantaloons and let them fall. Before she took off her stockings she washed herself, gingerly applying the wash cloth to her thighs and the tender, throbbing area between them. She rinsed the cloth in the bowl and could not help but notice that the water was soon tinged pink from her virgin's blood.

Her valise was still downstairs, but her other things were nowhere in sight. She pulled a man's silk gown from the closet and wrapped herself in it. The silk was smooth and cool against her overheated skin. Her fingers trembled as she took off the earrings and necklace Jason had given her. With a last glimpse

in the mirror, she noted the disbelief in the dull eyes that stared
back at her. But there was nothing she could do tonight. It was
well past midnight.

She went into the bedroom again, determined to get some
rest before she confronted Jason in the morning.

J.T. lay in bed in a darkened room down the hall, his eyes
covered by the crook of his arm. He couldn't get Jade out of his
mind.

He would not blame her if she had left, but he had not heard
her go. Nor did he expect it of her tonight—it was too late for
her to set out alone.

Since sleep was impossible, he spent an hour listening
intently to be certain she did not try anything as stupid as
leaving in the dark. Finally, when the house was so still that all
he could hear was his own heartbeat, he worried that she might
somehow have eluded him after all. He rose, naked, and crept
down the hall.

At the door to the master suite, he paused and listened, but
heard nothing. He pushed the door open and silently stepped
inside. As he drew near the bed, he could barely make out
Jade's silhouette beneath the bedclothes. She was curled on her
side, her legs drawn up protectively, and much to his chagrin,
she was sleeping.

Well, why not? He shrugged. She had everything she
wanted. She had gotten him to marry her without having to
crook her little finger. Now, because of his unbridled lust, their
marriage had even been consummated. She had every reason to
sleep peacefully.

He grew hard just looking at her. Pushing aside any regret he
was just beginning to feel for using her so callously, J.T.
thought about her lost innocence. She had offered no resistance
when he took her, which only led him to conclude that she was
willing to submit in order to further entrap him.

The longer he watched her sleep—stood listening to her soft,
even breathing, and breathed deeply of the orange blossom
scent in the room—the more determined he became to hold
Jade to her marriage vows. Why should he let her go now?
After all, she had tricked him into this marriage. To release her

from this bond would be far too easy on her. Theirs might be a loveless union, but at least he could make it convenient for himself. Marriage meant he could have Jade anytime he wanted her. Jason smiled a joyless, cynical smile.

The longer he stood and stared down at her lying there in his bed, the more he knew that there would be no divorce. No annulment.

✠ CHAPTER 14 ✠

It is easy to know men's faces . . .
But not their hearts.

J.T. had not slept all night. His eyes itched, his head ached. Seated on the side of the bed, he pulled on his boots and reached for his hat. He ran his hand along its crown before he put it on, and then walked over to the chair where he had tossed his saddlebags the night before.

The sun was up, but the day was gray and overcast, adding to the heaviness in his heart. He gave the room one last glance to be certain he had all of the things he would take with him to Monterey. Last night he had grabbed his pants, vest, and a clean shirt, and then shoved his razor, leather strop, and shaving soap into the saddlebag before he left the master suite. For a tense moment he thought he might have to go back, until he remembered that his duster was downstairs in the hall closet. He wanted to leave before Jade woke up.

The kitchen was cold and damp. He lit a fire in the stove and set some coffee on to boil before he went out to feed El Sol. When he returned from the stables, the coffee was ready. As he poured himself a steaming cupful, he heard a knock at the front door.

Coffee cup in hand, he went to answer it. Matt Van Buren stood on the doorstep. The man started to say hello, but stopped and stared at Jason intently.

"You look like hell. What's wrong?" Matt asked.

"Come in."

Matt followed Jason back to the kitchen. Still silent, Jason sat at the worktable in the middle of the room. Matt looked through the cupboards, found a cup, and poured himself some coffee. "Well?"

Jason shook his head. "I'd rather not talk about it, Matt. Not now."

"Is Jade all right?"

"She's asleep."

Matt did not push for further explanation. Instead, he reached inside his coat and withdrew a bulky envelope. "Here's the cash you wanted for the trip to Monterey."

Jason's tone was grim. "Thanks."

"Jason, look, I know it's none of my business but—"

J.T. couldn't put what had happened into words. Even if he tried, he didn't want to hear Matt say, "I told you so."

"You're right," he said, pinning Matt with a chilling stare. "It isn't any of your business."

Jade sat up in bed and pushed her hair away from her face. She pulled the edges of the silken robe together, threw back the covers, and stood, amazed to discover her legs were still able to support her. She had expected to feel worse.

Pausing to listen for some indication that Jason was up and about, she walked to the door and opened it as silently as possible. Jade walked down the hall, carefully opening and closing doors, but in each room all she saw was furniture draped with holland covers. The house was cold and damp; not a single fire was lit in any of the fireplaces. Although the rooms were huge and well appointed, there was a feeling of lifelessness about the place.

Near the end of the long hall she came to a door that was already open. Screwing up her courage, she glanced inside. The curtains were open, the bed unmade. Tentatively, she stepped over the threshold and peered around.

Jason was gone.

Relieved, she decided to slip downstairs. Before she faced him, she needed a strong cup of coffee.

Jade was halfway down the staircase when she heard Jason's voice echoing in the foyer below. She recognized Matt Van Buren's hushed tones, and wondered if Jason had already taken steps to end their marriage.

Tempted to run back to the safety of the suite, Jade paused in the middle of the staircase and held her breath. Suddenly aware of her presence, Jason spun around and stared up at her.

Her heart contracted at the sight of him, but the first thing she noticed was that his stunning blue eyes were still shadowed with distrust and anger. She would have given anything at that moment to see him look at her the way he had before last night.

J.T. stared up at Jade and cursed himself because he wanted her more than ever. She looked warm and kissable—the way a woman should look in the morning. Her hair, a wild cape about her shoulders, demanded to be touched. Her lips were full, the lower one slightly bruised and pouting. The fact that he had done her that slight harm did little to ease his already strained composure. She had on the peacock blue silk robe he had seen hanging in his father's closet. He watched her nervously push back the sleeves that hung to her fingertips. Her bare toes peeked out from beneath the hem. J.T. didn't have to open the robe to know she wore nothing underneath, for the silk caressed every inch of her.

Matt cleared his throat and tried to slip away, but Jason stopped him. "I'm leaving for Monterey," he said abruptly, his eyes on Jade. "I'll be back as soon as I've bought the horses I want." His narrowed gaze preceded the ultimatum he then issued to her. "I'll expect *you* to be here when I get back."

Without waiting for her response, he turned to Matt. "See that my *wife* has whatever she wants. She earned it last night." With that, he left them both to stare after him.

Jade was too humiliated to move as she held the robe closed at her throat. Matt coughed again uncomfortably and waited until they heard the back door slam, then walked to the bottom of the stairs and said, "There's hot coffee in the kitchen. It looks like you need a cup."

Attempting to smile, Jade felt her lips tremble and cursed her own weakness. "That would be fine," she said as she made her way down the stairs.

The kitchen, at least, was warm and welcoming. When she was finally seated at the same table where she and Jason had shared lunch that first day, Matt stoked the fire in the stove, served her a cup of coffee, and then refilled his own.

"Now, maybe you should tell me what's going on," he said quietly.

Jade looked at the man seated across from her. His open expression told her that he, unlike Jason, was willing to listen. In many ways he reminded her of a school boy, with his unlined face, sandy hair, and thick spectacles. The way he wore his high, round collar added to his scholarly demeanor. He certainly lacked the aura of masculinity that Jason exuded.

She did not know this man at all, but he was her husband's attorney. She had to talk to someone.

She started slowly, and over the next hour told Matt about her arrival in San Francisco, the details as she knew them about her father's murder, and Babs' plan for her to marry someone with money. As she explained how she had met Jason, how she was deserted by Babs at his front door, Jade could not help but realize how calculated it all sounded, even to her own ears. She went on to tell him that she had had no intention of marrying Jason at all. She told him of her attraction to J.T., the circumstances that led him to propose—which Matt said he already knew—and of how she had decided, even before the wedding, to turn her adobe and the Chinese collection over to the bank.

"I would have given over the adobe to pay the debts before the ceremony, but we had only one day to make all the preparations and there was simply no time," she finished.

She leaned back in her chair and toyed with the handle of her cup, then said, "Matt, I looked forward to a new life with Jason. I was even growing excited about moving to New Mexico. Then, last night after the ceremony, Babs confessed that she was the one who sent the *Chronicle* reporter here to interview Jason. She knew the man would find out we had been together and that the scandal would push Jason into marriage. I don't know how much of it Jason heard, but he most certainly didn't hear my shock and objection. I was on the way to tell him what Babs had said, when he burst into the room and confronted me.

"He thinks I only married him for his money," she said. She leaned forward, desperate to have this man believe her. "Nothing could be farther from the truth."

"I'll help in any way I can," he said.

"I never expected you to believe me."

"To be honest, neither did I. I even warned Jason away from you when he said he was going to propose. But I know Babs Barrett, and I know all about her hare-brained schemes.

Besides, I'm a fairly good judge of character. It's my job to know when someone is telling the truth. Now, what can I do?"

"I would like for you to deliver the deed to the Page adobe to Arnold Arvin at the Hibernia Bank. I'm hoping the land will help pay off some of my father's debt. Tell him," she added, drawing a shuddering breath, "tell him that I have decided against taking the collection back. They can keep that, too." She thought of the jade pieces, the paintings, the everyday implements that were decorative in and of themselves. Each item had been painstakingly categorized and dated by her grandfather. He had held each of them lovingly in his hands; they were as much a part of Philo Page as they were of China. But the collection meant nothing to her now that it had cost her happiness and brought Jason's distrust. "If that is not enough, please let me know, and I will find a way to get the rest of the money."

When she leaned her forehead on her hands, her hair fell forward like a curtain about her face. She tried to shut out the pain, tried to pull into the center of herself and know that this day would pass, but her mind was still reeling from all that had happened in the last few hours.

"Where is the title to your grandfather's home?" Matt asked softly.

She wiped her eyes on the wide sleeve. "Upstairs with my things."

"It's very likely the land itself is worth a small fortune."

"What makes you think so?" Why, she wondered, was she so very knowledgeable about things that were worthless and so lacking when it came to the practical side of life?

Matt carefully explained. "There's very little land around here that hasn't been bought up by the railroad or isn't still part of an original land grant. Whenever a piece of property opens up, no matter how small, it is usually sold for an exorbitant sum. The city is spreading faster than a wildfire."

He looked thoughtful for a moment before he asked, "If you had this Chinese collection, what would you do with it?"

She shrugged, and the robe started to slip off one shoulder. Coloring, she grabbed it and pulled it back into place. "Grandfather's dream was to house it in a museum, a place people could go to see the collection and learn about Chinese

culture." She looked thoughtful for a moment. "I would foun
one in his name."

Matt drummed his fingers on the tabletop as he stared at th
brick wall behind them. Suddenly he snapped his fingers.

"What?" She said, feeling a small stirring of hope.

"Did you ever stop to think of how a museum operates?"
She shook her head.

"They are funded by wealthy patrons, people willing t
donate money to a museum foundation."

"Mr. Van Buren, I don't think the good people of Sa
Francisco would be willing to lend me anything. Not now."

"The name's Matt. And I think you might be wrong. You'r
a wealthy woman now—"

She snapped to life, her tone angry. "I won't take a nickle
Jason's money. Not one cent."

"You might not have to, at least no more than a loan."

"No!"

He ignored her protest. "As the wife of one of the wealthie
men of San Francisco, you will, despite what you think, b
quite a curiosity to the society crowd. Money sometimes eras
all manner of scandal, especially here. If you were to spons
a certain worthwhile cause, such as saving this collection
rare Chinese art—"

"The pieces are not all that rare," she interrupted. "They'
merely representative of Chinese culture and history."

"That's beside the point. You know as well as I do th
lengths San Franciscans will go to just to prove they have
much culture as Easterners or Europeans. Why do so many
the city's debutantes find it necessary to travel to Europe
marry titled men? Why rush to establish the opera, the theate
Why is it the first thing a new-made millionaire invests in
art? These newly rich haven't been raised with culture, so th
buy it. All you need to do is host one afternoon tea or a soire
and display the pieces. Educate them, tell your guests—wl
will be among the crème de la crème of the city—that you a
willing to donate all of the pieces to a museum when there
a place to house them. You'll need to raise enough money
hire a curator, too, assuming you don't want to care for the
yourself."

Jade was astounded. The plan was so very simple, she wondered why she had not thought of it herself, until she realized she had been out of touch with San Francisco society for so long it would never have occurred to her that there might be the slightest interest in the collection. She felt a glimmer of excitement.

"What do you think?" Matt asked.

Forgetting the bruise, she toyed with her bottom lip and then winced. "I can't let myself get excited until you go to the bank and find out exactly what I have in assets. And I meant what I said. I won't use any of Jason's money."

"Not even on loan?"

"Not even then."

Matt shook his head. "I know he loves you, Jade," he said honestly.

"Loved," she corrected.

"*Loves*. Give him time to cool off. Try to reason with him again. He'll get over it."

She looked at him, her eyes full of pain. "I don't think so. Too much has happened."

"Give it time." He reached into his pocket again and withdrew some cash. "I'm leaving this with you. From what I can see, this place needs some staples and you should look into hiring some help, even if it's temporary."

"Please, Matt, I don't want your charity."

He shook his head with a smile. "Don't worry. I'm your husband's lawyer. I'll see that he gets the bill."

She looked around the cavernous room. "I don't belong here, but there's nowhere else to go."

He shrugged. "Jason will be gone at least a good week. You have until then to get your own life straightened out. Things will look different by then, and you can work on setting Jason straight."

A vision from last night flashed before her eyes. She closed them momentarily until it passed. In a voice that was a mere whisper she said, "I don't know if things will ever be the same again."

"Do you love him?"

She searched his face, then let her gaze drop to the tabletop.

It was hard to face the truth, even after the way J.T. had treated her. "Yes," she whispered.

She reminded herself so much of her mother then that she felt physically ill. She had become everything she had sworn she never would! How many times had she seen her mother weep over her father's latest indiscretion? How many times had Melinda Douglas used tears and money to win back her husband's love?

So many things were fast becoming clear to Jade. It had been easy to judge her mother, easy to be so very wrong. She understood now why Melinda Douglas had endured pain and heartache. The woman had truly loved Fredrick Douglas.

Jade wondered how far she would allow herself to go before she gave Jason up forever.

Matt reached out to pat her hand. "I'll go to the bank today. Is there anything else you need right now? From everything you told me concerning the tong and your near-abduction, I would suggest you take care. Don't go out. Buy whatever you need from the vendors that come to the door."

Jade had a sudden thought and asked, "Will you get word to Detective Chang that I want to see him?"

"Of course."

They stood and Jade reached out for his hands. "Thank you Matt. I don't know what I would have done without you. As I said before, I never expected you to believe me."

"All we can do is hope Jason will be half as receptive when he gets back," Matt replied.

Jade spent her first day alone exploring the cavernous mansion. Aside from the drawing room, the kitchen, and the foyer—with its sixty-foot ceiling topped by a domed skylight—she found a small parlor and two servants' bedrooms just off the kitchen. There was a pantry bigger than the help's parlor, and a service porch that ran the length of the back of the house. Further exploration revealed a library, lined floor to ceiling with books so new their spines were still uncreased. Ebony-paneled walls inlaid with ivory gave the room a closed-in warmth that the rest of the house was lacking. The dining room was seventy-five feet long. With additional tables sixty guests could easily be served. She gasped aloud when she threw open the double doors that led to the ballroom, then quickly closed them again.

As she roamed from room to room, she tried to imagine the house as it might have been when Jason's father was alive. There was nothing in the mansion that told what manner of a man he had been— no personal items other than his clothing. The place was so devoid of personality that she wondered if he really ever lived here at all.

Everything in the house was of the finest quality. Cut velvet draperies covered the windows, plush Turkish carpets protected the floors. As she wandered through the upstairs, Jade decided on the bedroom she wanted for her own. It was the smallest and coziest of the lot, the walls covered in yellow and gold striped paper. Swagged emerald drapes revealed Belgian lace curtains beneath. It was not as ostentatious as some of the other rooms, but she liked it because it had wide corner windows that looked out over the back garden and the stables. When she removed the dust covers, she discovered a library table that she immediately shoved across the room until it stood beneath the windows. It would be a good place to read and study.

She found her belongings had been delivered to the bedroom adjoining the master suite, and hauled them to her room. Since she did not know how long she would be staying once Jason returned, she unpacked a minimum of clothing. Then she took the time to uncrate her favorite books and stack them on the desk, along with some of her grandfather's papers. Alongside them she placed her horsehair brushes and a bottle of ink. When she had her things in order, she would practice writing Chinese characters.

As she carried her things in from the other room, she found it impossible not to let her thoughts drift to Jason. Matt said the trip to and from the Monterey Peninsula would take him at least a week. Jade knew that the only way she would be able to wait out the days would be to keep herself busy. It would not be wise to spend the time speculating on whether or not Jason would be of a mind to hear her out when he returned.

She would take one day at a time. At the Barretts' she had

longed for peace and quiet. Now that her wish had been granted, the emptiness of the mansion threatened to close in on her.

By evening she had her room arranged and had even found time to read and practice writing her Chinese. It was dusk before she thought about having something to eat, and her head was beginning to ache. She realized she had taken nothing but coffee and some stale bread at noon. As she was walking along the upper hallway, she thought she heard someone knock on the door downstairs and called out for them to wait.

Peering through the stained glass panels beside the door, she recognized Matt Van Buren and quickly let him in.

"Hello!" He moved past her into the foyer and looked around. "You need some light in here."

"I just came down," she explained as he set down the box he was holding and began to light the lamps. There was an overwhelming scent of sesame oil in the room. "What have you done?" She peered into the box he had set on a side table.

"I hadn't eaten and knew you were here alone without much in the pantry so I stopped by a Chinese restaurant and had them make up two covered plates for me."

"Wonderful!" she cried. He could not have thought of anything that would please her more.

"Don't let me forget the dishes though. They charged me a deposit, which will be returned if and when I take the dishes back."

"Whatever you paid, it was worth it," she said after inhaling the delicious odor again. "Is the kitchen all right? Or would you like to eat in the dining room?"

"The kitchen is fine."

Jade was relieved with his choice. She found the dining room far too imposing. The long, shining stretch of mahogany table surrounded by empty chairs would only call attention to the cavernous loneliness of the house.

Once they had eaten, both relishing the food and praising the cook, Matt gave Jade the news of his visit to the bank. "You'll be happy to know the property your grandfather left you is worth five times what he paid for it thirty years ago. And there's no problem as to his claim to it and his right to pass it on to you. Oftentimes land titles granted before statehood are found to be invalid, but your grandfather had new papers registered in 1850."

"Will it be enough to pay off the debts?"

Matt smiled and relaxed against the back of the chair. "The land is close enough to town to be highly desirable. Arvin says he even has a buyer interested in it. The bank is willing to accept it as payment for the debt and will return the art collection to you. And, you'll even have a small nest egg left over for yourself. They promised to have the crates delivered to you before the week is out." He crossed his arms and smiled a satisfied smile.

Instead of responding happily, Jade stared at him for a moment before she frowned and shook her head. Had she contacted a lawyer instead of listening to Babs or trying to find a way to save the collection on her own, she could have prevented this whole affair. But then, she thought sadly, she would have never met Jason.

"I would have thought you'd be a lot happier with the news," Matt said.

"I feel so ridiculous." She looked around the room, indicating the mansion with a wave. "None of this would have happened if I had handed the property over to the bank when I first arrived."

"You don't know anything about land values, and with the house in such disrepair it's no wonder you thought the place was worthless. Don't berate yourself, Jade. Go on from here."

"That's all I can do, Matt. But at least your news has given me a chance to start over." She did suddenly brighten as she realized she would have her own money and would not be beholden to Jason for anything.

"If all this hadn't happened, you would never have met Jason."

She traced the edge of the table with her thumbs. "No. No, I wouldn't have."

"And you love him, don't you Jade?" he asked softly.

She was surprised by Matt's frankness, but she answered again without hesitation. "Yes, I do."

"Then I hope things work out for you."

Matt stood up and prepared to leave, remembering to take the two covered dishes with him. Jade laughed when she walked him to the door, watching him balance the heavy china in both hands.

She opened the door for him, and he paused on the threshold to tell her that Detective Chang would be calling on her in the morning.

"Lock the door," he admonished, "and by tomorrow night I'll have someone here to help you."

"Please, don't worry with that. You've done so much for me already. Besides, I have the perfect servant in mind."

"I hope you find him."

"Oh, I will. I plan to ask Detective Chang to help."

Lieutenant Chang was as good as his word and arrived just after ten o'clock the next day. Jade told him of her recent marriage to Jason Harrington, which she learned he had already read about in the *Chronicle*. He congratulated her, then listened carefully as she made her request known. She asked for his help, described exactly the type of houseboy she was looking for, and was more than pleased when he said he thought he knew just the right man for the job.

Two hours later, she responded to a knock at the back door and ushered a young Chinese boy named Tao Ling into the house.

He was much younger than she had expected, and for a moment she doubted whether or not he had the special skills she would require of her house servant. He was tall, well muscled, yet thin. He moved with supple grace. His face was unlined, his dark eyes reflecting his intelligence. She was pleased when he bowed low and introduced himself in flawless English.

"Detective Chang told you the requirements for the position?" she asked.

"Yes."

"And you are qualified?"

"Yes." He bowed again. "I can cook, manage a household, decoct medicine, read and write English, and if you wish I can keep your accounts."

"And—"

"And I will serve as your personal bodyguard to see that no harm comes to you."

"You look so young," she said.

"I am twenty." He bowed again. "Born right here in San Francisco. And," he added with a broad grin, "I am wise for my years."

Jade could not help but smile. She liked this young man immediately. "You are certain you can protect me?"

"Should I demonstrate my skill?"

She shook her head. "No. I'm sure Detective Chang would not have sent you unless he knew that you would meet all my requirements. Did he tell you why I need a bodyguard?"

"May I speak frankly?"

"Of course."

"I know why you need a bodyguard. Your father's death is the talk of Little China."

"Are you a member of a tong?"

"Yes—"

She knew a moment of fear, but then she placed her trust in Detective Chang and relaxed.

Tao Ling continued, "—but the tong is not after you, Mrs. Harrington. The men who accosted you on the street work alone."

"Why?"

He shrugged. "Chang recently learned that the tong is no longer involved, but he is having a hard time learning anything else about the case."

"Consider yourself hired, Tao Ling. You may move into one of the bedrooms off the kitchen. The small parlor beside it is for your use."

"Very good, Mrs. Harrington. Does this house have a library?"

"Yes, it does."

"May I avail myself of the books?"

"Of course . . . if you'll promise to speak to me in Chinese on occasion. I want to keep my skills alive."

He bowed, and answered her in Cantonese. "I would be pleased. I would also like to teach you how to defend yourself, Mrs. Harrington. Some simple movements . . ."

She hesitated. "I . . . I don't know."

"Please think about it."

"I will," she promised. "That's all for now. You will need to get yourself settled." Then Jade took a deep breath and looked him square in the eye. "Please remember that I am the one who has hired you. I will be paying your wages. You work for me. When my husband returns at the end of the week, I will expect you to sleep on a pallet outside my door. He is not to enter my room unless I give my permission."

"I understand," he said, his expression unreadable. "I will collect my humble belongings and return within the hour."

❈ CHAPTER 15 ❈

While one misfortune is going,
To have another coming
Is like trying to drive a tiger out the front door
While a wolf is entering the back.

With three unopened letters in one hand, Jade closed her bedroom door and then crossed the room to her desk. She was more than comfortable in the room she had chosen at Harrington House. The floral-brocade chaise near the corner window offered just the right comfort and light for reading. Her desk, standing beneath the opposite window, always beckoned. The cheerful yellow and deep forest green of the wall coverings, bedclothes, and drapes were peaceful colors that soothed her whenever she sought solace in the room. Thanks to Tao Ling's efforts, everything was neat and tidy—except for her desk. Jade had told him not to bother with it, for she worked better surrounded by the familiar clutter of her books and papers.

Tao Ling proved to be a perfect houseboy. He attended to every task without having to question Jade as to how the work was to be performed. At the end of three days, the rooms they had decided to open were aired and dusted, the upstairs bedding changed. Cut flowers from the garden were distributed in the only rooms that they used—the foyer, drawing room, kitchen, and her own. She had also directed Tao to place cuttings in Jason's suite so that he could enjoy them when he returned. The colorful blooms helped give life to the otherwise mournful rooms.

She glanced out the window at the stables and wondered when Jason would return. He had been gone five days now, and with each passing hour she felt her apprehension build. Jade found herself listening for the jingle of his spurs, for the even tread of his footsteps down the long hallway. Each day at sunset, she wondered if he would arrive sometime during the night. If so, would he come looking for her? Each morning at sunrise, she wondered if this would be the day he returned.

To take her mind off of Jason, she looked down at the letters in her hand and shook her head. Matt Van Buren had delivered them just minutes ago. Two were from Babs, the other was for Jason from New Mexico.

She set Jason's letter atop a sheaf of papers on the desk. Then, she took up the heavier letter in a large vellum envelope that simply read, *For Jade*, in Babs' distinctively embellished handwriting. When she slit the envelope open, she found another envelope inside. A cursory glance attested to the fact that it was a letter from her father addressed to her residence in Paris and then forwarded to the Barretts. Her hands shook as she slipped her letter opener beneath the flap and neatly sliced it open.

The single-page letter was penned in her father's bold script, his words reaching out from the grave to haunt her. She tried to imagine his voice as she read aloud the words that had been written with an uncustomary tone of excitement and expectation:

"Daughter. I am writing to tell you that I am on the brink of possessing untold riches. I have devoted two years to this endeavor, and although I am nearly out of resources, I am confident that my present condition is merely temporary. I have discovered a way to achieve wealth beyond comprehension. Be advised that until I am able to acquire the capital I need to pay off certain debts, I am turning your grandfather's accumulation of Chinese objects over to the Hibernia Bank. Knowing you expected to claim them as part of your own inheritance, I feel it necessary to alert you to the fact that the pieces were not mentioned in his will and so rightfully reverted to me, as your mother's beneficiary. Fredrick Douglas."

She let the curt letter drop to the tabletop. *Wealth beyond comprehension*. The phrase echoed in her mind. Riches. Gold. Alchemy.

As bizarre as the story seemed, she had believed her father guilty of abducting the Chinese wizard the minute Lieutenant Chang had told her about the motive for Fredrick Douglas' murder. Now, in his own words, her father alluded to some fantastic money-making scheme. She could only assume it involved the missing wizard.

But if the alchemist *had* arrived in California, where was he now? Had her father masterminded the plan alone, or was Li Po now in the hands of an accomplice?

She refolded her father's letter, slipped it back into the envelope, and reminded herself to contact the detective. Then she picked up the enclosed letter and unfolded it. It was a note from Babs, begging her for forgiveness and asking for permission to call.

After she read the request, Jade ripped the page in half, balled it up, and set it aside. Elbows propped on the desk, she leaned her chin in her hands and stared down at the stables. Although she cared very little for horses, the long, low building seemed forlorn without the four-legged occupants it was meant to house. She reminded herself that all too soon the thoroughbreds Jason had gone to purchase would fill the empty stalls. And all too soon, she would have to face Jason Harrington again.

Even the swiftest horse cannot overtake the word once spoken.

How true, Jade thought, when the proverb came to mind. And how very sad. If only she could call back Babs' admission of deceit that Jason had overheard on their wedding night, they might have been able to go blissfully on their way, none the wiser. Now he blamed her for her friend's misdeeds. Jade would never forgive Babs for her meddling.

Tao Ling tapped softly at the door and Jade stood to answer his summons. Unable to shake her gray thoughts, she forced a smile when she faced him. Ever correct, dressed in a white Mandarin jacket, black trousers, and low-heeled slippers, he bowed. His queue was twisted into a figure-eight and pinned to his crown. He looked at her speculatively.

"A woman is downstairs asking to see you, Mrs. Harrington. Her name is Mrs. Barrett."

So, it had come to this. Jade had hoped never to have to face Babs again and had thought it would be enough not to respond to her notes, but as always, Babs had not waited for a reply. The woman had done irreparable harm to her marriage, and Jade could not find it in her heart to forgive her.

Jade shook her head. "Tell her I don't wish to see her. Tell her—" She paused, then shook her head again, refusing to take the coward's way out. "No. I will see her." She stiffened her resolve, knowing Babs would never take a simple no for an answer. What Jade needed to say had to be said face-to-face. She would deal with Babs now and be done with it.

She stepped by Tao Ling, who bowed again as she passed. Her black silk slippers sank into the rich Turkish carpet runner, silencing her steps. Color flared in her cheeks—she could feel it—even as she fought to appear outwardly calm. As she descended the stairs, Jade straightened the cuffs of her prim, high-collared blouse and ran her fingertips around the waistband of her gray serge skirt to be certain the blouse was neatly tucked in.

She paused at the top of the stairs and stared down at Babs. Perfectly outfitted in a burgundy morning dress of taffeta, her shining dark hair cascaded in a waterfall of ringlets from the crown of her head. Babs looked far more suited to life at Harrington House than she herself did, Jade decided.

Babs was waiting expectantly in the foyer, twisting the ties of her reticule in her gloved hands. She started forward as Jade reached the last few steps.

"Oh, Jade, I'm so glad you'll see me! You don't know how sorry I am. I just had to talk to you."

Cool and aloof on the outside, her stomach invaded by a thousand butterflies, Jade walked toward the drawing room. "Please, come in and have a seat."

Babs perched on the edge of the settee; Jade chose to stand before the fireplace. A low fire, the wood nearly reduced to ash and glowing coals, pulsed behind the grate. The remaining embers popped and hissed. As if objecting to death, they died explosively. Despite the heat from the fire, Jade was suddenly chilled, and thrust her hands behind her to warm them. She tried to avoid Babs' pitiful look of contrition.

Tao Ling hovered in the doorway. "Would you like me to serve tea, Mrs. Harrington?"

"Oh, that would be lovely, Jade," Babs said.

"No. Thank you, Tao Ling. Mrs. Barrett will not be staying."

The young man in the doorway bowed and slipped away quietly.

Babs' eyes flooded with unshed tears. "Please, Jade. Don't let this ruin our friendship—"

Jade held up her hand. "Our friendship, Babs, is over. If I were to forgive what you have done, it would be the same as condoning your actions."

"I did it for you," Babs said, her usual deep complexion stained with color. Her dark-eyed gaze flashed to the fireplace and back to Jade again. "I only wanted to see you well-settled."

"Your meddling has not only ruined my life, but Jason's. To make matters worse, I have learned that the land I held title to was worth more than enough to pay off father's debts. The Chinese collection will be returned to me tomorrow. So you see, Babs," Jade said sadly, "I didn't need to marry anyone. I should have seen to my own interests before I let you manipulate me."

"Jade—"

"I'm not through. In the short time I stayed with you and Reggie, it became clear to me that we no longer have anything in common, and—although that's no reason to discount years of friendship—it helped me to make the decision to exclude you from my life. Because of you, I am in a tenuous situation, married to a man who does not love or trust me. I doubt if he ever will again. I don't know what decision he will come to once he returns, nor do I know what I will do about this so-called marriage. What I do know is that I will no longer let myself be controlled by anyone or any circumstance."

"I'll talk to him," Babs volunteered, not fully comprehending Jade's blunt delivery.

"You've done enough."

"But surely you can't leave things as they are between us. I'd like to help you, Jade, since this is all my fault."

"Things will evolve on their own."

"Sometimes I hate that stoic philosophy of yours."

"I think we've said enough," Jade said quietly.

As Jade stared down at her, unwilling to say more, Babs' expression slowly became closed and sullen. She stood, pulled on the hem of her fitted jacket to straighten it, and assumed her own frosty stare. "I can see there's no talking to you. Your mind is made up."

"I'm glad you understand. I'd like you to leave now."

Without a word, Babs gathered up her taffeta skirt and whisked out of the room. Tao Ling was waiting at the front door, which he opened with a grand flourish as Babs brushed past. The last Jade saw of her was a flash of burgundy as the carriage door slammed shut.

Tao closed the door and smiled sadly. *"Hide your offended heart, keep your valued friend,"* he said sagely.

"There are times a woman should not hide her offended heart. Babs is no longer a valued friend, Tao. Too much has happened."

"Would you care for a cup of herb tea?" he asked.

She nodded, looking forward to the welcome warmth of the kitchen. Perhaps it would drive some of the chill from her heart.

In three short days, Tao Ling had made the kitchen his domain. He did the daily marketing, most often buying staples from the Chinese vendors who traveled door-to-door with their baskets of wares balanced on long poles supported across their shoulders. She left the menus up to him, and so far had been pleased with everything he prepared. He alternated between Chinese delicacies—roasted duck, egg rolls, wonton—and more simple fare, such as fish, steamed vegetables, and rice. He assured her he could prepare American meals as well, which she knew Jason would prefer.

As he measured the dry bohea tea leaves into a pot, she sat at the worktable lost in thought. Now she was truly alone. Babs, her last close tie to San Francisco, was out of her life forever.

As if he sensed her preoccupation, Tao drew her attention to the row of covered jars and crocks on a shelf above the dry sink. "Are you familiar with Chinese medicines, Mrs. Harrington?"

"A little," she admitted, suddenly attentive.

"My cousin owns an apothecary shop in Little China. I have

helped him out over the years. Perhaps you would like me to mix a curative for you?"

She smiled. "What makes you think I need one?"

"Your wistful smile. A faraway look in your eyes. The sadness of parting with a once-valued friend."

"What would you prescribe?"

He took down a small blue and white porcelain jar and wrinkled his nose. "Definitely not ground turtle shells. They are for weak kidneys."

"No, thank you."

Reaching for a corked amber-glass bottle, he shook the liquid contents and extended it to her. "Toad secretions. Very good for dog bite."

"I don't think so," she said with a laugh, and quickly drew back her hand.

Happy to see her spirits somewhat lifted, he smiled too. "Castor bean?"

"I know that one," she interjected. "For hearing difficulties?"

"Yes. Good." He nodded, then grew serious. "Perhaps when your husband returns, I should make him a love potion of sparrows' tongues. It will make you mysteriously enticing to him."

She held up her hand. "Please don't." Jason had experienced no difficulty on their wedding night, even though he no longer found her mysteriously enticing.

The water in the kettle soon came to a boil. Tao filled the tea pot and set it before Jade. "Do you wish to settle your problems with your husband?"

Instead of being offended by his open question, she was relieved that she had someone to talk to. "I hope so, Tao. But he no longer trusts me. When he left here, he was furious."

"And so it is out of fear that you ask me to guard your door when he returns?"

"Let's just say, I will refuse to live with him as his wife while hatred and distrust reside in his heart."

"I know a fitting proverb for such a circumstance."

She blew on the steaming tea and set the cup down without taking a sip. "I might have guessed."

"Curse your wife at evening, sleep alone at night," he said.

As she stared down into the steaming brew, Jade felt certain that Jason would be home soon. Then she shivered with something far less than happy anticipation.

J.T. had cursed himself for his impulsive marriage proposal all the way to Monterey. As he had ridden along the cliffs beneath the leaden autumn skies and watched the stormy gray Pacific beat against the rocky shoreline, he called himself all the derogatory names he could think of, not the least of which were "damned fool" and "idiot."

He had reached Monterey in two days and easily located Don Carlos Batista, a rancher with one of the finest herds of California golden palominos in the land. Jason knew the value of horseflesh and found Don Batista's price far below what he had expected to pay, so he bought seven golden ones as well as two Appaloosas and three Arabians. When he asked if he might hire one of Batista's *remunderas* to help him drive the herd back to San Francisco, the *ranchero* found one of his own hands willing not only to accompany J.T. to the city, but to go all the way to New Mexico.

Xavier Rojas was as experienced a hand as Jason had ever hoped to find. Bowlegged, short of stature but broad on smiles, the Mexican was in his early fifties. He had recently lost his wife and—since his children were already grown—Rojas had no reason to stay on at the Batista Rancho. By the time the two men had driven the small herd up the coast to the outskirts of San Francisco, they had become friends. There was something comfortable about the elder man that put J.T. at ease the moment he had met him. Perhaps it was the warmth and offer of instant friendship behind the snapping dark eyes, or the quick, sincere smile beneath the man's heavy black mustache. Whatever the quality was, Jason could not help but admire Xavier's skill with the animals and sincere love of his work.

It was afternoon when they rode into San Francisco on little-used byways, each leading a *remuda* of horses behind him. As they neared Nob Hill, J.T. felt himself become as tight as an overwound clock. His feelings alternated between anticipation and dread of seeing Jade again. One part of him hoped she had stayed at the mansion, while another hoped she had cleared out. His emotions still in turmoil, he hoped he would know what to say and do when he saw her. Each time he tried to envision a reunion, all he could think of was the crass, uncaring way he had treated her on their wedding night.

By the time they entered the gate and started up the long drive to Harrington House, he had convinced himself there was no chance of finding Jade there. J.T. and Rojas led the horses up the drive and then, telling himself it did not matter, but anxious to see if Jade was in the house, Jason left Xavier to tend the animals while he went inside.

Ten crates had been delivered to Harrington House that morning—crates filled with various and sundry pieces of Chinese art and decorative everyday utensils that Philo Page had deemed worthy of study. Jade stared at the strange Chinese characters drawn on the top of the boxes, and wondered if her grandfather had had the goods packed before he died. Since he passed away in his sleep quite unexpectedly, she felt certain that the pieces had still been displayed in the collection room at the adobe until after he was gone.

She tried to translate the words, but found none of the characters familiar. Some were similar to what she had learned, but unique in form.

"Can you read these?" she asked Tao as they stood in the foyer surrounded by crates and barrels of goods.

He studied the characters on the box nearest him and shook his head. "It must be an old form of writing. Or, perhaps your grandfather tried to leave you a message in Chinese but couldn't write it very well."

Suddenly, Jade leaned down to touch the black characters atop a crate. She let her fingertips graze the rough wood as she frowned in thought. "Grandfather knew some Chinese, but not how to write it. These might have been his attempt to label the crates, if he did pack them but . . . maybe they were left by someone else . . . someone who might have used an archaic version of Chinese to keep his words secret . . . Maybe—"

Tao moved to her side. They stared at each other, then at the top of the nearest crate as realization dawned. "Li Po?" he whispered.

"Exactly," Jade said.

"But, when would he have had access to these?"

Jade folded her arms and sat on a barrel as she tried to piece together a logical explanation. "Grandfather died," she said, thinking aloud. "My father immediately took possession of everything that wasn't mentioned in the will, but since my name was on the deed to the adobe, he could not legally sell it or use it as collateral. He probably stripped the house and had these things crated up—but there was no hurry to move them while I was in Paris. There was no one to evict him from the house."

Tao, caught up in the story, continued for her. "Once crated, he could have stored them in the house until he needed them. And when the alchemist was brought to California—"

"—father kept him at the adobe, too." Jade stared down at the crates and shivered. "But where is he now?"

"Perhaps this writing holds the key to finding him."

Frustrated, Jade stared down at the crate in front of her and tried to make out the meaning of the characters. "Wait here," she told Tao, and left him to run up the stairs to her room. She looked through the stack of books on her desk until she found a heavy volume bound in leather with gold detail. After serving as a missionary in Canton and Macao for twelve years, Samuel Wells Williams had compiled the works, *The Middle Kingdom: A Survey of the Geography, Government, Education, Social Life, Arts, and Religion of the Chinese Empire*. Published in 1851, the volume was one of the foremost references on China. Book in hand, she ran back downstairs to where Tao Ling waited patiently.

She leafed through the book until she came to the section entitled, "Antiquity and Origin of the Characters." Her fingers flew over the pages, scrolling as she read until she suddenly stopped and smiled triumphantly. "Listen to this! 'Chinese philologists arrange all the characters in their language into six classes, called *luh shu*, or six writings.' " She glanced down the page and then continued, " 'These pristine forms have since been modified so much that the resemblance has disappeared in most of them.' "

"I'd say *all* resemblance has disappeared," Tao said as he walked around the crate to stare at the characters from another angle.

" 'The characters are more like drawings of actual objects. Over the years they were modified into the characters we have today.' " Jade abbreviated as she scanned the pages. " 'There are only six hundred and eight characters in *luh shu*.' "

Tao shrugged. "Perhaps that will make translation easier. There are over twenty-five thousand now."

She set the book aside, and with hands on hips made a decision. "First, these boxes need to be stored somewhere out of the way."

"May I suggest the ballroom?" Tao asked.

"You may." Jade glanced at the closed double doors to the room that opened off the foyer. "That way, we won't have to carry them very far. I'd like to open them first, just to see what's in each box. I'll make a notation, and then we'll be able to go through them in detail later. I can't wait to try to decipher these markings."

He nodded. "I will go get something to pry them open."

Jade was as excited as a child at Christmas, and Tao was soon caught up in her enthusiasm as he pried off the tops of each and every crate in turn and Jade delved through the contents.

"Look, Tao!" she would exclaim as she lifted one piece after another out of its wrapping. Then, "Here's the clay camel! This was my favorite when I was a little girl." Almost reverently, she replaced the camel in the box. They opened all the barrels and crates and she found rolled scrolls, the lacquerware, jade, bronzes, rice bowls, blue and white porcelain vases—everything in excellent condition. Thankful that her father had not sold the collection off piece by piece, she could not help but wonder if anything was missing. There did not seem to be, but she had not located the original list of items. Nor did it appear that Captain Lennox or any of the other seamen who brought pieces to Philo Page had added anything to the collection since she had left for Paris.

Tao opened the last box while Jade noted aloud how strange it was that this particular box had none of the mysterious characters painted on it. They even lifted it up to look underneath, but it was devoid of any markings whatsoever.

As the top came off, Jade could not help but peer over Tao's shoulder at the contents. They were stacked beneath an old, moth-eaten blanket that had seen better days. Jade recognized none of the jumbled things as having belonged to her grand-father. She reached down and gingerly touched one of the jars on top. "What do you make of this?" she asked Tao.

He lifted out a lidded basket and opened it to reveal what appeared to be a three-armed glass bulb that was inverted on legs.

"What is that?" She wanted to know.

"A still. Alchemists use them to heat, boil, or transmute one substance into another." He carefully replaced the still and hastily closed the lid as if he had just opened Pandora's box. "These things belong to the wizard. They are his tools."

As Jade stared down at the box, a terrible realization hit her. "If these are his things . . ."

"I fear the man is dead," Tao said sadly. "If he was not, then he would surely have taken these with him, wherever he is."

"Let's take this box and hide it in my room before we move the others."

"Will you tell the detective what you have found?"

She hesitated for a moment as she tried to put her thoughts into words. "Not just yet, so I would appreciate it if you didn't tell Lieutenant Chang about this. I want to go through this box carefully before I turn it over to him. I feel so responsible, even though I had nothing to do with my father's scheme, that I would like to help solve part of this puzzle myself. Do you understand?"

He took a while before he answered, as if he was weighing her sincerity. "I think so."

She stood at one end of the box and waited for Tao to grab the other. "Well, are you ready to help me get this upstairs?"

"The oxen are slow, but the earth is patient," Tao said with a smile.

* * *

Jason stripped off his gloves outside the service porch, doffed his hat, and used it to beat the trail dust from his pants. His vest hung open; his shirt was sweat stained beneath his long duster. He ran a hand through his hair, and then mentally scoffed at such unusual concern over his appearance. His gut tensed as he reached for the doorknob.

As he swung open the back door, he paused to look around. He knew instantly that Jade was still there—a milk pitcher of flowers sat in the center of the kitchen worktable, and the aroma of roasting poultry filled the air. Utensils and pans were out in plain sight, and the table was set for two.

He frowned as he stared down at the two place settings, then closed the door and proceeded down the hall. As he neared the foyer, J.T. heard voices and tried to place the distinctive male tone that mingled with one that was definitely Jade's. He entered the foyer without making a sound and stopped dead when he caught sight of Jade and a handsome Chinese man struggling to carry a heavy crate up the stairs. Not yet one third of the way up, they carefully balanced the heavy load between them.

The striking young man was dressed as most of the Chinese J.T. had seen—in a baggy white jacket and wide, loose-fitting pants. What amazed him was that Jade was dressed in much the same fashion. Her clothing was dark—navy he guessed, not quite black. Unlike the man's unadorned jacket, hers was quilted and shot through with gold thread. Her hair was a riot of rich color, a vibrant red-gold against the dark clothing. Her hair hung loose and flowing, the way he liked it best, untamed by combs or ribbons.

He watched in silence while the pair struggled and laughed together. They had not even heard him come in. His heart lurched when Jade suddenly turned her merry eyes in his direction. Her carefree expression vanished immediately. She nearly let go of her end of the box, but caught herself and hung on. The young man turned to see what had distracted her and immediately sobered. He studied Jason warily, his almond eyes narrowing, his gaze intense.

J.T. strode to the stairs.

"What are you doing?" he demanded.

Jade stared down at him, her heart pounding nearly out of her breast, her face suffused with warmth. As always, he seemed larger than life, a natural force that somehow dwarfed his surroundings. And as always, she felt her blood stir at the mere sight of him. She tried to find her voice.

Tao looked to her for direction.

"It's all right," she said. "This is my husband." Then, to Jason, "We're moving this crate up to my room."

"*Your* room?" He arched a brow.

"As opposed to your room. That is, unless you object."

He didn't know what to say. Relief at finding her still in residence swamped him. He watched her poised on the stairs, indecision playing across her finely sculpted features. Finally, he said, "What I object to is your carrying such a heavy box." He nodded toward the servant. "Who's this?" Was this the man she was to have supper with in the kitchen? He did not really believe Jade was the type to take up with a servant, but then he had not believed she would try to dupe him into marriage, and she had.

"This is my houseboy, Tao Ling."

"And what exactly does your houseboy do?" Jason looked Tao up and down.

Jade stood her ground. "Anything I ask him to do."

Ignoring her frigid tone, he asked, "What is all this?" He indicated the boxes stacked about the foyer.

"Those are my things."

"I wasn't aware of the fact that you had any things. Do these contain the famous Chinese pieces you sold yourself for?"

Jade steeled herself and indicated with a nod that Tao was to back down the stairs. When they reached the floor, they set the box down gently. "You may go, Tao. I wish to speak to my husband alone."

Jason could see that she was seething beneath her cool exterior and was amazed at her ability to appear calm. The Chinese balked at her order. Jason crossed his arms.

"Go," she told Tao. "I'll be fine."

"I will wait in the kitchen. If you need me, all you need to do is call."

She nodded as he slipped past Jason.

Jason watched the man until he disappeared down the hallway. "He thinks he has to defend you from me?"

"No. *I* think he has to defend me from *you*."

"And you think that boy can handle me?" Jason looked dubious.

"I know he can."

More than the box on the floor stood between them. Jade watched him warily. He looked dusty and tired, his deep-set eyes marred by dark circles. *Good,* she thought, *he hasn't gotten much more sleep than I.* She waited to hear what Jason had to say, but he looked as indecisive as she felt.

Finally, when he looked away he said, "I don't intend to apologize for what happened on our wedding night."

"I didn't expect you to," she said.

"What did you expect?"

I expected to live happily ever after.

She wondered just what she could say in answer to his question. What exactly had she expected? For him to have initiated her to the act of lovemaking with gentleness and caring even after he believed the worst of her?

"I expected just about what I got," she said.

His gaze cut back to her.

She met his stare, unflinching.

"I didn't rape you," he ground out, as if he had to remind her, or perhaps reassure himself.

"No," she agreed. "You didn't have to. I was more than willing to live up to my part of our bargain."

"Bargain? Is that what you thought we were getting into?"

She shook her head and the sight of her sunset hair rippling down her back, brushing her hips, drew his attention. "No. I thought we were getting married, pure and simple."

"There's nothing pure or simple about all this." He suddenly looked exhausted.

"Arguing isn't going to accomplish anything. You look tired, Jason. Why don't you go to your room and I'll send Tao Ling up with water for your bath. Have you eaten?"

"Are we to go on then as if nothing has happened? Is that what you want?" He wanted nothing more than to follow her suggestion, but not with so much still unsettled between them. With his hands shoved in his pockets, he waited for her answer.

She held her breath for a moment as she tried to put her feelings into words. Then, she looked down at her hands. "I want what you want, Jason. If you decide to throw me out of here, that's your prerogative, but I fully intend to live up to the vows I made on our wedding night." She drew herself up and met his penetrating stare. "With one exception."

His smile twisted. "Let's hear it."

"I will not be manhandled again, nor will I allow you to use me the way you did on our wedding night."

Without a word, J.T. brushed by her. Jade held her breath as he paused with one foot on the stairs. Jason turned to face her again, reached out and took her chin in his hand, tilted her face to his, and stared down into the depths of her emerald eyes. He was afraid to dwell too long on her lips, on the luxurious gold-tipped lashes that rimmed her eyes or the spattering of freckles across her nose. "Allow?" His husky voice was laced with sarcasm.

Fear made her weak. She didn't know what she was more afraid of, Jason or her own reaction to him. Jade willed herself not to cry out.

An almost imperceptible rustle of clothing caused J.T. to look away from her for a moment. He discovered Tao Ling standing an arm's length away. Jason had not even heard the man approach until he was nearly upon him. Tao stood poised with both arms raised, moving them in circles at cross angles to one another. His bizarre, defensive stance gave Jason pause. The servant appeared to be in a trance. His eyes were intent on Jason, who didn't know whether to laugh or take a swing at the Chinese. Pounds lighter, two inches shorter, Tao Ling did not seem to be any sort of a match for a man of Jason's stature. Still, his eyes held a definite warning that gave Jason pause. He released Jade's chin.

"What's he doing?" J.T. asked her.

The tense moment passed. Jade was hard-pressed to hide a smile, but did. "He is a kung fu master."

"Ah." Jason said, still staring at Tao. "What's a kung fu master?"

"Tao is trained in an ancient way of fighting. He can kill with his bare hands or feet."

Jason swung his gaze back to Jade. "Would you let him kill me?" His eyes bored into her.

Resolutely, Jade shook her head, stepped away from Jason, and folded her arms across her breast. "No, but maiming isn't out of the question."

It was J.T.'s turn to hide a smile as he stared down at his defiant wife and then at her strange bodyguard. It wasn't exactly the homecoming he had anticipated, but then again, nothing that had occurred since he'd met Jade Douglas had been what he expected. Dismissing them both, he shrugged and started back up the stairs.

Tao relaxed his stance and bowed to Jade, but refused to leave her side.

"I'll take you up on that bath," Jason said over his shoulder. "And don't move another box. I'll do it."

Jade sent Tao to heat the water.

Jason paused near the top of the stairs. His eyes blazed with fury as he looked down on her and said, "I should warn you—if and when I decide to bed you again, no one is going to stop me."

Jade waited until J.T. had disappeared down the hall and then, weak with relief, she sat down on a crate. Nothing had been settled, but at least he had not thrown her out into the streets. She still had a chance to convince him that she had married him because she loved him, that she had not simply duped him into an alliance. Seeing him tonight, feeling the rush of need that swept over her at the sight of him, only made her that much more determined to try and win back his trust, and then his love.

She looked up at the empty staircase and whispered, "*If* and *when* you bed me again it'll be on my own terms, Mr. Harrington. Just you wait and see."

CHAPTER 16

A wife should excel in four things . . .
Virtue, speech, person, and needlework.

Ignoring Jason's curt order to leave the boxes until he could help move them, Jade had Tao help her carry the alchemist's possessions up to her room. She tried to dismiss the fact that Jason had explicitly objected to her moving the heavy goods, but could not help but wonder if he was just being gentlemanly or if he truly cared about her. With Tao's help she set the box on the far side of the bed, then picked up her brushes, ink, and paper, and set out to copy some of the characters from the crates downstairs.

"Mrs. Harrington?" Tao interrupted her in the middle of copying the third set of markings. "There is a man at the back door who says he works for Mr. Harrington. He says Mr. Harrington wanted to see him when he finished with the horses."

Kneeling before a particularly large crate, Jade set down her brush and stood up. "Thank you, Tao. I'll go see what I can do while you see to Jason's bath."

Hat in hand, an older Mexican stood on the service porch. Jade noted there was not a touch of gray in the dark hair that had been flattened by his hat. His thick, drooping mustache was equally black, his eyes a deep rich brown. He introduced himself as Xavier Rojas, and told her in heavily accented English that he had hired on as Jason's hand.

"Did he say where you were to stay?"

"There is a room in the barn for a stablehand, one where I can be near the horses. I have already put my things there, but if the *senora* wants me to move?"

Jade brightened. The less confrontations she had with Jason, the better. "That is fine, Xavier. Are you hungry?"

"*Sí, senora. Tengo hambre.*"

"Come back in an hour and you can eat dinner with Tao, the cook, here in the kitchen."

"*Gracias, senora.*"

"*Senor*, wait." Jade stopped him before he left the porch. If she was going to gain Jason's trust and affection again, she needed to learn about things she could discuss with him. "Will you show me Jason's new horses?"

Xavier's smile widened. He shoved on his sand-colored *sombrero* and led the way as Jade studied his clothing. Heavy chamois panels tied at the waist protected his trousers, while ornate garters held leather leggings on below his knees. He was much shorter than she was, but he carried himself with pride as he opened the door to the stables.

The interior was cool and dark, silent except for the sounds of its inhabitants, who occasionally stamped, snorted, and whinnied to each other. Jade jumped when one of them kicked the side of the stall nearest her.

"It's all right, *senora*," Xavier said. "The golden ones will not hurt you. Come, see the finest of the lot. El Sol."

She followed him to the end of the building and then stopped a goodly distance from the end of the stall and stared at the beautiful creature housed there. The horse's white mane hung along its magnificent neck. His hide looked as rich as the finest velvet; the deep golden color gave testimony to his name, The Sun. El Sol pushed his muzzle toward her and bared his teeth.

Jade jumped back.

"*La senora* is afraid of him?" Xavier sounded amazed at her timidity.

Jade nodded. "I never liked horses very well."

He held El Sol's head and beckoned her near. "Come, *senora*, come and meet the golden one and then the others your *esposo* paid for so dearly. He is a proud of El Sol. You should be, too."

Tentatively, Jade reached out and touched the soft muzzle. El Sol did not flinch, but watched her with wise, dark eyes.

"El Sol will have many children," Xavier predicted. "He is strong as a bull. He makes a good mount for the *senor*. If you want to know him better, bring a carrot or an apple with you next time, and soon he will look forward to your visits."

Afraid to stand near the massive animal much longer, Jade stepped away and smiled her thanks at Xavier.

"Anytime, *senora*. If you would like me to teach you to ride, I will be happy to do so. I taught all my children before they could walk—I can teach you."

"Thank you, Xavier. It's certainly something to think about," she said before she turned away and whispered to herself, "but not for very long."

J.T. leaned back against the rim of the tub and drew on his thin cigar as he let the warm water ease his trail-weary muscles. He blew a smoke ring, then another, then closed his eyes and tried to banish the provocative images of his wife from his mind.

How many men had to talk themselves out of taking their own wife to bed, he wondered. He couldn't help but smile around the cigar clenched between his teeth. She'd made herself quite clear, even had the reed-thin Chinese houseboy to back up her words. Were they bluffing? He'd never heard of anyone who appeared so defenseless who knew how to kill a man with his bare hands. And hadn't she said feet, too? Well, he'd never eaten Chinese food before he came to San Francisco either, and considering how hungry he had been afterward, he could see how a race of starved men might just devise a way to kill each other with their bare hands.

He heard a slight knock on the outer door to his room and called through the bathroom doorway, "Come in." He suspected it was Tao Ling again with the clean towels he had promised.

When he didn't hear any response, Jason called out again. "Come in!"

"I am in."

His eyes flew open at the lyrical sound of Jade's voice outside the open door. She was standing far enough away that she could not see more than the lazy trail of smoke from his cigar and his head and shoulders above the rim of the tub, but she was close enough for him to see that she was blushing a high color. She held a tall vase of flowers in her hand. Folded towels hung over her arm and her eyes were as big around as two moons.

Stiffly, she turned away. He heard her moving about the outer room.

"I need one of those towels in here," he called to her.

A towel flew through the open doorway and landed on the floor near the tub.

"Supper's in thirty minutes," she called.

He stood up, intent on embarrassing her further. Water sloshed over the side of the tub onto hexagonal floor tiles. Before he even stepped out over the side, he heard the outer door slam.

Jason shook his head and chuckled to himself, amazed to discover he was actually glad to be back, and relieved to find Jade still here. With things still as unsettled as they were, he knew he could be assured that life with Jade in the house would never be boring.

The cigar was no longer satisfying. He pinched the butt end between his fingers and touched the smoking tip in the bathwater, then caught the butt tight in his teeth. Half the pleasure of smoking was chewing on the stub of the cigar. Water ran from him in rivulets to pool about his feet and spatter the floor of the dressing room as he reached out for the towel. After ruffling the cloth through his hair, he wrapped it low about his hips and, bare-chested, padded into the bedroom. He noticed the fire burning behind the grate and decided having a houseboy in residence wasn't such a bad idea. The room was warm for a change, far more livable, and he hadn't had to light the fire himself.

J.T. sauntered across the room and paused before his guitar, which sat propped up in the corner. The battered old thing was much the same vintage as his hat, and like the hat, had been a gift. Lupita had given him the guitar shortly after his mother's death. She thought that music might help to ease his mourning, and she had been right in that. She had taught him to play herself—spent long hours with him after the day's chores were through to teach him to play the haunting, passion-filled melodies she had learned as a child.

He picked up the guitar, ran his hand over the worn surface

of it, and plucked the strings. It was out of tune. He sat on the edge of the bed and began to turn the frets and strum the strings until the notes blended and harmonized. His aunt and uncle both extracted a promise from him each and every time he picked the thing up. "Don't sing, *hijo*," Lupita would say. "Pleeeease don't sing," Cash would second.

As much as he loved to play the guitar, even though he was able to hear the notes and keep the instrument tuned, J.T. could not carry a tune to save his life. He missed them both—his dearest friends—as he sat on the edge of the bed hunched over his guitar. Wondering what they were doing tonight, wondering if they were well, he made a promise they could not hear. "I won't sing."

Jade changed into her skirt and blouse and waited in the drawing room for Jason to come down to supper. Ignoring the nervous fluttering inside, she looked over the drawings she had made and tried to decipher the strange characters. She was so preoccupied, she didn't know Jason had entered the room until she heard his rough voice directly behind her. She set her work aside.

"I thought you would dress for dinner," he said.

She spun around and looked up at him. Gone was the stubble that had shadowed his face. His hair was still damp, but neatly combed into place. His eyes were the color of a spring sky—and he was dressed in formal evening attire.

Nervously she smoothed her plain skirt and straightened her worn collar. Unlike Jason, she had nothing formal to wear. She had left her borrowed finery at Babs', except for the dress she wore on her wedding night, which was ruined beyond repair and hidden at the bottom of her valise. Too proud to tell him she was wearing her best, she pretended to ignore his statement.

She stood and led the way into the dining room, where she moved to the head of the table. Three tall candelabras were evenly spaced along the ten-foot table, which was covered with a starched linen cloth. Candlelight set the room aglow, reflected in the sheen of the gilded wall covering. Blue willow china stood out against the austere white cloth and napkins.

As Jason pulled out Jade's chair for her, he caught himself leaning toward her, longing to catch a whiff of the fresh citrus scent she always used. When she turned to thank him, he pulled back stiffly and walked silently to his own place at the other end of the table.

Neither of them spoke. As if on cue, Tao Ling walked in with a platter of roast duckling that he placed on the sideboard and then walked out again. Three platters later, he began to serve the meal. Steamed vegetables with sesame seeds and white rice completed the menu. He filled both of their plates, always careful to give Jason a larger portion, and then left the room.

Jade watched J.T. push the vegetables around with his fork, peering beneath them as if he expected to find some menace hidden there.

"Is this all we're having? No meat? No potatoes?" His appetite was such that he knew he could eat three times as much. He glanced at the sideboard. At least there was food left on each serving tray.

Fighting to control her temper, Jade explained. "We didn't know you would be here for dinner. Nor had we planned on Xavier."

"Where is he, by the way? Why isn't he eating?"

She looked startled for a moment before she said icily, "He's having his supper in the kitchen with Tao."

Jason couldn't help but think of the meal he would be sitting down to at his uncle's ranch. Stacks of warm tortillas, rich fresh butter, *frijoles*, steak, corn bread, mashed potatoes. Aunt Lupe's meals always made allowances for everyone's tastes. All the hands on the place ate together with the Youngers at long trestle tables in the kitchen. He tried to imagine the wiry Mexican *remundero* conversing with Jade's Chinese watchdog. "I'd like to see that exchange."

"Actually," she said, arching a brow and assuming her iciest tone, "they're doing very well together." *Better than we are,* she thought.

Jason's own reaction was much the same.

Chilly silence descended upon them again.

"Your father had good taste in china." Jade tried to open a

conversation, deciding to save the topic of her visit to the stable for later.

Jason failed to comment, so Jade went on as if he had shown a spark of interest. "There's a legend about the pattern on the plates. It's a Romeo and Juliet story, actually. It seems a father forbade his daughter to marry the man she loved. I think the tale says that he imprisoned her on an island in the beautiful palace you can see on the right side of the plate. But, her lover . . . found her. To escape, they became the two birds at the top of the painting, and flew away." When she mentioned the lovers, her voice faltered.

Although he had been pretending not to listen, Jason found himself staring down at his plate, shifting his meal about so that he could see the illustrations as she mentioned them. When he heard the catch in her voice, he glanced up and found Jade rapidly blinking away tears.

He felt his heart constrict, fought the reaction to her distress, and tried to convince himself that her obvious theatrics only infuriated him.

Jade nearly burst into tears when Jason suddenly began glaring at her down the length of the table. She felt like closeting herself in her room with her books and never laying eyes on him again. Instead, she reminded herself that he was her husband, and that he had loved her once. She refused to give up yet. As she tried to shake off the power of his chilling stare, a knock at the front door broke the tension between them. She dashed at the tears in her eyes with her napkin.

Jason threw down his napkin and stood.

"Tao Ling will get it," she informed him.

He glowered at her as he sat back down. "I'm not used to being waited on hand and foot. Nor am I used to everybody eating in different rooms. Obviously you are."

Her feelings were still too raw; she didn't have the courage to argue with him.

Tao appeared in the doorway and announced, "Mrs. Harrington, a Captain Lennox is here to see you. Shall I have him wait in the drawing room?"

Surprised to hear Jade referred to as Mrs. Harrington, Jason watched her reaction to her visitor's arrival. Her expression brightened instantly as joy radiated across her face. He felt himself tense as he watched his wife rush to meet her unexpected caller. It was all J.T. could do not to follow her to the foyer, but he stayed where he was, and as if nothing she did mattered to him, he casually asked Tao to refill his plate.

Jade ran to the door and immediately hugged the burly, ruddy-cheeked man standing outside. Everything about Emery Lennox, from his navy cap to his graying mutton chops, was dear to her. He pulled her into his embrace with strong square hands and pressed a wind-roughened cheek against hers. Bronzed from countless hours at sea, he was dressed as always in navy blue sea togs with shining brass buttons and a crisp white shirt. Heavy black boots completed his outfit. When he set her down, she pulled him inside, but did not let go of his hands.

"Oh, Captain Lennox, if you knew how many times I've thought of you in the past few days!"

"I just got into town, Jade darling, or I would have been here much sooner. I read in the *Chronicle* that you were married. Is that true?" His worried brown eyes studied her from beneath wild, salt-and-pepper brows.

She nodded, suddenly reminded of Jason sitting alone in the dining room. "Come on," she said as she led him by the hand through the maze of crates in the foyer, "meet my . . . come meet Jason," she amended.

He stopped in the middle of the foyer. "What's all this?" he boomed, arms wide, looking right and left at all the clutter and half-open crates.

She laughed, buoyant now that her grandfather's old friend had found her. No longer feeling like a ship adrift at sea, she found the captain's interest and friendship a welcome haven from the turmoil. "This is Grandfather's collection. It was just delivered to me today."

"Well," he said, showing little interest aside from a quick comment. "So this is where it ended up. Good. I know you'll take fine care of it. Now, let's meet that husband of yours."

Jason rose as Jade entered the room on the captain's arm. He offered a polite, if not enthusiastic greeting, then extended an invitation for the captain to join them for dinner.

"Don't mind if I do," Emery Lennox said, choosing a chair evenly spaced between Jason and Jade. Tao brought him a place setting and efficiently went about serving the new arrival.

"Captain Lennox was one of the men who brought my grandfather many pieces of his collection," she told Jason. "I remember looking forward to your visits," she said when the captain smiled her way. "Grandfather would always get so excited when he heard your ship was in port."

Lennox chuckled. "He did at that. He used to ride out to meet me when he got word that I was on my way to see him. I knew better than to return empty-handed from one of my trips." He took a hearty bite of honey-glazed duckling and then put down his knife and fork. "I was sorry to hear about your father's murder, Jade. Do you know anything about it?"

Jason listened carefully, content to stare down the length of the grand dining table at his wife. He had finished with his meal, and as Tao took his plate and poured him another glass of wine, Jason leaned back, his eyes hooded, as he watched Jade in the shimmering candlelight.

"No more than I learned when I first arrived," she began. "He was killed by the tongs, ostensibly because he abducted an alchemist from a small Chinese village."

"Preposterous!"

She shook her head. "On the contrary, I think he was capable of it."

The captain leaned forward with interest. "Do you have proof?"

Since she had not yet told Jason or Detective Chang about the alchemist's belongings she had hidden in her room, Jade chose not to tell Emery Lennox just yet. It would seem like another breach of confidence to Jason—one more secret she had kept from him. No, until she could tell her husband what she had discovered, the box would remain a secret.

She shook her head. "No, no proof. But I think my father was capable of anything."

"How could he have done it?" Lennox wondered aloud.

"He would have had no difficulty in hiring someone to do his dirty work. He was deeply in debt when he died, which leads me to think that whatever he was up to had cost him quite a lot."

The captain instantly showed his concern. "Do you need anything, Jade? If so, you would let me know, wouldn't you?"

If only you had arrived a few weeks ago, Jade thought, *I might not have married Jason.* Feeling Jason's gaze upon her, she glanced up and found him lazing in his chair, his eyes half-lidded. He was staring at her. Uncomfortable with that realization, she flushed, dropped her gaze, and then looked away.

"Have you been out to the adobe?" Lennox asked. "It was such a grand place when I first met your grandfather." He shook his head and studied the candelabra in front of him as he thought of other times. "As he and Chi Nu grew older, the place seemed to age with them. Now they're all gone. First Chi Nu, then Philo, now your father."

Jade blinked back tears. "Grandfather will be sorely missed. And Chi Nu was the best friend he could have ever had." She could not lie and say that she would miss Fredrick Douglas. "Jason and I rode out to the adobe when I first arrived. It's dilapidated, but it is no longer mine to worry about."

Jason sat up straighter in his chair and Jade tried to ignore his sudden move. She knew then he had been listening intently.

"You sold the adobe?" The captain looked genuinely dismayed. "Why?"

"I used it to pay off Father's debts. Jason's lawyer helped me find a way to save the collection. The land was worth far more than I ever thought possible." Her gaze shot back to Jason. "I even have enough money left from the transaction for my own use." She stared pointedly at J.T. "I'm not dependent on anyone."

Jason shoved his chair back and stood up.

Lennox did not seem to notice that his host was about to exit. "How did you and Jade end up married, Harrington? You're quite the lucky man, meetin' her and marrying her so quick."

As he took a cigar out of his coat pocket, Jason looked down at Jade and said, "My wife arranged it all, Captain. Now, if you two don't mind, I'll let you visit in private." With that he turned on his heel and walked out the door.

Jade watched him go with a sinking feeling. Once again, she had offended him. She had planned the scene far differently, wanted to tell him her father's debts were paid and that she was no longer beholden to him. She wanted to give him the chance to think things through knowing she was independent now. But instead, he had heard the news secondhand when she related it to Lennox.

She looked back at Emery and found him staring sullenly after Jason. "Captain? What is it?" She had never seen any but a jovial expression on his face.

"If I didn't know better, I would think that man just insulted you, Jade."

"I . . . he . . . he's tired. He just got back from Monterey."

"Well, that's no cause for him being rude to you, Jade." He patted his full stomach, wiped his napkin across his lips, and pushed away from the table. "Well, I feel as if I've overstayed my visit. I'm sure you'll want to get rid of an old man like me, so I'll be shoving off now."

She walked him to the door, sorry to see him go. "Will you be in San Francisco long?"

"At least a month. I just returned from the East Indies with a load of spices. Then I'm off for the Orient again. But before I go, I may just drop in at the bank and see if they've sold the adobe yet. Which bank did you deal with?"

"Hibernia. Are you interested in the old place?" Truly surprised, she tried to imagine the captain away from his ship and the sea. "They did say someone had been quite interested in it, even before I came back to town."

"Then wish me luck," he said as he put on his cap and buttoned up his double-breasted coat.

"Please," she said sincerely, "come back and see me again."

"You can count on it, Jade darling. You can count on it."

Tao was waiting to speak to her as she turned away from the door. "Mr. Harrington has changed and gone out to the stables."

"But it's dark," she said, disappointed because she had hoped they could talk. It appeared Jason had nothing further to say to her.

Tao shrugged. She thanked him, then slowly mounted the stairs to her room. Once there, she lit the lamp on the desk and sat for a while staring out at the stables. Golden lamplight radiated out of the open doorway. She tried to imagine Jason with his new horses. What care did they require so late at night? How often did they need feed and water? Was he truly busy, or had he simply preferred Xavier's companionship to hers? It seemed that no matter how she tried, she ended tripping herself up when it came to dealing with Jason.

She changed into a lawn nightgown, picked up a throw, and took her Middle Kingdom book to the chaise to sit down and read. Tomorrow, she promised herself, she would tell Jason about the alchemist's box and the strange Chinese writing, and she would apologize for not telling him about the resolution of her financial situation earlier.

Stalling as long as he could, Jason watched the upper corner window of Jade's room and waited for her to turn down her lamp. He did not trust himself to go near her, though he wasn' as angry as he was when she so blithely announced that she was now financially independent. After everything she had put him through, she no longer needed him. But if that was the case, why was she still here?

He leaned against the stable door, his hands folded over his chest, his teeth worrying the cigar clenched between them. "*Qué hora es*, Xavier?" he called out over his shoulder.

"Twenty minutes past ten, *senor*," the hired hand called back.

"Hell," Jason muttered. Not only had he been up with the sun, but he'd had a long day in the saddle. He threw the stump of the cigar on the ground, crushed it with his heel, and headed for the house.

Tao was still working in the kitchen. The house servant glanced up, his hands covered with bread dough, and watched Jason as he passed.

As he strode along the upstairs hall, intent upon getting

some much-needed sleep, J.T. could not help but notice the light streaming from beneath Jade's door. It drew him like a magnet until he stood in the hallway, his hand on the doorknob.

He opened the door slowly and warily moved inside. She was sound asleep on a chaise near the window, a heavy book open on her lap. He looked around the room and noted the way Jade was reflected in everything he saw. Her desk was a mountain of papers, books, pens, and brushes, all in organized disarray. Quietly he entered and paused beside the chest of drawers. Her hairbrush and button hook lay atop a thin piece of colored silk. He reached out to touch them. When Jade stirred, he nearly jumped, but then she quieted and he went on to peruse the rest of her things.

He paused at the desk and shook his head at the jumble it was in. The rest of the room was orderly, but it seemed his wife preferred to work amid disarray. He picked up one sheet and looked at the strange markings on it. Would he ever understand her? Jade didn't seem to need anything but her studies. That and the Chinese pieces downstairs. He paused at the foot of the bed and saw the low box almost hidden on the other side. Jason frowned. She had ignored his orders and carried it upstairs anyway. He rounded the foot of the bed, carefully lifted the lid, and stared down at the box. Unwilling to disturb her and be caught openly snooping through her things, he closed the lid.

Then J.T. walked over to the chaise where she slept. He gently slipped the book from her limp fingers and set it aside. Her hair was down, spread out wildly about her shoulders the way he liked it best. It looked as if she had just brushed it to life, it was so glossy and rich. With a feather-light touch he reached out and took a lock in his hand. It curled around his fingers. Unwilling to resist, he bent and breathed in the scent of her.

Jade moved in her sleep again, unconsciously trying to get comfortable. Without stopping to think, he reached down and picked her up, held her to him, and carried her to the bed. Unbelievably, she did not stir. He carefully pulled back the bedclothes with one hand and then lay Jade in the center of the bed. Tenderly he tucked her in and then straightened. He was halfway to the door when he stopped and turned around.

Jason stared down at her for a moment, wrestling with his own will—determined not to touch her again.

He lost the battle. Bending over her, he placed a light kiss on her forehead.

Before he turned out the light, he returned to her desk and picked up one of the books scattered there. *The Oldest and Newest Empire: China and the United States*. He opened the flyleaf and read the title again and then the author's name. William Speer, D.D., 1870. It wouldn't hurt to learn a little about the subject that occupied all of Jade's time. Besides, he thought, it would be a long time before he fell asleep now.

As he pulled the door closed behind him, he noticed Tao Ling walking toward him, carrying a bundle of blankets in his arms. His expression was grave.

"You were in Mrs. Harrington's room?" Tao asked, his tone crisp.

"I don't see how that's any business of yours," Jason whispered. He watched, dumbstruck, as Tao spread out the makeshift bed on the floor outside Jade's door.

"My mistress bid me sleep here when you are in the house. Please excuse." He turned his back, and much to J.T.'s amazement, prepared to lie down right there in the hallway.

Jason reached out to touch Tao's shoulder. Before he knew what had happened, J.T. found himself facing the other direction, as Tao twisted one arm high against his back. As the man continued to apply pressure to J.T.'s shoulder by raising his arm inch by inch, Jason managed to say between clenched teeth, "You're fired."

"I work for Mrs. Harrington. She pays me. When she fires me, I will go. Until then, I am to sleep here whenever you are home."

He let Jason go.

Jason stepped back, anxious to put space between them and asked, "Just when I'm home?"

"Exactly."

"I guess she means it," Jason mumbled, as he rubbed his shoulder and stared at the unshakable Chinese.

"Yes, sir. I believe she does."

Nonetheless, Jason gave Tao a look of warning. "I think you ought to know that if and when I really want to be in that room, no one"—he emphasized the words as he repeated them—"*no one* will stop me."

Tao Ling merely bowed.

Jason stalked down the hall to the master suite.

Behind the door in question, Jade had been awakened by the sound of voices and listened to the exchange and then Jason's retreating footsteps. She smiled into the darkness before she drifted off to sleep.

❧ CHAPTER 17 ❧

A gem is not polished without rubbing,
Nor is a man perfected without trials.

The next morning, wrapped in a plaid wool shawl over a skirt and blouse, Jade hurried to the warm kitchen. The temperature had dropped considerably before dawn. After she awoke, she had been too chilly to brave the cold and light a fire, so she quickly dressed, tied back her hair, and went downstairs. She told herself to slow down, that the pounding in her heart was because she had moved too fast, not because she so looked forward to seeing Jason.

The scent of freshly baked bread filled the kitchen, the results of Tao's efforts cooling on the table. He came in the back door with a load of vegetables in his hands, smiled, half-bowed, then set them on the worktable.

"I have tea ready," he said.

"Thank you, Tao, I need it. I'm freezing. Would you light a fire in my room for me when you have a chance?"

"Of course. A storm is blowing in. The clouds are gathering over the bay."

"Brrr!" She shivered, then as nonchalantly as possible, she said, "Have you seen Mr. Harrington this morning?"

"He left very early, dressed for business. He said to tell you he will return tonight, that he has a meeting with Mr. Van Buren today. Something about signing papers."

Her heart sank. Jade set down the tea and tried to think of all the reasons Jason might be seeing Matt, but only one came to her—he was ending their marriage. His innocent kiss of the night before had only been a gesture, nothing more. When she had revealed her independent status to Captain Lennox, she had sealed her fate. As she wondered how long it would be before she had to leave, her plans to spend the day unpacking the collection seemed a waste of time.

Suddenly both Tao and Jade looked up as a carriage pulled

in before the stables. At the same time hoping and dreading
that Jason had returned, Jade stepped out onto the service
porch. Chilled, she clutched her shawl closer and watched as
the carriage door opened to reveal Emery Lennox. He stepped
out and then extended his hand to someone inside. As Jade
watched, a diminutive Chinese girl appeared. The captain
helped her down and the girl teetered for a moment on bound
feet and then rocked forward, moving with a strange gait.

The girl, who was little more than a child, wore a costume
that was exquisite in detail—an emerald Mandarin jacket,
intricately embroidered with lilies and leaves of black, red, and
gold. The jacket was so long it covered her wide black pants to
the knees, while the sleeves hid her hands to the fingertips. As
the girl came nearer, Jade stared at her feet. Shod in gay satin
slippers that matched the girl's jacket, they appeared to be little
more than pointed stubs. Jade was so taken with the girl's
clothing that she did not notice the bruises marring her
otherwise perfect complexion. When she neared the house,
Jade saw that her left eye was nearly swollen shut.

"Come in," Jade said quickly as she opened the door for
them both. She gave the girl her hand. The child teetered up
the steps, amazingly agile given her handicap. Captain Lennox
came in on her heels. Waving them toward the kitchen, Jade
followed them inside.

Tao turned away from his work and bowed to the newcomers, but after the initial greeting, he had eyes only for the
young girl. Jade could not fault him for staring. By any
standards, the girl was beautiful, even though she had been
carefully groomed to appeal to men who sought out the
Chinese singsong girls.

Because a high forehead was considered a sign of beauty,
the girls eyebrows had been plucked clean. Delicate lines had
been pencilled in their place. Her hairline had been plucked
back a good two inches, just as the part down the middle of her
head had been widened. Drawn back tightly, her hair was
wound into an intricate bun in back.

"Please, sit down." Jade pulled out a chair, anxious to have
the girl off her feet.

Lennox pulled out a chair for himself, set his cap on the

table, and then smiled up at Jade. "I'm glad we found you at home."

She didn't tell him she had not left the place for nearly two weeks.

He ran his hand through his graying hair and dragged it down to scratch at his huge sideburn. His expression sobered. He stared down at the Chinese girl who sat beside him, her eyes downcast. She ignored the cup of tea Tao placed before her.

"I didn't know where else to turn," Lennox admitted to Jade. "I found this girl roaming on the Embarcadero at dawn. From what I can understand, she's a singsong girl who ran away from a brothel in Little China."

Jade remained standing, but she leaned against the table, still clutching her shawl. "She can't be more than thirteen," she said, astonished.

"I think she might be a few years older than that." The captain looked at the girl speculatively. "Twelve-year-olds are sold into slavery, Jade. This one is no exception."

Jade had studied the Chinese long enough to know that women had no status in the culture except to serve men. Parents who found themselves debt-ridden with too many mouths to feed often sold their daughters into servitude or prostitution. Because wives were not permitted to immigrate with their husbands, nearly all of the Chinese females in California were prostitutes, or singsong girls, as they were called. Still, knowing the facts did little to ease their harsh reality. Jade immediately took pity on the frightened girl.

"I would like to make a potion to take the swelling out of her face," Tao said, watching the girl carefully.

"Please." Jade gave him leave to do so.

After Tao chose the ingredients he needed and then disappeared into his room to mix them, the captain explained why he had come. "I was hoping you might keep the girl here, Jade. I don't know what else to do with her."

Jade did not know what to say as she looked at the old man. His expression was hopeful, almost expectant, but Harrington House was Jason's home, not hers. Even she might not be here much longer. If she agreed to shelter the fugitive, her own entourage would grow by one. But there was no way she could turn the girl away.

"I made certain no one saw me bring her here," Emery continued. "The Hip Yee tong protects the slave owners' rights. They charge the owners forty dollars a head for each girl, so the tong is very careful about recouping losses."

"She's a slave?"

"Most all of the singsong girls are, Jade."

"I don't want to put Jason in danger," Jade said. She was in enough trouble herself already.

"No one is looking for this girl," he assured her. "At least not here. No one saw her this morning and no one saw me. Who would think of looking for her here?"

He paused for a moment when he heard Tao moving around in his room. "What's he doing in there? Can you trust your houseboy?"

Jade was reminded of last night and the way Tao had taken his duty to protect her seriously. Coupled with the fact that he had been staring at the slave girl as if she were a berry on top of a cake, Jade was certain Tao would not give the fugitive away. "It seems to be bad luck to mix any medicine in the kitchen. And yes, I trust him implicitly."

"Good. Then as I said, the secret is safe."

Tao walked in with a thick paste in a mortar and stopped beside the girl. When he reached out to spread the paste on her cheek, she slapped his hand away.

He spoke sharply to her in Cantonese.

"Ask her name," Jade said.

The girl looked directly at Jade for the first time. "I Quan Yen, missee."

Jade smiled at Quan Yen's use of Pidgin English. She touched the girl's shoulder and spoke to her in Cantonese. "Welcome to my home, Quan Yen. No one will beat you here. You are safe."

Quan Yen's expression brightened. She glanced up at the captain, then at Jade before she shrugged and ignored them all, allowing Tao Ling to spread the paste on her cheek.

The storm blew in from the northeast, carried by a cold, furious wind until it slammed into the bay. Jade tried to relax as the sky darkened and the day lengthened. By noon they had to light the lamps. The house was built as tight as a vault, but the rain pelted the windows as the wind battered the strong block walls.

It seemed as if she started numerous projects, only to abandon them, mesmerized by the fury of the storm. Jason was out in the foul weather somewhere—safe and warm, she hoped. He had said he was going to see Matt, and if she guessed correctly, they were probably sipping brandy at Matt's club or in the smoking room at the Palace Hotel, waiting out the worst of the storm.

"How many will be here for dinner?" Tao asked, interrupting her reverie.

She turned away from the window. "At least five." Jade counted herself, Xavier, Quan, Tao, and Jason. "And Tao, we'll all fit at the kitchen table, won't we? Mr. Harrington will be more comfortable there."

But suppertime came and went, and Jason still had not returned. They waited, then ate without him. Jade spent the meal trying to talk to Quan, translating for Xavier so that he would understand, and worrying about Jason at the same time. Finally, the hours crept past and Jade decided that staring out into the rain-blown streets would not serve any purpose. Nor did it ease her mind to think that Jason might not be coming home at all tonight. She refused to let herself think of where he might be, not when the storm outside was still raging. Definitely not when she knew that San Francisco was filled with countless ways a man could indulge himself.

Instead of worrying, she took Quan Yen in hand, gave her one of her own nightgowns, and tucked her safely into the spare servant's room next to Tao's. For a brief moment, Jade wondered at the propriety of such an arrangement, until she remembered Quan Yen's former circumstances. She convinced herself that a word of warning to Tao would suffice. Besides, forcing the girl to climb the stairs on her bound feet was a trial Jade wanted to spare her.

Not long after her ward was settled, Jade went to bed herself—to bed, but not to sleep. She tossed and turned all night, balling her pillow into a wad and then smoothing it out again. She strained to hear any sound that might signal Jason's return, but all she heard was the steady downpour of rain off the eaves and wind against the windowpanes.

The clock on her mantel struck midnight and she groaned. Just as she was chanting to herself, "Damn, Jason Harrington. Damn, damn, damn!" she heard a door bang open downstairs and held her breath.

Nothing. No other sound followed for a short while; then she heard a man in the throes of agony. At least that was what she thought. Jade jumped out of bed and grabbed her robe, then stopped when she realized what she heard was J.T. trying to sing.

It was loud—more like bellowing—it was off-key, and he seemed to be making up his own words as he went along. She went to her bedroom door and cracked it open. Tao had stretched out on his pallet in the hallway and as she looked down at him, he shook his head, his finger pressed to his lips warning her to be silent. Jason's voice echoed in the stairwell as he tried to sing the "Battle Hymn of the Republic." The tune was almost unrecognizable: the tempo matched slightly, but the lyrics—although creative—were all wrong.

"My sides have seed the comin' of the comin' of the Lord, He is tramplin' and a tamin' and a sharpenin' His sword. Be swift my feet to answer him and don't forget the seed, dum-dum, de-dum, dum-dum."

By the time he shouted the dum-dums, Jade was back in bed with a pillow over her ears and laughing.

The singing grew louder until it ended just outside her room. Then, when something hit the wall outside her door, laughter turned to fear. She sat up. She had never seen Jason drunk before, not even after he had finished half a bottle of champagne. The only experiences she had to draw on were those of her childhood. Whenever her father came home drunk, she had learned to disappear until the storm was over.

"Get outta my way," Jason said, quite loud enough for Jade to hear. "And don't shush me. I hope *my wife* is listening. Now move. I'm goin' in."

Tao's voice was low and controlled. Jade crept to the door and pressed her ear against it, unwilling to miss the exchange.

If by some chance Jason made it past Tao Ling, she wanted to be ready.

"I don't think you really want to try it, Mr. Harrington. You are drunk. You would be no match for me."

"Ha!"

Another thud against the wall followed Jason's retort. Had Tao hit him?

"Careful, Mr. Harrington. You seem to have trouble standing. May I take you to your room?"

"Are you . . . are you always so right? I mean . . . polite."

"Yes, Mr. Harrington."

"The name's J.T. But 'snot to you. 'Stoo my friends."

Jade marveled. For someone whose words were so slurred, she was amazed that Jason was even standing.

"I got lots an' lots of friends," he was saying, "lots of 'em. What I don't got is a wife. Not anymore."

With her fingertips pressed against her trembling lips, Jade shook her head and fought back tears. He must have done it. He had seen Matt about a divorce.

"Go to bed, Mr. Harrington. Please."

In the silence that followed, Jade clutched her arms about her waist and bit back sobs. The chance to win back his love had been taken from her. It was over—and she had lost.

When she heard Jason shuffle away, stumbling once or twice as he made his way down the hall, she crept back into bed, curled into a ball, and listened to the mournful sounds of the wind and rain.

By morning the storm had abated, but the skies were still gray and drizzling. The lackluster light cast the huge rooms of the mansion in shadow. Fires burned behind every grate but they did little to alleviate the chill.

Bare from the waist up, Jason stood before the tall shaving stand in the dressing room of the master suite, fought to hold the hand that held his razor steady, and cursed himself for drinking so much last night. His head was ringing, his mouth as dry as the desert and twice as tasteless. In the middle of a downward stroke he closed one eye, but it did little to relieve the pounding in his head. He winced when he nicked himself. Then cursed.

He called out in answer to a knock at the outer door and then stuck his head around the doorframe to see who dared enter his domain. It was Tao Ling, carrying a cup of steaming liquid in one hand and a stack of mail in the other.

Without a sound, the man set the letters and tea on the washstand nearby. "Will you want breakfast soon?"

The thought of food did little to cheer J.T. "No, thanks. Is this coffee?" He eyed the cup suspiciously.

"No. It is an herbal tea. It should help your headache."

"I don't have a headache."

"No?" Tao did not hide his skepticism. "In any case, the tea will help you."

"Don't we have any coffee?"

"Some. It is not made."

"Make it," Jason barked, and immediately regretted it when his head throbbed. "Please."

After Tao slipped silently away, Jason finished shaving, then dried his hands and lifted the teacup. He sniffed it, blew on it, tasted it, and then poured it into the washbowl. Nothing that tasted that vile could possibly make him feel any better.

He sorted through the mail. The stack of letters reminded him he was long overdue writing to Cash and Lupita. There had to be pen and ink somewhere around here. Jade had plenty of them. If need be, he would borrow some from her.

The mail turned out to be a stack of invitations, some addressed to him, others to Mr. and Mrs. J.T. Harrington. It seemed all of San Francisco had put the scandal out of their minds now that he and Jade had married. The hypocrites. He knew he was included on the guest lists because he was one of the richest among them. As soon as the legal work had been untangled and he had liquidated his father's export holdings and this heap of stone, he was leaving. There was no need to hobnob with socialites. He tossed the missives aside and ran a comb through his hair until it lay slicked-back and shining. It wasn't a moment before the natural wave began to spring back, protesting his efforts.

He wondered what sort of mood his wife would be in this

morning. Hopefully it would be far better than his own. Who was she to give him ultimatums anyway? Or to bar him from her door? He tried to think of a way to pay her back, and as he stared down at the pile of opened envelopes he realized the perfect punishment had been laid at his doorstep. They would maintain their reclusive lifestyle, and she would soon come to hate being shut up alone in the mansion. They would not attend one fancy ball. He'd buy no frivolous gowns. Soon she would grow to hate the isolation and turn to him.

Wouldn't she?

She had certainly enjoyed herself the night they attended the ball at the Palace. A city girl like Jade would surely soon be bored with her life if all she ever did was read and draw and unpack those precious Chinese pieces of hers.

The longer he thought of it, the better he felt. It was a good plan. A fine plan. He'd drive her right into his arms, just like a wild mustang into a box canyon.

Feeling better about his future than he had in a long while, Jason pulled on a clean shirt and headed out the door. He could smell coffee brewing downstairs, and now that he thought about it, he realized his appetite had even returned.

He passed Jade's room, and when he saw the door open, he could not resist pausing to look inside. She was seated at her desk near the window, staring out at the rain. As much as he hated to admit it, he was not enough of a fool to deny that his blood still ran hot whenever he saw her. As always, she intrigued him. There was an aura of mystery about her that made him wonder if he would ever penetrate it, even if he lived with her for a lifetime.

She turned around, alerted by his footsteps when he was halfway across the room. He watched her expression change from an initial reaction of welcome surprise to one that was closed, almost defensive.

"Good morning, Jade."

She tugged at the neck of her blouse as if it constricted her breathing. "Jason." Her nod was polite, distant. "I thought you were Tao."

"What are you doing?" He stood over her, staring down at

the papers on her desk. He had seen her studying the strange figures before.

"Tao and I discovered that each crate had some very strange symbols painted on it. I think someone tried to leave a message, but I'm having no luck at all in deciphering them."

He needed to touch her. There was no denying the intensity of the feeling that welled up inside him. J.T. reached around her, brushing his arm against the side of her breast as he did. She stiffened at the contact, and drew back so that he could reach the page he was after. "This is certainly strange. What's that? A lion?"

It was hard for Jade to concentrate on an answer with him so near. She wanted to beg him to tell her what business he had conducted with Matt, wanted to know if he was planning to divorce her. Instead, she fought to quell the tremors his touch had initiated. She tried to focus on the page in his hand and not on the fact that he was so close. A four-footed figure was drawn beneath a moon and two stars. "It is a lion," she agreed. "Then again, it might be a dragon."

Feeling quite smug, he smiled, and tossed the page back onto the desk. "So what does it mean?"

"I haven't a clue," she said, tilting her face up to him.

It would be so easy to kiss her now. He caught himself staring and tore his gaze away from her lips.

Jade concentrated on straightening the pile of papers.

"Jason?" This tenuous situation between them was wearing on her nerves. She almost asked him outright about the divorce, but she lost her courage and said instead, "How are the horses? Did the storm bother them?"

"I haven't been down yet. Taking it slow this morning."

"I heard you come in last night."

He had the decency to be embarrassed.

"You're a terrible singer," she added.

"I wasn't trying very hard." He hid his smile. Somehow it satisfied him to know she had been awake and heard him outside her door. Did she know that had he been determined to get past Tao Ling he would have succeeded?

"Jason?"

"What?"

"We need to talk," she said, trying to gather her courage about her like a hen whose chicks had scattered. "I . . . that is, you went to see Matt yesterday and I wondered, I mean, I wanted to—"

"Did you want to see Matt about something?"

"No. No, I was wondering what you went to see him about."

His expression became immediately guarded. "Why?"

She couldn't help but notice the chill that had crept into his eyes. A lesser woman would not have pressed him, but her immediate future hung in the balance. "Did your visit have anything to do with me?"

"No, it didn't." Her relief was immediately visible. He wondered what she was afraid of. "Why?" he demanded.

"I thought, well, you told Tao you didn't have a wife anymore, and I thought—"

"You thought I'd gone to Matt about a divorce?"

Unable to speak, she nodded.

"Would it matter that much to you?" He tried to keep his voice casual, his tone light, but he knew he was was staring down to her too intently.

Jade knew a moment of hope. His expression was far from nonchalant. *He does care.* He cared what her answer would be, and because she could see it in his eyes she relaxed and said softly, "Yes, Jason. It would matter."

He turned away so that she would not see the overwhelming relief he felt, shut himself off from her so that he would not follow the impulse to take her in his arms. "I'm going down to breakfast."

He heard the chair legs scrape against the floor, knew that she was following him across the room.

"Please, Jason. We need to talk about this—"

Instantly, he turned on her, stopping her in her tracks. "Listen, Jade. We have nothing to talk about. You have shut me out of your room and made that ridiculous ultimatum that I'm not to touch you until I trust you. What if I never trust you again? Will we go on like this forever?"

"Do you think you can find it in your heart to forgive me? I didn't do anything to hurt you, Jason. I'm willing to do

anything to make this marriage work, but I will not sleep with
a man who thinks I lied to him. I can't sleep with you knowing
you don't trust me, to mention nothing of love. Can you go on
like this?"

"If I have to," he told her coldly. "But you can count on one
thing, love and trust aside—I don't intend on letting you go.
Not yet. I paid the highest price a man can pay when I put that
ring on your finger. It was like putting a noose around my
neck." He looked away, clenched his jaw, then looked back
down at her as if he had come to a decision. "But I'm damned
sure not gonna let you tighten it, and I'm not going to stand
here and talk about this mess we're in. I don't even want to
think about it this morning. If you're content with things the
way they are, then that's your choice."

When he turned away, Jade felt deflated. Then, unexpectedly, he paused in the doorway and faced her again. "Don't
spend all your time worrying about a divorce. You'll be the
first to know if I decide that's the only way out."

Their strange truce held. An uneasy week passed as everyone fell into a routine they all knew to be temporary. Jade
immersed herself in unpacking, cataloging, and setting the art
pieces up in the ballroom. Quan Yen stayed at Jade's side all
day, chirping in her high voice, often hiding her smile behind
her hand while she flashed her eyes at J.T. whenever he came
upon them. She even argued with Tao Ling over the evening
meal and the choices he made.

When Jade first told Jason about the girl, his only response
had been a puzzled shake of his head. He asked her if her
Chinese collection included people, and then, if she thought
the house had enough spare rooms.

She had not tried to hide her smile.

Whether he admitted it or not, she could tell Jason was
adjusting to the pattern she had set for their days. Tao kept the
house running smoothly, and everyone was well fed. She often
wondered what Babs would say if she ever witnessed a
mealtime at Harrington House with everyone gathered at the
kitchen table. It was an eclectic group to say the least: the
Chinese houseboy, the singsong girl, Xavier—who could not

take his eyes off of Quan Yen—and Jason, an indomitable presence in any situation. Not to mention herself, quiet, contemplative, observant.

By the end of the third week as his wife, Jade had made progress with her plans for the soiree, if not with Jason. At first she had debated whether or not to ask his permission to hold the small gathering. Then, the more she thought it over, the more she felt it was not up to him to grant permission, since she was using her own money to put on the event. He would not even have to attend if he chose not to. In fact, she thought as she opened the door to the third delivery that morning—this one a cart filled with flower arrangements—she would be just as happy if Jason never had to find out about the soiree. But with the party set for that night, there was no way she could hide the preparations from him any longer, not with Tao already hanging up paper lanterns in the ballroom.

Nearly all of the fifty guests she had invited had responded positively. Using Matt's original idea, she decided to limit the guest list to only the very wealthiest, most highly regarded members of San Franciscan society. Whether they would find the collection worthy of support, she couldn't guess, but at least the gathering would provide them with a look at her grandfather's pieces. Jade still thought of the collection as her grandfather's, not her own. It was just this feeling she hoped to convey to the guests when they gathered that evening. Philo Page had been an eccentric, but he had also been a wealthy land owner, one of the original American citizens of San Francisco. She hoped his name would help sway their opinions in her favor, and that by the end of the evening some of the guests would have made a commitment to funding a museum.

The last decision facing her was a major one that she had put off far too long. She couldn't decide what to wear to her own party. There was nothing in her closet except for two plain skirts and as many worn blouses with frayed collars and cuffs. Various sets of Chinese pants, two Mandarin jackets, and a silk robe completed her entire wardrobe. Unconcerned until the last moment, Jade found herself with no time to have a dress made, nor did she really relish spending her money on something she might never wear again. If Jason did take her to New Mexico with him, she would have no need of finery on a ranch.

It was late morning when she went upstairs to lie down and ponder her predicament. Lately she found herself drained by the slightest activity. She blamed a case of nervousness over the plans for the soiree, not to mention the anxiety of telling Jason about the affair. Now, with one thing and another, she was sure that when she did tell him, he was certain to say that she had purposely kept her plans from him.

During a moment's respite from the preparations, she stretched out on the settee in the drawing room and tried to concentrate on what she might wear for the occasion. She could go out shopping and perhaps find something already made in a dress shop, but the quality would not match the price. Besides, every gown had to be altered, and given her height, she most likely would not find anything suitable at all. Shopping seemed to be a wasted undertaking that she had very little enthusiasm for anyway.

Quan peeked in the open doorway, and Jade bade her enter. The young girl teetered in slowly, a tray balanced in her well-tapered hands. Jade smiled. The girl had taken to bringing her a soothing cup of tea each morning and afternoon. It was the one time of the day Jade felt truly pampered.

"Tea for missee," Quan Yen said softly. "Kine you like."

"Thank you, Quan. Please, sit down."

The graceful way Quan moved when she was off her feet never failed to fascinate Jade. Her fingers were long and elegantly tapered, every movement like that of willow branches swaying in the breeze. Jade wished there was something she could do for the girl whose feet had been maimed for beauty's sake, but it was far too late for that. Besides, according to Tao, Quan Yen's bound feet made her all the more valuable.

Jade had been appalled but curious the day Tao had taken time to explain the art of footbinding to her. When a girl reached six or seven years of age, it was her mother's duty to force her small toes toward her sole and bind them back with a ten-foot-long bandage. The large toe was left unbound and then the top of the foot was drawn forcefully toward the heel.

Although many girls lost their small toes when infection set it, they suffered the consequences to achieve the perfect golden lotus, a foot that was no more than three inches long.

Having golden lotus feet forced women to move with the curious lotus gait, the swaying walk that attracted men.

"How can a poor, crippled creature inspire anything more than pity? How could the men make them perpetuate this hideous thing?" Jade had asked Tao one morning when Quan Yen was still asleep.

"It is well know that a woman with perfect golden lotus has tighter flesh on her thighs. The lower half of the body must be tensed to walk—this strengthens the legs, enlarges the buttocks, tightens . . ." He had paused, as if wondering how to go on. Finally Tao had said, "The hidden cave behind the jade gate is so tight it gives a man great pleasure, not to mention the thrill one experiences when he is permitted to watch a lady unbind the foot, when he fondles it in his hand."

When Jade finally recovered from her revulsion she told him bluntly, "I think it's a hideous practice. Quan Yen has become a prisoner because of her feet."

Tao had smiled knowingly. "That was the original idea, Mrs. Harrington. When a man was afraid his wife would stray beyond the bedroom, he had her feet bound."

"Do you . . ." It had been her turn to pause, suddenly embarrassed.

"Do I admire Quan Yen, Mrs. Harrington?"

Jade had wanted to ask if he lusted after the girl, but was satisfied with the way he had phrased her thought. "Yes. Do you?"

He arched a brow and admitted openly, "I am mad for her."

"I hope you will remember that she was entrusted to my care, Tao."

"You need not worry. She wants nothing to do with me."

Jade had not needed to see the sorrowful look in his eyes to know what Quan Yen's rejection cost.

As she looked at the girl sitting so quietly beside her now, Jade wondered why she had rejected a handsome suitor like Tao Ling and what provisions could be made for her future.

She refused to think of this strange, beautiful child returning to the cribs of Little China.

Jason came in from his morning ride and knew immediately that something was going on. Tao held court in the middle of the kitchen, bartering in harsh, no-nonsense tones with three Chinese vegetable peddlers. Mounds of vegetables were piled on the tables, more were spread out on cloths on the floor. The men pointed and gestured, oblivious of J.T. as Tao haggled with them over the price.

Jason strode through the house unnoticed, looking for Jade. He stopped dead still in the foyer and stared at the flowers banked on tables outside the ballroom doors. Suspicious, he crossed the hall, opened the double doors, and paused dumbfounded on the threshold. Chinese lanterns were strung across the room. Cut flowers and potted plants filled every corner. Tables had been arranged everywhere—high ones, low ones, lampstands, card tables, pedestal tables, side tables, drawing room tables. He shook his head. They had to have come from every spare room in the house. Each and every table held a piece of Chinese goods on display. He glanced over his shoulder, but no one noticed he had entered, so he walked slowly around the room, studying the collection in silence.

Colorful blue and white porcelain pieces reminded him of his blue willow dinner plates. There were pieces of jade displayed in lacquer boxes lined with velvet; small bowls and teapots he recognized for what they were. The function of other pieces was more curious. There was a watchtower of green glazed clay standing in a bowl. Tiny figures were perched on every level.

Painted scrolls hung suspended from the light fixtures. He stepped close to them and studied the intricate details of the scenes. Warriors and their ladies were depicted on some, while others were of trees and mountains.

He paused beside each and every piece until he had seen them all, then he quit the room and stealthily closed the doors behind him. *Maybe it's my own fault,* he thought, *for leaving her to her own devices.* He had thrown himself into his work. He and Xavier spent long hours with the horses, and when he was not working with them, he spent his time with Matt downtown or visiting outlying ranches, lining up more stock to take home. But now it seemed as if he were not the only busy one. Jade was up to something again, and he wanted to know exactly what it was.

He took the stairs two at a time and walked into her room unannounced. Standing with her back to the door, she glanced over her shoulder at him with the startled, wide-eyed expression that he had come to expect.

"Hello, Jason."

He made note of the way she sounded so suspiciously casual. "What's going on downstairs?" he asked.

She turned around, but kept her hands behind her back, out of sight. "It's so nice to see you, too."

"Don't toy with me, Jade. What's all the fuss downstairs?"

She took a deep breath and shrugged. "I'm having a little gathering tonight. I didn't think you'd mind."

"How did you plan to find out if I'd mind or not? When were you going to tell me about this . . . gathering?"

"As soon as you came in. Which is now, I guess."

She appeared to be wiggling, struggling with something behind her back.

"What are you doing?" he said, stepping toward her.

"Nothing." She shook her head.

"Don't push me, Jade."

"Nothing, really."

"Let me see your hands. You're hiding something from me."

"Jason, you are getting ridiculous."

"Now."

She put her left hand in front of her.

"And the other."

Sheepishly, she stared down at the toes of her slippers, then extended the other arm. There was a vase wedged on it up to her elbow.

Jason planted his fists on his hips and grinned. "What am I going to do with you?"

She looked up when she heard the note of humor in his

voice. "Could you get this thing off me?" She even risked a smile.

He took off his hat and tossed it onto her bed. Then he stepped toward her. All his pent-up feelings for her, all the need he had tried to hold at bay, surged through him now that she was finally close enough to embrace. Jason found himself shaking as he reached out to take her arm. He paused, wiped his palms on his thighs, and then took the vase in both hands.

Jade closed her eyes when he took hold of her. He smelled delectably like Jason—of shaving soap and the outdoors. As he stared down at the vase, trying to figure out how to loosen it, she took advantage of her closeness to study the clean line of his jaw, the way his crisp hair waved over his collar, the sea-blue of his eyes.

He glanced up and caught her staring at him. He was close enough to feel her warm breath on the side of his face. He nearly let go of her, almost called Tao to have him get Jade out of this latest predicament, but he couldn't release his hold on her any more than he could let her walk out of his life forever. Their situation would have made him laugh if it had not been so pathetic. They lived together as husband and wife, but with none of the pleasurable benefits. He wanted her. Wanted her to the very core of his being, but he couldn't risk losing his heart again.

But there was only so much a man could stand.

As he wavered, trying to decide what to do, she blinked twice and then said, "Do you think you can get it off?"

He glanced down at the vase and then back up into her green eyes. "I'll hold. You pull." He tightened his grip on the vase.

She tugged, but nothing happened.

"What now?"

"Do you mind my asking why you put your danged hand in there in the first place?"

She glanced away. "I saw a piece of paper down inside it."

"Couldn't you shake it out?"

She shook her head. "If I could have, would I be standing here like this?"

He laughed out loud as she shrugged, her arms spread wide, one of them hidden in the vase.

"Do you have any cream? Any lotion?"

"On the chest of drawers," she said.

He pulled her across the room, where he paused long enough to open a jar of rose-scented lotion and spread it liberally around the opening. Then, he held the vase again and Jade twisted her wrist until her arm slid free.

The folded paper was still in her hand.

"I hope it was worth it," Jason said, staring at it curiously. "Who put it there? Your grandfather?"

"No. This came from a box of other things. Things I'm certain belonged to the alchemist."

Life had progressed at such an even pace lately, Jason had all but forgotten the mystery of the missing Chinese wizard. Since there had been no further attempts on Jade's life, he was fairly convinced that she and Babs had orchestrated the earlier tries. The whole affair was something he had tried to forget. But now, as Jade stood there with a letter she believed had been planted in the vase, only now revealing to him the fact that she had kept secret an entire box of evidence, he wondered when he would stop playing into her hands.

He watched as she unfolded the note. "What does it say?"

"I wish I knew." She held it up for his inspection. The page contained more of the mysterious symbols that had been painted on the crates.

CHAPTER 18

Happy people never count hours as they pass.

"Have you told Lieutenant Chang about these things?"
Sheepishly, she shook her head. "Not yet."

"Why not?"

"I wanted to try to work out the riddle to the symbols first,
ɔ make up for my father's part in all this. Besides, I've been
ɔo busy planning the . . . party." Before she thought, she
ad mentioned it again.

J.T.'s reaction was immediate. His expression darkened.
Which is why I came up here in the first place. Why don't you
ɭl me about this little 'party' of yours?"

"Matt suggested it," she began. "I want to house Grandfa-
ɭer's things in a museum—"

"Which you can do without a party. Besides, I thought those
ɭings meant everything to you. If I'm not mistaken, they were
art of the reason you married me."

"You are mistaken."

He went on as if she had not spoken. "Now you want to just
ɭve them away?" He couldn't believe what he had heard. First
ɭe married him in order to have the funds to retrieve the
ɔllection, then she gave up the adobe, and now she claimed
ɭe wanted to donate the Chinese pieces to the city.

"There's so much you don't understand," she said, rubbing
ɭr temples. Her head ached again.

"Obviously not, so why don't you take a minute to enlighten
ɭe." He strode over to her chaise and stretched out on it.

Against the bright chintz background, Jason appeared totally
congruous. His worn work pants, leather vest, and open-
ɔllared shirt appeared all the more masculine against the
ɭegant, floral print upholstery.

"Grandfather felt that if people were to be educated about
ɭe Chinese, that art was the perfect way to do it. No one will

273

want to help fund a museum if they don't see the value in th
items." She took a deep breath and struggled to explain.

"Little China is a city within a city, but all most peopl
know about the Chinese is their food and that they supply Sa
Francisco with cheap labor. When they were brought into th
country to lay the railroad tracks and work the gold mine:
everyone thought they would eventually go back to China. B
they stayed, and now over fifteen thousand immigrate a yea
They are looked upon as inferior people, Jason, inferior mere
because they look different, dress differently—their who
culture is strange when you compare it to ours. But China
thousands of years old. The Chinese were writing poet
before the Europeans were out of caves."

He watched her come alive as she spoke, her enthusias
adding high color to her pale complexion. Her hands moved :
her enthusiasm grew. Unconsciously she began to step towa
him when she wanted to emphasize a particular statemen
Jason had to warn himself not to be taken in by her beauty.

"I want the people of this city to care enough to want
house Grandfather's collection where it can be viewed a
appreciated by everyone in San Francisco. Perhaps then, ov
time, the Chinese will be appreciated for what they ha
brought to California. I've invited guests who are well able
donate funds to a museum. All I have to do is convince the
the idea is worthwhile."

J.T. felt in his vest pocket for a cigarillo, but his hand can
away empty. She was convincing, he'd grant her that. "It :
sounds very commendable. What's the trick?"

"Damn it, Jason, there is no trick. I was willing to give
the collection before we were married, but now, thanks
Matt, I think I've found a way to house it permanently, just
Grandfather wanted. I would never have let the pieces stand
the way of our future."

Abruptly, he stood up, turned his back on her, and stared o
the window. In the stableyard below, Xavier was training
dappled Arabian to work as a cutting horse, one that wou
separate cattle from a herd. But his mind was not on the sce
outside. "It's a little late for that, don't you think?" His voi
was stone-cold and lifeless.

Jade felt all the fight drain out of her. Her head was reeling. he wished he would leave so that she could lie down. She rned away from him and stood before the window. "The arty is going on as planned. Tonight. You can attend, or you an avoid it and me—just as you usually do."

"What?" He swung around to face her. "What's that upposed to mean? At least I'm not the one who has to hide hind *books* all the time."

She tossed back her head and glared at him. "No? That's :cause you're too busy living in the stables, that's why." Fcd) with his accusations, she turned away. "Since you are as ubborn as a mule that seems to be the best place for you ayway."

He didn't know exactly how she had done it, but she had furiated him again. "I suppose since I haven't taken you out any fancy social gatherings that you had to hold one here just spite me. Is that it?"

"What are you talking about?"

"I wondered how long it would be before you put up a fuss."

"You know so little about me." She shook her head. He was peless.

Angered when she would not turn around and face him, son crossed the room, grabbed her shoulder, and spun her ound. He could not ignore the fact that she flinched—the otective gesture maddened him enough to grab her arms and ill her close. "I know you must have needs, Jade. You're ore than the cold scholar you pretend to be."

She tried to push him away, but there was no moving him. er breath came faster as her pulse increased tenfold. She felt s searing gaze, felt the heat of him as he imprisoned her ainst his length. When her knees grew weak, she cursed him mply because he knew that her body betrayed her every time touched her.

His voice softened as his hold tightened. "And I know that matter how hard I try, I can't get you out of my blood. ju're like the opium the Chinese indulge in." His voice broke he fought his own feelings. "I can't stay away from you."

He smothered her lips with his own, but there was no nishment there, no brutality. The kiss was a welcome relief

after the heated tension between them. As J.T. enfolded her
his embrace, the world around them ceased to exist. No long
did they hear the sound of Xavier's commands as he work
the Arabian. Tao Ling's frantic instructions to the other he
and Quan Yen's high-pitched giggles faded away as Jade a
Jason became lost in the sensations evoked by their exchang

Suddenly, J.T. tore his lips from hers and stood her aw
from him. She swayed, disoriented for a moment, then focus
on him. His lips were taut, white about the edges like a man
pain. He was thinking about something. Wrestling wi
something that caused him to knit his brow as his gaze roam
over her upturned face.

The silence lengthened between them. Finally, in a to
laced with determination, he said, "You had better see to it th
your watchdog isn't on guard outside the door tonight. If
is"—he forced his lips into an unpleasant smile—"well, le
just say, I'd hate to hurt him."

"Jason, please. You can't mean this—"

"I do. You're my wife and I've ignored that fact lo
enough, Jade. I don't want to hear any more ultimatums abc
love and trust, either. I want you in my bed tonight, anc
intend to have you. Have your party. Do whatever you wa
But when it's all over, you're mine."

His hands dropped to his sides. For a moment he look
about to say more, but then he walked toward the bed. I
picked up his hat, fingered the crown, then turned back. "Y
don't need to look so scared. I promise you tonight won't
like our wedding night." This time he was determined to s
that she experienced complete fulfillment. Tonight he wou
take his time with her until Jade cried out for release and
from fear.

Afraid to stay in the same room with her any longer, Jas
shoved on his hat and walked out the door.

She watched him as he coldly walked away without
backward glance. He left her shaken and chilled. Jade sa
down on the settee, absently traced the floral pattern, a
wondered how she was going to get through the eveni
Running away was out of the question. He was her husbar
Until he was willing to let her go, he would come after he

Besides, she was not a coward. Running was not her way. Nor could she deny the fact that her body still responded to his. A slow, aching warmth had begun when he kissed her, building until it had spread throughout her body. She had wished for a chance to make their marriage work, but she had also told him he could not have her until he had learned to trust her again.

Why now? She stood on shaking legs and crossed the room until she stood before the mirror above the chest of drawers. Why did he have to give her such an ultimatum before one of the most important nights of her life?

Jade walked to the armoire, opened it, and stared inside, but nothing new materialized. Her thoughts were too scattered for her to concentrate on anything. Her head still ached. Unable to do anything else at the moment, she climbed up onto the bed and stretched out, hoping meditation would alleviate her inner turmoil.

In a dream that seemed to border on reality, she saw herself dressed in a vibrant, bloodred robe. An outstanding work of art in and of itself, the shimmering silk was covered with threads of gold and silver. Suns, moons, stars all vied with animal figures of dragons, lions, tigers, and cranes. Undecipherable Chinese characters had been embroidered in and around the figures, even down the sleeves that were wide and banded with bright yellow-gold. Because of the way she felt with the robe on, Jade knew the silk was endowed with a life of its own. In her dream, the curious robe was the perfect compliment to the display and the evening ahead.

When she awoke, Jade felt refreshed but disappointed that she possessed no such miracle robe. But the strange dream had helped her come to a decision about what to wear to the soiree. Still unwilling to think about Jason's parting promise, she took her navy Mandarin jacket and pants out of the armoire and dressed for the evening.

Three hours later, Jade stared around the ballroom and wished that the ground would open up and swallow her, and not because her preparations weren't executed as planned.

White-jacketed waiters hired for the evening moved unobtrusively among the crowd. Tao Ling, assisted by a cousin who worked as a chef in a restaurant in Little China, kept the food trays filled with Chinese delicacies. For those who did not care for such fare, he had purchased baked goods from a bakery. Another cousin's business, Tao explained.

The paper lanterns added a touch of gaiety to the formal ballroom; the gas chandeliers provided the perfect amount of light for viewing the collection. To anyone who merely passed by and looked in at the tableau, everything would seem perfect.

But in reality, nothing had gone right since Tao had opened the door to the first guests.

As she had suspected he might, Jason avoided the affair. She had not seen him since early afternoon, when he left her in her room. As a result, she welcomed her guests alone—a sad reception line of one—until Matt arrived early on and stood beside her. Her nerves were in such a state that his voluntary show of concern had nearly been her undoing.

It was apparent from the moment the first couple had walked through the door that they had not come to enjoy "A Night In China—A Reception Presenting the Chinese Collection of Philo Page, Presented by his Granddaughter, Mrs. Jason Terrell Harrington III," as the invitation announced. No, they had come to gawk at Jade and inspect the inside of Harrington House.

Matt was adept at making introductions. Jade was inept at recalling names. She had always been that way in a crowded situation. As the women were introduced to her, dressed in the latest fashion, bedecked in beaded gowns and adorned with jewels, feathered headdresses, and plumed fans, each and every one had paused to gape at Jade's unusual costume. Some, mercifully, were speechless. Others merely looked skeptical. Still others gave her backhanded compliments.

"How unique. How ever did you think of it?"

"Heavens! I would think you'd feel half-dressed."

"My goodness, don't you look . . . different?"

Through it all, Jade had smiled. And smiled. And ached to tell them all to go home.

She saw Matt standing across the room talking to two portly

gentlemen in cutaway tails. Their bored expressions said they would rather be anywhere else. She caught Matt's eye and motioned him over.

"Try not to look so worried," he advised as he grabbed an egg roll from a passing waiter.

"No one has even looked at any of the art except for a cursory glance here and there. They're all too busy gossiping among themselves. Look at the way the women have split up into those little groups of twos and threes. Do you think I'd have the courage to intrude on any of them? They remind me of hens in a barnyard. There's a definite pecking order to this, Matt, and I don't fit in." The men were just as bad. Worse, perhaps, because they spoke louder. No one had made any attempts to speak to her after they entered the ballroom.

"I think you should call them to attention, explain some of the more fascinating points about the collection. At least the highlights. That way they'll know what to look for."

Jade shrugged. "From the questions they asked at the door, I know now that all they came to see is Jason, not the collection. He's more of curiosity to them than art will ever be."

"You should try, at least, because that group by the door appears ready to bolt any minute now. All it will take to end this affair is for one couple to leave and——"

"You don't have to tell me. Grand exodus."

"I'm afraid so."

"Can you get their attention?" She was as nervous as she had ever been before, but tried not to show it. Jade didn't know which was worse, having to endure the unreceptive crowd, or face the end of the evening with Jason's ultimatum.

Matt clapped his hands to attract attention. One or two of the ladies' groups stopped talking. Half of those in attendance looked his way.

"Mrs. Harrington would like to give you a brief description of each piece of the collection. As she moves about the room, she'll be happy to answer questions." He leaned over toward her and whispered, "Where would you like to begin?"

For a moment she was tempted to say nowhere. Then it all became clear. She would start where it all began for her. "With the camel," she said, pointing toward the opposite end of the room, "near the tall double doors."

Unnoticed as yet, J.T. stood in the doorway trying to control his temper. He had been outside the foyer when Matt made his announcement to the crowd, and now he watched Jade at the far end of the room. She was trying to speak to the gathering in general, but the only ones paying any attention were the two oldest women in the room—and one of them seemed far more interested in what she was eating than in what Jade had to say.

No matter what barriers stood between them, Jason's heart went out to his wife as she valiantly tried to carry on with her presentation. He wondered what gave these people the right to be rude. Why had they come, if not to view the collection and hear what Jade had to say?

Although she had not noticed him yet, J.T. couldn't take his eyes off of her. Jade stood out against the crowd like an exotic orchid in a field of daisies. The dark background of her Chinese jacket provided a unique contrast to her red-gold hair. It reminded him of the impossible pairing of the sun against a midnight sky. The other women in the room appeared overblown when he compared them to Jade. Instead of wearing her hair in an intricate style of the day, she had braided it into one long, thick queue that swayed behind her, and into it she had worked the red silk sash that she had found in the adobe. A few unruly wisps and tendrils had escaped the braid to curl softly about her face.

She was so alone, and so vulnerable in this room full of strangers, that the unguarded moment reminded him of the time she had appeared in the doorway at their wedding. That night he had left his place before the judge to go to her. That night he had loved her more than he knew.

But even after all that had passed between them, he could not leave her standing alone in this hostile crowd tonight. Jason took a step in her direction, then stopped when he heard Matt Van Buren say, "Thank God you're here!"

J.T. glanced away from Jade just long enough to acknowledge Matt. He adjusted his cuffs, refastened a diamond stud that had nearly slipped loose, and kept an eye on his wife. He wished he could will her some of his strength. She looked about to wilt.

He couldn't keep the rage from his tone as he took Matt aside and said, "No one's paying any attention to her. I'm going to make them shut up and listen."

As Jason stepped forward, Matt pulled him back.

"Oh, no you don't. Not unless you want to cause her more humiliation. If you want to help, you'll get in there and give them what they came for—a chance to meet one of the five richest men in San Francisco—and act like these Chinese antiques of hers are the greatest things to hit the city since the trolley car."

"What should I do?"

"Just be gracious," Matt advised.

Jason scanned the room. "Sounds easy enough."

"Tell them you're all for this museum Jade is trying to establish."

J.T. didn't comment on Matt's second suggestion, but moved off into the room before Matt could add, "Above all, don't be yourself."

"This next piece," Jade said as she lifted a wafer-thin disk of jade from a lacquer box, "is called a *pi* disk. *Pi* being a symbol for heaven and earth. It's made of jade and adorned with two tiny dragons on the outer rim and one in the center. Grandfather felt it was of significance because he believed jade carved in this form dated back to China's late Warring period."

Her voice dropped away to nothing. It was apparent that no one in the room cared to hear what she was saying except for the two elderly dowagers standing in front of her. The room hummed with the conversations of the tight groups scattered across it. At least, she thought, she could be kind to the two women who had given her their attention for the last few moments. "Do you have any questions?" Jade asked.

One elderly woman, whose name Jade had promptly forgotten, looked at the other and asked, "Do you think they have any more of these cakes?"

Jade was about to signal to one of the waiters when she saw Jason working his way to her through the crowd. As he passed through the room, more and more people took note of him and turned to watch him walk by. She was surprised to see him in his formal attire, and noted with outright astonishment that even his boots had been polished to a gleaming shine. She remained speechless as he walked directly to her without pausing to speak to anyone else, took her hand, and placed a quick kiss on her cheek.

"Sorry I'm so late, dear."

Dear?

She shook her head to clear it. Had she fainted? Was she hallucinating?

The two women in front of them were immediately joined by two more. All of them sought introductions to J.T. He smoothly handled them while Jade remained able to do little more than gawk. He never once let go of her hand. Instead, he laced his fingers through hers and held them tight. When most of the crowd had gathered around them and he had their attention, Jason said, "I'm so happy you were all gracious enough to attend this little gathering of my wife's. I'm sure you realize the importance of viewing this collection that once belonged to Philo Page, but have you taken a close look at the craftsmanship of these pieces? Look closely at the paintings hanging to my left. They are as beautiful as any Rembrandt you've ever seen."

He beamed down on Jade with pride. "I find it quite astute of my wife to see the intrinsic value of this collection, but of course, anyone with an eye for quality and taste will recognize it in these pieces. Enjoy yourselves," he added. "Have some more champagne. Look around at your leisure."

Jade was so amazed by his impromptu speech that she could not move. She knew her eyebrows had risen nearly to her hairline, but she simply couldn't stop staring at Jason.

Just when she thought there could be no surprises left, someone nearby said, "Look, the Stanfords have just arrived."

Sure enough, when Jade looked toward the ballroom doors, she saw the former California governor and his wife entering the room. Although they were building their own mansion on the hill, one that would far surpass Harrington House, Jade had never met them. She glanced up at Jason, who was taking note of the stir the new arrivals had caused. He immediately pulled her along with him as he went to greet the Stanfords.

Within minutes J.T. had completed the introductions and had found a common ground of conversation with Leland Stanford. The man was passionately interested in horses. Jason was at ease talking to him about Occident, the first racing trotter in Stanford's stable. As smoothly as if he we a politician himself, Jason offered Stanford cigars and brandy in the library and left the two women to talk alone, but not before he gave Jade a parting kiss on the cheek and a reminder to "Have fun, dear."

"Well, my dear, the men have certainly become fast friends in no time at all," Stanford's wife said.

Jade was only half-listening to Mrs. Stanford. Still amazed, she was too intent on staring after Jason.

"May we talk, my dear?"

Jade finally turned to her guest. "Of course. I'm sorry, what were you saying?"

The woman smiled and tossed the edges of her opera cape back off her shoulders.

"I can have a waiter take that if you like," Jade offered.

"No, thank you, Jade. I'm still a little chilled. The wind has come up and it's quite foggy out. Now, as I was saying, I'm so sorry we arrived late. I told Leland I just had to see this collection. You see, we plan to decorate one whole room in our new home in a Chinese mode. Are any of these pieces for sale?"

Jade slowly and carefully outlined her plan for a museum foundation as she escorted Jane Stanford around the room, pointing out piece after piece of art.

Finally, Mrs. Stanford stopped her, well aware that most everyone in the room was watching. "I like you, my dear. And I knew your grandfather, although I'll admit I hadn't seen him for years before he passed on. I'm well acquainted with the California History Society here in the city—they do a fine service to San Francisco—but I agree that the Chinese need a museum of sorts, too." She glanced around the room and raised her voice a bit before she said, "I will be happy to be your first sponsor. In fact, I would be pleased if you would put me in charge of the whole affair. Will you leave this to me?"

Jade was so thrilled she almost grabbed the woman and hugged her. After viewing the entire collection, Mrs. Stanford met Matt Van Buren and agreed to have her own lawyer call on him in the morning to finalize the details.

It all seemed too good to be true. Jason had appeared in the doorway like a guardian angel and rescued her. Then the Stanfords had arrived and the most respected, highly regarded wife of one of the state's most influential men agreed to take charge of organizing the museum foundation. Jade was afraid she was going to awaken from the dream at any moment.

The evening gradually came to an end. J.T. returned to her side, and as they bade each of the guests good night, they were still holding hands.

As soon as the door closed and the last carriage pulled down the drive, Jason let go of her hand. He unfastened his collar and tie and shoved them into his coat pocket, shrugged out of his jacket and hooked it over his shoulder. Jade watched as he stopped one of the waiters carrying a champagne bottle toward the kitchen and then quickly relieved him of his burden. She thought he had forgotten about her until he started up the stairs with the bottle in his hand, paused midway, and turned to look down at her. He didn't say a word.

"Thank you, Jason." She felt she owed him that much for what he had done this evening.

"Don't thank me now, Jade." He pulled his watch out of his pocket and checked the time. "I'm giving you thirty minutes to finish up down here. Then, you'll either meet me in my room, or I'm coming after you."

For a few brief hours that evening, Jade had seen what her life would have been like if Jason's trust had not been broken. The experience had been wonderful. He had played the perfect mate. Then, just when she thought there might be a glimmer of hope for them, he had reissued his ultimatum.

She tried to maintain her calm as she went back to the kitchen to give Tao Ling the money to pay the waiters. Once the extra staff had left, Tao started to make her some tea. She did not think that even his soothing brew would calm her, so she refused.

"And Tao," she added before she could change her mind, "we won't be needing you tonight. You needn't sleep in the hallway." She looked down at her hands.

"If you are certain?"

He did not sound at all surprised, but then, she knew he had witnessed Jason's sudden attentiveness all evening.

"If you are certain," he repeated, "and do not mind, Mrs. Harrington, I would like permission to go to the *fan-tan* parlor tonight. It has been a while since I have had a night off." He shrugged.

Jade knew he was hopelessly addicted to gambling. Once a week on his day off, Tao went to Little China to play *fan-tan*, a game of odd or even, in one of the many gambling houses where the Chinese could also bet on *pai gow*, a domino game, or the ancient game of *Mah-Jongg*, played with tiles.

"Of course," she agreed. "You can take tomorrow off, too. I'm sure Quan can help out here in the kitchen."

He allowed himself to look doubtful. "I will return before morning."

The clock in the drawing room chimed and she hurried out of the kitchen. She had a quarter-hour left to decide what to do. Hurrying up the stairs, she took down her hair and shook it free. With the red sash she had used as a hair ornament in her hand, Jade ran down the hall. Once she entered her room, she quickly pulled a chair over to the door and jammed it beneath the knob. Its spindly, cabriole legs didn't look strong enough to keep anything out of her room, let alone someone as strong as Jason.

She closed her eyes and took a deep breath. Did she really want to keep him out? If she was to be truthful, she had to admit that she didn't. What she wanted was Jason, the loving, caring Jason she had known before the wedding—the man she had had another glimpse of tonight—and she knew with sudden clarity that locking him out of her room was not the way to go about getting him back.

As much as she did not want to, she thought of Babs. Naturally, Babs would have known what to do under such circumstances. What Jade decided she had to do was try to broaden her thinking and come up with a plan. She paced the room as she ticked off the facts on her fingertips.

She wanted her marriage to Jason to work.

She wanted his love and his trust.

In the three weeks that he'd been home, she had been biding her time, hoping he would learn to trust her again. For three weeks nothing had changed. They were at an impasse.

Today he had pledged, in no uncertain terms, that he meant to have her. Now. Tonight.

And she realized she wanted him, too.

But not just for tonight. For always.

The facts were clear, but she still didn't have a plan.

The clock on the mantel ticked loudly in the deep silence of her room. There were five minutes left.

They could fight it out again. She could try to hold him off as long as possible.

Or she could give in and go to Jason of her own free will to prove how much she loved him.

She removed her Mandarin jacket and tossed it over her bed, stripped off the silk trousers, then her pantaloons, her chemise, her slippers and stockings. Nude, she raced to the chest of drawers, grabbed up her brush, and ran it through her hair until it hung free and alive with curl.

Two minutes to go.

She leaned close to the mirror and pinched her sallow cheeks. The deep shadows beneath her eyes worried her enough to make her pause and stare back at the faded image of herself. Tomorrow she would go to the doctor. There was definitely something wrong with her.

One minute left. Jade donned her simple topaz robe and drew a deep breath. She tied the robe, crossed the room, and moved the chair out of the way, and once the door was open, Jade silently padded down the hall toward Jason's room.

A warm fire was burning in the grate in the master suite, providing the only light in the darkened room. Jason sat brooding before the fire, his eyes reflecting the hypnotic movement of the flames. He tossed back a glass of champagne and stared at the door.

She wasn't coming.

He sighed and ran both hands through his hair. He didn't look forward to arguing with her any more than he looked forward to having to force her into acquiescence the way he had on their wedding night. But he had given her no choice, and he was not about to back down now.

Clocks all through the house chimed midnight. He dashed the empty glass into the fireplace, furious that she had pushed him this far. He stood, crossed the room, and threw the door open.

J.T. didn't know who was the most amazed when he opened the door and found Jade on the other side, just about to knock. He could hardly believe his eyes.

"You needn't look so shocked, Jason," she said, trying to ease the moment. Then she bowed, much the way Tao might have. "I came to thank you for what you did tonight."

He stepped aside and she entered. Jason watched the way the silk robe caressed her every curve. He could imagine sliding his hands inside it and touching each and every inch of her smooth, warm skin, but he stood motionless, still unable to believe she had really come to him.

Jade turned, not exactly sure how to proceed, but intent on using every ounce of intelligence she possessed to help herself.

He closed the door but stood near it warily. What exactly was she up to?

"You stood by me, Jason. You let all those people believe you were behind the museum. Because of you, Stanford's wife has agreed to take over the whole project."

He shrugged. "It didn't take much doing, as my uncle would say."

"Oh, but it did." She walked toward him slowly, trying to emulate the movements of a cat. Jade reached up and began to unfasten the studs that held his shirt front and cuffs closed. "In front of all those people tonight, you acted like you cared for me."

"I've always had a knack for acting."

"It was a very convincing act."

She was right. It had been all too natural to cater to her, to stand beside her and play the adoring husband. It was too close to the way things might have turned out between them.

"Is that what you're up to now?" He wanted to know. Had to know. "Are you acting?"

She set his diamond studs on the bedstand. "Despite what you believe, I am not a good actress, Jason. I can't hide my feelings."

"No?" He moved closer to her.

"No." She licked her lips in anticipation of his kiss.

"What do you feel?" he whispered.

She whispered back, "Right now?"

"Right now."

She felt heightened anticipation. She felt her blood singing through her veins. She felt hot and wet between her legs, and her knees felt weak. She felt as if she would die if he did not kiss her soon.

But she could not bring herself to tell him what she truly felt or what she truly wanted.

Instead, she whispered, "Let me show you."

Jason couldn't believe what happened any more than he could control his body's instant response when she reached up and slipped her arms about his neck and drew his head down for her kiss.

Jason was shocked. But he did not let his amazement stand in the way of his passion. He clasped her to him and deepened the kiss, slashing his lips across hers, delving deep with his tongue. He heard her moan, felt her melt further into his embrace.

They fell upon the bed. Eager to possess her, half-afraid she would change her mind, J.T. pulled away and began ripping off his clothes.

"Wait!" Jade scrambled to her knees and pushed her hair back out of her eyes.

He stiffened. Had she changed her mind? Had the tease only been using him again?

"Let me," she whispered, and reached out to him with shaking hands.

Jason was speechless. He rolled over and lay perfectly still as Jade tugged his shirt out of his pants and then helped him pull his arms out of the sleeves. She tossed the shirt over the side of the bed and heard him laugh aloud.

She fumbled with his waistband, thankful for the weak firelight that hid the blush staining her cheeks.

He reached down and brushed her hands aside, flicked open the buttons, and then paused. How far was she willing to go to please him? He stretched out again and waited for her to make the next move.

Jade stared down at Jason, at his bare chest covered with crisp, brown-gold hair that trailed down past his navel and then disappeared into his trousers. She wanted to play the seductress, to make this night incomparable to anything she had ever known before, but her own naiveté inhibited her. With trembling hands she reached to him, then pulled back. She hid her face in her hands.

He sat up and brushed her hair back over her shoulder.

"Jade?" His voice was hushed, his breath warm against her ear. "Are you all right?"

She drew her hands down and shook her head. "I wanted to, but I can't." Her voice broke on a sob. "I don't know what to do."

He pulled her into his embrace and rocked her back and forth. "Shh." Pressing soft kisses against her temple, he whispered, "Hush. It's all right." He kissed her tenderly, teased her lower lip with his teeth, gently rubbed her back and calmed her nervous trembling. *How could she know what to do?* he wondered. Their wedding night had been a disaster. He had been angry beyond thought, and she had been a virgin. She had not known real passion, had not reached fulfillment. His little scholar needed to be taught. He took her face between his hands and slowly, tenderly, began to kiss her again.

Engrossed in his kiss, she barely noticed when his hand slipped inside the silk robe and cupped the underside of her breast. He pushed the robe open and dipped his head to her nipple. Jade moaned when his teeth teased the tender bud, then clung to him when his mouth captured her breast and he suckled there. Before he was through, he had gently untied the sash and bared both breasts. He teased her nipples with his thumbs until they burst into full bloom.

Jason's touch was scalding. Jade's response was one of building need until she lay back and pulled him down with her. As he devoted himself to exploring every inch of her with his lips and tongue, Jade reached down and ran her hands through his rich, thick curls. When his tongue lapped a fiery trail from the base of her throat to her navel, she writhed in wild abandon that drove him on.

Need consumed her. She felt like she was on fire, but found the sensation a pleasing contrast to the cool shimmering silk robe beneath her. When his lips neared the apex of her thighs, when his warm breath teased the throbbing, secret bud hidden there, she let out a startled murmur and shook her head. "No, no Jason, don't. Please."

He promised himself there would come a time when she would be at ease with him, but for now all he wanted was to make up for the way he had used her on their wedding night. For now, he could wait to introduce her to all of love's many pleasures.

"I'll take it slow," he whispered. "Slow." He kissed his way back up to her breasts, brushed them again with his lips, laved them with his tongue, and then pulled back. He stared down at her in the firelight. He could not resist running his hand through her hair. The firelight had set it aglow until it spread like glowing flames he could touch as it shimmered against the velvet bedspread. "My God, you're beautiful, my precious Jade."

She cupped his face in her hands. "You are too, Jason."

He laughed, but not in a way that would hurt her. She smiled up at him, her eyes warm with the glow of love. Her lips beckoned him to taste of their nectar again, but this time as he did, he slid his trousers off with his free hand.

He heard her swift intake of breath as he lay back down, this time between her thighs. He reached down and spread her legs and then probed the moist entrance to her womanhood with his erect member.

Jade ran her hands along his ribs and back up again. She raked her fingers through the tight hair on his chest, then down to the place where their bodies touched. When he groaned, a low, soulful sound issued from deep in his throat, she arched toward him. He pressed closer, but still did not enter her completely.

She wanted all of him, but he remained poised at the opening of her heated depths, teasing her, slowly dipping in and out, until a whimper of agony was forced from her lips.

"You want me, don't you, Jade. You want me inside you."

"Yes," she moaned again. "Yes, Jason. I do. I want you."

"Tell me what else you want."

"I want to feel you inside me. I want you now."

He pressed closer, becoming further enveloped inside her, yet not fully. Not yet. "How is it you always seem so cool, Jade? But you're not, are you?"

"No," she gasped, clinging to him, pressing her hands against his hips, trying to make him slide the rest of the way into her.

"You feel hot inside. As hot as the desert."

"Jason . . . please," she gasped.

"Do you love me?" he asked.

"Yes."

"Say it."

"I love you. I love you, Jason."

He thrust into her until they were fused together by the intensity of building pressure that was soon more than either of them could bring back under control. He began to dip and plunge and she followed his lead, arching to meet his demands until the demand for release became too great and Jade gave herself over to the blinding ecstasy that surged through her—radiating from the pulsating core of flesh that held him imprisoned—down to the very tips of her toes.

Inundated with her own pleasure, Jade heard him call out her name the moment his seed burst forth, hot and searing inside her. She held him tight, half-afraid of his ragged breathing and the way he continued to shudder with his face buried against her neck.

Stroking his smooth back, she held him close until his breathing matched her own. Finally, he raised his head and stared down at her, his gaze tender, the mask of doubt that had shadowed his expression since their wedding night gone.

He kissed her again, slowly, languidly, then rubbed his nose against hers.

Jade smiled and held him tight. He wrapped a handful of her hair about his wrist and then, lying across his wife, Jason slept

❈ CHAPTER 19 ❈

In a narrow lane . . .
Beware enemies.

Before the light of dawn brought color to the shadowed corners of the master suite, Jade awoke and carefully slipped out of Jason's arms. For a moment she thought he had awakened, then was relieved when he rolled over, hugged his pillow, and continued to sleep deeply. She smiled down at him when she recalled how sometime during the night he had awakened her, pulled her up and out of her robe, undressed himself, then tucked her into bed beside him.

She hated to leave his warm embrace, but was determined to be out before the city came to life. Each time she had awakened during the night, a growing suspicion kept her from immediately falling back to sleep; she thought she might be carrying Jason's child.

There was no other excuse she could give for her exhaustion and general malaise. For the past three weeks, she had grown more and more lethargic. Food did not appeal to her, and nothing she had tried had eased the pounding headaches. She had to know for certain before she told Jason. Their relationship was still too tenuous to handle any shock, and a baby would definitely constitute an upheaval.

She smiled as she slipped into her robe and quietly tiptoed out of the room. Last night had been wonderful, exactly the new beginning she had hoped for. This morning, it looked as if there was a chance that her dream of love might still come true.

Hurriedly, she dressed, buttoned on her shoes and her cloak. She took the time to write Jason a hasty note and put it in her pocket. When she picked up her black reticule and hung it around her waist, she was finally ready.

Downstairs, the kitchen was quiet and cold; the fire in the stove had burned out. Tao was nowhere to be found. She

293

quietly opened the door to his room, but he had still not returned from Little China. She hoped he wasn't gambling away his wages.

A sleepy-eyed Quan slowly wandered into the room and stared at the cold stove. She shook her head when Jade asked if she knew how to light it. It seemed that a singsong girl did not have any useful skills besides pleasuring men. Jade let her thoughts follow one on the other and eyed Quan speculatively. Little Quan Yen would know how to pleasure Jason far better than she did. It was not a reassuring thought, but Jade was bolstered by the idea that Jason seemed to enjoy teaching her the ways of love.

Bending over the stove, she cleaned out the cold ashes herself, fed in some kindling, started a small fire, and then added more split wood. When a pot of coffee was set to boil, she gave Quan Yen instructions to make certain she gave Jason a cup when he came downstairs.

"Where you go now, missee?" Quan wanted to know. "You want tea?"

Jade shook her head. She hoped the coffee would help jolt her out of her lethargy. "I'll just have a little coffee, Quan. Then I'm going out."

The girl suddenly looked panicked. "Where you go? I go too. Dress chop chop and go with missee." She started for her room.

Jade stopped her with a word. "Wait. Wait, Quan. I'm going to walk. It would be too hard for you to go along. Besides, I'm not going very far, just down the hill."

Quan's concern for Jade was evident in her worried expression. "Not good missee go alone. I go. I walk fast."

"Absolutely not," Jade insisted. "The best thing you can do is stay here and give Jason my note." Jade handed her a quickly penned explanation. For a moment Quan looked like she would argue, then changed her mind and took the note from Jade.

Outside, the morning was windy, but not foggy. The chilly air made her shiver, an excuse to walk faster. From the top of California Street she could see all the way down to the bay and Yerba Buena Island—a low mound of land surrounded by water that seemed to be floating offshore. She walked down the street past the narrow, bay-windowed homes that lined the hill as she headed for the heart of town. Jade had not seen Doctor Adams since her mother had died, but she assumed he was still in the same office housed in three small rooms on the ground floor of his home.

The city came to life around her. Chinese street vendors passed her on their way up the hill as they set out to sell goods to the houseboys who waited to buy their wares. As she neared a busy intersection, a milk wagon and horsecar vied for room amidst the growing numbers of buggies and carriages on the street. Shop owners pulled up the shades and swept off the sidewalks that fronted the many stores that lined the street. The city pulsed with a life of its own, and like a lumbering giant, awoke slowly, stretched, and finally opened its eyes to the new day.

By the time she reached her destination, even the foot traffic on the streets had increased. Slowly, Jade climbed the stairs to the building that, thankfully, still wore a sign that advertised her doctor's practice. A small bell hung over the door. It sang out a greeting as she entered the office.

Jason strode through the house at noon as mad as a bee in a bottle. It was bad enough he had awakened at dawn alone, but things only got worse as the day went on. He had no idea where his wife had gone. He woke up alone, and called her name. When there was no response, he raced down the hall to her room, which he nearly ransacked in his haste to see if she had left him for good.

There were so few clothes in her closet that for a second he thought she had left him, but as he sorted through them, he realized that she had left behind the clothes she always wore. Could it be these were all she owned? He shook his head. No wonder Jade had never worn any fancy dresses since she moved in with him. She had none.

His heart went out to her. He had few things by choice. Women, it seemed to him, needed clothing for every occasion. He thought of the way Nettie had been outfitted on the two occasions when he had seen her. But Jade had nothing more than the few sad pieces hanging in the armoire.

When he found her valise in the bottom of the closet, the tight pain around his heart eased. Curiosity made him open it. Embarrassment forced him to snap it shut again. In the dark interior of the valise, Jade had hidden away her ruined wedding gown.

Thankfully, Quan Yen had been in the kitchen waiting for him with fresh coffee, which was all he had for breakfast. When he asked the girl where Jade was, she had shaken her head sadly and said, "Missee go out. Not home." He asked after Tao Ling and received the same response. Frustrated, J.T. then went out to the stables to put the horses through their paces.

He spent the morning going through the motions of his work while his mind remained occupied with worry over Jade. Last night when she had finally come to him, she had given him more joy than he had ever known. He fell asleep, certain that things had changed between them. His father's business holdings had nearly all been liquidated. A buyer was interested in the house. Soon, he could return to New Mexico. Last night, he had been certain Jade would go with him. Now, once again, he did not know what she was up to.

When he saw Tao walking up the drive alone, Jason met the houseboy halfway. When he asked after Jade, Tao suddenly looked as worried as Jason felt, and said he had no idea where she was. J.T. was ready to set out after her, but he did not even know where to start looking. It was nearly noon. He decided to give her an hour.

Before the noon meal he went upstairs to wash up. Halfway down the staircase, Jason heard a knock at the door and hurried to open it, ready to give Jade a good talking to. Instead, he stood dumbfounded when he opened the door and faced Cash Younger and his wife, Guadalupe.

"Uncle Cash?" Jason couldn't believe they were standing there on the doorstep. "Lupita?"

"Don't stand there gawkin', J.T.! Open the door. We've come to visit."

It was Cash Younger all right. All six feet of him. But more stooped than Jason remembered. The lines about Cash's

sun-creased skin were a bit deeper, his skin pale—as if he had
not seen the sun in weeks. His uncle seemed to be favoring his
left side, which led Jason to assume he had suffered another of
his infamous accidents. Cash's full head of hair was almost
completely silver. The man appeared to be tired, but his blue
eyes were as full of life as ever.

Cash was outfitted in his one good suit, while Lupe was
dressed in the finest gown Jason had ever seen her wear. The
peach silk bedecked with ruffles was so far from the colorful
full skirts and muslin blouses she wore at the ranch that he
couldn't help but stare at her. Her hair was the same, rich
ebony plaited into thick braids wrapped about her head. Lupe
was reed-thin, a few inches taller than Cash, her skin brown
from tending her herb and vegetable garden. Lupe Younger
could make anything grow. She was known as a healer, a
nurturer. She had nurtured J.T. through his mother's death,
through his adolescent years. She always called him *hijo,* son.

Usually Lupe was in command of everything and everyone
on the ranch, but now as she stood outside and stared up at
Harrington House, she was more subdued than he had ever
seen her.

"Lupita? Did you come to see me or stare at this place?"
J.T. smiled down on her.

"*Hijo!*" Her attention then centered on Jason as she hugged
him and patted him on the back. "We were so worried about
you."

"I don't know why. I told you I'd be home just as soon as
everything was settled."

Cash and Lupe stepped inside and stared up at the forty-foot-
high ceiling in the foyer, at the overwhelming chandelier, and
then at the green and white marble floor. "*Dios!*" For a
moment all she could do was stare. Then she turned her
attention back to Jason and captured his face between her
hands. She turned him this way and that, reading his eyes with
her own as if they could tell her everything she wanted to
know. "When did you not answer my letter, when we heard
nothing from you even though your uncle was so ill, I knew
things were not right. So, as soon as Cash was able to travel,
we came to you."

Jason started to explain, but Lupe went right on. "Your

uncle was so sick. I could not believe how sick. For a few days he had no feeling in his left arm or leg and his face was frozen on one side. It was horrible. But, with prayers and good care, the trouble passed. Now he is well." She took her husband's hand and smiled, but was unable to entirely remove the shadow of doubt from her eyes.

He turned to Cash. Ill? Was that the reason his usually robust uncle appeared so frail? "When did this happen? I didn't get any letter. Are you sure you sent one?"

"*Sí, hijo,* weeks ago." She bobbed her head and her dark eyes flashed. "Cash fell ill the day after you left on your journey."

Jason frowned. No letter had come from them since he had arrived. At least not while he had been home, and Tao had brought him the mail every day. But if the letter had arrived while he was in Monterey, and if, as Lupe said, she wrote it weeks ago, that would explain its loss. Had Jade received it and not shown it to him? More to the point, why wouldn't she have wanted him to see it?

"Jason?" Lupe touched his arm, and his thoughts swung back to her.

"I'm sorry. I was just trying to think of where that letter might have gone. Let's get you both settled. Dinner will be ready in a while, and it sounds like we have a lot to talk about." He cast a worried glance at Cash. "I still can't believe you're here," he said, forcing a smile.

If their pile of luggage was any indication, Cash and Lupita were there to stay for quite a while. J.T. and Tao hauled it into the house and upstairs, where he gave the couple a choice of rooms. Lupe, ever sensitive to the needs of others, left the two men alone once the bags were in the room.

"I want to go and see the kitchen," she told J.T. "It must be grand."

Jason shrugged. "Turn right at the bottom of the stairs. It's at the end of the long hallway," he directed.

When he was alone with his uncle he said, "I'm sorry, Cash, I didn't know . . ."

"Hell, boy, nothin' you could do for me anyway. I told Lupe that, but you know her when she gets dramatic."

If his uncle's appearance was any indication, Lupe's worry had been justified. "You know I would have come home." Jason glanced down at his uncle's hands. They were gnarled and worn from years of hard work. J.T. hated to think he had almost lost his uncle now that he had enough money to turn the ranch into the place of Cash's dreams.

"So, this place is all yours, lock, stock, and barrel?" Cash stood up and slowly limped around the room. He paused beside an urn on a pedestal table, eyed it speculatively, then turned back to J.T. "You sure you want to come back to New Mexico and give all this up?"

"Sure as sunshine after a storm." J.T. tried to smile. He stretched and wished he could make Cash whole again. "The place has been for sale since the moment I saw it."

Lupe bustled back in and announced, "Dinner is almost ready. That man, Tao, said it is something Chinese."

J.T. could not miss her less than enthusiastic expression. "You'll get used to the food," he told them, "but I'll warn you now, eat a lot of it."

"Tonight," Lupe said, deciding instantly, "I will fix the meal."

"I was hoping you'd say that." Jason's stomach growled as he looked forward to real New Mexican cooking. "Before we go back downstairs I think I should tell you that I got married."

The second the words were out he realized that he might have put the news to them a little too bluntly. Lupe sat down abruptly on the edge of the bed and Cash barked, "Married? Who in the hell to?"

J.T. ran his fingers through his hair, sat down on a chair beside a reading table, and motioned Cash into the one opposite. "You better sit down for this. It's a long story."

"So that's it," Jason concluded a while later. "I married her, then I overheard Jade and her friend talking about their scheme after the wedding."

Lupe frowned. "But she argues that she is innocent and that she never wanted to trick you?"

"That's right."

"But *hijo,* maybe she is telling you the truth."

"You're too softhearted, Lupita," J.T. reminded her.

Cash, who had remained thoughtful throughout Jason's long explanation, finally spoke up. "You say she paid off the debt with her house when she found out she could, and that she's tryin' to find a home for this Chinese stuff—"

Jason nodded. "I was beginning to think she might be sincere. When I woke up today, she was gone. No explanation. Nothing."

"And you are worried," Lupe said.

"I'm mad as hell."

"From worry."

Trying to deny her words, Jason shook his head. "I was about to go looking for her when you arrived." His brow furrowed in thought. "I have no idea where she is, though."

"Maybe she went to see the detective you spoke of," Lupe volunteered.

"How about the attorney?" Cash asked.

"That's where I was going to start. I was giving her till noon to get back. I can't wait to hear the explanation she's concocted this time."

Cash leaned forward, his expression one of concern. "Do you think she has left you, J.T.?"

Has she? Jason couldn't be sure. "She didn't take any of her clothes or the jewelry I gave her. She certainly had good cause to leave, though."

Cash looked thoughtful, snapped his fingers and then said, "You didn't try singing to the poor gal, did you?"

Jason ignored his uncle's attempt at humor. His expression remained grim. "No. But I practically raped her on our wedding night."

"You didn't, did you?" Even Cash was aghast.

"No, I didn't have to, but if she had resisted, I don't know . . ."

Lupe stood up, refusing to hear more. "Well, I know. You would have done no such thing. Now, I think we should go down to eat and then, J.T., you will go look for your wife and bring her home."

Before he met them in the kitchen, Jason went into Jade's room and rifled through the papers on her desk, shook the pages of all of her books, and then sorted through the piles of notes until he found Lupita's letter.

He ripped the letter open and read Lupe's terse plea. She had asked him to come home. She had feared for Cash's life, and he had not even known the man was ill. And just as she had said, she had written to him weeks ago.

Why would Jade keep something like this from him? Did she somehow know what was inside? The letter did not appear to have been opened. Had she guessed? She must have feared letting him out of her clutches after what he had discovered on their wedding night.

He shoved the letter into his back pocket and went to join the others. Downstairs, Jason couldn't help but hover over Cash, pulling out his chair and then making sure the man was well settled before he sat down.

Cash Younger shook his head and requested, "Don't be making such a fuss over me, J.T. I don't intend to leave this earth for quite a while. Besides, this is one stubborn woman." He smiled over at Lupe. "She won't let me go."

Lupe's eyes flooded with tears. "Si, *mi corazón*, you are going nowhere without me."

Jason felt a pang of jealousy and wondered at the love he saw pass between them. What would it be like to share such love for a lifetime? Before he married Jade, he thought he would know, but now, after everything she had already done to disprove her affection, he doubted if he would ever be as lucky as the Youngers.

Their presence helped take his mind off of Jade. It was a relief to have them there. Seeing them both at his table only served to remind Jason how much he had missed them.

When Xavier came in from the stables to share the meal with them, Cash and Lupe were delighted to learn that he would be moving to the ranch. They both stared at Tao, who served the meal with Quan Yen's help, another sight that Cash and Lupe could not seem to get enough of.

Jason forced himself to slow down, to at least try to finish his food, even though he could not enjoy his meal with Jade missing. By the time he was through, he was certain of one thing. When he found her, she would definitely pay for the worry she had put him through.

"I'm not pregnant?" Jade did not know whether to be happy or sad.

Dr. Adams, a nondescript man of average height with brown eyes, thinning brown hair, and a brown suit, peered over his spectacles and shook his head. "I'm afraid not, Jade."

"Then what's wrong with me? I've never felt this tired in my life."

He shrugged and scribbled a note on a long sheet of paper. "I think you are just suffering from nervous exhaustion. That would explain your weight loss." He set the pen and paper down and then walked over to her again. He took her chin in his hand and tilted her face up so that he could study her eyes. "Get lots of rest, don't skip any meals, take some light exercise. Do you ever get outside?"

She shook her head. "Rarely."

"Well, start walking. Get that new husband of yours to take you out to the country." He patted her knee. "You'll be right as rain in no time at all. Now, you get dressed and stop by again in two weeks." He went on to prescribe a tonic, sold her a bottle of it, and sent her on her way.

Jade walked back along the street with her head down, watching the sidewalk pass beneath her. Lost in thought, she bumped into an old woman carrying a bundle of packages and stooped to help her pick them up. When she stood up, she felt dizzy.

There's nothing wrong with me.

She kept repeating the words as she continued along the avenue, but world was still spinning. She heard a horsecar bell ringing nearby and hurried to catch the car. After paying the driver, she stepped aboard.

Within a few blocks, Jade realized she had taken the wrong line and instead of nearing California Street, she was closer to the center of Little China. She tried to clear her head with a shake, but the movement only heightened her discomfort. She clung to the rail and stared out at the passing landmarks. The car was taking her farther from home when all she wanted at the moment was to get back to the house. And Jason.

At the very next stop, she stepped off, rather than go any farther out of her way. The streets were crowded with Chinese men. She looked about and tried to get her bearings, but her mind was growing fuzzier as she grew weaker. She rubbed her temples with her fingertips and tried to take a deep breath, but she was unable to fill her lungs. *It's only natural*, she reasoned, *to feel this way after having very little sleep last night*. The party and all the arrangements were more work than she was used to, and she had not eaten all day.

Now and again she glanced up to watch the clouds fly past a patch of open sky, framed by the tall buildings on either side of the narrow street. The structures, with their sagging, bamboo balconies, gave the appearance of two-story matchstick houses.

Up ahead, a fishmonger in his market stall wrapped an octopus, still water-slicked and dripping, in a newspaper covered with Chinese characters. He turned to shout to a companion half-hidden behind a stack of crates and barrels topped with round, flat baskets filled with Pacific crab. A jumble of goods formed the back wall of the stall.

Walking slowly, Jade watched as an overladen peddler tried to negotiate the press through the crowded byway, carefully balancing two huge baskets suspended from a pole that rested across his shoulders. He wore a proud look as he hurried through the crowd, hawking his goods.

With the ceaseless activity common to overpopulated places, the alleyway behind upper Sacramento Street vibrated like a tightly packed ant colony, its inhabitants ever mindful of money to be made or lost if they were not swift enough to grasp the opportunity.

She inhaled the cloying scent of tobacco and sandlewood that mingled with sesame oil and overused grease. Even the smell of the place was the same as she remembered it.

Little China was always the same. Foreign, intriguing, but never frightening. Not until today.

Jade stopped beside a corner vendor serving noodle soup out of a huge steaming caldron. She bought a bowl, drank the rich broth, deftly used the chop sticks to shovel the noodles into her mouth, and then quickly moved on. As her head began to clear, she became more aware of her surroundings, and with realization came fear. She had ventured into Little China alone. If someone still wanted her out of the way, she was a perfect target.

She glanced over her shoulder. No one seemed to be paying her any mind. When she came to the middle of the street, she realized she could be out of Little China in minutes if she took a short cut through the narrow alleyway to her left. She looked behind her. She looked ahead. There was no one in the alley. Jade ducked into the passageway, which was wide enough only to accommodate foot traffic, and stealthily walked alongside the tall buildings.

The sky was still gray. The hour seem later than it actually was. Still, if she did not get home soon, there was no telling what Jason would think. The beat of her footsteps accelerated, keeping time with her racing heart. She was near the end of the alley when she stopped to catch her breath. This time when she looked over her shoulder, Jade caught sight of a tall, bearded Caucasian at the other end of the path.

The sight of the burly man at the end of the alley gave her the energy to run. She did not pause to see if he was running too. She did not have to, for soon she could hear him bearing down on her.

Jade rounded the corner. Fear quickened her steps and helped overcome her exhaustion. Her breath was coming in heaving gasps, but still she did not stop. Instead, she ducked into the first door she came to, and found herself enveloped by a cool, dark world heavily scented with incense.

She recognized the interior of a *joss* house, a place were medicines and fortunes were dispensed. She stood in what appeared to be an anteroom. Incense burned in a brazier on a small altar in the corner near a statue of Buddha. Colorful ceramic bowls of oranges, rice, and sweets were arranged around the base of the statue. Thankful that the room was deserted, Jade hid there until she heard voices approaching from behind an inner door. With a furtive prayer to every god in existence, she stepped back out onto the street. Up ahead, moving away from her, was the man who had chased her down the alley. Unmindful of the curious stares of passersby, she pressed up against the building.

A firecracker exploded beside her. Jade nearly jumped out of her skin. Gongs sounded. A long string of firecrackers exploded in rapid succession. When a funeral procession turned the corner, Jade saw a means of escape. She waited for the hearse to roll past, and barely glanced at a draped portrait of the deceased that was propped up on the seat beside the driver. Red strips of paper "road money" were being tossed in the air by members of the funeral procession. The paper money was meant to appease any evil spirits who had not been frightened away by the gongs and fireworks.

Jade darted across the street between the hearse and the wagon that followed behind it, which was loaded with paper replicas of the dead man's most prized possessions and enough food to leave at the gravesite to help send the man off to the hereafter. She prayed that the noise and confusion would hide her escape.

Not until she had struggled to run two blocks more did she pause to take a breath and reconnoiter. Her pursuer was nowhere in sight.

Afraid to take another trolley, she ran up to a well-dressed man standing near a hitching rail and grabbed his sleeve.

Gasping for breath, she tried to make her need known. "I . . . I have to . . . rent your horse."

An Englishman in a bowler hat looked shocked. He untied the reins of what appeared to be the tallest horse in the world. "Really, madam, I—"

"I'll pay you. Please. I'll pay you five dollars. I only need to ride it to California Street."

The man stared back at her in amazement. A hired hack was only a dollar and a half a mile. "This is really quite strange." He shook his head.

Jade glanced over her shoulder, afraid the bearded man would catch up to her. "Please, have you heard of Harrington House? It's the biggest house on California Street. That's where I have to go. You can come get your horse in a few moments, but I need it now!" She fairly shouted the last words at him.

He stepped back to get away from her.

I'm becoming a madwoman. But there was no help for it, she thought. She tugged the reticule off her arm and opened it. Jade pulled out a wad of bills and waved them in the man's face. "Here! Take what you want."

"Well," he said, his eyes on the money, "I think five is a fair price, but . . ."

"Take it!"

He took it.

Jade snapped the strings of her bag tight and looped it over her arm. "Now help me up onto this thing." She looked her rented mount in the eye and shuddered. The man stepped up beside the horse and cupped his hands together. Jade grabbed the saddle horn and tried to pull herself up, managed to drape her stomach across the saddle, then wriggled as the man shoved on her foot until she righted herself. When she threw her right leg over the saddle, she then tugged on her skirt, trying to cover her calves and ankles. At the last minute, she remembered to tuck the ends of her cloak beneath her so that it would not flap and spook the horse.

He handed her the reins.

She had never ridden without someone beside her.

She was shaking like jellied consommé. "Don't forget Harrington House. Your horse will be there."

I hope. As she rode away, holding onto the reins and pommel for dear life, she wondered what the poor Englishman thought as he watched a mad woman with wild red hair flying about and tears streaming down her face bounce away on the back of his horse.

The small group assembled for dinner at Harrington House had just finished their meal when someone began pounding on the front door. Jason waved Tao aside and pushed back his chair. He ran his hands through his hair. The sound of his boot heels rang out loud and clear in the foyer as he hurried to answer the summons. He whipped the door open and felt a rush of relief followed by anger as he gazed down on Jade.

Her hair was a mess. Her eyes were deep emerald pools of fear that streamed tears. She looked confused and disoriented

He glanced out the door and saw a strange horse munching on the lawn beyond the drive.

"Jason?" she whispered, a tremulous smile on her lips.

He did not move aside. Instead, looming over her in the doorway, he all but shouted, "Where in the hell have you been?"

Her reticule dangled from one wrist as she pressed her hands to her temples. "Please, Jason, don't yell."

"I'll damn well yell when I want to yell!" Then, suddenly remembering his guests, he lowered his voice. "You have a lot of fast talking to do, Jade." He reached out and took her by the arm, dragging her inside. She was trembling; he could feel it even through her thick cloak, and it angered him. He had every right to be furious, and he wasn't about to let her fear curb that anger. "Where did that horse come from?"

"I . . . I gave a man five dollars to rent it. I . . . he'll come to get it in a while." The morning's escapade had taken its toll. She couldn't think clearly with her head pounding so. All she wanted to do was get upstairs to bed. "Should I have tied it up?"

"Xavier!" Jason called over his shoulder. Wiping his mouth on the back of his hand, the man appeared almost immediately.

"Get that horse tied up out front. Someone's coming for it." J.T. then turned to Jade. "What's the man's name?"

"I don't know." She shook her head. "I didn't ask him."

As Xavier scooted past them and ran out the door, Jason closed it behind him and turned on her. "Where have you been?"

She drew a shaking breath. What had happened to the loving man she had left curled up in bed? "Didn't you get my note?"

"What note?"

"I left a note with Quan Yen. I went to the doctor," she said softly. "I'm sick."

Fear made him shake her. "What's wrong with you?"

"Nothing."

"You aren't making any sense."

"Dr. Adams said nothing is the matter with me. But I'm sick, I know it. I'm dizzy, my mouth is always dry, my stomach aches, and I can't catch my breath."

He reached into his back pocket and pulled out a crumpled letter and waved it in front of her face. "Why did you hide this from me?"

She squinted, trying to see what it was he was shoving at her. "What is it?"

"Don't play coy with me. You know damn well what it is. It's the letter my aunt sent me weeks ago. Why did you hide it?"

"I didn't hide it. I've never seen it before." She tried to pull away from him. "You're hurting me."

"Were you afraid I was going to leave town before you had a chance to seduce me again? I'm surprised you waited until last night. You must have been pretty sure of yourself, putting it off for so long."

Jade buried her face in her hands and tried to think. Her mind was a jumble of thoughts that would not straighten themselves out. When had that letter arrived? From New Mexico, he had said. She rubbed her eyes and memory of it slowly came to her—the letter arrived the day Matt had brought her Babs' note and her father's letter, just after J.T. left for Monterey. She had tossed it on the desk, and somehow it had become lost amid the clutter.

"I did receive that letter," she admitted, no longer caring whether or not Jason would ever forgive her. All she wanted was to crawl into bed and pull the covers over her head. "Matt brought it the day after you left for Monterey. I put it on the desk and forgot about it."

He frowned with the dark expression she was coming to know all too well.

"Go ahead and beat me." She sighed and looked up at him with a weary expression. "I feel so bad already I don't think I would feel it."

His expression turned to disgust at such an absurd notion. "I'm not going to beat you."

"No?"

"No!"

"Then will you please stop yelling? It hurts my head."

"We have guests I want you to meet."

He hauled her into the dining room, where he paused on the

threshold and announced, "Uncle Cash, Aunt Guadalupe, this is my wife, Jade."

Cash pushed himself out of his chair and said hello.

Lupe stared, trying to find words to say, but failed.

Jade fainted dead away.

Hauling her into his arms, Jason carried Jade up the stairs to her room. Lupe followed close on his heels. She had been a healer all her life; the fact that Cash had recovered so quickly from his illness was testimony to her skill. She did not comment when her nephew carried his wife to a guest room instead of his own, but quickly set about loosening the girl's clothing while J.T. got a wet compress for her head.

Lupe sat on the bed beside Jade and smoothed back her hair while Jason hovered over them both. When Jade's eyelashes fluttered and she opened her eyes, her gaze immediately focused on Jason.

"How do you feel?" Lupe asked.

Jade licked her lips.

"Get her some water," Lupe directed, and J.T. disappeared.

"I'm all right," Jade finally said, weakly trying to sit up. "Really, I am."

"Stay," Lupe said, pressing her back with a gentle hand. "You're still dizzy."

Jason returned with the water and handed it to Lupe, who held Jade's head while she sipped at it. Lupe then looked at Jason.

"How long have you been married?"

He shrugged. "About five weeks."

"Are you carrying a child?" Lupe asked Jade.

The mattress sagged when Jason abruptly sat down beside Lupe.

Jade shook her head. "No. I . . . I thought I might be. That's why I went to the doctor."

You fool. Jason berated himself. When would he learn to think before he jumped to conclusions? The idea that Jade might be pregnant with his child had never entered his mind.

Lupe felt Jade's forehead, then the pulse at her neck. She asked for a detailed description of Jade's symptoms and listened carefully. "What did the doctor say to you?"

"He said I was suffering from nerves and told me to come home and rest. And walk." She looked at Jason and then away. "He said I should go to the country."

Lupe watched Jade for a moment longer. Then she decided: "I will bring you something to eat."

"No, please. Just tell Tao I would like some tea. That's all."

"I will make you some tea. Later, I will bring you a tray of food. You need to eat."

Jason was still too worried to smile as he listened to the exchange. Lupe's cure-alls always revolved around food. She often said that a person is only as healthy as what he puts into his body.

When Lupita left them alone, Jason, who was still seated on the edge of the bed, scooted closer to Jade.

"Jade, I'm sorry for the way I acted downstairs."

She refused to look at him and picked at the bedspread. "No, you're not."

"Yes, I am. Very sorry. It's just that I woke up this morning and found you gone, then when I found that letter among your things, something inside me snapped."

"Did you send someone to kill me, Jason?"

He looked stunned. "What are you talking about?" He studied her carefully to see if she was serious.

She tried to put her jumbled thoughts into words. Everything was so confused. "I got lost today, I don't know how I did, I know the city so well. My grandfather used to say—"

"What happened?" He tried to get her back to the point.

"I was on the wrong horsecar. I got off in Little China—"

"You weren't supposed to be there, Jade. In fact, I can't understand why you went out alone at all. Why didn't you tell me you wanted to see the doctor? I would have taken you."

She frowned, trying to pull her jumbled thoughts together again. "A man was following me. A big man. I ran down an alley, and I heard him run after me. I slipped across the street when a funeral went past and finally lost him."

"Was he one of the men who chased you the night we ate in Little China?"

"No. He wasn't Chinese. That's why I thought that maybe

you . . . you wanted to get rid of me so badly that you hired someone."

It hurt him deeply to think that she would even suspect him of wanting to cause her harm, especially after last night. He reached out and smoothed her hair back off her forehead. "Do you really think I would do anything to harm you, Jade? How could you think that after last night?"

"Because you're always willing to think the worst of me. *You* thought I kept the letter from you on purpose." Her green eyes glazed with tears of exhaustion and despair. In a broken whisper that tore at his heart she asked, "Will it always be like this between us, Jason? If it will, I don't think I have the strength to take it anymore."

He gathered her into his arms and held her close. She did not reach out to hold him back, but seemed content to simply lie there. He closed his eyes and kissed her temple.

He wondered what they were doing to each other.

She wondered how long they could go on this way.

❧ CHAPTER 20 ❧

Trouble neglected becomes still more troublesome.

A fire crackled behind the grate in the drawing room at Harrington House, lending a false sense of hominess to a room that had only been furnished as a showpiece. Jason stood with his hands in his pockets, staring out at the fog-shrouded gardens, and wished he was looking out at a clear, crisp New Mexican morning instead of another damp, dreary one in San Francisco. Lieutenant Jon Chang had just arrived, and Jason was waiting until Tao Ling poured the man a cup of tea. The small task was nearly a ritual, J.T. noted, as Tao carefully filled one of the small bowl-shaped cups.

Jason watched the detective take a sip, then set the cup down and look expectantly in his direction. After he cleared his throat, J.T. sat down in one of the tall armchairs near the fireplace. "I asked you to drop by because I want this mess involving my wife cleared up. Do you have any more information than you had a few weeks ago?"

Jon Chang showed no reaction to Jason's outright hostility. Instead, he took another sip of tea, then said, "No. Nothing. It is as if Li Po, the alchemist, has dropped off of the face of the earth. Has something happened recently that I have not been made aware of?"

"Yesterday my wife went to the doctor and on her way home became disoriented. A man, a Caucasian, followed her through Little China, but she managed to lose him."

"She was warned against going back to Little China."

"I know that and you know that, but you don't know my wife."

"Did she recognize this man?"

"She said she didn't."

"I see."

"There is also something that she has been working on that she hasn't told you about." Jason stood and walked over to a table laden with crystal decanters and glasses. He picked up his chair. "I took these off of Jade's desk."

Jon Chang reached for the pages and stared down at them in mute interest. "I don't recognize the characters."

"Neither did my wife. She's been trying to decode them for the past two weeks, ever since the crates arrived."

"Crates?"

"They contained the Chinese art pieces that her grandfather collected. To make a long story short, she wants to set up a museum here in San Francisco to house the collection. Anyway, each crate of goods delivered from the bank was marked with these characters, except for one, and that one contains what Jade is convinced are the alchemist's belongings."

For the first time since they had met, J.T. watched Jon Chang's face register surprise.

"She has the alchemist's possessions?" Chang asked. "Why wasn't I told?"

"Because she wanted to figure out what these symbols meant before she turned them over to you, but I want them out of here now, along with that box. I don't want my wife involved anymore. Someone still wants to find the alchemist, or whatever he left behind, and they are out to get my wife in order to have him. I want you to take the box and get the word out on the street that Jade Douglas Harrington is no longer involved in this in any way. She's innocent of any knowledge of her father's schemes."

"Of course, I'll do whatever you ask, but that isn't going to ensure your wife's safety."

"I intend to see to that. My business here is nearly through, and when it is, I'm taking her to New Mexico with me."

"I see. How does your wife feel about your turning these things over to me?"

"She doesn't know I've called you here. Besides, she's too sick to care."

"I am not," Jade announced from the doorway.

Both men turned at the sound of her voice. She was standing in the doorway, her emerald eyes huge in her pale face. She had donned the comfortable Mandarin jacket and pants, along with her silk slippers. Jason was on his feet in an instant. He crossed the room and escorted her to the settee.

"Do you want some tea?" Jason asked. "I'll have Tao bring in another cup."

She shook her head. Lupita had taken full charge of her, and Jade was amazed at how much better she felt this morning. At least the world had stopped reeling and her stomach cramps had lessened. She turned to Jon Chang.

"I'm afraid Jason is acting out of worry. I wanted to decipher the meaning of those symbols before I gave them to you. Would you mind if I worked on them a little longer?"

"Are you getting anywhere?" Chang leaned forward, anxious to hear her reply.

"Now wait just a minute—" Jason interrupted. He knew when he was being railroaded, and Jade was a master engineer.

"Yes, I am," Jade said without paying any attention to Jason's outburst. "But I don't understand the messages. For instance," she began as she reached out and took the pages from Chang, "this one says, 'The sun is in hiding. The earth is cold and damp and so is the clay.'" Jade shrugged. "Or how about this one? 'The devil rides a winged bird.' I haven't figured out the second half yet."

"Hardly a clue to where Li Po might be."

"No," Jade agreed, shaking her head, "but I thought they might at least lead us to him once I translated them all. Jason obviously told you I opened a box of items I believe were Li Po's. It was with my grandfather's collection."

"I understand that. So the alchemist was able to write on the crates that housed your grandfather's art? When?"

"I think that father must have kept him at the adobe. That would explain the silk sash I found there. There was nothing to match it among Grandfather's things."

Chang looked at J.T. "I can see why you want these things removed, but I am on horseback, Mr. Harrington. Would you mind if I send a man over for the crate later?"

Jade came to life. "I don't want you to take it yet!"

"Your husband is concerned for your safety. As am I."

"But, those things were with my grandfather's. Legally, they are mine," Jade argued. Her head was beginning to pound again. "And we really don't know for certain that they belonged to Li Po."

Chang asked, "What does the box contain?"

When she looked as if she would stubbornly remain silent, Jason indicated with a nod that Jade should answer him.

"A small glass still, bottles and vials containing cinnabar, slivers of jade, silver, gold dust—" She looked quickly at Jason, afraid he would accuse her of trying to steal it. "A very little bit of gold dust. Some bark and pieces of twigs, peach pits, herbs." She shrugged. "That's all."

"The presence of the still indicates to me that your assumption is correct. The items must have belonged to the alchemist," Chang said.

Jason stood up abruptly, signaling an end to any further discussion. Jade was beginning to wilt before his eyes and he did not want to see her collapse again. "I'll have the box ready for your man, Detective."

Chang stood. He looked down at Jade, his expression apologetic. "I think this is for the best, Mrs. Harrington." He held out the stack of pages she had drawn the symbols on. "Would you mind if I take one of these? I will try to locate someone who might know some of the ancient Chinese characters."

She took the stack from him and handed him the top sheet. "Do you really think you can find someone who might help?"

He bestowed one of his rare smiles on her. "I hope so. It is strange you have not yet come across a formula of any kind. I'm convinced there is no hope of finding Li Po. If indeed he could transmute lead into gold, or at least a fair imitation of gold, then his formula is what the men who tried to harm you are still after."

Jason put his hands in his back pockets. "That's why I want that box out of here."

"Turning the box over to me will not insure your wife's safety."

"No, but my getting her to New Mexico will," Jason said.

Jade turned to him, her eyes wide in amazement. He wanted to take her to New Mexico—and he had just said so as casually as he asked Tao to pass the peas at dinner.

Chang bowed toward Jade and picked up his bowler hat. "I'll be in contact with you again as soon as I find someone who can help with these." He folded the page of symbols and slipped it into his vest pocket.

Jason walked him to the door.

Chang paused in the doorway. He looked thoughtful before he spoke. "I will keep Li Po's things safe for you. When the case is solved, I will turn them over to you so that they can remain with the rest of the collection."

"Thank you," she said, before she met Jason's gaze. "It sounds as if my husband has his mind made up, so if we have already gone to New Mexico, please give the things to Mrs. Leland Stanford. She has volunteered to head up a committee to establish the Philo Page museum."

He nodded again and bade her good day. Jason walked him to the door and then returned to Jade's side. He sank down on the settee and stretched out his long lean legs and crossed them. He picked up her hand and toyed with her fingers.

"Will you go to New Mexico with me?" he asked.

Jade nodded. "Of course. If you'll have me." She turned toward him. "All I ever wanted was to be your wife, Jason."

He stared down at her and willed himself to believe her. Jason was tempted to seal her words with a kiss, but her pallor and the violet circles beneath her eyes kept him from it. There would be time. Years and years of time for him to do more than merely kiss her. He could wait until she was stronger.

Lupe entered the room, concern for Jade still evident in her eyes. Her tone was stern, for she had taken over Jade's care with enthusiasm and insisted everyone follow orders. "I thought you were upstairs in your room," she said to Jade. "What are you doing down here?"

"I was lonesome," Jade said.

Jason squeezed her hand.

Lupe scowled. "*Hijo*, you should know better than this. Take her back upstairs and put her to bed."

"I'd be happy to."

Jade colored when she recognized the warm sensuality behind his tone. Sneaking a glance at Jason, she found him smiling at her cockily.

"I want you to put her in bed and leave her *alone*. Then you must come right down and I will give you her tray." Lupe added a determined nod as she planted her hands on her hips.

Jade loved to watch Guadalupe Younger deal with Jason.

His aunt was reed-thin, long of limb, with midnight eyes that flashed like lightning. Lupe smiled as readily as she scolded both Jason and his Uncle Cash.

"All right. Let's go." Jason reached over and lifted Jade, then stood up with her. She looped an arm around his neck, certain that any protest would go unnoticed.

Jason strode into the hall with Jade riding high in his arms and started up the stairs. A knock at the door halted him. Lupe, who was still in the foyer below, opened the door. Captain Emery Lennox stood beyond the threshold, his cap in his hand, a wide smile puffing his already rotund cheeks.

"I'm here to see Jade."

At the sound of his voice, J.T. turned with his wife in his arms and Jade waved down at the captain.

"Come in, Captain Lennox," she welcomed him from her safe haven before she turned pleading eyes to Jason. "Take me back downstairs."

He began to protest. "Lupe said—"

Jade leaned close and whispered against his ear, "Just for a few minutes."

Aware that soon enough he would have Jade all to himself, Jason silently consented and carried his wife back downstairs. The group was soon reassembled in the drawing room.

The captain took a seat beside the fireplace and studied Jade, whom Jason had set back on the settee. Emery watched them carefully, with his hat resting on his knees. "You don't look well, Jade. Are you all right?"

"I haven't been well lately, but I'm feeling better already. Lupe is taking fine care of me." She introduced Jason's aunt to Lennox. Lupe excused herself after inviting the captain to stay for dinner, which he declined. He had just come for a short visit, he explained. But when J.T. offered him a brandy, Emery accepted.

"I came by with some wonderful news, Jade. At least, I hope you'll consider it wonderful."

"Really?" She sat up straighter, eager to hear.

"I have purchased your grandfather's property from the bank."

A feeling of relief swept though her when Jade realized what his words meant. No uncaring stranger would own the land her grandfather had loved. "Are you thinking of giving up the sea?"

"Not at all. I will still own a thriving shipping business. Why, I'm even trusting my shipping to pay off the property. But when you told me you had given the place up, I knew I had to have it. Keep it in the family, so to speak. I even plan to fix up the old adobe and live there when I'm in port."

"That is wonderful news," Jade agreed. "I wish you the best of luck. You can be certain I'll think of you often and picture you there."

"What do you mean, think?" Emery leaned forward to emphasize his point. "I want you and Jason to feel free to come out to the adobe whenever you want to. In fact, I planned to fix up the old room you always used when you stayed with your grandfather."

Jade looked at Jason, who was once again seated beside her, and gave him the opportunity to give the captain their news. The look he gave her in return was one of hope.

"My wife and I are leaving for New Mexico, probably as soon as the end of the week. But, if we ever get back here to visit—"

"Which we will, because it looks like there will be a Page museum after all. Mrs. Leland Stanford has agreed to take over for me. I'm sure I'll get a chance to visit, though." She glanced hopefully at Jason.

Unable to hide his surprise, Emery looked from one to the other and then finally smiled again. "That's very sudden, isn't it, Jade?"

She shook her head. "Not really. Jason has been trying to get his business concluded since the day he arrived. Now, he's anxious to get home."

The captain looked at J.T., then back to Jade and paused before he said, "Do you want to go, Jade?"

Jade turned to Jason and smiled. "Yes. I want to go."

"Well then," Emery continued, "I hope you'll have a chance to drive out and see the old place sometime this week. That is, if you're up to it."

"I hope I can. And Captain, don't worry about Quan Yen. I'm going to make certain she has a place to go before we leave."

He leaned back. "Now, that's one thing you don't need to worry your pretty head over. I found her, so why don't I find a place for her? After all, I have lots of contacts here in San Francisco."

"I was thinking we should see about giving her over to the missionary school," Jade said.

"Then I'll check into it for you," Lennox volunteered.

"That would be good of you," J.T. added. "I know I would appreciate Jade's not having to worry about Quan Yen."

"Captain, I know you were responsible for finding so many of the pieces for Grandfather. If there is anything you want to keep, any one piece in particular, you are welcome to it."

The elder man shook his head. "That's very generous of you, but I don't think so, Jade. The collection should stay together. But, if there were any papers among your grandfather's things, or your father's, anything that would help me restore the adobe and the gardens to their original state, well, I would be happy to have them."

"I didn't notice anything like that when I went through them, but I'd be happy to look again."

"Once you've rested," Jason cut in before he turned to the captain. "I hope you won't be offended, Captain Lennox, but I'd like to see my wife get some rest now. It's the only way she's going to get over this bout of exhaustion."

Lennox immediately stood and set his glass on a side table. "Of course. You shouldn't have had to ask—I'm sorry."

"Please, come again before we leave," Jade said, suddenly aware of how much her strength had waned over the course of the morning. She was looking forward to Jason carrying her back upstairs.

The captain took his leave and she got her wish, but instead of Jason taking her directly to her own room, he carried her to the master suite, pulled back the covers, and set her in the middle of the sleigh bed.

"Jason?" She looked up at him, uncertain what his decision to bring her to his room actually meant.

"Don't worry, Jade. I've no intention of making love to you now, but once you're well—"

The look he gave her said more than mere words ever could.

Lupe came in bearing a tempting tray of aromatic dishes. "Here is Jade's dinner. I decided to bring it up myself. Yours is downstairs, *hijo*. Cash is at the table already. You know how grumpy he is when he is hungry."

"Don't I know it," Jason said, on his way to the door.

Lupe carefully set the tray on Jade's lap before she turned to him.

"Wait for me, J.T., and we will go down together."

"What do you mean, you think someone has been trying to poison her?" Jason stopped in midstride and stared down at Lupita Younger.

They were at the top of the stairs, far enough away from the master suite so that Jade would not overhear, and even farther from the dining room where Cash, Quan Yen, and Tao Ling awaited them.

Lupe shook her head and signalled him to be silent. "I know what I see. She is pale, weak, and those dark circles beneath her eyes tell me that she is being drained of her strength. Her stomach hurts. She has dizzy spells."

"But, that could be any number of things. Her doctor did not seem concerned," Jason argued, unwilling to think that Jade might be close to death.

"She was well not two weeks ago, from what you have told me. Now, she is fading away, *hijo*."

He had told them all that he knew about Fredrick Douglas, Li Po, and the tong and Jade's connection to them.

"Have you seen all of the bottles and glass jars Tao Ling keeps in the kitchen?" Lupe asked.

J.T. shook his head. "I never paid them any attention. You don't think that Tao—"

"He is the one who prepares the food. Jade is the only one suffering. What am I to think?"

"But, Jade hired him—and from what she told me, she did so on the detective's recommendation. If that's true . . ." He stared off into space. Could Jon Chang be involved? Is that why the man had been so surprised to learn Jade had the alchemist's possessions? And so willing to take them?

Jason wondered if he had played into the detective's hands by telling him what Jade had discovered and insisting he take the alchemist's crate away. He leaned against the banister, his thoughts racing. Lupe remained silent beside him.

"I hate to accuse Tao unjustly," he finally said. "Jade thinks so much of him."

"I have not given her any of the food that he has prepared since she collapsed yesterday. If you will give me permission, I will continue to fix special things for her. That way, if she makes progress, we will know if he is responsible for her illness."

"No need to ask. You're in charge from here on, Aunt Lupe, but I would feel better if I just threw him out of the house."

"Only to cause your wife anger and the man hurt if he is innocent."

Jason knew she was right, but the idea that he had harbored one of Jade's enemies right here in his house infuriated him. He started down the stairway, his eyes dark with anger. Lupe reached out and stopped him simply by laying a hand on his sleeve.

"We must act as if nothing is wrong, Jason. You need to smile, *hijo*."

He tried. He really did.

Lupe shook her head. "Perhaps you can tell everyone you are worried about Jade. That will explain your ill humor."

"I *am* worried. Just when it seems everything is about to work out between us, you tell me my wife might be dying of poison."

"Not dying," she ammended. "Whatever harm she has been done is hopefully still reversible. Someone has been giving her small doses of a poison, one that kills slowly over time—if what I suspect is true."

"*If* you're right and *when* I find out who's responsible, I plan to get even." His jaw set, his eyes burning with raw anger, J.T. moved aside and let his aunt precede him down the stairs. With every step, he thanked God for sending his Aunt Lupita to him in time.

When Jade awoke the next day she expected to find Jason in bed beside her, but he was already up and gone. Last night, it had been heaven to sleep in his arms—he had been kind and solicitous, kissed her tenderly on her forehead, tucked her in beside him, and held her close without making any demands. It had been one of the only times in her life when she felt thoroughly safe and cosseted.

Lupe brought Jade breakfast, her excitement mirrored in her shining black eyes. She and Cash planned to take in the sights of San Francisco that day. Jade insisted they go to the Cliff House for dinner and to the Palace Hotel, just to take in its elegance. Lupe wanted to walk by the sea. Jade suggested they ride along Cliff House road and told them where to find tide pools.

"J.T. will be here all day to watch after you. I have left plenty of food for you both, and I told him to be sure you spend the day in bed," Lupe instructed.

"But Tao Ling—"

"Is going to have the day off. This is good, yes? He works very hard."

Jade agreed, but at the same time she wondered why Lupe's expression sobered when she mentioned him. Perhaps Jason's aunt could not adjust to Tao's ways in the kitchen.

"And Quan Yen?"

Lupe smiled again. "She is in her room. I looked in on her and found her painting her face. I hope you like *albondigas* soup," she added.

Jade nodded. "I do. I love it."

"*Bueno*. Then I will go."

"Have a wonderful day," Jade said with a smile. When Lupe left, Jade stretched and took a deep breath. For the first time in days she felt like meditating. Her head had stopped whirling, her stomach had calmed, and she actually felt rested for a change. She closed her eyes and took three deep breaths. Perhaps after a few minutes of silence, she would come up with an idea of how to wile away the rest of the day.

Her meditation was short-lived, for within moments there was a light knock at the bedroom door. Jade plumped up the pillows against the headboard, pulled the bedclothes up to her chin, and called out, "Come in."

Tao Ling's head and shoulders appeared around the door. "Do you need anything, Mrs. Harrington?"

"No, Tao. But I hear you have the day off. Don't lose all your money on *fan-tan*," she teased.

He shook his head and his long queue swayed behind him like a live snake. "No, Mrs. Harrington. I will take care. *The rich man plans for tomorrow, the poor man for today.*"

Jade laughed. "I should have known."

Still standing outside the door, he nodded. "If I may say so, it is good to see you smile, Mrs. Harrington."

"Thank you, Tao."

"I am happy that you have made peace with your husband at last. Anger is a little fire, which, if not timely checked, may burn down a lofty pile."

"I'll try to remember that, Tao."

"If you would like me to, I will make a love potion for you of dried sparrow tongues, snake saliva, and honey."

Her stomach lurched. "I don't think—"

"Taken before you make love, it promises to make you and your husband irresistible to one another."

She raised her hand in protest. "Really, I don't—"

"Or how about chrysanthemum powder and butterfly wings ground into paste? This, too, is a fine love potion once it is hidden in the sleeve of the beloved."

"Tao Ling?"

"Yes, Mrs. Harrington?"

Jade tried not to laugh outright. "I really appreciate the offer, but . . . well . . . Mr. Harrington and I are getting along just fine at the moment."

He bowed and then smiled. "Please let me know when I can help."

"I'll see you later."

Jade sighed. She smoothed the bedspread. She shifted her pillows. Glancing at the window, she found it too far away to see the grounds below, where she knew Jason and Xavier would be busy with the horses. She twirled her thumbs.

At this rate I'll go crazy within an hour, she thought. Lupe had told her to rest, and Jade was determined to be very well rested by tonight when Jason tucked her in again.

Very well rested.

Jade forced herself to close her eyes.

❊ CHAPTER 21 ❊

Even in a bamboo tube . . .
Snakes try to wriggle.

"If you want me to do this for you, *patron*, I will be happy
to." Xavier, unused to seeing an employer of his—let alone a
male—dishing up food for his wife and his hired man, sat
uncomfortably at the kitchen table and watched as Jason
carefully ladled the steaming *albondigas* soup into a bowl.
This was the third time he had offered to take over the task.

Jason shook his head. "No thanks, Xavier. Believe it or not,
I can do this. I like to cook."

"Cooking is a woman's work, *patron*."

"My wife is sick. Should I have her come down and serve
us anyway?"

Xavier shrugged. "What about the girl?"

J.T. looked at Quan Yen, who sat at the table smiling
vacantly at them, and shook his head. "She's just a child." He
had a hard time accepting the girl's past. How anyone could
sell an innocent child into a life of prostitution was beyond
him. His pity for her, coupled with the fact that he could not
bear to look at her misshapen feet in their tiny satin shoes, kept
him from asking anything of her. He had not even berated her
for forgetting to give him the note Jade had left him yesterday.

J.T. finished serving and set the soup on a tray just as he
heard the faint sound of a knock on the front door. After a
second thought, he took the bowl off of the tray and handed it
to his hired man. "You eat this one before it gets cold. I'll see
who that is."

Xavier pulled the bowl toward himself as Jason went to
answer the incessant knocking.

He was more than surprised to find Nettie Parsons on his
doorstep. He was speechless.

"Nettie." He nodded, but failed to respond more hospitably.

"Invite me in, Jason," she said boldly. "You used to have better manners than this."

He took in her upswept hair with its intricately woven cascade of golden locks, the rich, deep pink velvet gown that had far too revealing a neckline for modest day wear. That, coupled with the high color in her cheeks and the gleam in her eye, made J.T. hesitate to guess at the purpose behind Nettie's surprise visit.

Out of courtesy, he stepped aside. As she swept past him, the heavy scent of rose water assailed his senses. She headed straight for the drawing room and paused dramatically before the fireplace until she was certain she had his undivided attention.

"Where's your wife?"

"You don't waste words, do you Nettie?"

"No. And I don't waste time, either."

"She's upstairs, asleep I think. She hasn't been well."

Her brows arched suggestively. "Really?"

"Yes, really. What do you want?"

"Word around town is that you don't sleep together."

He couldn't believe her audacity, and it showed on his face. "What?"

"You heard me. I hear you two have separate rooms."

It seemed that someone had a big mouth. He wondered exactly who. "Where did you hear that?"

"It's all over the city. I heard it from Winslow, who heard it in the smoking room at the Palace." She studied her carefully buffed nails and then looked up at him from beneath lowered lashes. "Is it true?"

"That, Nettie dear, is none of your business."

She smiled, smugly satisfied. "Then it is true."

"My wife is upstairs in my bed right now."

"But you're obviously not with her," she jabbed back.

"Get to the point," he said without a trace of warmth in his tone. "I have things to do."

"I just came to let you know that since you and your wife don't seem to have a real marriage, that I would be willing to give up Winslow's . . . protection, for yours."

"You mean you're offering to be my whore?"

"Don't you know the word 'mistress' has a nicer ring to it?"

"I guess a few million dollars cancels out the fact that I didn't see fit to serve in the Confederacy."

"That was years ago, Jason, and as I told you before, I have learned to do whatever it takes to survive. Anyway, I thought you might be following in your father's footsteps. I've done a little digging and found out he kept a mistress 'til he died."

Even though he knew Peoney was nothing more than that to everyone concerned, he hated to hear Nettie talk about the woman that way. "You seem to like groveling in dirt, Nettie. Somehow I never thought of you that way."

"Shut up, Jason, and give me an answer. I don't have all day, you know."

After three hours of solitude, Jade was ready for a change of scenery. Jason had not appeared at her bedside all morning, and much as she tried to tell herself that the rumbling of her empty stomach was the reason she wanted to go downstairs, in her heart she knew she was looking forward to his company. She had just gotten up and walked down the hall to change out of her Chinese jacket and pants—now hopelessly wrinkled after a night of sleeping in them—when she heard someone knocking on the front door.

She stopped in her own room long enough to change into fresh undergarments and slip into a long silk robe before she tried to work her hairbrush through the tangled mass of curls that streamed loose about her shoulders and down to her hips. Anxious to see who might have come to call, one quick brushing and the promise of more was all she allowed herself.

Jade tiptoed to the top of the stairs and paused long enough to peer down and ascertain that Jason was not in the foyer. She heard voices coming from the drawing room—one of them decidedly a woman's. It definitely wasn't Lupe.

Could it be Babs trying for another reconciliation? She wondered at first, but from the upper landing she could not quite be certain.

She descended halfway and paused again. Although Jason's voice was recognizable, she could not hear his words clearly. Nor could she identify the woman.

When it sounded as if they were moving toward the door to the foyer, she turned and crept back up to the upper landing. She had no business greeting anyone the way she looked. Besides, she refused to be confronted by Babs again.

Hidden in the shadows at the top of the stairs, Jade pulled the edges of the robe together at the base of her throat and stood immobilized, listening to the exchange between Jason and the woman whose soft southern drawl she now easily recognized as Nettie Parsons'. The voices of the pair echoed up the open entry.

"You know what I wanted the last time I was here, Jason," Nettie said. "You should be glad it's not too late."

The last time I was here? Jade wondered exactly when Nettie had been at Harrington House. It must have been before she and Jason were married. She looked down at her bare feet, at the robe she had hastily tied around herself. Her long hair hung around her in curly disarray, even though she had brushed it just moments ago. The image of Nettie Parsons as she had seen her at the Palace, impeccably dressed and coiffed, looking every inch the southern belle, made Jade cringe when she thought of what she must look like compared to the striking blonde.

She listened to the sound of their footsteps as they neared the door and chanced a hasty peek down at them. Jason towered over Nettie, who stood with her shoulders back and head high, as if challenging Jason to turn down whatever it was she had requested.

"Well?" Nettie asked him when he failed to answer. "Aren't you interested? Do you know how many men have approached me, begged me to leave Winslow for them, since I arrived in San Francisco? And here I've lowered myself to come beggin' to you, Jason Harrington." She paused long enough to bat her long lashes at him.

Jade wished she could see Jason's reaction, but he had his back to her as he stared down at Nettie.

When Nettie reached out with familiarity to straighten Jason's collar, it was all Jade could do to keep herself from running down the stairs and throwing the woman out. It suddenly became quite clear to her exactly what Nettie was offering.

Would Jason accept?

The question burned in Jade's mind. After what he had been through with her, it would not be a surprise if he chose Nettie. Nettie and Jason had been together in the past and that, coupled with the fact that the woman was still a beauty, made Jade uneasy. Besides, why wouldn't any man succumb to the charms of an obviously experienced woman?

Why? Jade took a deep breath and instantly knew the answer to her own question.

Because she wasn't about to let Jason Terrell Harrington III do any such thing. Not if she had anything to say about it.

Their relationship had made great strides in the past two days, and she refused to let it slip backward because of Nettie Parsons.

She cinched her belt tighter, shook back her hair once more, and then, barefooted, walked down the stairs as if she were a queen.

Both Jason and Nettie immediately turned toward Jade. Nettie's face wore a look of shocked disdain. Jason did not appear the least bit surprised to see her. In fact, he appeared to be biting back a smile.

Jade walked directly to her husband's side and slipped her arm about his waist. She relaxed a bit when he accepted her by resting his arm across her shoulder and drew her near.

"Nettie, I believe you know my wife, Jade?" Jason said.

Nettie nodded, her eyes cold blue chips of ice.

Jade spoke without preamble. "Miss Parsons, I'm afraid my husband won't be able to take you up on your generous offer. You see, we're moving to New Mexico Territory in a few days, and I just don't see how he'll have much time. What do you think, Jason?" She turned to him with as innocent an expression as she could muster.

He shook his head, a wry smile twisting his lips, then he shrugged in resignation. "I'm afraid she's right, Nettie. As you can see, I've got my hands full." He pulled Jade closer.

Jade watched as Nettie's complexion went from pink, to white, to mottled red. The blonde balled her hands into fists and then, head high, turned around and tried to open the front door. Her cascading curls bobbed furiously with every yank.

"Allow me." J.T. reached around Nettie, unbolted the lock, and pulled the door open wide.

Nettie left without turning around.

Jade pulled away from Jason. "Allow me," she said, and slammed the door on the sight of Nettie's retreating figure.

As the slam echoed through the house, the smile she had managed for Nettie's benefit faded. "Just when was she here before?"

Jason just stood there and laughed.

"Well?" Jade prodded. "When? Don't stand there laughing at me, Jason Harrington."

"Am I crazy, or could it possibly be true that you are actually jealous?"

"Of course not." Jade glanced at her toes, uneasy with the speculative way he was looking at her.

"No? What other reason would you have for coming down here and practically tossing that poor thing out of the house?"

Her eyes riveted on him as soon as the words "that poor thing" were issued. "Now listen here, Jason," she began, but before Jade could say another word, he swept her into his embrace.

Nose to nose, they stared into each other's eyes.

"She was here before we were married," he said softly. "The day after we saw her at the Palace Hotel. I was planning on turning her down today the same way I did then."

"Really?"

He didn't answer at first, just stared down at her with a slow burning warmth creeping into his deep blue eyes. Finally, he pulled her to him, lowered his lips to hers, and kissed her until there was no room for doubt.

"What do you think?" Jason whispered after she had been thoroughly kissed.

Jade smiled. "I think I'm starving. Is there anything to eat around here?"

After a light meal they all ate together in the kitchen, Jade promised Jason she would rest. But then after a short nap, she collected the pages of Chinese writings, her own notes—keys to translating Chinese—and two books on the language, and moved downstairs to the library.

There was something about the close, dark room that was comforting. She lit the lamps, started a fire behind the grate, and then, before she became too exhausted, spread her work out on the massive cherrywood desk. She pored over her notes for a good hour, copying characters and searching for identical ones in her guidebook. Quan Yen appeared with a pot of fresh tea and hovered over her for a while, trying to persuade her to go back upstairs and sleep, but stubbornly, Jade refused. She felt far more rested than she had in days, and her stomach had calmed considerably.

The tea was rich and warm. She had hesitated to ask Jason to make it earlier, knowing he cared little for tea, and took coffee with the noon meal. Now the tea and the comfortable room offered her peace and quiet. The afternoon sun had dipped low enough to come streaming into the windows, highlighting the wood-paneled walls with a rich warmth. Jade paused to study the way the sunbeams played across the patterned Turkish carpet before she set aside her work and tried to relieve the tension in her neck by rotating her head and shoulders. After a second cup of tea, she decided she had been sitting long enough and stood up, stretched, and walked over to the window, hoping to catch a glimpse of Jason in the paddock area behind the house, but he was nowhere to be seen.

When she experienced another bout of nausea, Jade attributed it to being up and about too soon, and so poured herself another cup of tea, determined to fight off this irritating illness.

"Let's bring out one of the Arabians, Xavier. How about that little mare? Let's see how she takes to the bit today." Jason stood at the door of El Sol's stall and absently rubbed the big stallion's nose as he waited for Xavier to lead the other animal out of its stall. The proud little beauty would make an excellent mount for Jade.

He glanced up when he caught a flicker of movement at the other end of the long, open building and noticed Quan Yen walking toward him in her strange, weaving gait. Crossing to her, he saved her many yards of walking as he wondered at her sudden appearance at the stables. As far as he knew, she had never left the house before. Suddenly worried that something had happened to Jade, he questioned the girl at once and prayed she would be able to communicate more than a giggle.

"What is it? Is Jade all right?" He tried not to frighten her, towering over her as he did, but his one concern was his wife.

Her almond eyes widened, but the expression in them was as unfathomable as always. "Missee good. She sleep. This come for you." From the wide sleeve of her quilted jacket, Quan withdrew an evenly creased note and handed it to him.

Jason read it quickly. The brief note asked that he meet Jon Chang immediately at the apothecary shop on Washington Street in Little China. He smiled appreciatively at Quan Yen, thankful that she had not forgotten to give him the note.

J.T. called out to Xavier. "I have to go meet Lieutenant Chang in Little China right now. Saddle El Sol for me, then I want you to work where you can watch the house, all right?"

"*Sí, patrón.*"

"Better yet, go into the house and wait there until Cash and Lupe come home. I don't want to have to worry about Jade while I'm gone, and I don't think Quan offers much protection."

"*Sí, patrón.*"

"And Xavier, I don't want her worried. Don't tell her I've gone to meet Chang if you can help it."

Within moments, J.T. had strapped on his gun, swung himself into the saddle, and headed down the drive. As he rode through the front gates, he hoped that Chang had finally found whoever was behind Jade's near-abductions. He sincerely hoped so, because his fist was aching to connect with the scoundrel's jaw.

"Caves in the earth houses circles of the sun."

The words made absolutely no sense. Jade stared down at the translation she had penned and shook her head, immediately regretting the motion. She had been poring over her thick book of Chinese characters for hours, until her headache had returned and with it, her lethargy. She had finally given up her post in the library and had taken to her bed again. She wanted to blame her relapse on inactivity, but recognized her symptoms as the same ones she had suffered for two weeks. She looked up in surprise when Quan Yen entered the room. Jade set the page down beside her on the bed.

"There was no need for you to climb the stairs," she told the girl. "It must be very uncomfortable for you."

"No pain for me, missee. Always walk, chop chop, since little girl. No pain now." She pointed proudly at her feet. "Most beautiful feet. Small as hummingbirds." Quan moved closer to the bed and bowed, then held out a note to Jade. "Melican captain send one kine carriage. Driver say this for you."

Jade took the note and opened it. She squinted, trying to bring the words into focus. "I'm afraid my headache has returned," she told Quan, who immediately became solicitous.

"You likee tea? Someting eat?"

Absently, Jade told her no and then read the note. It was from Emery Lennox, explaining that he had found a guardian for Quan Yen and that he would like Jade to accompany the girl to the adobe. He extended an invitation to her and Jason for dinner, and promised he would have them home by early evening.

Quan helped her out of bed. Jade washed her face and hands, changed into a long skirt, blouse, and fitted jacket, put on her many-buttoned boots. Quan fastened the buttons with the silver handled hook while Jade wound her hair into a figure-eight twist. With a final straightening of the hem of her jacket, she picked up her reticule and was ready.

When they reached the bottom of the staircase, Jade was surprised to find Xavier seated in the foyer, leaning over a length of rawhide he was tightly weaving into a lariate. She paused for a while and silently watched as his callused brown fingers expertly braided the tough hide strips. He was lost in his work, absently worrying his mustache with his teeth. He wore his work clothes and chaps. Although she found his presence curious, she had no objection to him sitting alone in the foyer.

"Xavier?"

"Ah, *senora*." He stood up so quickly the chair toppled over behind him. He spoke as he righted it. "The *senor* asked me to sit and watch."

"Watch what?"

"Watch out for you," he explained with a smile.

"How kind," Jade felt even more confused as she wondered why Jason had sent the man to watch over her. "Why did my husband suddenly feel the need to send you in here?" She knew a moment of dread when she realized Jason must have had good cause to send the man in to protect her.

"He is not here, *senora*. So he sent me in to watch." The man smiled as if that were all the explanation she needed.

Jade felt as if she were at the beginning of the conversation again. She sighed. "Xavier, where is Jason?"

Xavier looked down at the pencil-thin braid of leather in his hands. He looked at the curled, dusty toes of his boots. He glanced at the front door. Finally, after considerable concentration, he looked at Jade and said, "He went to meet a man."

One of Jade's finely etched brows arched. "Oh? What man?"

Still reluctant, Xavier dipped his head and shrugged. "The Chinaman detective."

Immediately, Jade became concerned. "When did he leave?"

"Not very long ago, *senora*."

"Did he say where he was going and why?"

Xavier shook his head. "No, *senora*. He said he had to go quickly. He told me to watch and wait."

If Jon Chang had sent for Jason, he must have found some clue to the mystery surrounding her father and Li Po. Perhaps he had learned who the men were who had followed her. She was torn between sending Quan Yen to the captain alone and following Jason, or going out to the adobe. Since J.T. had left no word where he was meeting Chang, it would be impossible, not to mention dangerous, to go off looking for him.

Jade looked down at the invitation in her hand. She handed it to Xavier. "I am going to Captain Lennox's home. He has sent a carriage for me. Please give my husband that note when he comes in."

Xavier frowned.

Jade thought for a moment that he was not going to let her leave.

"*Senora*, I do not think—"

"My husband knows the captain is an old friend of the family. Besides, he's sent a carriage for me and has promised to drive me home before the evening gets late. Jason will understand. Tell him I've taken Quan to meet her new guardians. Tao Ling should be back very soon to see to dinner."

"But *senora*—"

She reached out and gently touched his arm. "Xavier, really. I'm fine. I'll be back soon. This way you can get back outside and do whatever it is you have to do. Just don't forget to give Jason the note. I'd hate to have a repetition of what happened yesterday."

He nodded, but his expression was still one of doubt.

"Come, Quan." Jade found she was actually looking forward to the ride out to the adobe. The short trip would help her take her mind off of her failing health for a while. She hoped they reached the place before dark so that she could see all the repairs Emery Lennox had undertaken.

The heavy scent of sandlewood blended with the lilting sound of wind chimes on the breeze as Jason paced Washington Street. The sidewalks in Little China were as crowded as always. He found himself constantly stepping aside to make way for peddlers stooped beneath their poles from which swung baskets ladened with goods. There was not an inch of space in the tightly packed community that did not attest to the crowded conditions in Little China. When he gazed upward, he could see balconies strewn with drying wash. Cooks squatted on the street stirring blackened pots over open braziers. Glancing around for Chang, he noticed one vendor seated on a windowsill selling cigars from a small table. Jason bought a cigar and bit off the end, but did not light it. Instead, he held it tight between his teeth as he waited outside the apothecary.

After a quarter of an hour, Jason stepped inside the shop to look around. The place reeked of incense that burned in a bronze, caldron-shaped brazier on an altar set in a niche in the wall. It was a moment before Jason realized that all the people crowded into the small interior of the shop had stopped speaking to stare at him. Six men stood before a long counter that reminded him of saloon bar. A wizened old man who was barely visible behind the bar had stopped in the midst of measuring fine white powder out of a blue and white porcelain jar.

Jason nodded. The man finally turned his gaze away from Jason and continued his work. One by one the others stopped staring in his direction and Jason was free to browse. He noted the rows and rows of many-sized jars with pewter lids on the shelves that lined the walls. Black enameled boards lettered with golden characters hung behind the clerk. These were frequently consulted by both the pharmacist and the customers.

Chomping on his cigar, Jason stood in the doorway, his back to the men in the shop, his hands jammed into his pockets, and stared out into the street. The sun had lowered; it would soon be dusk. He pulled his watch out of his Levi's and checked the time again. He had waited nearly thirty minutes.

Finally, realizing that Chang's small room was not far away, Jason stepped out onto the street and began to weave his way through Little China until he came to the fragile-looking building that marked the entrance to the alleyways that led to the jewelry shop where Jon Chang lived.

In some places, the network of passageways was no wider than his arm span. The tall buildings all but blocked out most of the sunlight. As he moved through the twisted labyrinth Jason thought to himself, *You are crazy, J.T. Harrington. Crazy as a loon.*

Even as he went deeper into the maze he repeated the words. He felt in his pocket for the copper coin Jade had given him before their wedding. He had tried to leave it in his bureau drawer, but somehow always found himself putting it in his pocket when he dressed in the mornings. Now he held onto the coin for luck.

Anything worked in a tight spot, he reckoned.

Finally he thought he recognized the building where Jon Chang had taken them. He climbed the narrow stairs, stepping

ver a kitten and some astonished children who did not attempt
hide their curiosity. The heavy scent of old grease, rotting
arbage, and sesame oil weighed heavy on the close air in the
arrow alley.

He found Jon Chang's door and knocked. There was a scurry
feet inside, and finally a toothless old woman came to the
oor. Jason could not tell if she was stooped or afraid to raise
out of a bow. He took the old woman to be a relative of
hang's, but the thought crossed his mind that he might be in
e wrong place. She smiled up at him, but her eyes betrayed
r suspicion.

"Is Jon Chang here?" Jason spoke slowly and distinctly.

The old woman shrugged and shook her head.

"I'm supposed to meet him here," Jason said, more loudly
is time.

Again, a shrug and a head shake was his only answer.

He tried once more. "Jon Chang. Here?" Jason tried to peer
ound the old woman, but she held the door half-closed. All
could see of the inside of the place was the corner of a table
vered with bowls.

"Thanks anyway," Jason mumbled as he shoved his hands
his pockets and dipped his head so as not to hit it on the low
lcony ceiling on his way downstairs. A door down the way
ened and three young men walked out. They offered no
lp. In fact, the look on their faces made his skin crawl.
essed all in black, the men's hard stares belied their young
es. He guessed they were all in their early twenties. Two
od with arms folded across their chests and stared at him
enly. The third slid down the wall into a squat and folded his
ns on his knees. They seemed to issue him a silent warning
leave.

Happy to comply, J.T. tipped his head in their direction,
ned, and went down the stairs.

Miraculously, he made his way back through the alleys to
ashington Street, where he checked at the apothecary once
ore. There was still no sign of Chang. Growing irritated, he
pped inside. "Anybody in here speak English?"

The sound of his voice brought all activity in the room to a
lt again. All eyes turned in his direction, but no one said a

word. Jason felt the hair on the back of his neck stand u
suddenly all too aware that he was the foreigner here. And
was a hell of a time to remember that Jade had told him th
Fredrick Douglas had died with a meat axe in his skull not f
from this very shop. Jason pushed his hat down lower on h
head and turned to go.

"I speakee English. Mebbe you likee speekee me?" A m
dressed much like the others in dark, nondescript pants and
wide-sleeved jacket stepped forward. He wore a black sku
cap and bowed low when Jason turned to him.

"You know Jon Chang? Policeman Chang?"

The man's face shuttered. "No sabe."

From the Chinaman's quickly guarded expression, Jas
knew he was lying. "I was supposed to meet him here. Ha
you seen him? You see Chang here?"

"No Chang. No see no place. You go now."

The tension in the air was so thick Jason thought it mig
choke a horse. He studied each of the men one by one. Sor
were far younger than he, others far older. None of them we
armed. He thought of Tao and his supposed talent for killing
man with his bare hands. They all seemed to be waiting for h
to make the next move. Jason thanked the man who spo
Pidgin English and left.

He walked to the hitching rail where he had left El Sol a
flipped a coin to the boy he had hired to watch his horse. T
thought of Jade at home alone had begun to nag at him, and
the time he had mounted and turned the stallion toward the h
he was certain something was definitely wrong. Why wou
Jon Chang send him an urgent message and then not even se
a messenger to let him know he had been detained? He felt si
to his stomach when suspicion came to him. Had the summe
really come from Chang, or had someone just wanted him e
of the house?

He kicked El Sol into a gallop when he remembered that r
even Tao Ling was at home with Jade—only Xavier, who w
too old to be of much protection. By the time he had gone t
blocks, J.T. had convinced himself he should never have l
the house. He could not even trust Tao Ling now that Lu
suspected the man of poisoning Jade. Tao knew the Young

vere going out. He might very well have sent the note to be
ure Jason was out of the way. Perhaps Tao sensed they
uspected him of poisoning Jade.

El Sol's hooves pounded out a tattoo that echoed the word
unning through Jason's mind. *Why?* Why would Tao want to
arm his wife, unless he had been hired by one of the tongs to
ill Jade, just as they had her father? But Jon Chang had
ecommended the man to Jade. Was Chang behind the scheme?

By the time Jason reached the brick that marked the entrance
o the drive, he had succeeded in whipping his worry into a
ever pitch. He was furious at himself for falling for such an
bvious ploy and feeling more anxiety than he ever had in his
fe. If anything had happened to Jade it would be his fault.
He knew he would never forgive himself.

The captain's carriage reached the adobe just as the clouds
aat streaked the deep turquoise sky were highlighted with pink
nderbellies. Jade strapped her reticule over her wrist and
epped out of the carriage. She stood in silence, taking in the
inset sky in the distance and breathing in the tranquil peace of
hat had once been her grandfather's garden. Here, at the end
f day, the tall oak in the middle of the garden was gilded by
ie sun's dying rays. Jade took a deep breath and then looked
vay from the glorious sunset sky. She was glad to note that
e captain had already begun work on the long-neglected
irden. The earth had been turned over in many places and
arious leggy shrubs had been uprooted.

The sound of hushed voices caused her to look up. Two
orkmen were on the roof replacing some of the missing tiles.
ne could barely see them in the waning light. Her attention
as then drawn to the doorway as Emery Lennox stepped out
ito the veranda and moved to take her hand.

"Jade! I'm so glad that you could come. Is Jason with you?"
e looked around behind her at the closed carriage.

Jade shook her head. "No, he had to go into town and I
asn't certain when he was coming home, so I brought Quan
en with me and left him a message. Maybe he'll join us
ter."

"Yes, indeed. Maybe he will. In the meantime, welcome Come in and see what I've done with the place."

They went inside, Quan Yen following close behind them Jade paused just inside the threshold and looked around i wonder. The captain had furnished the adobe in carve teakwood pieces from the Orient. Dragons with ivory ey adorned a pair of matching chairs near the door, whi deep-carved figures of villagers ornamented tall chests, lo trunks, and table legs.

Bronze locks and other ornamentation on the furnitu glinted brightly in the candle- and firelight. A huge gong hur from a teak frame near a window. Statues of the various go and goddesses reigned over the room from where they stood o tables and chests. Shimmering red and gold silk cushior rested on chairs and benches.

The ragged remains of serapes that had hung in the doo ways had been taken down, giving the house a flowing, op effect. Jade moved through the large, central room that serve as parlor and dining room and ran her hand over the shinir surface of a massive ebony dining table. She had alwa imagined the captain on his sailing ship, so she had nev thought of him in such luxurious surroundings before. A though the adobe itself was still in need of repair and a fre coat of whitewash, she could see that, combined with h exquisite pieces, the place would be quite a showplace.

She paused to study an eight-paneled screen framed in bla lacquer. The scenes depicted on the panels were of Chine ladies in low-cut gowns wandering in a garden where th watched fish swim among the lotus blossoms. What attract Jade to the piece was the fact that the scenes had been creat out of gems and stones. Inlaid amethyst, carnelian, and pi tourmaline all combined with moss green jadeite, mother-o pearl, and soapstone.

"These panels are wonderful!" She couldn't hide her enth siasm for the intricate work. "Have you been collecting the things long?"

"For years. I've had them stored here in San Francisco un the day I decided to run my shipping business from land a give up the sea."

"I would never have thought these pieces would look so at home here." She turned to face Lennox and caught him staring intently at Quan Yen.

"Is everything all right?" Jade asked, aware of a subtle tension between the two, yet unwilling to admit to herself that the look on Captain Lennox's face had been blatantly sensual. Suddenly uneasy, Jade asked, "When is Quan's guardian going to arrive?" She smiled at the girl, hoping to put her at ease, but Quan Yen had become as distant as she had been the day Lennox had first brought her to Harrington House.

"I just received word that the people from the mission won't be driving out tonight, Jade. I'm afraid there is no guardian for Quan yet."

"Did they change their minds? I'm certain that once anyone were to meet her that they would see how very pleasant she is. Why, she's been a great help to me lately, always trying to cheer me when I feel low." Jade walked to the girl's side. She spoke softly in halting Cantonese. "Are you all right, Quan? Do you want to leave?"

The girl looked at Jade, then at Emery Lennox and slowly smiled. "I all right. I want stay."

Lennox cleared his throat. "Quan isn't the only reason I wanted to see you, Jade. Why don't you sit down?"

She was not certain when she began to feel uneasy, nor did she know why, but by the time Jade was seated on one of the carved dragon chairs, she sensed that something beyond her knowledge had definitely passed between Emery Lennox and Quan Yen.

CHAPTER 35

❈ CHAPTER 22 ❈

*An avaricious man, who can never have enough . . .
is as a serpent wishing to swallow an elephant.*

Jason reined El Sol to a thunderous stop, swung his leg over the saddle, and dismounted. When he noticed that the house was well lit, he told himself to calm down—Jade was safe inside. She had to be. He would open the door and find her tucked safely in bed, bent over her books and papers, or sleeping peacefully with her radiant red-gold hair spread out about her on the pillow, just as she had been last night. Jade was fine.

His calm was shattered when he saw Xavier running from the stables to greet him.

"Why aren't you inside? Where's my wife?" Jason was already pounding up the walk toward the service porch door.

Xavier trailed behind, puffing as he tried to keep pace with Jason's long stride. "She's gone, *patron*."

Jason halted abruptly and turned on Xavier. "What do you mean 'gone'? Not again!"

"Only to her friend's house. I have the letter." Xavier began digging the note out of his pocket.

Babs immediately came to mind. J.T. willed himself not to grab the little Mexican and shake him as Xavier tried to fish the letter out of his pocket. Finally, when the man pulled it crumpled from the depths, J.T. grabbed the note.

Without waiting for Xavier, Jason continued toward the house. The sky was growing dim and he was forced to wait to read the note until he reached the well-lit kitchen. The back door banged behind him as he strode across the porch and into the kitchen. Earlier, Xavier had lit the lamps and started the fire in the stove and fireplaces throughout the house. Jason leaned toward a lamp in the center of the worktable and read the note.

When he saw that the note was from Lennox, J.T. was relieved. "Why didn't you tell me she went to see Lennox?"

343

"You did not let me, *patron*."

A wry smile curved Jason's lips. He shrugged, embarrassed at his own impulsive behavior. He was not a little amazed at the way he had reacted to his fear for Jade's safety. Still not exactly elated to find she had left home when just yesterday she had been so ill, he was relieved all the same. Despite their rough beginning, she had managed to gain hold of his heart. This afternoon, when he thought he had left her in danger, J.T. realized just how much of a hold she had. No longer could he imagine his world without her.

The note said that she would be back early. In a more controlled tone Jason asked, "Have my aunt and uncle returned?"

"No, *patron*, not yet."

"Good." Jason stood and started down the hall. "In that case, I'm going to go change and wash up. They should be home soon."

Cash and Lupita Younger arrived shortly after Jason had freshened up, changed into a clean flannel shirt, and slicked back his damp hair. Lupita came in clutching armfuls of small packages, her smile radiant. To Jason's relief, his uncle still seemed to have energy left as he ushered them both into the drawing room.

"Don't mind if I do sit a spell," Cash said as he took the snifter of brandy that Jason offered him. "This little lady ran me ragged today."

Lupe gently hit him on the arm. "You are the one who insisted we go to one more store," she said with a laugh. To Jason she said, "Your uncle acts as if he has never been to a city before. For me it was the first time, but for him—"

"It's been years, woman! 'Sides, last time I was in a town it was Santa Fe, and that watering hole doesn't hold a candle to this place."

Jason stretched out on the settee. "Want to live here? I can let you keep the house," he offered.

Lupe and Cash both looked appalled.

"No thanks, J.T."

"Oh, *hijo*, no!" Lupe cried. "We must go home."

"That's what I thought you'd say." Jason smiled.

Lupe's gaze strayed to the pile of packages on the side table near the door. "Is Jade awake? I have a surprise for her. It is not much," she apologized, "but I think she will like it. Does she have a shawl?"

Jason shrugged. "From what I've seen, she doesn't have much of anything, a fact I haven't had time to alter. But you'll have to give it to her later, because she's not at home."

Lupita quickly sat up straighter, all signs of exhaustion faded. "What? Where did she go?"

"She got a note from Emery Lennox, the sea captain you met yesterday, and accompanied Quan Yen to the adobe to meet her new guardian. Lennox is going to have her driven home after dinner."

"But, she is still weak. She should not be out tonight in the damp air. She should—"

"Lupe, there's no use telling her what to do. She has her own way of doing things and the will to see it through."

Cash finished off his brandy and handed the glass to Jason for a refill. "I could have told you not to marry a woman with a mind of her own," he said, sneaking a glance at Lupita.

"Yeah, well, I probably wouldn't have listened," Jason said.

Lupe glanced toward the doorway and lowered her voice. "Is Tao Ling home?"

"Not yet," Jason said.

"Maybe this is a good time to open the jars in the kitchen—" She sounded unsure.

Jason disagreed. "He'll probably come home any minute. Besides, he hasn't been anywhere near Jade today and I made sure she only ate the food you left. Since Jade did hire him, there would be hell to pay if she hears about this and we don't find anything."

"You should have told her about my suspicions," Lupe said. "I should have told her myself, but I was waiting until she was stronger."

"As I was," Jason added. "How was I to know she would be up and out this evening?"

"Sounds like you need to put the woman over your knee," Cash volunteered.

Lupe shot him a dark scowl.

"Only teasin' " he quickly added.

Just as Jason predicted, Tao appeared in the doorway within a few moments. He bowed to Jason and announced, "The detective arrived just as I was entering the house. Will you see him?"

"Send him in. I'd like to know why he kept me waiting for him in Little China for over an hour."

Jon Chang was not alone when he entered the drawing room. He bowed to the Youngers and then to Jason, who made the introductions and then waited expectantly for Chang to introduce the old man with him.

"This is Sung Ho Sin. He has some knowledge of ancient versions of Chinese as well as alchemy. He has come to try and translate the messages your wife found on the crates."

"We'll leave you two alone," Cash Younger volunteered as he started to rise.

Jason stopped him with a shake of his head, then turned to Ho Sin. "Thank you for coming to help."

"I hope I can," the old man said slowly.

To Jon Chang, Jason said, "I wish you'd have sent someone to tell me you couldn't meet me this afternoon."

It was immediately evident from Jon Chang's confused expression that he had no idea what Jason was talking about. "I am afraid you have me at a disadvantage, Mr. Harrington. I know of no meeting."

It was Jason's turn to look confused. "That's what I was afraid of." He still was not certain he could trust Jon Chang. Someone had sent him the note, someone who had wanted him away from the house. Either Xavier's presence had discouraged any attempt to harm Jade, or Lennox's invitation spoiled someone's well-laid plans. Jason reached inside his leather vest pocket and handed Chang the note that was supposedly from him.

"This is not my handwriting," Chang said. "I made no plans to meet with you."

"That's what I was afraid of." Jason walked over to the liquor table and poured himself another drink. He nodded toward the newcomers. "Detective? Mr. Sin?" They declined his offer. He crossed the room again. "That means someone did want me out of here." He silently cursed himself for being so stupid. It would not happen again.

"And Mrs. Harrington?" Chang asked, concerned.

"She's at an old friend's for dinner."

"I see. I'm glad to hear that she is feeling better. Will it still be possible to see the copies she made of the letters on the crates? If you would like us to return when Mrs. Harrington is at home—"

"No." Jason was adamant. "I want this over with as soon as possible. We're leaving here within a day or two. If you'll wait here, I'll go up and get the notes off of Jade's desk."

He was on his way back downstairs when he passed Tao Ling on his way up. Jason stopped the man in midstride. "What are you doing up here?"

Tao's expression shuttered immediately. "I want to ask Mrs. Harrington if there is anything special she wants me to prepare for dinner."

Jason squelched the urge to grab Tao by the lapels and throw him down the stairs. If the young man *had* tried to poison his wife, Jason wondered seriously if he could see him brought to justice when he would rather deal with Tao himself. "Mrs. Harrington is not here. Lupe will prepare dinner as soon as she has rested," Jason said tightly. He stepped around Tao and as he did, sensed rather than saw the other man tense.

"Where is Mrs. Harrington?"

"That's none of your concern, is it?" Jason faced Tao squarely, certain it would do him a world of good to get into a real knock-down, dragged-out brawl. Tao had yet to prove the mysterious fighting skills Jade claimed he had. Perhaps now was the time.

"She hired me to protect her. I was not told she would be going out today. I beg your pardon, but I do believe I have the right to know where she has gone. I could not help but notice that Quan Yen, too, is missing."

"Missing? They're not missing. I know exactly where they are."

"But I do not."

"You were hired as a servant here." Jason's temper had

reached its threshold. He clenched the papers in his right hand.

Tao remained seemingly calm, yet persistent. "Since it was Mrs. Harrington who hired me, I have every right." He turned around and started back down the stairs again. Jason watched the man's soundless movements. Tao paused and said over his shoulder, "I will ask the detective to intercede."

Great, Jason thought. *A united front.* "Hold it, Tao." As long as the detective knew where Jade was, what harm would it do to tell Tao? Chang was likely to do so anyway. Besides, she was out of harm's way. "She has gone to visit Captain Lennox. It seems he's found a guardian for Quan Yen."

At the bottom of the staircase, Tao folded his arms and hid his hands in the wide sleeves of his jacket, then bowed to Jason. His queue swung forward over his shoulder as he did.

Without a word of thanks, a sign which caused J.T. to believe the man thought he had every right to know where his mistress had gone, Tao Ling turned and walked into the drawing room ahead of Jason.

The group awaiting for J.T. sat in stony silence. The old man was sitting in one of the high-backed armchairs by the fire. Cash and Lupe waited uneasily on the settee. When Jason walked in, he immediately handed Jade's carefully copied pages to Chang and prayed he was doing the right thing.

"I would like permission to stay," Tao Ling explained to Jon Chang. "Whatever is revealed concerns my mistress. I may be needed."

"Permission is not mine to give." The detective looked to Jason.

Jason glanced at Lupe and Cash. At least if Tao remained in the room, he would know where the man was and what he was up to. He shrugged, his feelings obvious. "If you want."

Chang handed the old man the first of the pages. It was a while before he spoke. When he did, in halting English, his voice was thin and weak. "This is a very ancient, very rare version of Cantonese."

"Can you read it?" Jason pressed.

"Some of it. But you must remember, alchemists often wrote in symbolic language. Red is a holy color, cinnabar is a red compound of mercury and sulfur that can be liquid or solid.

The word dragon is often substituted for mercury, tiger for lead."

Jon Chang looked thoughtful. "So, these may be the formulas Fredrick Douglas wanted Li Po to use to produce gold?"

Ho Sin shook his head. "No. An alchemist would never write down his formula, for to do so would break the spell. These messages are not formulas, but they do indeed seem to be written symbolically. They might have been left as directions to the alchemist's whereabouts."

Jason watched, his impatience barely curbed, as the old man took a deep breath and closed his eyes. His movements were so slow that Jason feared he was falling asleep. Ho Sin leaned back, his head against the high back of the chair. Lupe, Cash, Tao, Lieutenant Chang, and Jason collectively held their breath until the old man's eyes opened a moment later. He raised the first page. "The goddess cannot find the hidden sun," he read aloud. He picked up a second page. "Caves in the earth house circles of the sun."

"What in the hell is that supposed to mean?" Cash blurted out.

Lupe shushed him.

The old man read another page. "The devil rules the sea. The wind and weather are his to command."

Chang looked at Jason. Jason shrugged.

"Make any sense to you?" Jason asked the detective.

"I am afraid not. Perhaps when your wife gets back from her friend's home?"

Jason pulled out his watch. It was still early. "She may not return for another hour. Or more." He looked at the Ho Sin, certain the old man would not be awake when Jade came home.

"The dragon has been buried beneath the earth." Although no one was paying him any mind, Ho Sin shuffled the pages and droned on.

"Excuse me, old one," Tao interrupted Ho Sin. "What does the word 'earth' symbolize? It is used quite often."

"Forgive me, I do not know." Ho Sin sadly shook his head. Tao slowly began to recite the passages that had already been translated. "The goddess cannot find the hidden sun. Caves in the earth house circles of the sun. The dragon has been buried beneath the earth."

"Didn't he say dragon means mercury?" Cash stood and stretched.

Jason looked to Chang who nodded. "So, mercury is buried in the earth. The sun is buried, too. What's the sun supposed to mean?"

"The male entity," Ho Sin volunteered.

Cash shrugged.

They barely heard Ho Sin's next words. "The sun could be the alchemist himself."

"How could he write these messages if he was already buried in the earth?" Lupe wondered aloud.

"Mrs. Harrington felt that the crates were probably stored beneath her grandfather's home," Tao told them.

Chang clarified. "The old adobe."

"Which," Lupe added, "is a house made of earth."

"Jade and I visited the adobe weeks ago. Someone tried to shut her up in the cellar but we never saw anyone, nor was there any sign of the alchemist ever having been there. But she did find a piece of red silk. A belt, I think."

"An adobe with a cellar?" Cash asked. "Never heard of it."

"Not a cellar, exactly," Jason explained patiently, "more like a small, cold storage room beneath the kitchen. Captain Lennox bought the place. I'm sure if he finds anything he'll let Jade know."

Ho Sin sat forward in his chair showing more signs of life than he had since he began translating. "A sea captain?"

Jason gave him his full attention. "Yes. Why?"

Shuffling back through the stack of pages, Ho Sin finally paused and read aloud, "The devil rules the sea. The wind and weather are at his command."

"Devil could mean any foreigner," Chang explained.

"Wind and sea," Jason muttered to himself. A sea captain had to have helped Fredrick Douglas transport Li Po to California. And Captain Emery Lennox had conveniently been a friend of Fredrick Douglas's father-in-law . . . Jade's grandfather, Philo Page.

* * *

A chill shook Jade as she tried to focus on Emery Lennox. The teakwood chair was beautiful but uncomfortable, the dragon carving on the back pressed into her shoulder blades. Nerves made her fiddle with the straps on her reticule until she became aware of what she was doing and set it on the floor beneath the chair. The captain had pulled a similar chair closer to her own and leaned forward, his hands on his knees. Her mouth gone suddenly dry, Jade licked her lips.

"Do you remember when you were a little girl and I would come to visit your grandfather?"

"Of course," she said, but even the happy memory did little to put her at ease. She asked him, "Is there something special you want to talk about?"

"As a matter of fact, there is. I've become quite concerned about this business of giving Philo's collection to a museum foundation. Are you certain they'll know how to take care of it once you've gone off to New Mexico?"

"I'm not concerned, especially since Mrs. Stanford has taken over for me. She has the connections to hire the best curator, and with her background for charity work, I'm certain she'll be able to keep the funds coming in."

He leaned back and stared at her. "Still, shouldn't there be someone in charge who genuinely cares about those pieces? Someone who's family, so to speak?"

"Well, I hadn't thought—"

"I would be happy to see that the Philo Page Museum becomes a reality. In fact," he said as he drew a wad of pages out of his pocket, "I took the liberty of having this document drawn up that gives me the right to see that the entire collection is maintained satisfactorily."

With her headache it was hard to concentrate, but despite the distraction, Jade knew that she had already made up her mind. Besides, before she got herself embroiled in any more legal predicaments she was determined to contact Matt Van Buren.

"I wish you had mentioned this before now," she said, trying to sound sincere. "I really can't do anything until I contact my husband's lawyer."

Lennox scoffed. "Since when does such a headstrong girl

need anyone's advice?" His expression saddened. "Don't you trust me, Jade?"

She answered too quickly. "Of course, it's just—"

"Let's make this easy. Your husband wants to whisk you off to New Mexico far sooner than I would like—why, we've just gotten to know each other again—and it would ease my mind to know the collection will be well managed."

"Well . . ." Hedging, Jade glanced over at Quan Yen, who was still staring openly at Lennox.

Before she could say more they were interrupted by a tall, wide-shouldered man with a full, grizzled beard and dull gray eyes. He paused in the doorway, glanced Jade's way, and then spoke to Lennox. "Cap'in, I need to talk to you."

Emery scowled at the man, then tucked the unsigned contract back into his pocket and stood. Jade had the overwhelming feeling she had seen the burly man in the doorway before, but could not remember where. Then, when he turned and followed Lennox out the door, she felt her heartbeat quicken. The man with Emery Lennox was the same man who had chased her through the streets of Little China.

J.T. couldn't do more than stare at the wizened old man in the armchair. Ho Sin, whose feet did not even touch the ground, looked no bigger than a child's life-sized doll. As much as he wanted to deny the fact that Jade might be in danger, J.T. slowly pieced together the facts. "Someone wanted me out of the house today, so they sent me a note supposedly from you, Mr. Chang. Then, while I was gone, a carriage came for Jade with a note from Lennox. He knew I wouldn't be here, and just as he hoped, Jade went to him without me."

"If indeed he is the 'devil that rules the sea,' your wife's friend might be the one who has been after her all along." Jon Chang, who still stood behind the old man's chair, placed his hand on Ho Sin's shoulder.

"He wants the alchemist, or the formula if that's all that's left. He must have searched the adobe and come up empty-handed."

"But why would he want to harm your wife?"

"I don't know," Jason said as he began walking toward the door, "but I'm sure as hell not going to wait around to find out. I'm going out there."

"I am going, too," Tao Ling said to no one in particular.

"Mr. Harrington, may I remind you this is still my case?"

Jason paused in the doorway. "Remind me all you want. Are you coming or not?"

"May I leave Ho Sin in your care?" Chang asked Lupita and Cash.

"Of course," Lupe said before she called out to Jason. "Take Xavier with you."

"I'm goin', too," Cash volunteered.

"Oh no you are not, Cash Younger. Not if I have to sit on you," Lupe warned. "I didn't nurse you back to health only to have you fall ill again."

"Damn, woman!" He yelled as he watched Jason open the closet in the foyer, take out his duster, and strap on his gunbelt. "I'm going to miss all the fireworks."

Lupe crossed her arms.

Cash Younger contented himself with a loud grumble as the other men left the house.

Her mind in turmoil, Jade watched Emery Lennox and the bearded man leave the room. She wondered if her legs would hold her, knew they had to, and stood up. Quan Yen was at her side in seconds.

"Where Missee go?"

"Home," Jade managed. "I have a headache."

"Am I to stay, or go?"

"You're going with me, Quan. I can't leave you here alone." Jade was beginning to doubt her own sanity. Had the captain lied to her all along? Why had he sent the bearded man after her? And what of Quan Yen? Had Lennox found her wandering the Embarcadero, or had that story been a lie, too? Jade knew one thing for certain: she had to get out of this house and get out now.

On shaking limbs she crossed the room and stepped out into the entry hall. Lennox was in hushed discussion with the bearded man. They stopped speaking as soon as Jade arrived.

"What is it, my dear?" Lennox asked.

I have to act as if nothing is wrong. I have to get home
Jason will take care of me. Everything will be fine.

She forced an apologetic smile. "I hope you'll forgive me
but I suddenly have a terrible headache. I would like to go
home."

Lennox looked up at the big man in the doorway. "Take care
of it, Burke. Now."

❈ CHAPTER 23 ❈

The tiger's cub cannot be caught . . .
Without going into his den.

The moon was not yet full, but it was bright enough to cast the land in shadows of light and dark. The hills, yellow in daylight, were now shades of gray. The high branches of the oaks looked like crooked black arms reaching up against the night sky. Jason and the other men stopped on a hillside above the adobe and stared down at the yellow rectangles of light glowing in the windows. He pulled his coat closer to help ward off the damp night air. He thought of the Sangre de Cristo range in New Mexico and knew he was far warmer here than he would be this time of year if he were home, but that knowledge was little consolation. Besides, he was certain part of the cold he experienced was due to his fear for Jade. If Captain Lennox was the man who had wanted to harm her all along, then they had both played right into his hands.

El Sol snorted and pawed the ground, anxious to run. Jason nudged the big horse closer to Jon Chang's mount. "I'll ride in alone from here," Jason told him, "in case they have a guard out. That way we won't spook him into harming Jade if we're right. Lennox will just think I've taken him up on his invitation."

Chang nodded. "If our suspicions are wrong and everything is fine, walk outside and wave us away and we'll head back to town. We'll wait as close to the house as we can. If we don't see you by eight o'clock, we're coming in."

"I don't want Jade hurt."

Jon Chang smiled. "Don't worry. We won't come in with guns blazing, if that's what you're afraid of. Besides," he added, nodding toward Tao, "I have my secret weapon here."

Jason snorted. This might be the night he would get to see the mysterious Tao in action—still, for Jade's sake, he hoped not. He nudged El Sol forward and started down the hill.

355

* * *

"I really do have quite a headache, Captain," Jade said again. "Do you think you could have one of your men take me home?" Suddenly it seemed important to her to try to remember exactly how many men she had seen since her arrival; there had been the driver who had brought her from town, the two men on the roof, and the bearded man in the hallway. Had he been one of the men repairing the roof? If not, there were at least four men at the adobe with Lennox.

"Surely you can have dinner? You'll feel better after you eat something." Emery stepped forward, took her by the arm, and turned her back toward the dining room.

Jade fought the urge to stiffen, tried to act as comfortable as she should have been with him, and hoped she was succeeding, but his easy dismissal of her request did little to calm her frayed nerves. She forced herself to smile up at him, to remember he was her old friend, after all, and told herself she was being ridiculous.

The dining table was set for three. Emery placed Jade on his right and Quan Yen on his left. The cook, another burly man with muscles that bulged beneath his shirtsleeves, carried in the food. Jade added him to her tally of four—or now possibly five—men. A huge pheasant that was artfully arranged on a platter along with potatoes and carrots proved to be simple but delicious fare. Jade wished she was calmer so that she could enjoy the meal. As it was, she pushed the ample helping Lennox had carved for her around the plate.

"Evans has been my galley cook for over eight years," the captain said to break the ominous silence that hovered over the room.

"He's very talented," Jade said.

"I think so. Eat up, Jade. You look far too pale and thin."

She stared down at her plate, then across the table at Quan Yen. The girl was watching her carefully.

"More wine?" Emery asked as he filled his own goblet.

Jade shook her head.

"Some tea?" Quan asked in Chinese.

"No, no thank you," Jade said again.

As the captain ignored her distress and began to tell a story

about the worst storm he'd ever seen at sea, Jade let her mind
wander. Why had he suddenly taken such an interest in the
collection? As far as she could recall, he had never paid it
much mind. When he had come to visit her at Harrington
House that first day, he had barely even noticed the crates.
Why now?

Obviously he wanted something of her or he would not have
gone to such lengths to have the burly man follow her through
the streets of San Francisco. Had he also hired the two Chinese
who had nearly abducted her in the alleyway?

If, she decided as he rambled on, what he really wanted was
to get his hands on the collection, the only way she could gain
knowledge of his true motives was to deny him that which he
wanted most. She would push him to play his cards. She
waited for him to finish his tale, put down her fork, and then
said, "I've been thinking about the provision you have had
drawn up and, although as you say you want to do what's best
for the collection, I'm determined to leave things as they are.
Mrs. Stanford has promised to do her very best and I'm certain
she will. Besides, she'll add prestige to the list of founders."

Jade watched Emery Lennox's expression shutter as easily
as she might close the draperies in her room. Then he smiled.

"I hope you aren't being too hasty, dear."

"Oh no. I've thought it all through." Jade tried to take a sip
of wine, but found it nearly impossible to swallow.

She watched as he set down his knife and fork. His hairy,
broad-backed hands rested on each side of his plate as he stared
at her. Jade stared back. There was not a sound in the room
except for the pounding of her own heart.

Lennox's tone hardened, as did his gaze. "That's really too
bad, my dear. I hate to have to kill you."

Jade's fork clattered to the plate and bounced off onto the
table. "What?"

"I tried to make this easy for you," Lennox said nonchalantly as he lifted his goblet to his lips. "All I asked for was
your signature."

Jade pushed back her chair.

"I wouldn't do that if I were you," he warned.

Jade stood up and turned to run from the room. The bearded

man was standing directly behind her. She had not heard him enter.

"Sit down, Jade. I don't intend to ruin a good meal simply because you are not willing to cooperate."

"Are you mad? My husband will kill you for this." It sounded good, she thought, to say so, but even as the words were out she wondered if Jason would really avenge her death. Perhaps he would celebrate being rid of such a difficult wife.

"And why would your husband want to do that? By the time the search for your body is over and they find you dead in Little China, I will have sailed back to Canton."

Jade's mind raced ahead as she tried to comprehend his plan. "And I suppose that when I turn up missing tomorrow and you arrive on the doorstep with that piece of paper making you the trustee of the collection that no one will associate you with my disappearance?"

"I'm not that stupid. I intend to let things progress just as they are. After your death is discovered and your bereaved husband clears out and goes back to New Mexico, I'll wait a few weeks, sail back into town, and collect my prize."

"A collection that most people view as far from valuable."

"Don't be a fool. You know what I really want."

Jade knew exactly what he wanted. "The alchemist's formula?"

For a moment she thought he was going to reach across the table and grab her. "Did you find it? Have you already translated it?"

She shook her head. "No."

"I don't believe you. Quan Yen said that you're working on those pages every day in your room."

Jade's gaze cut to the girl across the table from her. "Quan Yen? Has this all been a trick, then? You set her up in my home to spy on me?"

"It was very easy. When I told you she was wandering along the waterfront your heart was in your eyes. The truth of the matter is that the slut is mine. I bought her two years ago in Canton. She's the one who told me about Li Po. In fact, he was her grandfather."

"She betrayed her own grandfather?"

"Why not? He was the greedy bastard who sold her to me."

"But her bruises, she'd been badly beaten—"

Lennox smiled openly, suggestively, at Quan Yen and said something to her in Cantonese that Jade could not translate. "She likes a heavy hand," he said, staring hungrily at the girl. "Now, what have you learned of the formula?"

"Nothing. The writings are in a language too archaic for me to decipher."

Her own calm attitude amazed her. Here they were, chatting as if they were two old friends talking about the weather. Jade realized all too clearly that her only hope was to stall for time. How long would it be before the hulking guard behind her snapped her neck?

"I can't imagine you are this in need of money, that you would go so far as to . . . to . . ."

"To kill you? Since when does a man have enough money? Besides, it's not just the money. Quan said Li-Po had been working on a secret elixir, a tonic that would restore youth and make a man forever young."

"Surely you don't believe that?"

"Oh, but I do. And so did your father."

"Then where is the alchemist? If he had an elixir that would make him immortal, where is he?"

"He's dead."

Shaken, Jade asked, "How do you know for certain?"

"I had my men dig up every inch of the garden. Your father told me he died, but at first I didn't believe him. I thought he was lying, but when I couldn't find a trace of Li Po, I realized your father had buried him somewhere and that the formula might be buried with the body. It's not. I know, because we found the grave earlier this afternoon. So you see, this dinner is sort of a celebration."

A very macabre one, Jade thought. *A celebration of death*.

Lennox looked about to rise, so Jade said, "Tell me exactly how my father became involved in all of this."

"I returned from a voyage and came here to deliver a brass gong to your grandfather for his collection. I had recently purchased my little joy-girl here and she had told me all about Li Po. When I arrived with the gong, I learned your grandfather had just passed on. Your father was here, selling off furniture and crating up the collection. We had a drink, then another, then a bottle or two, and that's when I decided he was the perfect partner to bring into my scheme. I told him that I planned to abduct Li Po and use the gold he could manufacture to lure investors into shares in a fictitious mine. But what I really wanted was the elixir of life that Li Po was supposedly able to concoct. Can you imagine what the wealthy and powerful men of the world, the Crockers and Stanfords and Rockefellers, would pay to live forever?

"I sailed back to Canton and had my crew capture Li Po. We were no sooner ashore than word came in on another ship from China about the old man's abduction. At that point, the tongs still didn't know who brought Li Po into the country, but naturally, they wanted him for themselves. I secreted him out here and left him in your father's care. Then, I set sail the next morning, intending to hide out until things cooled off. But when I returned, Douglas told me Li Po had taken sick and died. I thought he was lying in order to keep everything for himself. He wouldn't tell me anything about Li Po, he just insisted the man was dead. So, I leaked word to the tong that your father was behind the abduction. They killed him."

"And then?" Jade glanced back over her shoulder. Burke was still there, his arms folded across his chest, his attention centered on Quan Yen.

"Then I decided to hide out until I thought the tongs were satisfied that they had avenged Li Po. When I came back, intending to get my hands on the collection and the house to search for the formula, you were here. You'd bailed out the collection and gotten yourself married. It would have been far easier if you hadn't done that, Jade, but the rest was simple. Quan Yen watched you day and night and reported to the men I sent by disguised as peddlers. She was also very adept at slipping a toxic herb into your tea. Consumed over a period of time, it leads to convulsions and then death."

Jade spread her hands wide on the cool tabletop and stared aghast at Quan Yen. "You were poisoning me?" she whispered.

Quan Yen stared back without a sound. *So young*, Jade thought, *and yet so very deadly*. She tried to imagine the girl pleasuring Emery Lennox, but her mind refused to accept the image.

Lennox answered for Quan Yen. "I wanted you in a weakened state. That kept you at home where we could watch you, except for that little unexpected jaunt you took to the doctor yesterday."

"And the urn that nearly killed me at the Palace, the men in Little China? Were you behind those attempts on my life?"

"You hadn't married yet. If you met with an accidental death, or ended up a victim of the tongs like your father, then I could have simply paid off the bank. Now, you have a beneficiary. But, I'm sure you'll be willing to sign this contract before I'm through with you." He patted the papers in his side pocket.

"What would you have done if my husband had come with me tonight? Would you have killed us both?" At least she could be thankful for one thing, that Jason was safe at home. If she had died knowing she was responsible for his death, too— The thought did not bear thinking.

"Who do you think sent Harrington the note that took him away from the house when my driver arrived? I had it delivered to Quan Yen earlier with instructions that she was to give it to him just before three o'clock. At three thirty my carriage arrived to collect you, did it not?"

"So if I had stayed home today, your plan would have been foiled?"

"Merely postponed."

She still could not fathom the truth. This man was willing to kill her for a formula that might not even exist, and if it did, would no doubt prove to be a hoax. "Why didn't you just ask me for the collection, or for the formula for that matter?"

He rose half out of his chair and leaned forward over the table, his eyes wide. "Do you have it?"

"No," she repeated, shaking her head.

He sat back down. "Would you have given me the collection?"

"No." She lied cooly, knowing she probably would have, had he asked her early on.

The thin-faced man who reminded her of a rat burst into the

room. Lennox stood and walked around the table and as he did, Jade turned in her chair to watch.

"Captain, there's a rider comin' in," the man announced.

"Jason!" Jade said triumphantly.

Lennox did not move. "Is he alone?"

"Aye."

It was Lennox's turn to look triumphant. The captain turned to Burke. "Lock her up in the cellar. See that she can't make a sound. A few hours down there and she'll be ready to sign anything."

"No!" Jade was up and out of the chair. She began backing away from the bearded sailor but there was no escape. He reached out for her arm and pulled her toward the kitchen door.

"Take away her place setting and Quan Yen's." He issued the order to the thin-faced man before he turned to the Chinese girl and said in Cantonese, "Go to the kitchen. Hide in the pantry if need be." She hurried to do his bidding.

In her weakened state, Jade was no match for the man who held her securely by the wrist as he dragged her into the kitchen. She saw everything in a blur—the cook standing in the center of the room, holding the trap door open, his grease-spattered apron, and his brawny, hairy arms.

"Stop!" She tried to plead with them as she struggled against Burke's hold. "Let me go."

As the dark hole in the earth yawned before her, Jade shrank back. A fetid, decaying smell issued from the cellar.

"I'm not going down there without a lamp," her guard grumbled. "Get me a lantern, Dick." With one hand on Jade and the other on the trap door, the bearded man relieved the cook of his burden. She twisted and tugged, trying to wrench free, but he held her as easily as she might hold the stem of a blossom. Finally, tired of her antics, he gave her wrist a vicious twist that nearly drove her to her knees.

The cook returned with a lantern. He held the door open again and handed the light to the bearded man, who growled at Jade. "You can climb down the ladder under your own power or I'll throw you down."

He kept hold of her wrist until she turned around and felt

with her foot for the top rung of the ladder. Once she had started down, he released her.

The dank, putrid air seemed to cling to her. Jade tried to breath through her mouth to avoid inhaling the stench. Had the cook used the cellar for garbage? When she was halfway down, the guard above her began his own descent. The lantern cast a bobbing, swaying circle of light around the ladder above her. It danced off the ceiling and walls of the small, square room below.

Jade did not look down. She concentrated on each careful step as she tried to avoid tangling her feet in her skirt hem. Her hands shook and she gripped the rails tighter. Her captor's heavy boots were on the rung inches above her head. His rapid descent forced her to move faster.

Finally she felt the packed-earth floor beneath her feet and stepped back. The waving lamplight flung their shadows against the four walls. Once the man had reached the bottom of the ladder, he raised the lantern high and swung it to the left. Jade followed his gaze and gasped.

"At least you'll have company." His hollow laughter filled the air.

She stared down at an open grave that had been sunk a good four feet beneath the cellar floor. Although the badly decomposed body was unrecognizable, Jade had no doubt as to the identity of the corpse. Li Po, the renowned wizard, lay moldering in the grave. At the foot of the gaping hole in the ground lay an open wooden chest, its contents strewn over the floor. Two embroidered shoes with thick heels lay in juxtaposition to one another. A tall, crumpled hat and a red silk robe lay wadded together near the shoes.

Jade backed away toward the opposite wall. "You can't leave me here." She could barely whisper. She shook her head. "Please. Don't do this."

"Look, lady, I don't have a choice. Shut up and get over in the far corner."

"But—"

"Move!" He raised his hand as if to strike her.

She backed away from him until she felt the cold wall

behind her. Pressed against the earthen surface, Jade watched him suspiciously.

"Sit down," he growled.

She slid down the wall and crouched there.

"Sit!"

She sat on the damp earth and stared across the room at the open pit not far away. A shiver ran down her spine. She closed her eyes and tried to will herself out of this horrible situation.

The lantern rattled as the guard set it on the floor a few feet away. She felt him standing over her and she opened her eyes, only to see that the man had a dishtowel in his hands. He tore it into strips and bound her ankles and wrists. When he reached out with one final strip to gag her, Jade cried out and tried to twist her face away.

There was a sharp sound of boot heels overhead and she recognized Emery Lennox's voice. "What're you doing down there? Get it done and get up here!"

Jade continued to shake her head to avoid the gag. Burke backhanded her so hard she fell over on her shoulder. He jerked her upright again and shoved the strip of cloth over her mouth and yanked it into a knot in back.

Her head was reeling. Jade tried to focus on the lantern that was just out of reach. Double vision caused her to see two wavering flames where in reality there was only one. Finally, the two flames merged and she gently shook her head to clear it. She blinked and tried to focus. Heavy, rapid footsteps on the ladder alerted her to the fact that the man had left her alone. She silently gave thanks to him for leaving the lamp behind.

The trap door overhead banged shut. Jade jumped. She could not take her eyes off of the open grave on the opposite side of the room. The sight of the bloodred robe haunted her. It was exactly like the one she had worn in her dream. Covered with golden threads, it shimmered in the lamplight as if it was alive. Willing herself not to stare at the grisly remains of the wizard, she told herself that Li Po could do her no harm. The man was dead. All that remained was the empty shell that had housed his soul.

As footsteps thudded overhead, she tried to imagine where Li Po might be now. Was he in a place where souls awaited reincarnation? She hoped he was among an assembly of souls waiting to be reborn. She hoped his spirit was anywhere but here. Jade tried to convince herself that no matter where the wizard's spirit was now, she was in no danger. A pile of bones and rotting flesh could do her no harm.

But Emery Lennox could, so she concentrated on what might be happening on the floor above her. Had Jason truly come after her? She wondered what excuse Lennox would give him as to where she had gone. Would Jason believe him? Rocking to and fro, she tried to make a noise that would carry to the room above, but only succeeded in hitting her head against the wall and then issuing a muffled, throaty moan.

Certain that he was being watched, J.T. waited on the veranda for Lennox to answer his knock. He tapped his hat against his thigh and glanced over his shoulder at the darkened hills shadowed against the night sky. Footsteps from within sounded on the plank floorboards. He turned his attention to the door, which swung wide to reveal Emery Lennox.

The man was dressed in impeccable navy with gold braid trimming the cuffs. His white shirt was starched, his hair glossed into place with hair oil. He smiled when he recognized Jason, and ushered him into the hallway.

Jason glanced into the room beyond and marveled at the change in the place. He recognized the heavy, dark furniture as Chinese in origin and could just imagine what Jade must have thought when she saw them. He came quickly to the point.

"I've come after my wife."

"I hate to say it, but she left over an hour ago." Lennox's face registered concern. "She was terribly tired and complained of a headache, so I sent her on home. Quan Yen has already gone with her new guardian, a missionary from Stockton."

Jason looked around. The man was believable, the story more than plausible given the way Jade had been feeling; still, Jason bridled at being so smoothly dismissed.

As if he sensed Jason's hesitation, Lennox said, "Can you stay for a drink?"

Preoccupied, Jason nodded. "That would be great. I'm

anxious to see the changes you've made here." As the two of them walked into the central room, Jason added, "I was only out here once, just long enough to walk through the rooms. You've really accomplished quite a lot in a short while."

Lennox paused before a tall teak chest carved with scenes of the Chinese countryside and poured two glasses of whiskey. He handed one to Jason, toasted him, and then bolted his down. Jason nursed his drink, walking around the room, seemingly interested in every detail of the furnishings. He was aware of movement in the room beyond the dining table. That would be the kitchen, he recalled, and realized Jade could be hidden anywhere. Determined to search the entire place before he left, he turned to Lennox.

"Would you mind showing me everything? I know Jade will want to talk about it all, she's bound to drive me crazy with it. I really can't believe the change."

Carefully, Lennox set his glass on the table. "Of course." He bowed and waved Jason toward the hallway.

"That old kitchen was a real mess. What have you done there?" Without waiting for Lennox to suggest he go in, Jason rudely opened the kitchen door and stuck his head and shoulders in. A huge man stood over the stove stirring a simmering pot of liquid. He frowned at J.T. and then turned his back to the door. If there was ever a man he'd hesitate to tangle with, Jason knew the cook was that man. He smiled, nodded, and said, "Sorry, just looking."

The cook remained unmoved while J.T. peered around. His eyes went to the closed trap door in the floor of the kitchen. If Lennox had locked Jade downstairs, how could he get to her without outright asking to see the cellar?

He stepped away from the kitchen door and walked back through the dining room. Lennox followed close behind. Jason feigned a gift of gab as he found himself complimenting the changes in the place, the repairs, the furnishings. He had Lennox show him the upper rooms. J.T. asked questions. The captain mumbled replies, to which Jason paid little attention. He was too busy looking for any sign of his wife.

By the time they reached the first floor again, J.T. realized he had better walk outside and alert the others not to come barging in, for it appeared Jade had truly left. There was no sign of her or Quan Yen anywhere.

Holding out his empty whiskey glass, Jason smiled at Lennox. "Thanks for the tour. I'm impressed," he said, stretching before he shoved his hands into his pockets. He scratched his head and then rubbed the back of his neck. "Wonder why I didn't pass your carriage on the road?" He said half to himself. "When did you say Jade left?"

His brow wrinkled in thought, Lennox mused, "I guess it was about, oh, say nearly two hours ago."

"Two hours?"

"Give or take a few minutes."

"Then she should have been home before I left."

Lennox shrugged. "Barely. Besides, I told my man to take it slow."

Jason paced to the chair where he'd tossed his hat. "I hope to God nothing's happened to her." He swung on Lennox. "You do know someone's been trying to harm her, don't you?"

Lennox nodded. "She told me as much. That's why I put an extra guard on the carriage." He drew a gold watch out of his coat pocket and flicked it open. Worry darkened his features. "The carriage should arrive back here within the hour. If it doesn't—"

"Then someone's abducted her." J.T. silently cursed himself and the situation. If Lennox was telling the truth and Jade had left earlier and had been waylaid by the real villain while he, Jason, was here on a wild goose chase, then he had played right into his enemy's hands.

"What time is it?" he asked Lennox.

"Two minutes shy of eight."

Jason had two minutes to walk out the door and call off the others. He wished to God he knew what to do. He had stalled long enough. Retrieving his hat, he started to leave. Just as he turned toward the hall, his eye caught a patch of black against the shining hardwood floor beneath the low dragon chair near the fireplace. Without staring at it, he quickly identified the object on the floor as Jade's black velvet reticule. He had seen it often enough to recognize it; she usually hooked it over her wrist.

He sensed that Lennox spied the bag at the same time, for the captain paused momentarily and placed himself between Jason and the chair. J.T. feigned ignorance of the entire incident. Instead, he tarried near the door that led to the hallway.

"Just one more thing, Captain—" Jason began. It was almost amusing to watch Emery Lennox's anticipation of his departure. "I was wondering if you happened to find anything down in that old cellar." He hoped the man was beginning to squirm inside, for unless Jason missed his guess, that's where Lennox had hidden Jade.

He wanted his wife out of that hole and out fast, but without knowing how many men Lennox had about the place, Jason was hesitant to act alone.

"No," Lennox said almost absently, "I didn't find anything down there at all. Why do you ask?"

Jason's gunbelt rested heavy on his hips. He felt good knowing it was there. He resisted reaching down to finger the weapon hidden beneath his coat. "I just wondered. The day we rode out here, Jade somehow managed to get trapped down there. She hadn't seen anything of interest, but then, you know women. Like the rest of them, she's a bit scatterbrained." He was glad Jade couldn't hear him now.

Lennox yawned and stepped out into the entry hall. With one hand on the door handle, he made his intentions all too clear to Jason, who dragged his feet as he carefully centered his hat on his head.

Come on, Chang. Jason silently prayed that the men outside were nearing the house. He knew he could take Lennox then and there. He wasn't so sure about the man in the kitchen. How many others would there be to contend with?

In the end it would not matter. Even if Lennox had an army there to stop him, Jason didn't intend to leave the house without his wife.

❈ CHAPTER 24 ❈

Though the sword be sharp . . .
It will not wound the innocent.

"I'm not here."

With her eyes closed tight, Jade whispered the words over
nd over. "I'm in my room. I'm safe. I'm not here." But the
old earth at her back and the smell of death that permeated the
ir were ominous reminders that she was still captive in the
ellar. From beneath shuttered lids she sensed the flickering of
e lantern's light. Her eyelids flew open as she fought to
ntrol her mounting panic. The flame leapt and danced
lthough there was no draft in the room. Terror gripped her.
he lamp was running out of oil.

Even with her eyes closed she could still see Li Po's open
rave. He had been buried deep beneath the floor of the
asement, the earth repacked tightly over his grave until, in the
adowy darkness, she had seen no sign of recent digging.
ow, mounds of dirt were banked on the opposite side of the
ave, and the defilers' picks and shovels were still propped in
e corner.

She opened her eyes, struggled against her bonds, then
oaned aloud. There were worse fates, she was certain, than
ing trapped underground with a dead man, but at the moment
ne came to mind. She glanced at the ceiling and prayed that
son would get away safely. Lennox would surely tell him
at she had gone. Hopefully, J.T. would believe him and
ave. Above all else, she wanted Jason to be safe. Her only
gret was that he might never realize how very deeply she had
me to love him, or how much she truly wanted to be a good
ife to him.

To keep her mind from concentrating on the ever-dimming
mplight, she tried to picture J.T. at his home in New Mexico.
He once told her the sky was so wide and blue that it seemed
go on forever. She wanted to witness the peace of the desert.

And she longed to know what it would be like to finally se
aside the past and dream her own dream.

For so long she had carried Philo Page's dream in her hea
that she had put aside her own chance for happiness. But Jad
knew, too, she could never have let her grandfather's dream di
any more than she could have turned aside the hand of fate th.
led her to Jason.

The binding at her wrists numbed her fingers. She trie
twisting her hands to gain some comfort, but nothing hap
pened. The lamplight flared, sputtered, and then died. Jad
shut her eyes tightly against the darkness and choked back
scream.

Loud footsteps echoed overhead, faster and more frant
than she had heard them before. Someone was pounding c
wood. She strained forward, her head tilted sharply toward th
trap door so that she might hear what was happening in th
kitchen above her.

"Open up in the name of the San Francisco Police Depar
ment!"

Although the words were muffled, she thought she reco
nized Jon Chang's voice.

Jade started screaming against the gag.

At the sound of the commotion at the back door, Jaso
smoothly palmed his revolver and drew it on Lennox. He ke
the man backed against the wall in the entry hall as the
listened to the cook shouting in the kitchen. No more than
moment or two passed before Lieutenant Chang and Tao Li
ran through the dining room and halted in the entry. Jason ke
his gun aimed at Lennox as Tao and Jon Chang warily stepp
forward. A swift glance at Chang alerted Jason to the fact th
the detective was well armed. Tao was not.

"Xavier?" Jason asked.

"In the kitchen, guarding the cook," Chang said.

Before Jason was able to move, the door behind him swu
open. Unwilling to risk wounding J.T., who stood directly
front of him, Chang held his fire. A tall, bearded seaman thr
a shotgun into the small of Jason's back and warned, "If y

know what's good for you, you and your pig-eyed friend will drop your guns."

Jason glanced at Chang. Neither of them moved. The man behind Jason nudged him hard with the barrel of his gun. "Do it."

Jason dropped his gun.

Chang followed suit.

Lennox bent to retrieve Jason's weapon. "Good work, Burke. Now get over here and hold that gun on all three of them while Miles ties them up."

Burke forced Jason to cross the room and stand beside Chang and Tao. The smaller man, Miles, his sharp face scowling, slipped into the room behind Burke. "I'll need some rope, Captain," he said.

"Then you better goddamn go get it!" Lennox blustered. His nervousness apparent, he pointed Jason's own gun at him while Burke's shotgun was aimed at Tao and Chang.

"Let my wife go, Lennox, or you'll live to regret it."

"How did you know she was here? How did you even come to suspect me?"

"Does it gall you that your little plan was so easily upset?" Jason asked.

"Not upset," Lennox assured him, "merely hampered by your sudden appearance."

"The lieutenant here found a man who could decipher the writing on the crates." As J.T. baited him, Lennox became excited with the news. "He's the one that led us to suspect you."

Lennox moved closer to Jason. "Did he translate the formula?"

"Wouldn't you like to know?" Jason felt Tao tense beside him. He continued to taunt Lennox. "Has all this been worth the trouble, Lennox? What did you hope to gain?"

"In a few minutes when you're dead, Harrington, you'll wish you had what I've gone to all this trouble for . . . immortality."

Before Jason could say another word, Tao Ling moved. His right foot shot out with lightning swiftness and blinding force. The rifle in Burke's hands flew across the entry hall. Burke spun and ran for the door.

When Lennox turned toward Tao, Jason lunged at him
knocking the man's gun hand upward. Chips of adobe show
ered down on them as the gunshot reverberated in the smal
room. Chang ran forward and wrenched the gun from Lennox'
hand, then J.T. pushed him back until the captain was pinne
against the opposite wall.

Jason held Lennox against the wall with his forearm presse
across the man's larynx. He glanced over his shoulder in tim
to see Tao fly through the air and lash out with a kick t
Burke's midsection. When Burke doubled over, Tao choppe
downward with a precise movement of his hand that connecte
with the back of Burke's neck and sent the huge man crashin
to the floor.

Chang turned to Jason with a nod and a smile.

"My secret weapon," he said.

Jason was suddenly thankful he had not tried to get past Ta
when the man was guarding Jade's door.

The front door opened and Miles rushed in carrying a coil c
rope and a knife. He froze when he saw Burke on the floor an
Lennox up against the wall. Jon Chang turned his gun on th
intruder and Miles dropped his knife.

"I'll take over from here," Chang said, stepping towar
Jason. He trained his gun on Lennox, then looked at th
rat-faced Miles and pointed at Burke and the captain. "T
them both up, then we'll take care of you."

The little man complied without argument. Burke la
unconscious on the ground where Tao had left him.

"I'm going after Jade," Jason said. Tao followed hi
toward the kitchen where Xavier stood with two pistols traine
on the burly cook. He smiled when Jason walked in. "Tie hi
up, Xavier," J.T. ordered. Then he reached the trap doc
grabbed the hatch, and threw it open.

"Jade!"

He could see nothing in the smelly, black pit below. Cursi
Lennox for leaving Jade in the dark, he climbed down th
ladder. "Get a light, Tao," he called out, carefully feeling h
way down.

"Jade!?" He paused at the bottom of the stairs. Some lig
from the kitchen filtered down into the depths, so he waited

ioment while his eyes became adjusted to the darkness. The
lace stunk like hell. He heard a scrabbling sound and moved
oward it. Above him, Tao started down the ladder with a
imp.

"Jade?"

Jason hunkered down and reached out with shaking hands as
e felt for his wife. He connected with her hair first, and his
ingers became tangled in it. Then he moved his hands to her
houlders and tried to still her tremors by pulling her into his
rms. "Shh. It's all right, Jade. I'm here." He tried to soothe
er with words as his fingers tore at the gag's knot behind her
ead. Her hair became tangled in the rag and his fingers, and
he complained with a groan and a jerk. "Hold still," he said
oftly. "Almost done."

Tao stepped close to them and held the lamp high. Jason
orked faster. He pulled the gag away and Jade sucked in a
eep draught of air and coughed. Jason drew her into his arms
nd held her tight.

"My hands," she whispered. "Please."

He drew back and struggled with the knot at her wrists.

"Wait!" Tao interrupted Jason's task. He reached around
ehind him and drew a small knife out of a hidden sheath tied
his calf. He handed it to Jason who slit open the binding and
eed Jade's hands. Jason bent to undo her ankles and then took
er numb hands in his own and began to rub life back into
em. A dark bruise purpled her cheek from her jaw to the
orner of her eye. Her sleeve was torn.

The wild look in her eyes frightened him more than the cold
umbness of her hands. He followed her gaze and glanced over
s shoulder. A grave yawned wide on the other side of the
om. Dirt still clung to the partially decomposed body resting
the open grave. A small chest with its contents strewn about
ood open at the foot of the grave near a mound of earth. Had
stepped the wrong way at the foot of the ladder, he would
ve fallen in.

"Get me out of here," Jade said through chattering teeth.

"Gladly. Put your arms around my neck," he said. Jason
cked her up and headed for the ladder.

Jade clung to him as he adjusted her and held her close with one arm while he climbed upward. She buried her face against his neck, breathing in the warm, familiar scent of him. He was alive. He smelled of the outdoors, tobacco, and life.

The world brightened as they emerged from the cellar. Jade blinked, raised her head, and looked around. She smiled at Xavier, who helped her stand. A wide smile of his own brightened his features. Emery's cook was tied to a chair near the kitchen table.

"The captain?" she asked. "Where is he, Jason? Is he—"

"He's not dead, if that worries you. Jon Chang has Lennox and the other two tied up by now."

When they entered the drawing room, Jason set Jade down on one of the dragon chairs.

"How did you find me?" she whispered.

Jason reached beneath her chair, picked up her reticule, and took her hand. Lowering himself to one knee, he slipped the string ties over her wrist. "I almost believed him when he said you had gone home." J.T. shook his head. "I nearly left, then I saw your bag under the chair and knew you were still here."

"What made you come after me?"

"Chang came to the house with an old man who deciphered the symbols. That's how we found you."

The symbols. The reason Lennox wanted her dead. They seemed so very unimportant now.

Jade was so tired she couldn't seem to concentrate on anything but the sight of Jason. Staring into the depths of his eyes, she recognized the look of relief in them. Relief coupled with something more. Her eyes filled with tears. Jade felt them spill hot and heavy down her cheeks as she stared down at Jason.

"I do love you, Jason," she whispered, "whether you ever believe me or not, I love you. I married you because I love you. I'll always love you."

On one knee before her, Jason opened his arms and pulled her against him. He buried his face in the cascade of shining hair that had tumbled around her shoulders. He squeezed her tight, lifted his head, and then kissed her deeply. Then he pulled back and brushed her hair back away from her shoulders.

"I love you, too. And now that all of this is behind us, I want to start over."

"Oh, Jason, I do too."

Before she could say any more, they both turned at the sound of footsteps behind them. Jason stood up as Tao walked over to them.

"I'm sorry to interrupt," he said. "Chang has Lennox and his men tied up in the buckboard outside. Xavier will ride guard for him. I will drive you both home in the carriage."

J.T. reached down for Jade's hand. "Good. I'm sure my wife is ready to go home."

Tao looked concerned. "Where is Quan Yen?"

Jade stood up and looked around the room. She hesitated to tell Tao all that she knew about Quan Yen, but the girl was dangerous, and apparently still hiding.

"Lennox told me she left with a missionary," J.T. told Tao.

Jade shook her head. "She's still here." She shook her head sorrowfully as she told them, "All this time she was slipping poison in my tea." Ashamed of her own gullibility, she was unable to meet Jason's eyes. She watched Tao carefully as his expression changed from surprise, to sorrow, to an immobile mask devoid of feeling.

"I will find her," he said.

J.T. stayed with Jade and took her hand in his. She chanced a look at him. "I'm quite a fool, aren't I?" she asked.

"Because you felt sorry for Quan Yen? Or because you trusted a man you thought was your friend?" He shook his head. "No, I don't think you're a fool. In fact," Jason continued as he placed his fingertips beneath her chin and tilted it upward until their eyes met, "I think it's time I learned to trust."

"Oh, Jason. Don't make me cry again." She tried to smile.

"When you look at me like that, I want to carry you off and make mad, passionate love to you," he whispered.

Jade couldn't help but laugh. Then her eyes widened and she cried out, "The pantry!"

Jason shook his head with a wry smile. This wasn't exactly the time or place he had in mind, but if she really wanted to make love in the pantry— "I know you're a bit eccentric, Jade, but . . . the pantry?"

"No! Quan Yen! That's where the captain sent her—to hid in the pantry."

"Stay put." Jason was on his feet in seconds, heading for th kitchen.

Jade stood up in an attempt to pull herself together. Tao' footsteps echoed overhead as she ran a shaking hand throug her tangled hair and tried to pull it back in a knot. Tugging the torn shoulder seam of her sleeve, she surveyed the damag and then let it droop again and brushed off her skirt. Sh shivered when she thought of the man buried in the cella Tomorrow would be soon enough to see to it that Li Po had proper burial. She would remember to ask Lieutenant Char about arrangements. Perhaps the tong associations would unit to give the old wizard a proper Chinese funeral with gongs an fireworks.

An eerie feeling crept over Jade as she stood there thinkir of Li Po. Slowly she turned around, and there in the doorwa between the sitting room and the hallway stood Quan Yen. Th girl's heavily painted face was as flawless and guileless ever, her cheeks glowing with high, bright spots of color. was not until Quan took a teetering step forward that Jac realized the girl clutched a gun in her hand.

It was aimed directly at Jade's heart.

Jade lifted her hands in protest and slowly backed across t room. She meant to use a tone loud enough for Jason to hea but the words were issued barely above a whisper, "You dor want to do this, Quan Yen."

"Yes, missee, I do. You make all kine trouble for me. F captain. I kill you. I kill everybody. Let captain go."

"Even if you kill me, you will never be able to kill them a There are too many of them. They are stronger."

"I find gun. Now I kill one at time." Quan Yen's expressi became one of joy as she spoke of killing.

The singsong girl wobbled across the room. The g wavered in her hand.

"If you shoot, the others will hear the gunshot and run here," Jade warned.

"I ready. I know hiding place. Missee maybe should before. Easier with the tea. Much nice for you. This is not nice as fall asleep forever. Messy. Alla time messy. Now I kill missee. Captain get secret and no die."

Jade shook her head. "There is no formula. Only an old man's messages that were a cry for help."

"Much magic. Li Po find magic drink. Captain and Quan Yen live all time forever."

Jade knew then that there was no reasoning with her. Seeking a path of escape, she glanced over Quan Yen's shoulder. To her relief, she saw Jason quietly sneaking across the room toward the girl. He mouthed the words, "Keep talking," and although her voice quivered with fear and anticipation, she complied.

"Perhaps you should not kill me," Jade suggested. "You could tie me up. Make the men let the captain go. Then you can both escape."

The idea gave the girl pause to think. It was during that very moment that Tao walked in the room. Quan Yen spun toward the sound just as Jason lunged at her from behind. He was directly in the line of fire when the gun went off.

Jade screamed. Jason fell forward, nearly knocking Quan Yen off her feet. The girl kept the gun clutched in her hand while she tried to regain her balance. Across the room, Tao took a step forward and spun around on one leg while he kicked out with the other.

Quan fired. The bullet lodged in the wall behind Tao. He spun again, whirling like a top as he lashed out, kicking and spinning, moving faster and faster toward the girl.

She fired and missed again.

Tao's foot finally connected with Quan Yen's arm. Jade gasped when she heard the girl's arm break as Tao's powerful kick snapped the bone. The gun flew out of Quan's hand and hit the floor. Quan Yen screamed, then clutched her arm and crumpled.

Unable to hide his sorrow, Tao picked up the gun Quan had dropped, stepped over the fallen girl, and knelt down next to Jason. He rolled J.T. onto his back and then turned to Jade. "He's not dead. Can you see to him while I get her out of here?"

Finally able to breathe, Jade choked back a sob and nodded.

She ran to Jason's side and stared at the blood that seemed to be everywhere. The whole right side of his face was covered with it, as was his neck and his shirt. She had no idea where he had been wounded.

"Jason?" She whispered frantically to him, reached for the hem of her skirt, and tenderly began to wipe away as much blood as she could without hurting him.

Behind her, Tao jerked Quan Yen to her feet. The girl sobbed as she held her crippled arm tightly against her. Issuing curt orders in Cantonese, he marched her out the doorway just as Jon Chang came running in. He went immediately to Jade and knelt down beside her.

With her hands and skirt hem covered in blood, she implored him to help. "I don't know where he's hurt. There's so much blood." She grabbed the front of Jason's shirt and balled it into her fists. "Damn you, Jason Harrington! Don't you dare die—not after all you've put me through already!"

Chang drew a wide, white kerchief out of his pocket and wadded it up. Slowly, beginning at Jason's hairline, he began to pat away blood and search for a wound. The copious amount of blood was coming from a crease that ran along Jason's temple. When it appeared that Jason had suffered no more than a surface wound, Jade let go of the death grip she held on his shirt.

"I can do that for him," she whispered, willing to relieve Chang. He gave the task over to her and Jade pressed the wad of fabric against Jason's temple. She did not like the idea of having only Tao and Xavier watch over so many prisoners. She doubted if she could take any more surprises. "I'm fine. Maybe you should see to the others."

"Call out if you need me."

Chang left after she reassured him that she would be fine caring for Jason alone. With one hand still on the kerchief, she placed her other open palm alongside Jason's cheek. "Jason?" she whispered softly. "Can you hear me?"

As he lay there with his eyes closed, she noticed his exceptionally long lashes before his eyes opened. The momentary confusion in his gaze quickly became one of recognition and understanding.

"Where's Quan Yen?" He tried to look for the girl, but Jade's hand at his temple kept him from moving his head.

"Tao took her outside with the others."

"I want to sit up."

"Wait." She lifted the wad of blood-soaked cotton and checked his wound. The flow of blood had slowed to a trickle. "All right, but slowly. I don't want you to black out again."

"Yes, ma'am." He grinned up at her.

When he was seated cross-legged in the middle of the floor, Jade finally relaxed. "Are you all right?"

"Still a little dizzy," he acknowledged, now holding the cloth to his temple on his own. "But I'll live."

"You'd better," she mumbled, half to herself.

"Don't you relish being an extremely rich widow? I thought that was the plan?"

Unaware that he was only teasing, Jade caught her breath until she met his eyes and saw his smile.

"That's nothing to tease about, Jason. In fact, I don't ever want you to refer to that part of our lives again. It was all a misunderstanding that I thought you wanted to leave in the past."

"Didn't anyone ever tell you not to yell at a wounded man?"

She remained stubbornly silent.

"All right. Agreed. If you kiss me, I won't mention it again for the next fifty years or so."

"Is that blackmail?" she asked.

"My kind of blackmail."

"Then I have no choice, I guess." She feigned a sigh of resignation and leaned forward to kiss him.

"Now," he said when their lips finally parted, "if you'll help me up, we can go home."

She slipped her arm beneath his and helped him to his feet.

❊ EPILOGUE ❊

In bed, be wife and husband . . .
In hall, each other's honored guest.

The next afternoon, an overcast sky produced sheets of drizzling rain outside Harrington House. Inside the master suite the flames of two dozen candles arranged around the room mingled with those from a blazing fire in the fireplace to dispel the gloomy weather.

Jason's capable hands roamed over Jade's willing body as she lay back against the pillows propped against the high, curved headboard. The candlelight gilded her fair skin; the flames were reflected in the shimmering highlights of her hair. Where he touched her, she felt her body tingle. As his lips followed his hands, every nerve beneath her flesh jolted to life with a quiver.

More roughly than he intended, Jason pulled his body across hers. He was hot and heavy with need, she was pliant and welcoming. He took his hands off Jade and braced them on either side of her. "Tell me again," he growled low in his throat, "now."

Her voice was breathless, her tone urgent. "I love you."

"Again."

She opened her eyes and stared into his. "I love you." Her words were louder, stronger. Then she gasped, "Don't make me wait, Jason. Please don't make me wait." With eager hands she reached out and cradled his face between her palms. She pulled him up and held him captive while she kissed him deeply, and reveled in the taste and smell of him. Jade gently bit his lower lip, sucked it between her teeth, and then plunged her tongue into his mouth.

When the kiss ended, he raised his head and stared into her eyes. "You want me again?"

"Yes."

"You're sure."

"Yes! Oh, yes, Jason, yes!"

Jason moaned, raised himself between her open thighs, and drove into her. Jade's eyes flew open wide. She called out his name and grasped his hips, pushing until he filled her. He crushed her in his embrace as her fingers traced a frantic pattern on his hips, thighs, and buttocks, driving him wild. He withdrew his hardened shaft and then plunged over and over again until she writhed beneath him. He knew when she climaxed, felt the walls of the moist sheath that encased him convulse wildly, heard her cry of release, and let his seed burst forth inside her.

Jade felt the white-hot, liquid heat of his climax and another release of her own began even as the first had yet to fade entirely. She shuddered and clung to him, afraid to let go, afraid that if she did she would spiral out of control and lose herself forever. When she was in charge of her senses again, when the searing fire that had raged inside her began to abate, she decided that dying of ecstasy would not be such a terrible fate.

She listened to the sound of their commingled, ragged breathing. Jason's weight was heavy, but not unbearable. She ran her hands over his rib cage, felt the smooth, rippling muscles beneath his taut flesh, and counted herself the luckiest of women.

When he was in command of his senses again, Jason rolled to his side and took her with him. He buried his face in her hair and smiled a secret smile of contentment when he felt Jade reach down and draw the covers over them both.

It was an hour later when Jade awoke to find Jason seated in a comfortable rocking chair near the bed, strumming his guitar. He smiled when he saw that she was awake.

She smiled when she saw that he was nude.

"Do you think we should dress at all today, or just wait until tomorrow?" he asked.

"I don't think I've ever seen a naked guitar player before."

"I don't think you've ever seen a naked man before," he said.

She blushed prettily. "You're right." Then, to change the subject, she said, "Sing a song for me."

"No."

"Why not?"

"I love you too much," he told her.

"Then sing me a love song."

He shook his head. "I don't think so. You're sure to leave me forever if I do."

"It can't be that bad—"

"Cash and Lupe made me promise never to sing. That's how bad it is." He set the guitar down next to the rocker. He walked over to the bed and slipped in beside Jade.

"I'm counting this as our honeymoon." J.T. leaned down and kissed her tempting lips.

"I thought you said we would honeymoon in New Mexico." She kissed him back.

"That will be our second honeymoon. This is our first."

When someone tapped at the door of the suite, Jade instinctively pulled the covers up beneath her chin. Jason looked down at her and shrugged. "Looks like the honeymoon is over."

Lupe called out from beyond the locked door. *"Hijo?"*

"What does that mean, anyway?" Jade whispered.

"Son," Jason explained in a whisper. "She's always called me son." Then he called out to his aunt, *"Sí*, Lupita. *Qué pasa?"*

"The detective is here to see you. Should I have him wait or tell him you are not well?"

Jason looked to Jade to decide. "Your choice," he said.

She sighed. The brief respite had been glorious, but the world was waiting outside the door. There was much to do before they left the city. "I suppose it's inevitable. Besides, we have to get up sometime."

"If you insist." He threw back the covers and called out to Lupe. "Tell him we'll be right down." Jason stared around at the candles Jade had placed on every piece of furniture in the room. "There are wax drippings everywhere."

"Do you think the new owner will mind?" she asked.

"Not if he has a good housekeeper."

Jade climbed out of bed and began pulling on the silk trousers Jason had so expertly removed earlier. "Are you taking anything from the house back with you?" She paused to tie her hair in a knot and then slipped on her Mandarin jacket.

"You."

"How about that rocking chair Matt delivered yesterday?" The night before, while they had been at the adobe, Matt had left the rocker with Cash and Lupe.

J.T. looked at the worn arms of the chair and at its lopsided seat cushion. He thought of the empty place it once occupied in Peoney Flannagan's parlor. She had asked Matt to give it to Jason with a note of thanks for the generous trust fund he had established for her.

"Is it special to you?" Jade asked.

He almost denied it, then stopped. He thought of what loving Jade had taught him—that there really were two sides to every story. He looked at the rocker again and said softly, "Yeah. It's special to me. It was my father's." Then he shrugged on his shirt and looked over his shoulder at her. "Is there anything you want to take with us?"

"No. Not really. I want to start out with things we acquire together. No more ties to the past for me, Chinese or Californian."

He finished buttoning his shirt and crossed the room to take her in his arms again. "Exactly what I was thinking." He looked around the room and said, "My father never intended this house to be a home."

"Maybe it will be one for the new owners."

"Maybe." Jason kissed her forehead and then released her. "I hope so."

"You go on down," she urged. "I'll blow out the candles and then follow you."

When Jade arrived downstairs, Jon Chang was seated on the drawing room settee between Cash and Lupita. Cash wanted to learn every detail of the capture of Emery Lennox from the lieutenant's viewpoint, while Lupe focused her attention on offering him more of the sweets she had baked that morning.

He stood up when Jade entered the room. She greeted him warmly and then took a seat near Jason by the fire.

She looked across at her husband and smiled at the rakish appearance the cut near his forehead gave him. Then she turned her attention to the detective.

"The captain has pleaded guilty to kidnapping, both yours, Mrs. Harrington, and Li Po's. Your written testimony is all we need to hold him now. You are free to leave for New Mexico."

"Thank you," Jade replied, nodding. She could not help but feel saddened by Emery Lennox's fate, even though she knew he had caused his own downfall. "And Li Po?"

"The poor man," Lupe interjected. The story of the wizard had intrigued her since her arrival. Jade and Jason had explained the entire affair to Cash and Lupe after they returned from the adobe.

"Li Po will be buried with all the honor he would have been given in his village. The allied tongs have agreed to it."

Cash frowned and grumbled aloud. "What's honorable about an old man who sold his own granddaughter to that lecher?"

Jon Chang appeared unruffled as he answered quietly, "In China, a woman has very little worth. In families with too many daughters, the girls are often sold in order to feed the others. It is not frowned upon."

"Damned sick if you ask me," Cash mumbled.

Jade tried to direct the conversation elsewhere. "How is Tao? He was in love with Quan Yen, you know."

Jason looked surprised. "Really?"

"Really," she said.

"Tao is well. Anxious to get to work again."

"We'll miss him," Jade said.

"I hate to think I ever suspected him of poisoning you," Jason said with a shake of his head. "I guess because Quan Yen seemed so young and helpless that it never occurred to me that she might be the guilty one."

"If she'd had her way, I'd be dead now," Jade said with a shiver.

Lupe crossed herself. "Don't speak of it, *hija*."

Jade's eyes smarted with tears, and she smiled when she heard the woman use the endearment.

Chang shook his head. "I wish you would have told me of your concern regarding Tao Ling. I could have relieved you of your worry." He smiled one of his rare smiles. "Not only is he my cousin, but he often works for me. I'm sure now that you've witnessed his prowess, you know why."

"He's a detective?" Jason was stunned.

"Unofficially. So you see, you were never in any danger." Jon Chang stood and straightened his jacket. "Excuse me, please. I have brought you something." His long queue swayed behind him as he walked to the foyer and then returned with a small wooden chest.

Jade recognized it immediately as the one that had been buried with Li Po. The detective opened it and held it out for Jade's inspection. Inside, carefully cleaned and folded, was Li Po's crimson robe, his odd, tall hat, and his shoes. She reached into the chest and unfolded the robe to study the intricate patterns on it.

Dragons leapt and intertwined with tigers. Crescent moons, stars, sun symbols, and Chinese astrological signs were painted around the embroidered animal figures. She recognized many of the symbols as those painted on the crates. Although the symbols were archaic, the silk was obviously new. It was the finest piece of handiwork Jade had ever seen.

"The tongs realize you were an unwilling pawn in all of this," Chang explained, "and they know of the work you have done to help establish the Chinese museum. They wanted you to have the robe for the collection. Li Po will be buried in new finery."

Jade bowed. "Will you thank them for me and tell them that I will present the robe and other contents of the chest to Mrs. Stanford, who has agreed to preside over the museum foundation? This piece is exquisite." She accepted the robe, but did not tell him that she had reservations about putting the piece on display. Each time she looked at it she experienced an eerie feeling she could not put into words. Unable to forget that she had dreamed of this exact robe long before she saw it, Jade wa determined to instruct Mrs. Stanford to store the chest in the museum, but never to display the contents.

"How are the plans for the museum progressing?" he asked, interrupting her thoughts.

"Wonderfully," she said, carefully refolding the robe as she spoke. "Mrs. Stanford hopes to acquire a building near Little China so that both races might visit the museum. After all, the pieces are Chinese, they should be viewed by the Chinese as well as the Americans of San Francisco."

Jon Chang nodded. "Perhaps it is enough that the Americans see the antiquities and know that there is more to 'John Chinaman' than pigtails and yellow skin."

"We can only hope," she said.

Jason realized the lieutenant was ready to leave and so he stood and extended his hand. "Thank you, Mr. Chang, for your help."

"Good luck to you on your journey and in your new home," Chang told him. "Please come to see me whenever you return to the city. Perhaps there will be another case you can help me solve."

"Does that include me?" Jade teased.

Chang bowed. "Most especially."

"You can bet I'm not coming back," Cash said. All eyes turned his way. "The wife spends too damn much money shoppin' here. Too many stores."

Jason and Jade left the Youngers playfully sparring in the drawing room as they walked the detective to the door. When he was gone, Jade slipped her arms around her husband's neck and pulled him down for a kiss.

"Weren't we in the middle of our honeymoon?" she asked with a gleam in her eye.

Jason faked a heavy sigh. "Let me grab a handful of cookies to keep up my strength and we'll go back upstairs." He draped an arm across her shoulders and started toward the kitchen. "You know what, Jade?"

"What, Jason?"

"They told me I was wealthy when I inherited my father's money—but I never felt as rich as I do now that I have you."

She stopped him by placing her hand lightly on his arm. Her

pulse quickened as she thought of all the love he had to give
and all he could still teach her about the art of making love.

"Do you have to have those cookies?" she whispered.

"I think I can hold out until dinner."

Jason swept her into his arms and started up the stairs.

*   *   *

SAN FRANCISCO CHRONICLE
October 27, 2000
ARCHAEOLOGISTS, CHEMISTS,
METAPHYSICIANS ARGUE OVER
SIGNIFICANCE OF LATEST DISCOVERY
BENEATH THE CITY

AP WIRE SERVICE

SAN FRANCISCO—An archaeological dig on a construction site downtown has revealed a treasure-trove of
Chinese artifacts believed to have been part of a
collection housed in the basement of a museum on the
sight before the 1906 earthquake and fire destroyed the
building.

A strict interpretation of the California Environmental
Quality Act forces developers in certain areas of the city
to see that archival research is completed, and if
warranted, archaeological excavation must take place
before permits are issued.

More than thirty pieces, some dating from as far back
as the Sung Dynasty, were excavated from the site.
Among pieces of ceramics, lacquerware, bronze, and
jade was a small chest containing a crimson silk robe
that has become the object of heated dispute.

According to Harold Scrimpton, an expert on Chinese
antiquities from the University of Stanford, the robe is
of great significance because the symbols embroidered
on the piece predate the Shang-Yin Dynasty—one of the
earliest in Chinese history—and yet the robe shows no
signs of age or decay. "Even if it was made in 1906, the
year the museum burned down, there is still no explanation as to why it is still in perfect condition,"
Scrimpton said.

To add to the mystery, local metaphysicians claim the symbols on the robe are of a highly mystical nature. Chu Kwon Loo, self-proclaimed mystic and leader of the Masters of the Visions of Light Ashram, claims that the symbols were often used in ancient alchemical practices. Working with scientists from MIT, Loo has translated the symbols into chemical formulas which he alleges will produce a gold-based life-extending elixir.

Although expert chemists remain skeptical, they have agreed to test the formula.

A moving novel of sweeping passion

WINDS OF EDEN
by
Justina Burgess

In the tradition of Barbara Taylor Bradford's
<u>A Woman of Substance</u>

India, at the dawn of the 1800s, is a strange and turbulent place for a young Scottish girl to come of age—but Desiree MacKenzie is captivated by the astonishing beauty of this exotic land. There, her future is threatened by her ruthless guardian uncle. And there her heart is awakened by the love of two remarkable men. Captain Kirby of the 78th Highlanders vows to love her forever, but it is Hector MacLeod, a successful trader, who valiantly wins her hand in marriage.

Only the test of time will reveal her ultimate fate—from the intrigues of India to the beauty of Scotland and England, from the joys and heartaches of love, friendship, and betrayal, to the bittersweet storms of unexpected change...

A Jove Paperback
On Sale in October